THE
DOUBLE
AGENT

THE
DOUBLE AGENT

A NOVEL

WILLIAM

CHRISTIE

MINOTAUR
BOOKS
NEW YORK

First published in the United States by Minotaur Books, an imprint of St. Martin's Publishing Group

THE DOUBLE AGENT. Copyright © 2022 by William Christie. All rights reserved. Printed in the United States of America. For information, address St. Martin's Publishing Group, 120 Broadway, New York, NY 10271.

www.minotaurbooks.com

Designed by Omar Chapa

Library of Congress Cataloging-in-Publication Data

Names: Christie, William, 1960- author.
Title: The double agent: a novel / William Christie.
Description: First edition. | New York: Minotaur Books, 2022.
Identifiers: LCCN 2022029866 | ISBN 9781250080820 (hardcover) |
    ISBN 9781250163011 (ebook)
Subjects: LCGFT: Spy fiction. | Novels.
Classification: LCC PS3553.H735 D68 2022 | DDC 813/.54—dc23/eng/20220624
LC record available at https://lccn.loc.gov/2022029866

Our books may be purchased in bulk for promotional, educational, or business use. Please contact your local bookseller or the Macmillan Corporate and Premium Sales Department at 1-800-221-7945, extension 5442, or by email at MacmillanSpecialMarkets@macmillan.com.

First Edition: 2022

10 9 8 7 6 5 4 3 2 1

For my friend, Philip

PROLOGUE

1943

TEHERAN, IRAN

It was past midnight in the British embassy. Alexsi Ivanovich Smirnov was still wearing his purloined Russian uniform. The buttons that ran halfway down the shirt tunic were open, exposing the elasticated bandage binding up his broken ribs. Sticking plasters covered the glass cuts all over his face and neck. He sat with his hands folded calmly upon his lap, and through his clothing he could feel the hard outline of his lucky folding knife. The British were no better at searching you than anyone else.

A British officer wearing colonel's insignia sat opposite him, with a pad full of notes. They had been at it for quite some time.

The knob turned and the door opened. And the great man walked in with absolutely no fanfare. He was smoking a cigar and wearing that same ridiculous one-piece collared jumpsuit he'd had on before, with a cloth belt loosely buckled over his girth, two big breast pockets, and a zipper down the front.

Alexsi stood to attention.

Winston Churchill swung the cigar out of his mouth with a sweep of the hand. That famous voice rumbled out. "They tell me I owe you my life, young man. Give me your hand."

With the British colonel watching him like a wary guard dog, Alexsi leaned over the table and shook Churchill's hand.

Churchill released him and, with a gesture that was pure noblesse oblige, bid him to sit down. And took the colonel's chair for himself without a word.

Alexsi caught the aroma of the cigar. Cuban. Romeo y Julieta, Uncle Hans's favorite, too.

"Your story has been related to me," Churchill said, his famous lisp even more noticeable at close range. "Quite remarkable. If you don't mind, I have a few questions of my own."

"Your servant, sir." Alexsi hoped that was the right English, since it came from books.

In any case, it made Churchill's eyes twinkle with delight. Then they turned serious. "I am told you are a native Russian, is that correct? A Russian intelligence officer."

"Yes, sir."

"And that for seven years you have been posing as German. Eventually joining their army and becoming a German intelligence officer?"

"Yes, sir."

"Remarkable. Most remarkable."

Churchill sounded almost wistful at the thought of such an adventure. Alexsi wondered if he would have to disillusion the man by telling him he'd been dragged into the entire affair against his will. Blackmailed and threatened at every turn.

Serious again, Churchill said, "My question is this. As a Russian intelligence officer, was it possible that some lower-level official hatched this scheme without Stalin knowing of it?"

"No, sir," Alexsi replied instantly. "Out of the question. No one in the Soviet Union would dare such a thing. No one. Not even Beria. This had to be approved by Stalin personally. There is nothing more certain."

Churchill nodded gravely and drew on his cigar. He seemed lost in thought. And then, "I realize that only one man knows the answer to this question. But perhaps you can offer me some insight into why Stalin would do such a thing."

"You mean plot your death, sir?"

"That is correct."

"I can only guess."

"Please indulge me."

"You are an old-line anti-Bolshevik, sir. A dedicated foe of Communism since the time of the Revolution. If Stalin believes in nothing else, it is annihilating his enemies when the time is ripe."

Churchill didn't miss his hesitation. "And?"

"The Germans foolishly sneer at them. I do not know what the Russians think. But anyone with eyes can see that the Americans will be a great power after the war. Perhaps, sir, just as he was easily able to persuade them to reside in the Soviet embassy where the NKVD will be recording all their private conversations and reading their secret documents, Stalin feels that the Americans would be more easily persuaded in all things without you standing beside them."

Now Churchill was rumbling with outrage. "And he would accept this monstrous risk?"

"Not much of a risk, sir. All the NKVD did was stand back and let the SS assassination team they had been observing all along take position in the house I obtained for them but never intended to be used. I am told

3

the Soviets delayed you at the vehicle gate demanding proper identification? For a period of some time before I arrived? As if they had no idea who you were?"

Churchill nodded.

"They knew that a man such as yourself would never carry an identification card in his pocket. So you have an overzealous Russian private soldier delaying the prime minister of Great Britain over the proper identification required to enter a gate. Just stupidly following his orders to the letter. Anyone who knows soldiers would laugh. And I'm sure you laughed, sir, as you waited for someone in authority to come and straighten it out."

His face fixed into that famous bulldog glower, Churchill nodded again.

"So all the Soviets have to do is make you a stationary target, sir, long enough for the Germans to take a clear shot. Stalin would not care in the least if they mowed down a score of Russian soldiers in the attempt. If the Germans succeed all the Russians at the gate, and everyone who received the order to delay you, would be shot for criminal incompetence. The Germans who killed you would of course all die. Molotov would attend your funeral with an exquisite wreath of flowers, and most likely weep with emotion. They would perhaps name a street in Moscow in your honor. But if the Germans fail, heroic Russian soldiers gain the credit for saving the British prime minister. It was embarrassingly close, so everyone agrees to keep it secret from the world. And all the Russians along the line of the order will be shot just the same and silenced forever. Stalin takes his chance, and it costs him nothing. You are still his ally today, from necessity, and you will never love him in any case. This is how the man does his work, sir. He does not have to be this subtle in Russia."

Churchill concentrated on his cigar again. "And his work in Russia is as evil as I imagine?"

"There are more in camps than live now in your nation, sir. Unless they have been driven out to die in front of the German guns. Not including countless numbers shot out of hand in dark cellars all over the Soviet Union."

Churchill nodded, as if that was the answer he had been expecting. "One final question. Make no mistake, young man. I am deeply grateful to you for saving my life. But I am curious why you went to such extraordinary lengths to do so."

Alexsi knew this was a man of vast experience. He would not accept being told that it was someone risking his life because it was the right thing to do. His instinct told him to tell the truth. "Sir, when I was in Berlin I informed Stalin when and how the Germans would invade the Soviet Union. I am sure there were other warnings."

"I also informed him," Churchill interjected.

"Yes, sir. He ignored them all. Eventually, every Russian who gave him this intelligence will have to die. Stalin will never let it be known that he sat back and allowed Hitler to invade and nearly conquer the Soviet Union. He cannot."

Churchill went back to dreaming over his cigar.

Very much like Uncle Hans used to. Alexsi thought it was a fine way to make everyone wait while you thought things over. "And as I said before, sir. Sooner or later, every Russian with knowledge of this plot against you, even the very highest, will be liquidated."

"And a man of your abilities could not manage to disappear without a trace?" Churchill inquired.

"I chose not to, sir," Alexsi replied, boiling anger locked up behind his impassible Russian face. He'd saved the old bastard's life. He didn't expect them to kiss him like a Russian, but did he have to go down on his knees to beg the British Empire for refuge? Fine, he'd do it if he had to.

Churchill exhaled a puff of Cuban smoke. "You're quite an extraordinary fellow, aren't you?"

It did not come out as a compliment. Alexsi did not expect anyone to understand his story. All he said was "There is an old Russian saying, sir, that if you live among wolves you must act like a wolf."

A brief flicker of enjoyment crossed Churchill's face, as if he had been expecting another response and liked this one better. Now he rose, and Alexsi and the colonel rose along with him. He put out his hand to shake once more. "Thank you again, young man. We have high hopes for someone of your talents. Colonel—"

An undisguised warning glance from the colonel cut the prime minister off before he gave a name.

"Very well," Churchill said, with barely disguised petulance at being corrected. "The colonel here will discuss these things with you."

"Sir," Alexsi said, confused. High hopes?

They remained standing until Churchill left the room. As the door closed they both sat down.

The colonel rushed to light a cigarette. "The prime minister thinks cigarettes are unhealthy. Ten cigars a day, and they're unhealthy."

"High hopes?" Alexsi said.

The colonel waved out his match. "The German woman you were with crashed her car into a bridge on the outskirts of Teheran. Dead."

Alexsi nodded. No accident, there. The NKVD being thorough. "High hopes?" he repeated.

The colonel drew on his cigarette. "Having you with us is the most splendid opportunity. We intend to play you back into Germany as our agent. We've already begun negotiations through the Swiss to exchange you for a British intelligence officer in German captivity."

Alexsi only nodded. The Englishman smiled, thinking he was in accord. But for Alexsi it was more along the lines of: Yes, that was exactly what I should have expected.

This was what happened when you were foolish enough to tell the truth.

PART ONE

Fortune and misfortune live in the same courtyard.

—RUSSIAN PROVERB

1

Alexsi Ivanovich Smirnov sat on the edge of the army camp bed, as he had all night, listening to the British embassy settle down around him. After being awake for more than two days, he'd been afraid to lie down and perhaps miss his chance. Though that was doubtful with the combination of broken ribs stabbing like knives with every drawn breath and the iron-hard canvas of the folding cot. He knew the guards would never stop pacing the hallways, because Prime Minister Winston Churchill was still somewhere within the building, definitely in a more comfortable bed. But two hours had passed since Alexsi's ears told him the last shift had changed, and the footsteps were taking longer and longer to pass with military regularity before the door of the little room they had him locked into.

With an air of regretful necessity, it had to be said. Frightfully sorry, old chap—for your own safety, you understand. They actually spoke that way, just like in the English novels he had read. The Germans would have told him that he would be shot if he attempted to escape. The Russians would have shot someone in front of him to make sure he absorbed the message. The British were much more civilized about it, which slightly mitigated Alexsi's resentment. Though he had absolutely no intention of returning to Berlin as their spy. Since they did not seem open to discussion, especially now with their prime minister's endorsement, it was definitely time to leave.

The wristwatch the British had been either polite or careless enough to leave on his wrist read 3:10 in the morning. Everyone who wasn't asleep was tired, and he would have just enough time before dawn.

The footsteps creaked in front of his door, and he counted off the seconds it would take until they turned the corner out of sight.

Alexsi rose quickly. Too quickly, for he almost cried out from the pain. He'd blown a house full of German commandos down nearly on his own head, and the parts of his body that weren't in agony had stiffened up from the battering they had taken. He hobbled toward the door like an old man, suddenly fearful of being unable to move quickly if he needed to.

He plunged his hand down into his waistband, to the pocket he had sewn into the front of his underwear for the little Russian folding knife he had carried since he was a boy. A trick taught to him by Azerbaijani smugglers who shrewdly noted that even the most conscientious policemen searching for hidden weapons balked at putting their hands on another man's groin. Alexsi had found it to be true, with the exception of Soviet secret police guards of the Lubyanka prison, who ruthlessly examined every last possible hiding place, including the interior of your ass with an unsurprising lack of gentleness. Even so, he had gotten the knife past them, and it had saved his life on more than one occasion.

Alexsi had filed the smaller of the two blades down to his own specifications, and an old warded door lock was useful only to keep your friends from barging in on you. He jimmied it open as quietly as he could and peeked out.

The hallway was empty. He'd been locked in an interior room with no window, in what he judged to be the basement of the building.

Alexsi crossed the hall and tried the first door on the opposite side. He was looking for an outside window. No luck on the first two rooms. He'd noted the row of small ground-level ventilation windows as he was led into the embassy, a former Persian mansion.

A glance at his watch told him that the guard would be coming back soon. Alexsi closed the door behind him and stood silently in the darkness of the musty storeroom. Precious time was passing, but impatience was always the enemy.

The guard's footsteps trailed away again. As soon as Alexsi opened the next door down, the heightened visibility told him that there was a window. The room was filled with wooden file cabinets and a small desk barely large enough for a man to sit at.

Alexsi picked his way to the far wall carefully, since bumping into anything would sound like a bomb going off in the early-morning silence. And any light would be a beacon under the bottom of the door.

It was a small window, nearly square, and just slightly above the level of the ground outside. Alexsi eyed it warily—it would be a very tight fit. He tested his weight against a nearby chair, and propped it up against the wall. Standing on it, he examined the window carefully, feeling around the frame. Yes, there were two alarm wires joining at a contact plate just under the bottom latch. He found the wires by touch, as they were nearly painted over. They looked old enough to be long-disused, but this was not the time for foolish risks.

Alexsi used his knife to pry the wires away from their brackets around the window, and this gave him enough slack to gather them together. With his knife he carefully scraped away a section of paint and then the insulation on each wire to expose the core, finally twisting them together to keep the alarm circuit closed when he opened the window.

He raised it carefully, grimly awaiting an alarm bell. Nothing. With ears tuned to the sound of running feet, he locked the window open with the little metal rod on the hinge and poked his head out to see what the guard situation was like. It appeared that the landscaping was at least partially hiding him from sight of the walkways. Excellent. He waited a bit longer for someone to kick in the door of the room, but all was quiet.

Time to move. Alexsi pulled the bulky wool Soviet Army tunic over his head, trying not to cry out loud from the pain in his ribs. The wide elasticated bandage the British doctor had bound them with would have to remain on.

Pushing the tunic out onto the grass above, he tried to go out head-first. No, his shoulders were too wide for the window frame. He extended one arm through the window to turn his shoulders sideways, and with the extended hand pushing on the outside wall turned himself faceup.

His legs were off the chair now, dangling inside the building, and the pain in his rib cage was so incredible he was afraid he might lose consciousness. A cold sweat washed over his body. Alexsi was wedged tightly in the window frame with only one hand free and the other pinned against him. He realized that his agitated pushing was only making things worse, and there was no quick way through. He stopped, took a deep breath, and resolved that the only solution was to calmly wiggle an inch at a time.

The scraping sound of hobnailed boot soles on stone made him freeze. The low hedge in front of his face was bordering a walkway. Lying on his back on the grass, Alexsi looked up in despair to see a British soldier coming down the walk.

All the sentry would have to do was look down. The rifle was slung over his shoulder, and the fixed bayonet gleamed in the moonlight. Alexsi only hoped the soldier wouldn't panic and pin him to the ground with it, like a butterfly in a case. He closed his eyes, not only out of resignation but because he had been trained that all animal eyes gleamed at night.

The footsteps passed and nothing happened. Alexsi snuck a look up. The sentry had his hands in his pockets against the night chill, and was walking hunched over as if the helmet on his head was weighing him down.

Alexsi began breathing again. He was bathed in icy sweat that made it feel like Moscow in the winter. He resumed wriggling through the window, and every move was like being stabbed in the lungs.

Finally he was far enough out to get his left arm through the window frame, and both hands pressing on the outside wall speeded his progress.

Then he was free. He rolled over in the grass and leaned back in to close the window behind him. Starting to shiver uncontrollably, even though it was well above freezing, he pulled the placket-front *gymnasterka* tunic back over his head.

And that was the problem. It would be easy enough to slip back over the wall, which was how he had arrived at the embassy. But then he would be walking the highly patrolled streets in the ripped and disheveled partial uniform of a Red Army private soldier. With incredible luck he might make it a block or two before being picked up.

He had another idea. His twin careers as first a thief and then a spy had proven that a bit of unexpected boldness often paid off better than elaborate sneaking about.

The lush landscaping of the embassy grounds made it easy to stay out of sight. That and the fact that British soldiers on guard insisted on marching to and fro as if on parade, rather than waiting quietly in the shadows for some intruder to pass by.

Unfortunately, they might have been clumsy but there were a great many of them. It took Alexsi longer than he had hoped to ease his way through the trees to the rear side of the embassy. The approaching dawn was beginning to purple the horizon.

He was rewarded with the sound of a vehicle engine, and homed in on it. There was an open area of grass between the tree trunk that was concealing him and the hedge that was his destination. Alexsi surmounted this by crawling slowly along the line of shadow cast by the tree in the moonlight. Still on his belly blending in alongside the hedge, he peered through it to the sight of an orderly row of American jeeps. Even more perfect, these had fabric tops all neatly buttoned up around them to protect the driver and passengers from the elements.

Predictably, there was a sentry stamping around the perimeter of the car park. Alexsi waited until the fellow reached the side corner with his back turned, then made a little hop over the edge as if curling around the pole of a high jump. After a moment to get his breath back, he was up and inside the jeep. The door was only a simple metal latch.

Almost in spite of himself he had to pause to touch the flexible but clear plastic window in the canvas cover of the door. He had never seen its like before. The inside smelled of canvas, grease, and petrol.

Fortunately these vehicles had no ignition key. He'd had to teach himself to drive one shortly after arriving in Iran.

Now it was time for one of those decisions where you would either be patting yourself on the back for the next week or regretting everything for the rest of your life, however long that might be. Alexsi decided to wait, curling up in the well beneath the steering wheel, out of sight of the passing guards.

The sky progressively lightened, and he kept checking the luminous hands of his watch. Soon it would be too late, and he would have to chance it.

Then a jeep engine started, two rows of vehicles away from him. Alexsi popped up into the driver's seat and pushed his foot against the starter button next to the accelerator pedal. The engine briefly turned over and died.

Alexsi's stomach dropped, and he fought the urge to plunge his foot down on the starter again. He took a breath to calm himself and lightly tapped the accelerator to give the engine some petrol. Then he pushed the starter and accelerator pedal at the same time. The starter ground away sickeningly for a moment; then the engine caught. Alexsi pumped more petrol into it, and twisted the lever to activate the lights. Turning the wheel, he released the clutch and pulled out into the open space between the rows.

Alexsi held up a moment to let the other jeep get in front of him, then followed it toward the gate.

The jeep in front paused before the closed metal gate, and after a brief wait honked its horn. A soldier finally emerged from the guard shack, making a rude gesture as if to say, I'm coming, I'm coming. He opened the gate and angrily waved the jeep through.

Alexsi let the clutch out again and followed the first jeep through the gate. The soldier on guard had already positioned himself to close it, and didn't even look over at him.

The first jeep turned left. Alexsi turned right. He'd been worried that a single jeep might be seen as an interesting diversion in the boring small hours of the morning. But confronted with two the guard couldn't wait to get back into his warm little shack. Even in the German Army, soldiers were always vigilant about anyone trying to enter a guarded facility but never paid attention to anyone leaving. Now that he was driving about Teheran in exactly the right vehicle, it made no difference that he was in the wrong uniform.

2

1943

TEHERAN, IRAN

As a cold November dawn broke over the city, Alexsi in his purloined jeep was cheerfully waved through two British Army checkpoints. The reception might have been different if he were driving toward the high-security areas of the British and Russian embassies, rather than away from them.

In the poor southern district of Persepolis he came to a stop before the wide wooden doors of a ground-level garage that had originally been the ground-level animal stable of a very old building. From a nearby minaret came the *adhan* preparatory call for *fajr,* the dawn prayer. For Alexsi the timing couldn't be more perfect, as it had nearly emptied the streets.

Alexsi unlatched the jeep door, twisted halfway out, and yanked off one of his Russian *sapogi* knee boots. Shaking it, he was rewarded with a tinkling sound as the key he had secreted inside fell out onto the pavement.

Boot back on, Alexsi unlocked the garage doors and swung them open. In a moment the jeep was inside and the doors were bolted tight from the inside. He lit the kerosene lamp that had been standing ready on a tall shelf.

There was nothing inside the garage but that otherwise-empty shelf. Any thief would have immediately left disgusted, just as Alexsi intended. He dragged the shelf down the length of the wall and picked up the steel pry bar that had been hidden by its base. Picking his spot, he rammed the end of the pry bar into a seam in the exposed-brick wall. A dozen bricks removed, Alexsi reached into the cavity behind the wall and lifted out one of three large metal toolboxes and a full-length mirror.

After propping the mirror up, Alexsi stripped naked and examined himself critically, like an actor about to take on a new character. He had already decided which of his three emergency identities to use. Both the British and the Soviets would be searching for a European in Teheran, so that was what he absolutely could not be.

With hand clippers Alexsi cut his hair down to a rough stubble. His beard was already two days old, which was perfect. Then, using a sponge fastened to the end of a stick, he stained every millimeter of his skin and scalp with the contents of a large bottle of black walnut oil. As it dried he paid particular attention to his face, his neck, and inside the ears. Any streaking or uneven discoloration would give the game away. A few days of sun and dirt would do for him before the oil wore off.

When he was satisfied that the walnut oil had dried completely, Alexsi donned a complete set of terribly worn Iranian workingman's clothes. The jacket already had Iranian rial and British pound notes rolled up tightly and sewn into the seams, but only a few small-denomination coins went into his pocket. The battered leather belt had British sovereign gold coins sewn into the center, and its weight was comfortingly substantial. He finally laced up the scuffed shoes and again examined himself in the mirror. The final touch was a stained skullcap. The disguise was good. He could pass for a poor Iranian, even at face-to-face distance. A carefully soiled and aged Iranian passport and identity card were the extent of his papers. A cheap workman's sheath knife stuck in his belt supplemented the pocketknife returned to its hiding place in his underwear. Other than that, his only baggage was a frayed canvas shoulder bag that held a single change of equally shabby clothing and a few cheap toilet articles.

In the mirror he practiced the submissive posture of a poor Iranian, discarding for the foreseeable future the shoulders-back confidence of a rich European. To look tired, meek, and beaten all you had to do was feel it. And at the moment the only thing he didn't feel was meek.

With the garage door firmly locked behind him, Alexsi dropped the key into a sewer drain and left behind all his previous lives in Teheran.

Prayers were over, and the streets of Persepolis were now busy. As he walked, Alexsi was firmly rebuffed in his requests to hitch a ride in everything from a delivery van to a trash picker's horse-drawn cart. His disguise just might be a bit too perfect, Alexsi thought; in reaching for anonymity he had left himself looking too disreputable for his own good.

He turned a corner. A rickety cargo truck was just rolling out of a warehouse door onto the street. It immediately caught Alexsi's thief/spy's eye, because something just wasn't right. As soon as the truck was out, the warehouse doors were slammed shut with un-Iranian-like speed. Instead of just a driver there were five Iranians clustered around the cab having a cigarette and a quiet conversation. And just like birds on a roost, one by one they would periodically look up from their talk and carefully check the street. A group of truck drivers tended to look tough, but these were even tougher than usual.

No, it didn't look right at all. Which led Alexsi to believe that it might be the perfect situation for him. He walked up to the group, and they had a wary eye on him before he even got close. "Brothers, what chance of a ride?"

They looked him over even more closely, and one, not the obvious leader, said, "Got any money?"

The speaker was wearing a suit jacket of pinstripes so garishly wide that any street pimp would have discarded it out of pure sartorial embarrassment.

"I'm down to my last few rials," said Alexsi. "But I'm willing to work. I'll unload the truck for you."

The leader blew out a cloud of cigarette smoke, and said, "Bad luck in the city?"

Alexsi nodded.

"Where are you going?"

"Wherever you are."

The leader just looked harder at him for that, until Alexsi added, "I'm trying to go south."

The pinstripe jacket was behind Alexsi, lifting the flap of his shoulder bag. "You sure you don't have any money?"

His hand stopped when the blade of Alexsi's sheath knife came to rest, lightly but definitively, on the side of his neck just under the jaw. "You should not touch people's things without permission, brother," Alexsi said mildly.

There was always uncertainty in such moments. In that instant of tense hesitation, Alexsi was prepared for them to turn on him. But instead they laughed uproariously at the pinstripe jacket, who was frozen like a statue with Alexsi's knife still upon him.

The leader spoke for the pinstripe jacket. "He's learned his lesson," he said to Alexsi. It was a command.

Alexsi sheathed the knife in one smooth motion. There and gone.

"What's your name?" the leader asked.

"Farhad," said Alexsi.

"You're from the north?" said the leader.

Alexsi nodded. His Farsi had never lost the Azeri inflections from his boyhood, so that always had to be a part of his legend—the creation of which was the first lesson he'd ever been given by his Soviet spy trainers. A legend was everything from the assumed identity you used to live in a foreign country, that would withstand any scrutiny, to the tale you told a policeman who stopped you in the street. It all had to trip off the tongue as easily as the story of your own life, and be believable to every person you spoke to. If you gave a detail it had to check out, but overexplanation was the mark of an obvious liar. The trick was to have that different life already imagined inside your head, and knowing the kinds of questions different types of people asked.

The leader looked him over again, slowly, as if expecting Alexsi to buckle under the pressure and confess to something. Then he held out his cigarette pack.

"No, thanks," Alexsi said. "I don't smoke."

"Religious?" the leader asked, understandably skeptical after the knife demonstration.

"Too poor to afford the habit," Alexsi replied.

The leader laughed, and that made up his mind. "Are your papers all right?"

He meant for the British checkpoints.

Alexsi handed over his passport and identity card.

The leader gave the documents a cursory look, then handed them back. "We're going to Bushehr. You'll work, right? And not pull that knife unless you're told."

Alexsi was inwardly delighted. Nearly a full day's drive right to the coast, exactly where he wanted to go. "I'm your man, brother."

The leader nodded. "Climb in the back."

Alexsi made himself comfortable atop the bags of rice heaped up in the cargo bed. The truck began moving, and to his relief the engine and the road noise in the open back forestalled any conversation. Not that there would be any for a while. He was the stranger. He knew it would take a while for him to work his way into the group. The important thing was not to push it—he had to be patient and allow it to happen in its own time. Everyone was tying cloths over their faces as protection against the ever-present Iranian road dust, Alexsi using a scarf from his bag.

He was exhausted, and even though he'd comfortably wormed his way down between the bags out of the wind he couldn't sleep. His mind would not let him. Leaving Berlin had finished him with the Germans. They were a spent force—their defeat might be bloody and terrible, and they might be able to drag it out another few years, but it was still inevitable. No worries there. But as soon as he'd stumbled over the Russians' plot to stand back and let the Germans kill Churchill, he'd known his Russian masters would never let him live. At the time he'd thought that with the Soviet empire dedicated to his destruction the only thing that might save him would be the protection of another. So he'd stuck out his neck to save Churchill's life, counting on the thanks of the British Empire. Only to have Churchill himself endorse the idea of sending him back to Berlin, as a British spy this time. What they said about the gratitude of princes, it was all true.

He ought to have lain low and relied on himself, as he'd done all his life. Now he was in a fix. He had gold buried back in Teheran that he couldn't carry with him. He had money in a Swiss bank that he couldn't reach. With the war raging all around the world there were no such things as passenger liners and airplanes for casual civilian travelers. Especially civilian travelers who could not withstand being placed under official scrutiny.

Alexsi reviewed a few courses of action, and just as quickly discarded them. It was clear what he would have to do, even though he was unsure of exactly how he would go about it. At Bushehr find a ship, something small and inconspicuous like a trading dhow. Even the war couldn't stop those from crossing the Gulf in the thousands. Slowly make his way to

Africa and wait out the end of the war there. Once it was over he could move again, acquire new papers, and get ahold of his money. The end of every war threw up refugees, and he would be able to disappear among them. South America, perhaps the United States.

He contemplated the journey ahead of him grimly. For years he had come to enjoy a life of privilege in Germany, Switzerland, Teheran. This would be like going back to his days as a little street rat in Azerbaijan. Well, it was better than dying.

The truck bounced like an airplane flying through turbulence. One of the bags of rice digging into Alexsi's ass was harder than any bag of rice had a right to be. Turning on his side so his arm was out of sight, he surreptitiously unsheathed his knife and plunged it into the bag. Withdrawing it, he rolled over onto his stomach as if trying to get comfortable. No one was paying any attention to him. The point of the blade was slightly tacky with a rubbery residue. He rubbed it with his finger and lightly dotted it onto his tongue. Opium. He'd been sure of some kind of contraband. No wonder they were heading for the coast. There would be a dhow there to carry this out of the country. Signing on as a sailor instead of a passenger would almost guarantee anonymity. If they didn't get caught, that is. Then he would be waiting out the war in an Iranian prison, courtesy of the British. Not something to look forward to, but also better than dying.

Alexsi rolled onto his back and tried to make himself comfortable again amid the bouncing and the dust. One problem at a time. With his mind finally reconciled to that, he drifted off to sleep.

3

1943

TEHERAN-QOM ROAD, IRAN

Alexsi came awake. The truck had stopped. As he sat up to look out over the top of the cargo bed, his hand automatically grasped his knife.

It was a British checkpoint. A section of soldiers in a small truck, wooden barriers on the road to stop traffic. Alexsi ran a critical eye over the surrounding terrain. Low bare hills on both sides of the road. No way to drive around, nowhere to run. Unless you wanted to stretch your legs for a bit, however futilely, until the riflemen found the range on you.

A military truck sailed past in the other lane after being waved right through. But there was another cargo truck up ahead of them, and the soldiers were crawling over it like ants. It was something to pass the time, Alexsi thought. Or a particularly ambitious sergeant. Later in the day they might become bored and wave everything through. But not now.

The Iranian smugglers in the truck were seeing everything he was, and they were reaching under the rice bags for their guns.

A shoot-out, Alexsi felt, would be incredibly shortsighted. Even if they were able to kill every single soldier at the checkpoint, which was doubtful, they were not about to outrun any later pursuit in a cargo truck. Unfortunately, recent bitter experience had convinced him that these days no one was receptive to reason.

Nothing shook off the fog of coming out of too little sleep like a little naked terror. As sometimes happened when Alexsi was scared out of his wits, he was also hungry. If the smugglers had passed around bread, he had slept through it. And he had neglected to buy a loaf for himself when the bakeries opened after the dawn prayer.

Prayer. He glanced up at the sky and, yes, you could say that the sun had reached its apex. He looked over his shoulder, and other vehicles were beginning to back up on the road behind them. It was worth a try. Better than being without a gun in the middle of a gunfight.

Standing up to his full height atop the rice bags and cupping his hands around his mouth, Alexsi at the top of his lungs began reciting the call to prayer.

The smugglers all turned and gaped at him. Even the British soldiers up ahead stopped their searching and turned to see who was doing all the caterwauling.

Alexsi made a subtle motion to the smugglers to alert them that he actually knew what he was doing, and to follow him. He jumped off the back of the truck.

With the drivers behind opening their doors to try to see what was going on, Alexsi trudged across the road to a flat stretch of sand and spread his jacket down before him as a prayer rug. He began the *tayammum*, the ritual ablution with sand when water was not available. When he looked up, the leader of the smugglers had come out of the cab and instantly understood what Alexsi was doing. He pushed all the others into line before him.

Traffic was now backing up on the road as the other drivers came out to join in prayers. This kept an army convoy from going around, and the soldier drivers were hammering on their horns.

As a boy Alexsi had cut his teeth as a smuggler with Azeri tribesmen who felt that God was perfectly fine with them being thieves, raiders, and throat cutters as long as they prayed five times a day. Blending in, he'd pretended to be devout so as not to spoil a good deal. Now he was careful to keep to the Shia tradition, with the first *rak'ah* of standing prayers performed with the hands open. Sunnis, he knew, kept them clasped.

When they moved from standing to bowing, Alexsi saw the smuggler chief grinning at him. More and more drivers were leaving their vehicles to join in the prayers. It was open to conjecture whether it was because they were also devout or because the British sergeant had noticed the traffic backing up and was screaming for you fuckers to get back in your trucks. It would be uncharacteristic of anyone, and certainly of Iranians, not to enjoy tormenting their occupiers.

Another military convoy came down the road and ground to a halt. By the time they reached the second prostration, traffic was backed up a kilometer. The soldiers were screaming their lungs out and brandishing their bayonetted rifles but not daring to touch the worshipers. Which was prudent when dealing with a mob of Shia at prayer, Alexsi thought. More than a few of those idiots probably wouldn't mind throwing themselves right onto the bayonets in the assurance of a clear pathway to God.

When they performed the *taslim*—wishing peace and God's mercy upon each other, first to the right and then the left—the soldiers were ready to lose their minds. As the prayer group broke up and began moving ever so slowly back to their vehicles, the sergeant was screaming, "Go, go, go!" Waving everyone through without a search just to get the traffic moving again.

After the worshipers gave him a salaam of gratitude for leading prayer, the smuggler chief offered Alexsi a respectful nod as he climbed into the cab. The rest clapped him on the back as they climbed aboard.

Perched atop his rice bags, Alexsi was just enough of a Russian to praise his luck. These smugglers had all been careful not to give their names. Before he was the outsider, a convenient lamb to be carried along and sacrificed if the going got tough. Now he was suddenly someone clever whom it wouldn't be wise to part with.

The bread that they had waited until he was asleep to pass around now emerged from hiding, and he was offered a cup of hot tea from a vacuum bottle. Alexsi just smiled and thanked his new friends.

4

TEHERAN-QOM ROAD, IRAN

There was shouting, and this time Alexsi was rested enough to wake up grumpy. What now?

He raised his head just in time to see a black American sedan closing on them from behind. Alexsi didn't understand what the fuss was about; they were just being passed by a faster vehicle that didn't want to eat their dust.

The sedan swerved into the opposite lane and came abreast of them. Then from the rolled-down rear window came poking out the distinctive conical muzzle of a Bren machine gun.

Nothing could have made Alexsi shake off the cobwebs faster. The occupants of the automobile were Iranian, so the machine gun had certainly been stolen from the British. Someone had sold out the news of the shipment of opium, and they were about to be hijacked by criminal competitors.

Of course his compatriots couldn't argue with the machine gun. They would have to pull over. Alexsi quickly decided on the direction he'd run as soon as they stopped. The hijackers would be more concerned with securing the valuable cargo than in chasing a lone man down across the desert.

It was a decent plan. Unfortunately, the hijackers weren't in a threatening mood. The air split with the sharp chatter of the gun firing. The truck swerved hard, nearly toppling, and Alexsi knew they'd gone for the tires first.

He couldn't believe the stupidity. Why not try to take the whole truck intact and undamaged, and then shoot everyone at their leisure? Now they'd just have to carry all that opium to some other vehicle.

Alexsi had been waiting for the truck to slow down a bit, but the machine gun turned its attention upward and gusts of rice blew up around him as the next burst stitched across the top of the cargo bed and right through the bags. The whipcrack report of their passage echoed across the desert hills.

That was more than enough to send Alexsi into flight. He sprang up and dashed across the top of the rice bags with the bullets passing all around him, and leaped off the back. It was a case of the least bad decision, and he was desperately hoping for soft sand on the side of the road. An instant after his leap and still in midair, he was punched in the chest by a terrific burning blow. He never felt himself hitting the ground.

5

1943

TEHERAN-QOM ROAD, IRAN

Alexsi was somehow aware that he was dreaming, and frankly amazed that the dead were allowed to dream. When he opened his eyes to a familiar winter desert sky, his first emotion was genuine surprise. Then he looked down at himself and thought that being dead might have been a better resolution.

The side of his face was in the sand, so he couldn't help but look down. The front of his shirt was soaked in blood, which told him why he could breathe only in little electric gasps that felt like drawing air through water. His legs were twisted out unnaturally, like those of a broken doll thrown to the ground. He couldn't imagine why he wasn't screaming in agony—though he had seen people very badly hurt and about to die, and it was like they were numb. As if the lack of pain was nature's farewell blessing, whether you deserved it or not.

Then in the peripheral vision of his right eye was a young man, a boy really. Westerners would have called him ugly, but to Alexsi he was handsomely exotic. Wearing a short-sleeved khaki shirt and a darker brown slouch hat, with a grimly determined look in his eye. A British Enfield rifle was tucked under the Gurkha soldier's arm, and a bayonet was poised at Alexsi's throat.

A British officer suddenly appeared in his field of view, a Gurkha sergeant attentively at his elbow. Both were wearing the same hats. The officer looked Alexsi up and down contemptuously, then issued some orders in a foreign tongue that Alexsi assumed was the language of the Gurkhas.

The soldier lowered his rifle, and they all began to turn away. Alexsi knew that the order had been given to leave him there and let him die. He opened his mouth. If he was unable to speak, then his luck had finally run out.

Alexsi croaked out to the officer, in English, "Sir! Sir!" He knew his English had a deep accent that would sound German to British ears. Now the pain was there. It hurt so badly to speak that he was afraid he might pass out before he was through.

Surprised, the officer turned about.

Alexsi had to cough the words out in gasps. "If you . . . wish to . . . make your career . . . you will . . . take me . . . to a . . . British . . . intelligence . . . officer . . . alive."

The officer stared down at him, frowning now.

Dying might have hurt less than trying to talk any more. Alexsi watched him making up his mind.

The officer turned away. Alexsi didn't move his head to try and see where he had gone. He only felt resignation. After all, everyone's luck ran out sooner or later.

Then he was grasped and turned. The pain was unbelievable, and Alexsi screamed. That must have been shocking enough, because the hands abruptly left him still. His eyes were screwed shut against the pain, and when he felt able to open them there was a Gurkha wearing a white armband with a red cross upon it. The Gurkha was pulling a long cap off what looked like a small tube of toothpaste. Then Alexsi felt the needle stick into the skin of his stomach. It had to have been morphine, because he didn't feel like screaming when the Gurkha tore his shirt open a few moments later.

Now there was a small crowd of Gurkhas watching the medical orderly work. He removed the packaging from a battle dressing, but Alexsi had already lost consciousness before it could be applied to the bullet hole in his chest.

6

Alexsi awoke again, this time in a gummy haze. In a hospital room, alone it seemed, just his single bed with striated light bouncing off the wall from a barred window. It was impossible to tell whether it was morning or afternoon.

His head was too heavy to lift, but he could cast his eyes down enough to see the yellow rubber tube emerging alarmingly through a gauze-covered hole in his chest. It trailed off in the direction of the floor, and Alexsi was glad he couldn't see whatever was emptying from it. Both legs were encased in white plaster and elevated on traction ropes. Alive again, Alexsi thought.

As his head slowly cleared, he tried to move his arms. The right worked, but not the left. He could see the tube running down into it from the clear bottle hung above the bed. And then he became aware that his left wrist was handcuffed to the metal frame. Someone evidently felt that, despite his condition, somehow he could run away. He supposed he should take it as a compliment.

The days passed in a morphine dream. A succession of doctors and nurses treated him with brusque contempt, as if he were an enemy soldier. They ignored all his questions, and it did not take much imagination to guess they had been ordered to. Christmas came and went, and all that marked it was a strange sweet pudding in a tray dropped onto his bedside table. He could hear the New Year celebration, but it did not involve him.

He was rolled down hallways for more surgery. The rubber mask clamped over his face, and when he woke again the tube was gone from his chest. His broken legs had been let down from the pulleys, but were still in plaster. His wrist was still handcuffed to the bed.

It was not long after that last surgery when he awoke to the strong smell of cigarette smoke in the room. Sitting beside his bed was the same intelligence colonel who had debriefed him upon his arrival at the British embassy and silently observed his interview with Winston Churchill. A slight fellow, with a high forehead and intelligent, professorial eyes. A pencil moustache that did him no favors—though enough ribbons on his jacket to make Alexsi imagine he was one of those wiry British professors who plunged into trackless jungles in search of lost cities.

The colonel's legs were crossed. He was patiently smoking a cigarette and eyeing Alexsi dispassionately. The state of the ashtray told Alexsi that he had been waiting for some time. During their previous meeting the man had declined to offer his name, and Alexsi did not expect it now.

A good interrogator always wanted you at your worst. Such as when you were still loopy from morphine and sleepless from nurses taking your blood pressure and temperature every hour all night long.

Alexsi knew this would be the second most important conversation of his life, after his first meeting in the Lubyanka prison in Moscow with his Soviet spy mentor, Grigory Petrovich Yakushev. Yakushev had softened him up for that one by throwing him into a cell full of Russian thieves to fight for his life. The conditions here were much better, but it was equally life-and-death.

During Alexsi's training, Yakushev had deliberately worked him into a constant state of exhaustion and then made every lesson, every conversation into an interrogation. Alexsi hadn't realized the aim until much later, but now he gave thanks for the man's thoroughness. No matter how he felt, and he felt terrible, it was time to bear down and focus. It was not as if he hadn't been expecting it, and not as if there had been anything to do in that bed but prepare himself.

The colonel finally noticed him and stubbed out his cigarette. "Finally awake, eh? And, I must say, looking much the worse for wear."

Waiting and listening was usually best, but Alexsi had already decided to cut to the chase. "My offer of service still stands, sir."

The colonel uncrossed his legs and moved the ashtray from his lap to the small bedside table. "Well, that's quite generous of you, old chap. Sure that had nothing to do with you being caught. Thanks so much, though. No longer interested."

Alexsi let time pass by while they stared at each other. In a rare moment of praise, Yakushev had once told him that he would always be every interrogator's nemesis, because the best weapon was silence and people's universal need to fill it. Whereas Alexsi was one of the rare few with no fear of it. He waited until the colonel finally began to fidget, then asked the question. "Then why are you here, sir?"

"Curiosity. Here to find out what your game *really* was, after all."

"It is what I told you at first, sir. An offer of service."

"That's really what you're sticking with? A bit thin at this point, I must say."

"Then why did I save Churchill's life, sir?" Alexsi asked. "If I am not who I say I am. If I am whatever you imagine: a German agent, a Soviet agent, a confidence man of some sort . . . then why did I save your prime minister's life?"

The colonel frowned, and Alexsi knew that, for good or ill, he had just saved them both an hour of banter. He had also left the door open for the question that stood between them to be asked, and rather than answer it unsolicited he wanted the colonel to ask it.

Obliging him, the colonel said, "Then why run?"

"I will not go back to Berlin," Alexsi said. "I cannot. I am blown there. Inside a week I would be hanging from a meat hook in the cellar of Gestapo headquarters."

"That's rather vivid," the colonel observed.

"I have been there," Alexsi told him. "I have seen the hook."

Clearly, that was close to the last thing the colonel expected to hear, and he paled slightly as he took a moment to absorb it. "Then why didn't you just say that before?"

"Would it have made any difference, sir?" Alexsi countered. "After your prime minister endorsed the idea? I am sorry, sir, but I am a Russian and I have posed as a German in Germany, and in my experience there would be no debating such an order. I would be sent back to Berlin. And I will not be sent back to Berlin. But my offer of service to you still stands." His throat had been sore from the beginning, and his voice long unused. All this unaccustomed talking had lowered it to a rasp.

"Terribly good of you. But why should I trust you? After your little escape the provost marshal of Teheran is off to a new posting in Sierra Leone. I should not care to join him."

"I should think you would want a man who can disappear from an embassy surrounded by troops," Alexsi said. "But if I am mistaken . . ."

He was seized by a coughing fit, and with his free right hand snatched the small white enameled basin from the bedside table. Leaning over on his left side, which was painful enough already, he was racked by unstoppable coughing spasms. It felt as if his ribs were cracking. Then, on the verge of feeling like his lungs were about to come up, he coughed out an enormous gelatinous blob. A few more coughs and he was able to stop. Drained by the ordeal, he looked down into the basin with dismay at a huge quivering black blood clot.

Alexsi leaned back against the pillows, feeling completely drained of strength. The colonel left the room and fetched a nurse, who wiped his face with a damp cloth and whisked away the basin.

"Doctor said that might happen," the colonel said. "Good sign."

Alexsi just nodded weakly against his pillow. Nice to let him know, since he had thought he was about to die.

The colonel sat back down and handed him a glass of water. Alexsi took it and drank, nodding his gratitude.

Alexsi felt it would be a race between when he finally felt able to speak again, and when the colonel lost interest.

Sensing that the colonel was about to get up and walk out, Alexsi summoned up his strength and said, "Sir, whatever you imagine I might be, or what kind of conspiracy I might be attempting on you, let me ask. Does any possible scenario make sense to you except what I have already described?"

The colonel thought that over for a good long time. "Then what are your terms? Just out of curiosity, you understand."

"I would be pleased to discuss them with a senior officer of your service, sir. In England."

The colonel looked triumphant at that, as if he had finally heard what he expected. "So you want to go to England? That's your game."

"If I remain here," said Alexsi, "the NKVD will eventually hear of my presence. If they have not already. And I will be dead and of no use to you."

"You think the Soviets can get into a British Army hospital," said the colonel.

"Much easier than I got out of your embassy," Alexsi replied.

The colonel thought that over for a moment, then said, "That won't wash, my friend. If you have terms you'll discuss them with me."

But from his face Alexsi felt that it did in fact wash. "I think not, sir. With respect. Once in England I will either be of great service to you, or you will throw me into prison. Or shoot me, if you prefer."

"Spies are hanged," the colonel interjected.

"Then that would be my fate," Alexsi replied. "Please excuse me, but I am very tired, now. You have my curriculum vitae. You will let me know if I have the job."

And with that he closed his eyes and went to sleep.

7

1944

TEHERAN, IRAN

So much for a nap as a negotiating tactic, Alexsi thought. When he opened his eyes it was late afternoon and a tray of lunch was sitting on his bedside table. He couldn't believe he had slept that long. He also couldn't believe the nurses had left him undisturbed that long.

A nurse came in. "Ah, you're finally awake."

As she took his temperature and checked his pulse, Alexsi reflected that there were at least five different types of British accents he'd heard so far. Three of them were nearly impenetrable to his ear. The Scottish didn't even count.

She plucked out the thermometer and looked at his tray. "You need to eat to keep up your strength," she said sternly. All the British nurses spoke the same way, as if they could order illness from your body. "I'll leave it."

Despite the command, Alexsi thought her tone was markedly more friendly than he'd heard to date. Perhaps the colonel had put in a word to them.

As she left, he checked the doorway. No guard. It would have been no effort to put one on his door, so it was clear the colonel hadn't taken him seriously.

Alexsi examined the contents of the lunch tray with his spoon. Cold, hot, it didn't matter. He had gone hungry so many times in his life that food was food. British hospital food was creamed everything, with the entrée having the same rough consistency as the pudding. Though it was definitely not as sweet. The first spoonful gave Alexsi an unsettling thought. No, they wouldn't poison his food. Only because the meals were served all at once and if the right tray didn't reach the right victim it would cause an uproar. Not that they would care if anyone else died, but they would want it to be secret.

When the tray was empty, he lay back on his pillows to think things over. A Russian/German shot up with Iranian smugglers and a prisoner in a British Army hospital would definitely be a topic of conversation, and the NKVD had very long ears. The Soviets would never forget about him, not after he'd spoiled their plans and killed their men.

It would most likely be an assassin sent to his room. Done in a moment and out the door. A dead body for the British to scratch their heads over, and an object lesson for everyone else. In Moscow, just before he left for Berlin, Yakushev had shown him an album full of news clippings. All the Russian traitors the NKVD had tracked down and liquidated abroad.

Time was against him. Even with the colonel's endorsement, any decision to bring him to England would have to go all the way to England, and come back. No one would be in a rush to make a decision on his account.

Once again he was on his own. The British had of course taken his knives, wristwatch, papers, and everything else when they removed his clothes. Losing that little folder was like losing an old friend. It had been with him since Azerbaijan, and saved his life any number of times. Alexsi knew he was in no condition to fight off an attack with no weapons. Not with both legs in plaster and coughing up blood clots from a bullet through the lungs. Taking leave of the hospital was impossible for the very same reasons.

Alexsi was a Russian. A girl whose betrayal had nearly killed him twice had told him the most Russian thing he would ever hear: Your fate is your fate. Alexsi's Russian soul refused to dismiss fate, but he also had no intention of lying in bed and waiting for it to arrive at his door. He spent the rest of the afternoon thinking things over, and after making up his mind took another nap. He would need to be alert when the sun went down.

The hospital had quieted down for the night. Alexsi leaned over as far as the handcuffs would allow to look out the window at the track of the moon. With no clock it was the only way he could tell the time, and it was high. Time to move.

While examining his legs, one of his doctors had left his patient chart on the side table. Alexsi had acquired one of the metal paper-binding pins at that time. Now he retrieved it from his pillowcase. Handcuffs were not hard to open with the bent-open end of the pin, and in any case he had little to do but practice.

Now came the real problem. The plaster casts came up to his groin. Would the bottoms be flat enough to support him upright without him falling on his face and breaking both legs all over again?

As quietly as he could, he pushed down the folding metal side frame of the bed. Holding on to it for support, he swung himself out of the bed and tried to bring himself up vertically.

By the devil, he was weak. Already light-headed, he was teetering on the rounded plaster encasing his feet. At least his legs didn't hurt, though the ends of the casts digging into his groin were none too comfortable. He stayed close to the bed so he could fall back onto it if necessary.

Just about to give himself up to fate, he realized that his metal side table was on wheels. Feeling like a fool, he transferred the contents onto the bed. It turned out that he could even raise the table higher.

This was much better. He tried a few steps across the room, and the table supported him nicely.

The table made noise when he moved, but then people were always pushing noisy things around hospitals. Even at night.

Alexsi listened at the door. The nice thing about hospital hallways was he could tell how many people were about by the sound of their feet. He would be all right unless a nurse popped in unexpectedly.

While waiting for his moment, he practiced walking across the room. It was not going to be easy in the casts, never mind the table for support. That and his physical condition, which was close to nonexistent.

He lay back on the bed to rest as he listened intently to the hallway. After about an hour it seemed that the time had come. The night shift took their tea break at exactly the same time, like clockwork. The British were as humorously fanatical about their teatime as every book about them made out.

Up again, and moving slightly more confidently, he peered out the door. The hallway was empty. Nothing ventured, nothing gained. If caught he would just say that he was going stir-crazy, and they could drag him back and handcuff him again.

Lurching forward, he thought this was what ice skating must be like. But that only brought back dark memories of a freezing Moscow winter.

He kept one hand on the hallway wall for support, and the other balancing himself on the rolling table. Between the clicking of his plaster feet and the squeaking of the table wheels, he was making, to his mind, a tremendous amount of noise. As he approached the nurses' desk, hugging the wall for both concealment and physical support, he heard voices. But the desk was abandoned. The voices were coming from a room where, he guessed, the nurses and doctor were taking their tea. The door was half closed.

Good fortune had already put him on the opposite wall, where he needed to be to cross in front of the door without casting a shadow. Pushing hard against the wall with one hand to take as much weight off the table wheels as possible, Alexsi slid past the door in the widest lurching stride he could manage.

Once safely past, he had to lean against the wall for a moment to get his breath back. He certainly didn't have the strength to get out of the hospital. The odds were even whether he would have the strength to get back to his room without collapsing.

He'd been hoping, but there was nothing at the nurses' desk he could use. He hadn't imagined that the staff of a military hospital would be carrying sidearms, but you never knew. There was a wheelchair there, though. Alexsi fell back into it with relief, the wooden frame creaking under his weight. He'd been nearly all in. And now at least if someone happened upon him he could explain himself as a patient who was allowed to be roaming the halls.

That gave him pause, and he pondered rolling right out of the hospital in the chair. No. Foolish. He might make it out the door, but what then? He couldn't drive with his legs in plaster casts. What could he disguise himself as, a man with two broken legs in a wheelchair? If they caught him escaping again, all the bargaining in the world would do him no good. It would be prison or the hangman. The odds were even worse than remaining in the hospital.

Deciding to stick with his original plan, Alexsi left his rolling table at the nurses' station and continued on in the wheelchair. It was a surgical ward, for heaven's sake. There had to be something. And he had to find it before teatime ended.

Ah. On the other side of the nurses' desk the patient rooms ended.

There was a door marked SURGICAL SUPPLIES. Alexsi opened it, and pushed himself through in the wheelchair. He had to lift himself out of it to turn on the light. Getting caught was the least of his worries now.

Holding on to the counter for support, he made his way down the shelves. The instruments were arranged in metal trays, to be sterilized before surgery. He passed by the scalpels. Only if he had to. A scalpel, like a straight razor, was a decent weapon only if your adversary was conveniently immobilized, or you had all the time in the world to wait for them to bleed to death.

There. On the last shelf was an array of surgical trocars. Solid metal handles and a hollow spear point like a highly sharpened screwdriver.

Alexsi chose two and slid them into the drawstring waistband of his hospital gown, tying it tighter around them. Then he rearranged the tray to make the remaining instruments look symmetrical and untouched.

Light off and back into the chair. As soon as he got the door closed, he made speed down the hall and back to his room. The rubber wheels were much quieter than his rolling table. Halfway back down the hall he heard footsteps behind him. Once again he gave thanks for hospital floors.

Alexsi whirled about in the chair and saw the shadow down the hall. He wouldn't be able to make it. He opened the door of the nearest room and rolled right in.

Looking over his shoulder, he saw two empty beds and thought he was safe. But there was no way to hide in a wheelchair. Alexsi stood up, holding the wall for support, and with one hand pushed the chair around the corner. He slipped behind the door so he would be concealed behind it if anyone came in. And left it open a crack so he could see out.

Then a low moaning began behind him. Alexsi nearly leaped out of his skin. Teetering on his casts, he took a long moment to twist himself around, and as he did the moaning only grew louder. Alexsi's hand instinctively dropped to one of the trocars in his waistband. There was a bed in the corner that he hadn't seen in the darkness, and an Indian soldier was lying there, eyes so wide the white sclera was clearly visible in the darkness. Staring straight at him, moaning. Then, as Alexsi turned about, the moaning changed into some kind of chant in an Indian language. It sounded religious.

Alexsi was trying to think of something to say to calm the fellow down and quiet him, but he didn't even know if the Indian spoke English. He might just make it worse. Then he looked down at himself and realized. The moon through the window was shining on him standing there in his white hospital gown and white plaster casts. The poor fellow must have thought the angel of death had suddenly appeared to take him away.

Alexsi let go of the wall and spread his arms out in the most benevolent gesture he could think of. The Indian abruptly stopped chanting and violently threw the sheets over his head so he would no longer have to see what was happening.

Well, at least that had stopped the noise. Alexsi realized that these rooms must be only for patients just out of surgery, who were then moved to large wards as in German hospitals. They had just kept him in one by himself until they sorted out his fate. The Indian fellow, in addition to being superstitious, was probably drugged up to boot. And that had only made everything worse.

He turned his attention back to the hallway. The footsteps tapped past. Looking out the door a crack, Alexsi saw that it was the stocky unpleasant nurse he had nicknamed the dragon. Taking a break in the hospital from her regular duties, which he had imagined to be reuniting severed heads with the correct bodies from the battlefield.

She disappeared around the corner. Alexsi knew if he waited much longer the Indian might start moaning again. Grabbing the wheelchair and the doorframe, he swung himself back out in the hallway. At least the poor fellow could tell his friends that death had passed him by this time.

Panting from his exertions, he finally grasped the doorknob of his room. The wheelchair could not be explained, so he stood up and shoved it down the hall with all his might. It sailed away, finally bouncing against the wall and coming to a stop a healthy distance away.

No table, which he'd left down at the nurses' station. Lurching across the room, Alexsi piled everything that had been on it onto the meal tray, and dumped it all atop the chair that the colonel had left and that one of the nurses had tucked away in the corner.

The hallway suddenly came alive with footsteps as he jammed the trocars deep under his mattress, where they wouldn't be found when the nurse changed the bedding.

Alexsi collapsed back into the bed. He was still panting, but at least now he was winded and relieved. He was congratulating himself on a job well done when he was suddenly seized with alarm. He snapped the handcuff back onto his wrist just as the door opened.

It was the little redheaded Scottish nurse whose accent was totally impenetrable. "Awake, are ye?" she said. Then a frowning glance at the tray and pans and water tumbler piled up on the chair. "Where is ye table?"

At least that was what he thought she said. "I don't know," Alexsi replied. "It was like this when I woke up."

A despairing sigh at the foolish ways of people. "Och, roamin' wheelchairs, tables gone missin'. There's no end to it." She picked up his tray from the chair, and going out the door said, "At least ye ate somethin'."

Alexsi toweled the sweat off his face with his sheet.

The nurse was back in a minute, rolling the table before her and still shaking her head. She arranged everything back onto it and then examined his face. "Ye canna sleep? Do ye ken fur a draught?"

Alexsi didn't have the faintest idea what she was saying. "Perhaps a book to read? Please?" All his previous requests had been ignored.

"Wot language?" she asked suspiciously.

"English would be fine," Alexsi replied. He had always read it better than he spoke it.

"A comic?" she inquired. "Or somethin' deep?"

It still sounded like another language entirely coming out of her. Alexsi guessed that a comic book would be roughly the same in German or English. Unless she meant humor. In any event . . . "Deep would be fine," he said.

She turned to go.

"And might I have some water, please?" Alexsi added.

As she went off he made the instant decision to sleep during the day so he would be alert at night. Daytime would be best, of course. The wards full of doctors, nurses, orderlies, visitors. Wait until the hospital was at its busiest, then slip into the room, do the work, and then slip out among all those white coats and uniforms and anonymous faces.

But he was certain that if they came at all they would come at night. Night was the time of murder. As Yakushev would have said scornfully, they would mistake quiet for security.

The Scottish nurse returned with a full tumbler of water and the collected works of Shakespeare. As she handed the book to him she raised an eyebrow as if to ask whether that was all right.

Alexsi was actually overjoyed. At the University of Berlin he had read some of the plays in German translation, but never the original. "Thank you very much, miss."

She beamed at him and said something like "Och, dinna mention it."

Alexsi fondled the book's leather cover. This would definitely help pass the time. Waiting for his killers would be difficult enough as it was.

8

1944

TEHERAN, IRAN

They did not appear like the murderers in *Richard III,* garrulous and debating their mission. They came in silent and determined, dressed in white orderly uniforms, gliding in on soft shoes.

The hall light stabbed into the room when the door was opened and quickly closed again. Alexsi, pretending to be asleep, thought his Indian friend of the other night hadn't been too far wrong about the white angel of death. He was lying on his side, facing the door. Eyes only open a crack, feigning the deep regular breathing of sleep.

The first murderer stood still for a moment, looking over the room in the darkness. He reached inside his white jacket and Alexsi's stomach dropped. He had to stop himself from moaning. If it was a silenced gun then his attacker was out of reach. And he was a dead man.

But it was a leather case. The first murderer removed a hypodermic syringe and, overconfidently, set the case down on the rolling table next to Alexsi's head.

Alexsi fervently hoped that the other would remain at the door and keep watch, but that was not to be. The second murderer slipped around the other side of the bed. Two men to subdue one. Easier that way. Keep the victim from struggling and crying out until the work was done.

The first murderer leaned down, not like a doctor about to administer an injection, but with the tube clasped in his fist and his thumb on the plunger.

Even though he could not see him, Alexsi could hear the second murderer's breathing. He knew the man was poised over him, waiting until the first was ready.

Alexsi lashed out from under the sheets and with his left hand caught the wrist with the syringe. It was not his strong hand, so he only used momentum to jerk the wrist down and the needle into the mattress. They were face-to-face now, and those overconfident eyes were now wide and frightened. Slightly raised up, Alexsi swung his right hand in an arc past his ear. There was a sound like a knife plunging into a green melon when he drove the trocar into the side of the murderer's skull just above the ear.

The first murderer's eyes rolled up, and his body spasmed as if it had been galvanized by electricity.

All Alexsi needed was a second of stunned hesitation and a little luck. He got both. As he whirled about the second murderer grabbed for his throat. This one's job had been to hold him down for the injection, and so he had no weapon immediately at hand and no time to reach for one.

Alexsi didn't resist the hand on his throat. He wanted his man even closer than arm's length. The second trocar, carefully positioned under the pillow, was already in his right hand. He reached out with his left and yanked the front of the orderly jacket toward him, for leverage.

Alexsi had only been aiming for the head, but the trocar went in the left eye and buried itself up to the handle with much less resistance than the previous one. In what must have been a final parting message from his brain, the second murderer threw himself violently backward, struck the wall, and then crumpled to the floor.

Alexsi shouted, as loud as he could manage, "It's your time now, fucker!" In Russian, in case there was a third man outside the room covering the door. Out of weapons and strength, he collapsed back onto the pillows. If there was another assassin, who didn't run after hearing that, then he was done for.

He watched the door, awaiting the verdict on his fate. It opened and he was momentarily blinded as the room light snapped on.

Another figure dressed in white, but it was only the little Scottish nurse. She was looking down at the body of the first murderer on the floor, the gleaming polished trocar sticking out of the side of the head. With an edged weapon the only guaranteed instant kill was the brain, and the skull was too hard for most knives. His NKVD instructors had taught him that back in Moscow.

The nurse's hands were over her mouth, but that was not diminishing the volume of her screams in the slightest.

Alexsi was about to try and say something to her, but his arm bumped into something hard. He froze, and amid all the screaming calmly reached down and plucked the poison syringe from his mattress. He carefully set it onto the table.

He looked at his hands, but not to check them for spots of blood like one of Shakespeare's hero/villains. The first time he had killed a man with a blade, they shook for an hour afterward. Now they only trembled in time with his thumping heart. The Russians said there were two types of men. When their lives were in danger the first became frightened, then thought. They were the ones who died. The second thought, then became frightened afterward. They were the ones who lived.

9

1944

TEHERAN, IRAN

The colonel said, "They tell me there was enough potassium chloride in that syringe to stop the heart of a Bengal tiger." He was back in his chair by Alexsi's bedside. His uniform was still immaculate, but Alexsi knew the man had been called from his bed. The hair was slightly less meticulously combed back, and one corner of the pencil moustache had been nicked during hasty shaving. The neck was glowing with the rash of that, the same color as the bloodshot eyes. Though he was hiding it well, that usual air of upper-class English unconcern seemed a bit frayed when he had to reposition the chair to avoid the pool of blood on the floor, which had not yet been mopped up. "By the way, have you ever heard tell how one hunts a tiger?"

Alexsi shook his head.

"You stake out a live goat as bait," the colonel told him. "Never heard of the goat staking himself out, though."

"I had no other option," Alexsi said.

"No, *I* gave you no other option," the colonel replied. Then he sighed. "Good of you, though, not to rub it in."

There were now two burly military policemen stationed outside the hospital room door. That really had been all the apology Alexsi wanted.

The colonel appeared to be finding Alexsi's calm silence more unsettling than the blood on the floor. As if he would have preferred shouted recrimination. "You didn't happen to recognize those chaps by any chance?"

"I never saw them before," said Alexsi. "And they did not speak." He added, "Not in any language."

The colonel stared at him for a moment, as if formulating a reply. "Not carrying any papers. Unfortunate, that."

"They were not amateurs," Alexsi said. "European, though. Not Iranian. I am sure you will discover they were not British."

The colonel took another moment to reflect on that. Then, "Hospital stores were missing two surgical trocars. You wouldn't care to tell me how you got your hands on them, would you?"

"No," Alexsi said.

The colonel smirked at that. "Didn't think so. Well, you've certainly fleshed out your curriculum vitae. You're quite the survivor, aren't you?"

"Thus far," Alexsi replied. He was not foolish enough to think he had bent fate to his will. He had been skilled before, but still unlucky enough to be shot to pieces off a smugglers' truck. This time he had been both skilled and lucky.

"You'll be pleased to hear you're on your way to England."

"Thank you."

"That's it?"

"I apologize," said Alexsi. "Was something else expected of me?"

"No, I don't imagine so," said the colonel. "It seems the Russians certainly believe you are who you say you are. Probably past time I believed it, too."

Alexsi nodded, inwardly relieved. If the NKVD decided to try again, the two military policemen would be only a momentary impediment. He reached under his pillow and handed the colonel a pair of handcuffs, neatly coiled. "Now that my door is guarded, perhaps you could return these to their owner."

The colonel balanced them in his hand for a moment, as if testing their weight. Then he put them in his briefcase without another word.

PART TWO

However much you feed the wolf, he still looks to the woods.

—RUSSIAN PROVERB

10

TEHERAN, IRAN—WHITCHURCH, BRISTOL, ENGLAND

While they were cutting off his casts, the doctor stood so far away he was nearly out of the room. The better to escape, Alexsi imagined, if the patient suddenly began stabbing people in the head. That was what it was like with two dead men on your account. Two *more* dead men, he reminded himself. The orderly who did the work reminded him of an assault pioneer unscrewing the detonator from a land mine while wondering what sort of day they'd had at the mine factory.

They cut his hair and let him shave and shower afterward, and it was wonderful. Even though it was like learning how to walk all over again with knees that actually bent. Alexsi spent a long time scrubbing the flaking skin and plaster off his poor white matchstick legs. He tried a few deep knee bends. Getting down was no problem, but coming back up felt like fighting the weight of an anvil on his back.

When he emerged from the bath, there was the scratchy brown battle dress and side cap of a British private soldier waiting for him. The clothing smelled of mothballs. One of the pair of military police who hovered about like two guard dogs had to show him how to wind the absurd puttees. Both of them glowered their disapproval, as if he were being given something he had not earned. Alexsi understood their attitude but he appreciated the colonel's foresight. During a war a uniform was the best way to blend in.

His legs were so weak that he had to walk out of the hospital, if you could call it walking, with each hand on a military policeman's shoulder for support. Over his shoulder was a canvas valise pouch. Inside were his only current possessions: a canvas roll apparently issued to all British soldiers that contained, in pockets, shaving equipment and metal shaving mirror, eating knife, fork, and spoon, boot and clothing brushes, foot and tooth powder; also two enameled mugs, because apparently it was unthinkable to not have some means of drinking tea on your person at all times. The volume of Shakespeare was also tucked inside the bag. True to his thief's instincts, he had not asked to keep it. But then again, they had not asked for it back.

He left with no ceremony, and they bundled him into a jeep with even less. Alexsi remembered when he was only a boy traveling from Soviet Russia to Nazi Germany. A fledgling spy kicked out of the NKVD nest at the Lubyanka to fly on his own. Everything was so new, so bright, compared to what seemed to be the grayness of Russia. He never wanted the train trip to end. Now every journey was just something to be endured. Alexsi wondered if he had become jaded. Or perhaps it was just that now he knew how very long and boring it would be.

At the airport there was an American Dakota cargo plane with British bull's-eye roundels. The military police gave him up on the runway, but after he climbed up the ladder into the plane and was pointed toward the one remaining empty seat there was an Englishman in a suit but with obvious military bearing among the passengers who walked over, leaned down, and murmured, "Don't try to skip out, there's a good chap." The Englishman then opened his suit jacket to reveal a small Browning hammerless automatic in a leather shoulder holster. Just to get his point across. Then the Englishman returned to his own seat and never spoke another word the rest of the flight.

There were only twelve seats for passengers, with light cargo in crates along with passenger luggage strapped to the floor behind them. Alexsi was sure that, just as in the German Army, only the highest-priority people were allowed to make such flights. For everyone else it was slow trains or even slower ships.

Teheran to Baghdad. Baghdad to Cairo. Cairo to Tripoli. Tripoli to Gibraltar. It took that many days. At each stop a succession of army dining halls and meals of canned beef or canned fish, and always canned vegetables cooked down to a green slime. The beef was mostly suet by the time Alexsi reached it. Or else it had been suet all along. Also pudding that was not really pudding. And tea, of course. If you didn't have a watch, which he didn't, you could tell the time by when the tea appeared. On the airplane there was a crewman with a steaming kettle that had come from somewhere, hopefully not an open fire in the cockpit, and they all drank from those enameled mugs. With canned milk that everyone but Alexsi mysteriously had on their possession. He would have liked some, because raised on Russian tea, he could barely choke this English stuff down.

The final leg of the journey was Gibraltar to Lisbon. They spent only a short time there. Alexsi looked out the window longingly at neutral Portugal. There was the possibility of being able to draw on his Swiss money through a Portuguese bank, and false papers could surely be obtained there. But the suit-wearing Englishman with the automatic might as well have been reading his mind. He stationed himself in the door of the Dakota as long as it was open. But, interestingly, stepped out just as the door was shut and did not return. His seat was taken by a middle-aged English woman clutching a hatbox. When that happened Alexsi was sure this would be the final leg of the journey.

Once they were back in the air he realized that the stop in Lisbon had been carefully timed so the flight to England would be under the cover of night to foil any marauding German long-range fighter planes.

Only the darker darkness of land compared to the sea told Alexsi that they had reached England. The entire country was blacked out. Except for the runway, it was like a black carpet—not a single light visible anywhere.

After a landing so bouncy that only the seat belts kept everyone off the roof of the plane, the propellers spun down and the side door opened. When no one told him otherwise, Alexsi followed the rest of the passengers out and down a rickety metal ladder.

Someone with a shielded battery lantern was saying, with English politeness, "Stay together, please."

The lantern led them into a building, and only when they were all inside and the door with thick blackout curtains was closed did the lights come on.

Alexsi shielded his eyes with his hand until they adjusted to the brightness. The first thing he saw was a faded sign on the wall that read: THE BRISTOL AND WESSEX AEROPLANE CLUB. Trying to remember his geography, he had no idea where Bristol and Wessex was but guessed they had flown here rather than London to remain out of range of the Luftwaffe.

"After the baggage is brought in, kindly be prepared to present your passports, or your paybook and official orders," came the announcement from the other side of the room.

Having neither, Alexsi fell into the back of the queue that formed. Doubtless someone from British intelligence would show up to straighten it out.

The room lifted into a low roar of conversation, and cigarettes ignited like a forest full of trees on fire.

Double doors opened, and four carts of luggage were rolled in. Everyone pushed forward with their tickets. Alexsi's luggage was the canvas bag already slung over his shoulder, so he remained against the far wall.

There were two podium desks with long wooden benches behind for customs inspection. Curious considering how few passengers there were, but both were manned.

After no one approached him, Alexsi could only assume that the customs agent would know who he was. Upon reaching the desk as the last in line, he only stood there and waited.

The customs officer said, "Paybook and orders, Private."

As if speaking to a simpleton, for which Alexsi could not blame him. "I have neither, sir."

The customs officer's eyes narrowed at Alexsi's heavily accented English. "Passport?"

Alexsi shook his head.

In a tone that could only be described as cautious, "Did you come off that plane?"

The customs officer was a younger man, though not as young as Alexsi. Pale and reedy enough to make Alexsi imagine that asthma or something similar had kept him from military service. The question was so incredible that Alexsi thought he might be on the receiving end of the legendary British sense of humor. He briefly considered replying that no, he had parachuted onto the airfield but then walked into the terminal to clear customs because it would be wrong not to have his passport stamped. Briefly, but then he actually replied, "I was placed on the aircraft by British intelligence, sir. I suggest you inquire to them."

"I see," said the customs officer, as if that was absolutely the last thing he had expected to hear that evening. The other customs officer, an older man, was now standing behind him. Then, after a pregnant pause, "You may leave your bag with me, and take a seat over there." He was pointing to a bench seat against the far wall, far away from any door.

That order had been accompanied by enough dry swallowing to make Alexsi think that the issuer was worried about it being obeyed. Not fancying his chances in the darkness of wartime England with no money or papers or even a remote idea where he was, Alexsi only sighed and said, "Yes, sir."

From his seat he watched the customs officer speaking animatedly on the telephone. He wondered how long it would take to straighten out. All the other passengers had disappeared out the door, presumably to some sort of transport.

On the bright side, it was the first time in five days that no one was offering him any tea that he would feel obligated to choke down out of politeness.

An hour later the terminal door opened, along with Alexsi's hopes. Then he sighed again as they fell back to earth. Two English policemen in the uniforms familiar to anyone who had been to the cinema.

As they approached, Alexsi looked up at them from the sitting position.

"Come along with us, son."

They were both middle-aged, and burly, buttoned up tightly in their blue wool. One had a wooden truncheon ready in his hand.

For an instant Alexsi's Russian suspicion thought this might be some kind of test. Then his German practicality dismissed it. It was possible to appreciate the irony, though. After all the trouble it had taken to get to England, to be arrested the instant he arrived, by mistake, because someone had forgotten to do their job or send the right message from Iran. It was his destiny, it seemed, to be arrested by his masters each time prior to becoming a spy.

It would have been funnier if he hadn't been tired, and hungry, and positive this would not be straightened out any time soon.

His lack of response had the bobbies glancing anxiously at each other. "Do you speak English?" the second one demanded.

"Yes, sir," Alexsi replied. His own accent might be poor, but this was yet another nearly impenetrable English regional dialect.

"Come along quietly, then," said the first.

Other than the truncheons, they were both unarmed, but then so was Alexsi. He'd lost his knives after being shot in Iran, and the period since then was actually the first time in nearly twenty years when he was not carrying one. He would come along quietly, though. When he was first arrested as a boy by the NKVD, they had beaten him senseless when he tried to run. The Gestapo would have, if he had given them the opportunity.

He stood up and walked to the door, flanked by the policemen on both sides.

Before they reached it the customs agent ran up and handed one of the bobbies Alexsi's shoulder bag.

"Anything in there?" the policeman who accepted it inquired.

"I didn't look," said the customs agent.

The bobbies both stopped, along with Alexsi because they were grasping his arms. "Correct me if I'm wrong," said the older policeman to the customs agent. "But that's your job, isn't it?"

"There might be a bomb in there," the customs agent replied lamely.

The policeman holding the bag held it up in front of Alexsi's face. "Is there a bomb in there?"

Alexsi shook his head.

"Right, then," the policeman said witheringly, in the direction of the customs agent. And they carried on out the door and into an automobile. Which had burlap sacking over the headlights.

One policeman driving, the other sitting beside Alexsi. His bag on the front seat.

They drove without a word between them over dark country roads that ended in a village, and a village police station.

Immediately through the door, screened by blackout curtains, there was a desk behind an open window. Alexsi was familiar with the three arm stripes the British used to identify a sergeant. Though this was another policeman, not a soldier. The man's ruddy face almost matched his ginger hair. "Name?"

Alexsi remained silent.

The sergeant's face turned hard, as if any noncompliance was a challenge to his authority. And the challenge would soon be stamped out. Alexsi had seen the same expression on the face of both Soviet and German policemen. "Name!"

"These gentlemen ordered me to come quietly," Alexsi finally said.

There was a snicker from behind, and the sergeant directed that withering gaze past him at the two bobbies. "That's not what it bloody means."

"I am not supposed to be quiet?" Alexsi asked innocently.

The sergeant's face turned a deeper hue of red. He took a breath, as if to steady himself, then said slowly, enunciating each word, "Tell me your name."

"No, sir," Alexsi replied. And then quickly, to forestall any possible violence, "I will give it to a British intelligence officer."

As if this was something he could manage, the sergeant picked up his pen and began writing. "Right. You refuse to give your name."

Alexsi considered a few possible replies, then decided on "Yes, sir." And then added, "Without malice." He had enjoyed that word reading Shakespeare. He hoped it was still in general use.

The sergeant was still bent over his papers writing. Without lifting his head, he spoke as if to no one in particular. "Lock him up."

The bobbies each took one of Alexsi's arms.

11

1944

WHITCHURCH, BRISTOL, ENGLAND

Say what you would about English jail cells, they were more comfortable than airplanes. And the smell of vomit and urine, just like Soviet and German jail cells. Alexsi used the chamber pot, though it seemed a previous occupant had either not bothered to or was making a statement of his displeasure.

After dawn they brought him a plate of ersatz scrambled eggs, along with a fried slice of some tinned pork product that was previously unknown to him. The bread was quite good, though, toasted and spread with margarine. Of course there was tea.

In midmorning two policemen unlocked the cell, though not to release him. They took him to a room and sat him in a chair. Obviously an interrogation room. A protective wire screen around the lightbulb, and otherwise bare except for a heavy wooden table. Even if it had not been fastened to the floor like the chair, it was too heavy to throw. But no tie-down rings on the table or meat hook fastened to the ceiling, which made it almost cozy compared to a Gestapo interrogation room.

They made him wait there alone, which was always the preferred technique. Then a young man walked in. Wearing a suit but definitely the military type. Specifically the officer type. Not a military reject like the young customs agent of the previous night. University man.

"Hello," the young man said brightly as he came through the door.

Bustling and friendly was how they would start, Alexsi thought. Inviting him to be helpful, to clear things up. If he were in the hands of the Russians or Germans they would begin by beating him like a drum. And he would be talking his head off, at first not of anything consequential, but as long as he was talking they would not be pulling his fingernails out. But if the English were going to be friendly then he would keep his mouth shut until he found out what was going on. Information was a currency like any other. You did not want to empty your pockets foolishly.

After taking the seat on the opposite side of the table the young man unpacked a notebook from a slim leather case, and unscrewed the cap from his fountain pen. "No worries, we'll get this all sorted out. Right. Let's begin with your name."

"You are a representative of British intelligence?" Alexsi inquired.

"As it happens, I am," came the reply.

"Might I ask your name?"

"Ian," the young man said, still bright as a penny.

"Then what is my name?" said Alexsi.

"Pardon?"

"What is my name?" Alexsi repeated.

"That was my question to you, if you recall."

"I will speak only to a representative of British intelligence," said Alexsi.

"Which I am." Wary now, though still outwardly friendly.

"Then you would know my name." Or at least, specifically, the name he had given to the British colonel in Teheran. When Alexsi had been trapped by the NKVD as a young thief and a smuggler, they had revealed an encyclopedic knowledge of his life. A name was something that was entered into an archive and remained there forever. Anyone might read a file and betray the information to a new set of masters. And so Alexsi had always found a new name for every new occasion of his life. Even after saving Churchill he had not given the British his real name. The Russians would always be searching for Alexsi Ivanovich Smirnov, and he would offer them no assistance.

"Your name is for my confirmation," the young man whose name was almost certainly not Ian said.

Alexsi could see him flustered. Anyone at all might enter an interrogation room, identify themselves as British intelligence, and invite you to empty yourself of all your information. If this was a test, he was not about to fail it. If it was, as he now suspected, the next act of a monumental fuckup on someone's part, he was not about to make it any worse by participation. He would know that the right people had found him when he heard the name he had given them in Teheran. He said dispassionately, as an observation, "That is quite weak."

"I must warn you against adopting this attitude. Considering your position, you do not wish to be seen as uncooperative."

"And what is my position?" Alexsi asked.

"A German spy."

Alexsi would have laughed in his face. Would have, if he had any confidence in ever meeting British intelligence in Britain. "Do you often allow German spies to enter your military airfields, board your planes, and fly to England? You should not let the Abwehr find out, they would rejoice at you making their work so much easier."

"Then if you are not a German spy, why are you refusing to answer my questions?"

Enough was enough. "Tell your masters, whoever they are, that I will not speak to an endless procession of flunkies. Send me someone with authority. Who knows what is going on here. Until then, I will say no more."

The young man choked down his obvious anger. "If you will not answer my questions you will be sent directly to Brixton Prison." He then paused, as if to let that sink in.

Alexsi reflected, to himself—because he had already decided on silence, and anyway had been taught that you only provoked an interrogator in order to throw them off their path of inquiry—that what the French called *sang-froid* was merely a matter of experience. If you had already killed a man then you were unlikely to be shaken by killing. If you had already been terrified out of your wits then you were unlikely to be frozen by fear. And if you had already been imprisoned in the Lubyanka then you were certainly unlikely to be intimidated by the mention of some English prison, however medieval. He stared right through the young man who called himself Ian.

The pen was furiously capped, and the notebook slammed shut and thrown back into the case. The goodwill was gone, and the young man not named Ian was furious at having failed in his mission. "I'll have you know we hang spies in this country."

Alexsi broke his silence at that. "They do everywhere."

12

WHITCHURCH, BRISTOL, ENGLAND

The English, it seemed to Alexsi, were almost as dedicated to drink as the Russians. All night long the inebriated had been dragged into the police station. Considering the uproar, the cells must have been full. Sleep had been impossible. Alexsi dreaded the sound of the metal chamber-pot cover scraping open in the cell of the drunken old man next door. It was just the prelude to what sounded like the poor fellow trying to shit out a live rat.

Instead of breakfast, just after dawn a policeman unlocked the barred door to Alexsi's cell and swung it open. "Out you go."

Motioned down the hall with the policeman following, Alexsi found himself at the desk he had arrived at. Though a different sergeant was behind it this time. An older man, in his forties, wearing a waterproof overcoat with the legs of a heavy brown suit poking out beneath it, was bent over signing some papers. Another, about ten years younger, in a belted khaki trench coat, had been standing back observing but was now watching Alexsi like a hawk. They had the look and feel of policemen, but that was true of both NKVD and Gestapo agents also.

The outside door suddenly crashed open and two policemen dragged in a drunk and thrashing young soldier.

"That's right!" the young soldier shouted.

"Shut your gob," one of the policemen ordered, twisting his arm roughly as they tried to position him in front of the desk.

"Go ahead, sort me out!" the young soldier shouted. "Why don't you fucking sort me out!"

Alexsi wondered, did he mean "sort" as in "to arrange"? Between the accents and the usage, English was seeming to be an almost insurmountable problem.

In his urge to make himself heard, the young soldier had been spraying spittle in the direction of the desk. Directly in the path of this onslaught, the older civilian bent over the desk put down his pen and touched the back of his neck. He pushed himself upright and turned around quickly.

The drunken young soldier said, "What's your fucking . . ."

The civilian hit him in the face with a single punch. The two policemen helpfully released their grip on his arms. No longer supported by them, the young soldier fell back straight onto on his ass with his legs splayed out in front of him. He put his hands over his face and immediately burst into tears.

The police sergeant, who while all this was happening had acted as if nothing at all were happening, picked the papers up off his desk and flipped them around, as if to see whether the signature was in the proper location. "Right," he exclaimed. "He's all yours."

Alexsi took that to mean him, and was proven correct when the khaki trench coat pointed toward the door. Alexsi had to step around the soldier on the floor, who was still crying piteously while cupping his hands around his bleeding nose. Once Alexsi was past, the two policemen dragged the crying soldier to his feet.

"Shut up, ya prat," one of the policemen said. "Asked for it, now, didn't ya?"

With the example before them, the two civilians did not bother to deliver any warning. Alexsi thought perhaps he had underestimated the English. They were seeming more interesting by the moment. He just looked at his escorts and nodded as if to say, Point taken, gentlemen.

It appeared he was not about to get his canvas bag and Shakespeare back. Alexsi guessed they would sell it. So British policemen were the same as any other. All thieves, except they didn't have the courage to be *real* thieves.

It was pouring rain outside. A black saloon car was parked in front of the police station, and the khaki trench coat opened the back door. Alexsi was not an automobile fancier; one was as good as another to him. This had the manufacturer's logo of a griffin holding a flag. He also noticed that both men had carefully positioned themselves, without making a show of it, to cut off any avenue of escape. Professionals. Well, they were the first he had encountered in a while.

The older one drove, and the trench coat slid into the backseat next to him. The rain-wet wool of Alexsi's British Army battle dress was giving off a strange odor that it had not had when dry. The wet made the rough fabric itch.

As they drove through the English countryside, the driver kept looking at Alexsi in the rearview mirror.

Alexsi could only guess that most of the people they transported were full of questions. As a boy he had been as full of questions as any other. But a father who beat you whenever you annoyed him taught you not to ask questions. And everything Alexsi ever did seemed to annoy his father.

Later his NKVD trainers praised and encouraged his silence. A spy who asked too many questions only attracted attention to himself. Why are you asking so many questions? In any case, if you only listened attentively people told you everything anyway. Even what you had not thought to ask.

Besides, being in the hands of the authorities was like being in the hands of your father. Asking where you were going or what was happening would at best get you laughed at, at worst beaten up.

This was Alexsi's third time as a prisoner in an automobile on the way to somewhere. The first had been with the NKVD on the way to the Lubyanka in Moscow. The second had been with the Gestapo on the way to Prinz-Albrecht-Strasse in Berlin. He could only hope that this trip would end better. The prison called Brixton would have to work hard to match the tripe soup and rubber truncheons of the Lubyanka.

They drove for three hours by his calculation. In total silence. Then Alexsi saw the first road sign for London.

13

Alexsi had once found a picture book of London on a dusty shelf in a Baku library. In Azerbaijan, on the far edge of the Soviet empire, the censors were much less dedicated to their work.

The real London was just like the pictures, except with more modern automobiles. Though they would turn a corner and there was just a pile of rubble where a building or two had been, courtesy of German bombers. All in all, much less damage than Berlin. Alexsi felt qualified to make the comparison, since the Royal Air Force had done their best to kill him in the Nazi capital.

Some of the roads were so narrow that it seemed a miracle an automobile would fit. Horses, Alexsi thought, remembering narrow dirt lanes through dark Russian forests. The roads had been made when there were only horses.

They came to a stop before a sand-colored office building. An office building, Alexsi thought. Not a prison, at least. The street sign said BROADWAY. The number on the building was 54.

The policeman next to him opened the door, and Alexsi followed him out. A brass plate at the door read: MINIMAX FIRE EXTINGUISHER COMPANY.

Despite all that had happened, for the first time in England Alexsi felt a flutter of panic. It seemed certain that his guards were not making a quick stop to purchase a fire extinguisher. In Moscow everyone knew NKVD headquarters. In Berlin they pulled their coats up around their ears when walking past Gestapo headquarters, as if screams might somehow carry through the sandstone walls. What could be so terrible that it had to be kept a secret in your own capital? It didn't have to look like a prison to be a torture chamber. After all, the Lubyanka had been a department store before the Russian Revolution.

They walked in, and down a narrow hallway. A middle-aged man with graying hair neatly pomaded back sat at a desk behind an opening in the wall. He critically eyed Alexsi in his now-rumpled British Army battle dress and then accepted the credentials of his two escorts. After careful examination and a check against a list on a clipboard, he made a notation in the ledger lying open on his desk. Sliding a narrow strip of flimsy paper from the tidy stack in front of him, he selected a rubber stamp from a rack, struck it violently on an ink pad, and handed the stamped paper over the counter. "Top floor is waiting," he said with mild disapproval.

Sandwiched between his two guard dogs, but as always without being touched, Alexsi was herded down the hallway.

He decided on a test. "I need the toilet," he told the policemen.

The older one looked at his wristwatch. "Can it wait?"

Alexsi shook his head.

The younger one sighed, but they detoured him down another

hallway to a subtly marked men's toilet. One blocked the door while the other stood in the way of the frosted glass window. The same as they had done at the roadside cafés where they had stopped for tea during the drive.

Alexsi really didn't have to go, but he made a show of it nonetheless. The Russians had pounded their lessons into him so effectively that he gathered, catalogued, and analyzed the information around him with hardly a second thought. On the road they had stopped for tea more times than even an Englishman needed, and his escorts carefully pocketed each receipt. So they would be claiming their expenses. They definitely knew their way around this particular building, so they either worked here or brought prisoners often. They were late, which meant they were expected. If he were on his way to interrogation they would not have let him piss. They would not have wanted him to be comfortable.

Ironically, for what was supposed to be a fire extinguisher company, there were only red-painted buckets of sand in the corner alcoves. The walls had once been white but the paint was so old they were now gray. The floor was linoleum, peeling upward at the seams. The lighting was all bare bulbs, but dim. Not like the blinding 200 watts the NKVD favored for the Lubyanka, bright enough to see into your soul and keep you from sleeping until the final bullet in your neck.

There were open doors, unlike in the Lubyanka, where they shot anyone careless enough to leave their office door open. Alexsi could hear loud murmurs of blended conversation, see outside windows of frosted glass, desks separated by scratched wooden partitions. In the Soviet Union everything was shabby but the Lubyanka was the shabby best. Nothing too good for the secret police. This was just shabby.

The elevator was one of those with the sliding metal gate for a door. It activated with a sudden jerk, and as they creaked their way upward it made a noise like the lamentations of the damned. They seemed to be moving a meter a minute. It would have been faster, Alexsi thought, to shut off the motor and for all of them to raise it by pulling on the cable.

They stopped on the fourth floor. The incongruous sight of a man in a suit sitting at what looked like a children's school chair with a desktop attached. The man only glanced up at them and made a notation in a green ledger that an accountant might enter figures into. Down a hallway to the right. The door at the end had a small lit bulb above the sill. Alexsi wondered if that was a signal that someone was in, or that someone was not to be disturbed, or that some visitor urgently needed to be dragged out and dealt with.

Through the door and into a waiting room with two secretaries behind two desks, flanking another door like a pair of guard dogs. One mild-looking and almost attractive, the other a massive dragon that made her desk look small by comparison.

They sat down under the dragon's disapproving eye. She glanced up at the clock on the wall without changing expression. Alexsi thought that was so much more effective than simply announcing that they were late. Both his escorts shifted uneasily in their seats. She had that effect.

The dragon pressed a button and spoke with her hand over the mouthpiece of the telephone so they could not hear. She put the handset back in its cradle and just stared at them without a word.

The door they had just come in opened and a man of about seventy walked in. Alexsi thought he looked like an undertaker in his dark three-piece suit, white shirt, and dark tie. Bald, jowly, wearing circular horn-rim eyeglasses. He just stood there and looked them over like an old owl. Alexsi felt himself being taken in head to toe, with purse-lipped disapproval as if he had dared laugh during a funeral service. With no change of expression that would indicate that his opinion on the subject had changed, the undertaker strode past the dragon's desk and went through the door behind her without a word.

A minute later the phone buzzed. The dragon picked up the handset, listened without speaking, then set it down in the cradle again. Her eyes flicked up to Alexsi, and she said, "You may go in."

Alexsi just sat there until the older policeman elbowed him in the ribs. He stood up, but his two escorts remained seated. He just stood there until the secretary gestured with an impatient open hand toward the door behind her.

It wasn't much of an office. The desk was good wood, but scarred, and nearly bare except for a small stack of files and three telephones. NKVD offices always displayed a portrait of Stalin. Hitler gazed down on the Abwehr with those blazing eyes. There was no sign of the King here. A large green safe stuck out against a back wall. Repository for, Alexsi allowed himself to imagine, all the greatest secrets of the realm.

The undertaker was seated in a padded leather chair beside the desk with his legs crossed. There was only one other man present, behind the desk that was obviously his. Younger, in his fifties, though clearly the one in charge. Also balding, but not to as pronounced a degree as the undertaker, with a full but carefully trimmed moustache encompassing his upper lip. Dressed immaculately in a three-piece pin-striped suit. A strange combination of apparently tall yet almost delicate-looking. This one, Alexsi thought, was the schoolmaster that everyone mistakenly decided was weak until he broke a stick over a pupil's head.

They were both staring at him. Alexsi came to attention before the desk, though just in time catching himself before clicking his heels together like a German officer.

The gentleman behind the desk, and no other description suited him so perfectly, said, "Good morning, young man."

"Good morning, sir," Alexsi replied.

A slight flicker of a reaction to his heavily German-accented English, then, "Please sit down."

An empty chair was waiting before the desk. Alexsi took it.

The man behind the desk said, "I am C, the head of C Service. The organization that, I believe, you have offered your services to."

Alexsi was now beginning to accept that he was finally back in the hands of MI6, the British secret intelligence service, though it was hard to reconcile with this appalling building. The Abwehr headquarters in Berlin was a repurposed mansion even though it was also totally unsuitable to its mission.

In any event, this was really something. In his time Alexsi had also had a personal interview with Admiral Canaris, the head of German military intelligence. The only one missing now was Comrade Beria, the head of the NKVD. Though it was said that meeting Beria was like meeting the angel of death—the last face you would ever see.

"Please excuse me, sir," Alexsi said. "I do not wish to be impertinent. But would you please tell me my name?"

The man who called himself C looked mildly amused. He glanced down at the file folder open on his desk blotter. "Ivan Pavlov," he said.

"Thank you, sir," Alexsi replied.

"That is a question I would have imagined you already knew the answer to," said C. "Might I inquire as to the reason?"

Alexsi said, "Sir, from the moment I arrived in England no one seemed to know who I was or what I was doing here. I assumed that anyone who knew why I was sent from Teheran would know my name. You are the first who did." Actually, Ivan Pavlov was his own joke on the English. It was the Russian equivalent of John Smith. There were so many Pavlovs that they had given up listing them all in the Moscow directory. And those were just the ones whom the state had allowed a telephone. Paper wasn't cheap, after all.

That first night in the British embassy in Teheran he had been truthful with them about everything but his name. Something had held him back. Names were how intelligence agencies unlocked their searches for people. They would go to their files of index cards and look for a name, whether it was real or an alias, and on the card would be other names and places associated with it. Then down to the archives for the files on the names. If you used a different name each time, and never the same one twice, it made their job all the harder and any search for you that much longer.

"Quite," said C. "I feel I owe you both an explanation and an apology. In an unforgivable blunder, the fool who was to meet your flight allowed himself to be delayed. Because of this, normal procedure placed you in the hands of the security people, who are a separate service and of course were not read into your arrival. It has taken us until now to extricate you from their hands and bring you here."

As a Russian, Alexsi would have been inclined to believe that conspiracy was at the heart of every reversal. But as a German, after five years of war, he was now certain that there was little on earth that could not be explained by simple incompetence. All he said was "Yes, sir."

A brief blinking of the eyes was all that conveyed C's amazement. "I must say that's quite decent of you. After saving the prime minister's life the thanks of the nation seemed to involve being shot, abandoned to assassination, and incarceration after being conveyed to England. Any resentment on your part would be understandable. Which was why I wished to meet you personally."

"Yes, sir," Alexsi repeated.

C gestured down at the file folder before him. "Your history as related is so remarkable that my first impression upon reading was that it was either entirely truthful or the product of a deranged mind."

Alexsi sat in silence, until it was clear they were waiting for him to speak. "I am sure you will decide for yourself, sir."

"Where were you born?" C began.

"Soviet Azerbaijan," Alexsi replied. "You would call it, I believe, a state farm."

"Collective farm," the undertaker interjected. His voice was as rude as his manner.

Alexsi shrugged, as if conceding the point.

"When did you volunteer for Soviet intelligence?" C asked.

"I did not volunteer, sir. I was given the choice of service or death."

"You don't say," C replied. "If you would, please expand on that."

Alexsi realized that he was now in the middle of the third-most-important interrogation of his life. "My mother died when I was very young. My father was not an attentive parent, and overly fond of alcohol even by Russian standards."

"So you are Russian, not Azeri?" C said.

Alexsi nodded, realizing that the extent of the British Empire gave its servants special insight into the Near East.

"Please go on," said C.

"Because of this, I regarded a family of Germans as my own."

"German Communists?" the undertaker interrupted again. "Émigrés?"

"Yes, sir. Through them, I learned to speak German."

"Fluently," said C. "With a German accent."

Alexsi nodded.

"That was what brought you to the attention of Soviet intelligence." The undertaker, interrupting again.

"Yes, but not the way you suppose," said Alexsi. "The family was denounced, arrested."

"The purges," said C.

Alexsi nodded again.

"Bloody Communists are always eating their own," stated the undertaker. "Cannibals. Serves them right, what?"

Alexsi struggled to maintain both his silence and his countenance. "My father was also denounced and arrested. I was sent to a state orphanage. I ran away." All true, but he saw no reason to offer more context.

"To what end?" said C.

"I became a thief, sir."

"How remarkable," said C.

To forestall the undertaker's inevitable interruption, Alexsi said, "In the Soviet Union, if you do not wish to serve the state you become a thief. I did not steal from people, since the state owns everything of value. I stole from the state."

"Armed robbery?" said the undertaker.

"You would call me a burglar, sir," said Alexsi. "Later, a smuggler."

"Smuggling what?" the undertaker demanded, before C could open his mouth.

"Arms," said Alexsi. "Across the border from Azerbaijan to Iran."

"In return for . . . ?" the undertaker pressed.

"Livestock," said Alexsi. "Opium. Money, gold, is useless in the Soviet Union."

C gave the undertaker a look across his desk. Chastened, the undertaker leaned back in his chair and folded his hands in his lap.

"Please continue," C told Alexsi pleasantly.

"I did not know it at the time," said Alexsi. "But the NKVD was searching for me. I was arrested in Baku and sent to Moscow on a prison train. In the Lubyanka, I was taken to a ranking officer who offered service or death. I chose service."

"Remarkable," said C. "How old were you at the time?"

"Sixteen, sir."

A glance from C to the undertaker told Alexsi that the British would never contemplate anything like that. "I was told, sir, that Hans Shulz, an official in the German Foreign Ministry, had written to the Soviet Union asking that his nephew join him in Germany."

"The son of the family you grew up with," said C.

"My best friend," said Alexsi.

"Dead?" C said gently.

"I assumed so," Alexsi replied.

"You were to impersonate him," said C. "Because you spoke German, and knew the family intimately."

Alexsi nodded again.

"I'm sure we knew the Russians were baroque," C said to the undertaker. "But dear Lord . . ."

"Sixteen," the undertaker said in reply.

"So they trained you," C said to Alexsi. "If you had failed?"

Alexsi mimed a pistol to the head.

"Incredible," said C. "Off to Germany, then. Join the family. War comes, join the army. Abwehr due to languages, I assume?"

"Also my uncle's influence," said Alexsi.

"Posted to Iran," said C. "Eventually given the assignment of assassinating the prime minister, President Roosevelt, and Marshal Stalin at the Teheran Conference. Simply incredible. Normally spying is a rather mundane business. But this would make a cracking novel, what?"

"Quite," said the undertaker.

"It is in your file," said C. "But just to make it explicit. You lit out from the embassy because you did not wish to return to Berlin. Correct?"

"That is correct, sir," said Alexsi, relieved that finally someone in England was able to grasp that essential truth. "I would not have lasted a week. It would have been suicide."

"Asking people to risk their lives happens to be the mission of this service," said the undertaker. . . .

Unlike the rudeness of people who were simply blunt and had no idea how they were coming off, Alexsi felt, the undertaker's rudeness was intentional. "There is risk, sir," he said, turning to face him. "And then there is suicide. In my experience those who propose suicide missions are always very careful to never be a part of them."

C smiled faintly at that. "Yes, well, the prime minister has been known to let his enthusiasms run away with him on occasion. As have our own people. What did you happen to think of Colonel Nicholson?"

So that was the name of Colonel Pencil Moustache. Alexsi filed it away for future reference. "I think it is good he is in Teheran, sir. Rather than some other post more vital to your war effort."

The undertaker beside the desk chuckled out loud. "Prisoner exchange. That wouldn't have raised any suspicions in Berlin, what?"

"A pity, though," said C. "A source in Berlin would pay great dividends these days."

"If you are asking me to reconsider, sir," said Alexsi, "I must decline again. After Teheran, I am blown as Captain Walter Shulz."

"Quite," said C.

The undertaker spoke again. "If your identity as a German officer is compromised, then what, may I ask, is the value of your services?"

Alexsi was ready with his preferred solution first, but he answered facing C. "Sir, I know you have captured German spies, and therefore are informed how the Abwehr trains its agents. But I was trained as a Wehrmacht infantry officer, and then as an Abwehr military intelligence officer. Perhaps you might find some insight into that process helpful. I served at Abwehr headquarters in Berlin from 1940 to 1941. Abwehr Switzerland and then Iran in 1941. Then back at Abwehr headquarters in charge of the Near East Desk until the end of 1943. Abwehr headquarters is quite small, considering, and I believe I may offer insight into senior officers, organization, agents, and operations in many other theaters. Also communications and coding systems. In addition, I am familiar with the German Army general staff field headquarters at Zossen. I was briefed on my first mission into Iran by Admiral Canaris personally. And on the attempted assassination of Prime Minister Churchill, President Roosevelt, and Premier Stalin by General Schellenberg of the SD personally."

"So it wasn't Canaris?" C interrupted quickly.

"No, sir," said Alexsi. "The mission came directly from Himmler to General Schellenberg, and was exclusively an SS operation. I was the only Abwehr officer, and that was only due to my experience in Iran. I was quite literally picked up on the street by the Gestapo, taken directly to General Schellenberg's office, and ordered under pain of death not to say anything to anyone at Abwehr."

"I'll wager that gave you a turn," said the undertaker.

Alexsi ignored him. He was watching C, who was leaning forward in his chair. The Russians had taught him to be alert to anything that provoked undue interest in an interrogator. If you listened carefully you could learn more from them than they were trying to extract from you. C seemed overly anxious to exonerate Canaris from the attempt on Churchill's life. Every German with a brain knew the war was going badly, and thinking carefully about what would happen when they lost. And the SD, the SS Security Service, was constantly attempting to take over intelligence from the Abwehr and would probably succeed in the end. Alexsi wondered if perhaps Admiral Canaris had decided the time had come to feather his nest with the British.

"Your impressions of Canaris will be very helpful, of course," said C.

"Shouldn't wonder if you've shaken Hitler's hand, too," the undertaker said facetiously.

"Since you mention it, sir," said Alexsi. "I have."

Both men stared at each other, then at him.

When Alexsi didn't say anything further, C said, "Would you care to expand on that?"

"I was commissioned along with thirty-six hundred other lieutenants at the Reich Chancellery," said Alexsi. "Hitler addressed us and shook all our hands. Though I must say that with thirty-six hundred hands to shake, they nearly ran us past him at double time."

After a moment to absorb that, C said, "Nonetheless, any impressions you'd wish to share?"

"He is shorter than you would imagine," said Alexsi. "As a matter of fact, he was standing on a wooden crate behind the podium."

C chuckled appreciatively at that.

"Pity you didn't shoot the blighter," said the undertaker.

"As I told you before, sir," said Alexsi, "I am not suicidal."

"But you are interesting, nonetheless," said C.

Alexsi said, "Meaning no criticism, sir, but from the time of my arrival in your embassy in Teheran, through my entire stay in hospital, no one has shown the slightest interest in debriefing me."

The two Englishmen just looked at each other once again. Finally, C sighed slightly and said, "Yes, we shall definitely have you sit down with a stenographer and an officer who knows to ask the proper questions."

"Just make damned sure you're aboveboard with us," the undertaker said to Alexsi. Then to C, "Five said it was like interrogating a rock."

"Yes, well, that is how an agent is supposed to conduct himself under interrogation, isn't it?" said C. Then to Alexsi, "You do realize you're among friends now?"

"Of course, sir." Alexsi knew that Five was MI5, the British counterintelligence service. He kept the satisfaction he felt to himself. If he did not allow himself to be hurried, his life story might just keep him safely in London until the end of the war.

"Speaking of hospital," said the undertaker. "We understand you killed two chaps while abed."

"I had to let them come to me, sir," Alexsi replied. "Both my legs were broken and in plaster." It was the same at Abwehr headquarters. All the men safe behind a desk loved a good war story. As for himself, he would rather be safe behind a desk.

Both men glanced at each other silently for a moment. Then the undertaker said, "With an icepick, wasn't it?"

"I was informed that they are called trocars, sir. They were all I could lay my hands upon."

C just coughed politely into his own hand.

"Well, at least that finally spurred Colonel Nicholson into action, what?" said the undertaker.

It seemed more a statement than a question to Alexsi, so he did not reply.

"So, what are the terms of your service?" the undertaker demanded.

"Not to sound too mercantile," C interjected with mild disapproval.

Alexsi remained focused on the man behind the desk. "Sir, I am effectively stateless. If my work for you is acceptable, I would appreciate British citizenship after the war is won."

"By whom?" said the undertaker.

Alexsi turned to look at him, said nothing, and then turned back to C. C nodded solemnly.

"I suppose you'd like that in writing?" said the undertaker.

Alexsi did not look at him this time. It was a ridiculous question. Paper burned, or found its way into the waste, and promises were easily forgotten. To C again, "Your word is enough for me, sir."

"You have it," C replied. "And I am making a notation in your file, in my own hand, for future reference when your service comes to be evaluated."

Alexsi's ear was sharp enough to pick up the threat behind the perfect courtesy. General Schellenberg of the SS favored the same kind of silky threats. But he did watch C write, upside down of course, and for some bizarre reason the ink in his pen was green.

"Hope you realize the full value of that," said the undertaker. And as if Alexsi might not have gotten it, added, "British citizenship."

"One might say it pales next to the prime minister's life," C said mildly.

That shut the undertaker up.

"Other than that, sir," Alexsi said to C, "I would only expect to be paid the same as any of your other officers." No sense in letting them think he was some kind of patriotic fool. The slight emphasis on the final word hopefully told them he would prefer not to be paid as a sergeant.

"You'll have to pay tax on it," said the undertaker.

Alexsi now turned to look at him, as did C.

"Service didn't have to in the past," the undertaker grumbled.

Still feeling resentment over it, Alexsi thought idly. Because it was what the NKVD had taught him to look for. Anyone's resentment about anything, but especially money.

C glanced at his wristwatch, and stood up.

Alexsi automatically came to attention.

C walked around his desk and put out his hand.

He was even taller than Alexsi had guessed. Alexsi shook the offered hand, which was very firm. He returned the handshake with equivalent firmness.

"I must say it has been a pleasure meeting you, young man," said C. "I look forward to hearing of the good work you'll be doing with us."

"My honor, sir," said Alexsi.

The undertaker opened the door as a signal that it was time to leave.

Alexsi stepped into the waiting room, and saw that his escorts were gone. He almost laughed aloud at the two secretaries this time. Because Admiral Canaris in Berlin was guarded by a pair almost exactly like these.

He felt quite fine. He had never felt free in his life. He wondered if that was what he was feeling now.

14

1944

LONDON, ENGLAND

Alexsi was in the MI6 canteen having tea with his stenographers. No choice, really, since the entire nation stopped at the stroke of 4:00 P.M. anyway for an extra little meal of tinned meat or vegetable sandwiches and iced cakes. As a Russian, he found it difficult to get used to cucumber in a sandwich. As a German, he found it impossible.

They had started with one stenographer, but when the first's fingers went numb they brought in another to give her a rest. Alexsi completely sympathized. During his Russian spy training he had been made to write so many reports he'd had to soak his aching hand in a bowl of snow every night. Here all he had to do was sit and talk, with regular tea breaks.

And talk he did. He had no intention of mentioning Russia until they asked. They never did. The British could not have been less interested in the NKVD. They couldn't get enough of the German Army and

Abwehr, though. Every detail he related would take his questioners off on another tangent. Alexsi was more than happy to oblige. Organizational charts? He was happy to draw them, then expound upon each name.

The problem was, after two weeks and the first flood of questions, he felt the British losing interest. He'd answered all their urgent queries, which he could tell dealt with German intelligence and what must surely be an upcoming invasion of France. Then the officer detailed to question him kept slipping out more and more often to deal with his other work. Alexsi sensed that they were more interested in what *their* spies on the continent were radioing every day than what he had to say. It was really just like Abwehr headquarters. Everyone had too much to do, too much to read, and by necessity their interest became exclusively focused on their own little fiefs.

Soon it was just him and the stenographers. So he just began with the day he entered the German Army and went on from there. Which was boring, but all right. Enough tea breaks and it might be 1945 before he ever reached Iran in his story.

They were looking at him expectantly. He said, "A man walked into the records office in Berlin. He wished to change his name. The clerk said, 'This is war—we don't have time for such foolishness.' The man looked so sad that the clerk finally asked his name. He said, 'Adolph Smellybum.'"

The stenographers giggled, pretending to be shocked.

Alexsi said, "At that the clerk took pity on him, and said, 'Fine. What do you wish to change it to?' The man said, 'Herman Smellybum.'"

They shrieked with laughter. Alexsi was quite pleased with himself. If you could translate a joke into another language, and get a laugh with it, then you were becoming fluent.

Unfortunately, either by accident or by design, all the stenographers were of a matronly age. They mentioned their daughters only to show the photographs of the dashing young soldiers they were engaged to. Alexsi didn't know whether it was the famous British reserve, following orders, or perhaps trepidation at still considering him a German enemy. They might laugh at his jokes, but at the end of the day they packed up their shoulder bags, wished him a pleasant evening, and left.

Of course, it could have been depression rather than reserve. The London winter was mild compared to Berlin, and almost tropical compared to Moscow. But he could not recall a day when it did not rain. St. James's Park was just to the north, but Alexsi did not relish sitting on a bench in the rain. At the end of a day of dictation he turned in his pass to the 54 Broadway doorman and walked a few minutes through the dripping mist to his room at a posh hotel called St. Ermin's, which MI6 had mostly taken over.

Every time he walked through the lobby he had the same strange feeling from the English sitting there, as if everyone was staring at him yet would only keep staring if he tried to talk to them. The bar held no interest. The one time he'd looked in he'd been instantly repelled by all the spies and agents and special forces soldiers. You could practically taste the conspiracy in the air along with the cigarette smoke.

The old man who ran the elevator was chatty with everyone, but not with him as soon as he heard the accent. Alexsi went straight to his room without stopping at the hotel restaurant. He could readily remember all the times when he never had enough to eat, but he was never hungry in the evenings after English tea. He had been given a ration book that he never used. Restaurants were allowed to charge no more than five shillings for a meal, and the British were paying him nearly ten pounds sterling, or two hundred shillings, per week. After sitting down for an MI6 photographer, he had an alien registration card and an Allied military identity card. He was adamant about not being a Russian, and at first they'd wanted to make him a Pole. He'd heard there were a great many Poles in London, and it would hardly do to bump into one carrying Polish papers and speaking no Polish. Many fewer Czechs, though, and from what he'd heard in Berlin the British had parachuted most of them back into Czechoslovakia to be betrayed to the Germans by other Czechs.

Alexsi was familiar enough with Czechoslovakia, having invaded it early in his German Army career. Not that the Czechs put up any fight at all. So now he was Adam Novak, another name as common as John Smith. And another little private joke, Novak being "new man."

His hotel room was one of the small ones, but very nice. Looking out over the foggy London dusk before it was time to pull the blackout curtains, Alexsi remembered when his only dream was to have a room of his own. Now he thought there was nothing more lonely than the sight of a city at night.

It all would have provoked bitter laughter from the boy he had been, the one who dreamed every night of escaping his father and the shitpile of a kolkhoz in Azerbaijan. That at age twenty-three, and after Moscow, Munich, Berlin, and Teheran, he would be staring out a window dreading the prospect of learning another city and another language and another people.

15

At dictation the next day there was a knock on the door. Then nothing. This had never happened before. The English officers usually just barged in after a perfunctory tap, Alexsi usually instinctively beginning to move his chair out of the way, because their room was only slightly larger than a broom closet.

He and the stenographers just looked at each other.

Alexsi shrugged.

One of the ladies ventured a timid "Come in."

"Pardon the intrusion," came a voice from behind Alexsi.

Alexsi turned about. A head was poking in the room with a boyish smile, though the face belonged to a man as old as the century. The rest of his body entered gradually. Lean and athletic, and by his bearing clearly a military man even though he was not in uniform.

"Ladies," he said, with that English charm Alexsi was still getting used to, a jarring contrast between Russian habitual rudeness and German brusqueness. "Forgive me. Could I ask you to take an interval for a cup and a fag, and leave this gentleman to me?"

Alexsi's English had improved to the point where he could recognize one of those requests that was really an order. As did the stenographers. "Certainly, sir," they both murmured. Which told Alexsi that here was another officer, and he was familiar to them.

While they were still gathering their women's things, the middle-aged boyish Englishman offered his hand. "I'm Ken."

Alexsi shook it. One of those gentleman-athlete grips that was prepared to match you all the way from soft to bone-breaking, your choice. He sat down.

As the ladies left, Alexsi automatically stood up and bowed slightly to them. The German manners he had learned, and which never failed to produce smiles in British matrons. They closed the door behind them.

Ken just grinned at all that. Hugging the walls of the room, he folded himself around the desk and took one of the stenographers' seats. Arranging himself back and forth as if trying it out, he elbowed the stenotype machine out of his way so he could get a clear view of Alexsi. "I'm in charge of training, among other things," he said, sprawling back in the chair. "I've been reading your reports with great interest."

The statement would have been unremarkable, except that Ken made it in Russian. English-accented Russian, but very good. Alexsi guessed he had learned it from Russian parents. He replied, also in Russian, "Are we speaking so we will not be overheard, or for another reason?"

Ken just gave an equivocal smile. "I don't get much chance to practice my Russian these days."

Alexsi sat there with perfect stillness, prepared to frustrate another interrogation if necessary.

Ken just looked him up and down, still with that boyish grin. "I was most interested in your account from the German side of the debacle in Holland. We already knew, of course, but you very helpfully filled in all the details of the infiltration of our sister service."

"The Special Operations Executive," Alexsi said. "Since the Germans of course know all about it, perhaps we could dispense with all these euphemisms in the name of security."

"Quite," said Ken.

A sergeant in the SD, the SS Security Service, had broken the British agent codes both by the incredible carelessness of the captured agents and by the very un-German practice of being kind to prisoners rather than torturing them as a matter of course. The Germans then began playing back the captured radio operators under their control. It was common practice among all intelligence services to give their agents a security check to either add or omit from their messages to indicate whether or not they were captured and forced to transmit under duress, but the British blithely ignored them. Perhaps thinking that the agents had somehow forgotten them. Soon the Germans had all the Dutch networks under their control, yet the British persisted in dropping guns, explosives, radios, codes, and more and more agents into their hands. The Germans called it *das Englandspiel*. The England Game. When the British finally awoke to what was going on, the Germans ended the game by sending them a nicely insulting radio message in the clear.

Ken hadn't mentioned, Alexsi thought, and he himself would not mention out of tact, that many of the agents parachuted into the Germans' hands were MI6's also.

Ken said, "I'm worried we're having the same problems in France. Could you perhaps offer some insight."

"I'm not aware of any large-scale penetration like Holland," said Alexsi.

"Relieved to hear it," said Ken.

"But your problem is radio," said Alexsi.

"How so?"

"Shall I be blunt?"

Ken seemed amused by that. "Why not?"

"Your radio operators have poor technique. They send slowly. They remain on the air for unbelievable amounts of time. They send from the same locations, time and again, on regular schedules, and on the same frequencies. They make the German direction finding easy."

"That bad?" said Ken.

"In France the direction-finding system is located at Gestapo headquarters in Paris," said Alexsi. "The Avenue Foch," he added helpfully. "I have seen the equivalent equipment in Germany. Thirty clerks at a shift keep watch on banks of cathode tubes, and every frequency from ten kilocycles to thirty megacycles is monitored. Three hundred tubes, one clerk to every ten. When a radio begins transmitting in France it shows up as a luminous spot on the tubes. The clerk telephones the goniometric stations at Brest, Augsburg, and Nuremberg, and they begin to take cross bearings to triangulate the location of the transmission. Within fifteen minutes they can place the radio set within a . . ." He paused to make the conversion from kilometers to miles. ". . . a ten-mile triangle. At the same time they move mobile detection vans from regional bases throughout France into the triangle. Even if the operator finishes sending the message, the vans remain in place. If the operator acknowledges a reply to the message of only a few seconds they can narrow it down to a half mile. If the transmission continues the Germans send men with portable detectors to determine the exact location, even within a town."

"Forgive me," said Ken. "You say they have portable detection equipment?"

"It is called *Gürtelpeiler*," said Alexsi. "The apparatus is shaped to the body and strapped around the waist, the antenna looped about the neck. The signal-strength meter on a cable running down the arm is worn on the wrist like a watch. The equipment is completely concealed under an overcoat. The operator simply walks through a neighborhood and turns his body to establish the direction of the transmitter."

"This answers a great many questions," said Ken. "I was just about to ask you why I hadn't heard of it until now. But I imagine the answer is that no one bothered to ask you."

Alexsi only nodded.

"How did you happen to know so much about it?"

First Russian, then German, and now English. You always heard the suspicion in their voices when you told them something they did not want to hear. "They nearly caught me transmitting in downtown Berlin," Alexsi replied. "I had to leap from a hotel window and abandon my set. I believe they were looking for another transmission and happened upon me by accident. Bad luck. After that narrow escape, I took a greater interest in countermeasures."

Ken paused to digest that. "Then what is the solution?"

"Transmit for no longer than five minutes," said Alexsi. "No regular timetables, no regular frequency. And for pity's sake, your people have to stop keeping copies of their sent messages. If they are captured with them, which a great many are, it makes the German code breakers' job child's play."

"We only have six weeks in which to train our wireless operators," Ken said defensively.

"I understand," said Alexsi. "Quantity over quality. Given sufficient numbers, a few will survive to complete their mission."

That caused Ken for the first time to have trouble meeting his gaze. "Anything else?"

"If you ask an agent to repeat a message because the wireless operator on your side couldn't hear it, or had trouble unbuttoning the code, it is like you are shooting them yourself."

"What if the message really didn't come through?"

"Have them repeat it a day later, at another location."

"What if the message is vital and time dependent?"

Alexsi only smiled sadly. "I congratulate you on having agents who are more self-sacrificing than myself."

Ken just gave him that boyish smile back. "I congratulate you on having survived so long in the lion's den. I'm sure prudence had everything to do with it."

Against his better judgment, Alexsi liked the man. Though this was just the sort of earnest patriot who would get you killed for all the finest reasons.

"Great stuff," Ken said enthusiastically. "Could I prevail upon you to give a short lecture on it to a few of the heads of our sections? And perhaps a bit on the Abwehr?"

Alexsi felt as though it was one of those requests that wasn't really a request. He also felt that there was no good way to avoid it. He had not yet banked the amount of goodwill that would allow him to refuse any request that was not suicidal. "Of course."

"Super," Ken said with that bright smile.

16

Rather than the heads of sections originally mentioned, his lecture attracted quite an audience. Alexsi hadn't cared for that one bit—the fewer people who knew about him and knew his face the better. But there was no way out of it. Afterward was a drinks party in the canteen. Alexsi wasn't under the illusion that they were celebrating the excellence of his talk. Rather, they had him hold it at the end of the day, which gave everyone an excuse to drink afterward. The crowd was too large for the bar, which he had been told was invitation-only anyway. Not that he cared about that. He found the British second only to the Russians in their enthusiasm for alcohol. A violently drunken father had cured him of any desire for drink, as had Germans spilling their guts while awash in beer. Both his sobriety and others' drunken stupidity had saved him on more than one occasion.

The British were all walking about with beer and whiskey. He was holding a glass of their tonic water minus the gin. He had hoped to find a line of retreat once everyone became drunk, but that hope was quickly dashed. As the interesting new attraction they had him pinned into a corner and were peppering him with questions.

"My remit is counterintelligence," said a dreamy-looking man in his thirties.

Alexsi had no trouble imagining him in a university professor's robes. Which was probably where he had come from. "Yes?" he said politely, acutely conscious of his still-thick accent.

"The German agents we have captured to date," said the professor. "Not to put too fine a point on it, but generally they're quite a rum lot. Perhaps I'm not framing this properly, but . . ."

"I believe I understand your question," said Alexsi. The Russians would interrogate and shoot someone in the time it took an Englishman to frame a question. "To an intelligence officer, when you see the absence of the thing you expect, your instinct is to assume only that the enemy has been diabolically clever in hiding it from you. Not that it does not exist."

The professor nodded.

"My focus was the Near East," said Alexsi. "When I inquired whether there were any high-level agents in Britain that could offer insight into future plans in this area, I was told there were none. My first thought was that I was being lied to for security reasons. But I discovered that it was the truth, and there were two reasons. The first was that Hitler in 1935 forbade any spying against Britain, because he regarded you as racial allies and hoped to ally your naval power with Germany's land power."

Uneasy shifting from the crowd at that.

"The second reason," Alexsi went on, "was that Admiral Canaris felt that recruiting high-level agents in place who would take years to bear fruit was putting too many of his eggs in one basket. So his emphasis, and I feel your experience will bear this out, was on recruiting a great many medium- and low-level agents who would report on things like troop locations and airfields that the German Army could use in its day-to-day operations."

"That does mesh with our experience," said the professor. "And I confess I'm relieved to hear it. Does seem to be missing an opportunity, though. What?"

"Look at it this way," said Alexsi. "If you intend to conquer France, you need to know the roads through the Ardennes, and whether the bridges will bear the weight of tanks. You do not need to know what the inner circles of the French government will do if you invade, since you have already made up your own mind about it."

"Quite," someone in the back said. "That was bloody well put."

The crowd had now pressed in around him tightly enough to make him uncomfortable. Alexsi left unstated that they were no doubt doing the exact same thing in preparing for their own invasion of France. They didn't need to know what the Germans would do. Everyone knew what the Germans would do. They needed to pick the right ground to fight on. Preferably the ground with the fewest Germans in the immediate vicinity.

"That raises the question," said another donnish-looking fellow in spectacles. He was the local Abwehr expert, named Trevor-Roper. The one person in the building who had sought him out. And Alexsi had been impressed, thinking that he knew more about the Abwehr than Canaris himself. "Are we then right to think of German intelligence as second-rate? Or are we underestimating them?"

"The big picture?" said Alexsi. "Do I have the correct idiom?"

There was silence, then a helpful voice in the back said finally, "Spot on."

Alexsi said, "The big picture is that the German Army regards tactical excellence and battlefield leadership as their highest priorities, and assigns officers accordingly. Those who are found wanting, second-raters if you would, are moved to intelligence and logistics, and as such these are their greatest weaknesses. They are excellent in wireless interception, especially on the battlefield, because signals are highly valued. They are very interested in tactical intelligence, such as battlefield reconnaissance, and much less in the strategic intelligence provided by spies. The Abwehr reflects that. But since their goal is to rule the world, they emphasize counterintelligence and are excellent at catching spies. It is a matter of emphasis, not overall incompetence."

Trevor-Roper nodded, as if he were marking Alexsi's paper. "You have a gift for being precise, sir."

Alexsi left unstated his own opinion that spying, essentially, was useless. Even if you were able to pull off a brilliant coup and tell your masters something that their enemy intended to do, as he had told the NKVD that Hitler was about to invade the Soviet Union, they still had to believe you. And even if they did, which Stalin clearly did not, there was still the small matter of having to stop a million Germans and thousands of their tanks pouring across your border.

"Yes, quite illuminating," said the first professor, the one in counterintelligence. "Might I call upon you, if any other questions come up?"

"Of course," Alexsi replied. The more people who wished to be briefed, on any subject, the longer he was safe in London.

A hand lightly touched his arm. Alexsi did not particularly like to be touched without his leave. He turned, and with effort kept the annoyance off his face.

The hand belonged to a young man in his late twenties or early thirties, a fleshy face broken by an inviting smile. "I say, that was a smashing talk!"

They really did speak like that. The English. Just like in the cinema. Alexsi nodded pleasantly.

"I'm Kim," said the young Englishman, extending his hand. His hair, pomaded down in the fashion, was uncut to the point where it seemed to bulge out and threaten to break free from its watery bonds at any moment. The eyes were blue and wide in that well-fed face, which was beginning to announce a second chin.

"Adam," said Alexsi, shaking the hand with much less enthusiasm than it had been offered.

The blue eyes, though watery from drink, seemed to sparkle confidingly, as if to say: Of course you are. "Created out of the dust, so to speak."

Chuckles from the audience around them.

Alexsi only stared back blankly.

"Perhaps that was a bit too biblical," Kim said to warm laughter.

Alexsi offered up his best perplexed expression.

"Quite," said Kim, undaunted. "Wonder if you'd care to join us for a drink. Show you a bit of the town, meet the troops as it were. It'll be fun."

In his head Alexsi heard the ponderous voice of his Soviet spy trainer, Grigory Petrovich Yakushev. *As a spy we have taught you to be alert to the personal vulnerabilities of others as a means of gaining information from them. However, you must always be alert to your own vulnerabilities. There is nothing more difficult, but it is a matter of life and death. We have taught you when making an approach to arrange the circumstances so that your target feels that they, not you, have initiated contact, as this is much less suspicious. In the same vein you must always consider yourself the target. Beware the moments you are at your worst. If you were not friendless you would certainly ask why a complete stranger suddenly sought your friendship. If you were not loveless why, out of the blue, a woman would urgently require your love. Why the fellow inmate in your cell is so very interested in helping you. In those moments the people who come to you have come to recruit you. Or compromise you. Or betray you.*

Alexsi was quite familiar with betrayal. He himself had been the betrayer more than once. They would never have let him out of the Soviet Union unless he had proved himself to them that way. When he was young and weak he would never have had his revenge without betrayal.

In Berlin he had known he was under suspicion when a captain named Ressler in SD counterintelligence made a clumsy approach to him. Not quite knowing what to do, at the time, he had thought to play along. It had been no end of trouble, and nearly ended with him hanging from a meat hook in the cellars of Gestapo headquarters. Live and learn, the English saying went. If you were lucky enough to have lived, then you had damned well better learn.

"Thank you," he said to the only Englishman he'd met who liked foreigners. He lifted his glass. "I do not drink spirits."

The fleshy face pinched slightly, but the voice was undismayed. "Well, there's plenty of fun without drink."

"Is there?" said a voice in the back, and everyone laughed.

"Speak for yourself," said another, to more laughter.

"Yes, there is," the young man named Kim said over his shoulder, as if slightly cross at being interrupted. Then, more confidingly to Alexsi, "Plenty of fun in London these days. Girls are treating the war like there's no tomorrow, what?"

Alexsi just looked at him, puzzled, as if he did not understand the reference.

"Perhaps a spot of dinner at my club," Kim said doggedly. "White's? Meet some of the best people?"

"Thank you," Alexsi said again, his tone pro forma. "Some other time."

"Standing offer," said Kim, his smile now being maintained by effort. "Ta-ta." He turned and left, his entourage following.

Alexsi took advantage of their movement to make his escape in the opposite direction. He abandoned his glass to the nearest flat surface and set his pace quickly enough that no one would be inclined to stop him to talk. But as he slipped through the door of the canteen and turned, he nearly collided with Ken, whose tall frame was slouched against the side of the hallway as if he were holding it up.

"Dandy talk," Ken said, voice slowed by drink.

"Thank you for arranging it," Alexsi replied, without much sincerity.

Ken wasn't too drunk to not pick up on that. He grinned and said, "I should offer congratulations."

"Didn't you just?" said Alexsi, trying to keep moving, though he'd already sensed this was not someone to push past.

"Not the talk," said Ken. "On being one of the few immune to the Philby charm."

"Is that his name?" said Alexsi.

Ken nodded.

"And congratulations *were* in order?" Alexsi said. As soon as it came out of his mouth he was uncomfortably aware that by pressing the point he was telegraphing his anxiety.

Ken just grinned again. He took a drink, and that was enough for Alexsi to bob his head in acknowledgment and slip down the hall.

There was an orderly line of unsteady drinkers queuing at the lavatory, which the British called "the gents'." Unable to wait, a man in a pinstriped suit was bent over vomiting into one of the fire buckets. Another man was standing behind him as if in support, like a squire to a knight, but instead of a lance he was clasping a bowler hat in both hands.

17

LONDON, ENGLAND

Northwest across St. James's Park, rain pattering the lake. Not the bridge—the training still so deeply ingrained in him said that bridges were traps that could be closed at both ends, with the only way out into the water. And then even into the water, your enemies would just be waiting for you on the bank, laughing. So he skirted the bridge, passing through trees that were brown skeletons with arms raised up in surrender against the winter that would not end. Buckingham Palace to the left and St. James's Palace to the right. And so he found his way across Green Park to Piccadilly.

Alexsi told himself that he has been a prig. A German prig at that, and there was no worse. So the English do not care for foreigners? Well, who does really? No one knows suspicion of strangers better than a Russian. He has watched carefully, as he was taught, and purchased an English suit and English shoes to blend in. Also the acquaintance of an English barber, though he drew the line at pomade. He doubted he would ever feel like an Englishman, but at least now he would not stand out until he opened his mouth.

He went to the Suivi, the nightclub on Stratton Street everyone talked about. He ought to have known better. Such places were where you went with friends, not to find them. If you walked in alone everyone who approached you was the opposite. The drink cadgers who would be your friend as long as you were buying. The confidence men who would lead you to a friendly game of cards or dice. The women wearing too much makeup who would slip chloral hydrate into your drink so they could roll you for your wallet. His training let him see through them like glass, and even if he had fought his way past those there were still the British in their tight little groups, American airmen so loud they sounded like flocks of parrots cawing. Desperate drinkers, desperate dancers. It made him think that was why people drank alcohol, so other people would no longer bother them.

It was useless. On the street, walking back toward Westminster, thinking: I tried. The streets were blacked out, of course, against the Luftwaffe, who came over only infrequently these days. But there was a three-quarters moon, just enough to see by.

Why was Teheran so easy and London so hard? The Iranians meant nothing by their smiles; they smiled so you would look at their face while they were trying to reach into your pocket. But at least they smiled.

He stopped, suddenly, on the street. Letting the other pedestrians swirl around as it suddenly occurred to him. He had been pretending then. In Munich, Berlin, Zurich, Istanbul, Teheran. He had always been playing someone else, and it was easier. Even in Russia he had been many people. Now in London he had to be himself. He hadn't been himself since he was a little thief in Baku, who would rather just go to the library and read.

Perhaps he should just go to the library.

Ahead on the next corner, in the moonlight, one of the streetwalkers was eyeing him. She didn't look half bad, and he was tempted. He hadn't had a woman since Teheran, and the last one was a German who tried to kill him.

Then a female voice a few short meters away said, "You don't need to do that."

Alexsi whirled about. She was standing still as everyone else passed them on the sidewalk. Blond, real or not it was impossible to tell in faded moonlight. Wearing a khaki trench coat. Not the most sexy outer garment, but it was winter. At least the trench coat was belted tight against her waist and accentuated her hips and bust.

Now that she had his attention, she said, "A good-looking man like you doesn't need to do that."

Alexsi just stood there, looking at her.

She said, "Come home with me. You don't have to pay. I'll be glad for the company."

Rather than be alarmed, Alexsi was thinking that this, at least, was exactly like Berlin. Their men were away at war. They were lonely and needed a man, but they needed one who would be away before dawn, before the neighbors could begin gossiping and writing letters to the front.

He smiled and held out his arm, bent elbow pointed toward her. She smiled back, a flash of teeth in the moonlight, and grasped the crook of his arm. "I'm Nan."

Alexsi had been about to tell her that it was all right if she didn't wish to give her name. "Adam," he said. "Do you live far?"

"Still in Piccadilly," she said. "Just a bit north. It's a pleasant walk, if you don't mind."

"Not at all," Alexsi said.

The moon was suddenly covered with overcast. The street went black. It was crowded, because it was war and no one knew what tomorrow would bring. She moved in close, and he drew his arm tight to bring her in closer. He could hear the tap of her shoes on the wet pavement.

"Are you Polish?" she asked.

"Czech," Alexsi replied.

"Oh," she said. "It's horrid what happened to Lidice. Nazi bastards." She squeezed his arm. "Sorry. Language."

At the end of May in 1942 two Czech commandos who were parachuted in from London assassinated Reinhard Heydrich on the streets of Prague. Heydrich was Himmler's number two, and some said Hitler's next-generation successor. The commandos were betrayed and killed in a gunfight with the SS. To underscore Heydrich's importance, in an action extravagant even by the German standard of reprisals against innocent civilians, the entire village of Lidice was bulldozed off the map. All the men were shot, the women and children packed off to concentration camps. Unlike their countless other massacres of the war, the Germans publicly boasted of this one, probably to forestall London contemplating any other high-level assassination attempts.

Ironically, Heydrich's death cleared the way for General Walter Schellenberg of the SS Security Service to step up to Himmler's number two. Schellenberg had been the one who sent Alexsi to Teheran.

As they passed the next intersection, she said, "These are my rooms."

There was a plate full of ringers and names by the door of the building, but it was so dark Alexsi couldn't make out any of the names. There were at least four floors, though.

He held the door for her. Once they were past the blackout curtain there was light again. Dingy bulbs, perhaps, but they still made Alexsi blink as his eyes became used to it. Once they adjusted, he got his first good look at Nan, whether or not that was really her name. Not a classic beauty, but Alexsi liked women more than he liked men and liked women who looked interesting and intelligent. This girl was that. Pale like all the

English, with a prominent nose compensated for by full lips and brown eyes that were large but perhaps just a bit too far apart.

The eyes were very nervous. Alexsi stopped and took her hand. She turned slightly to face him. "I just want you to know that I am a gentleman," he said.

She looked at him frankly. "I knew that the moment I saw you."

Alexsi brought her hand up to his lips and kissed it. "But not too much of one."

She laughed at that, thankfully, and flushed into a lovely shade of pink. "I'm just up the stairs."

They went up to the third floor. She led the way down the hall, which was covered in a flower wallpaper that must have been truly hideous before it faded into merely ugly. It was peeling at the seams.

There was a loud creak of door hinge behind them, and Alexsi whirled about. The door shut quickly.

She had lost her grip on his arm, and took it up again. "It's just my busybody neighbors. Too much time on their hands."

Alexsi only nodded. It had given him a start.

She unlocked the door to her apartment. Alexsi had to grin at that. A German girl would have given him the key to unlock it for her.

The lights snapped on. The apartment was small and neat, with a mishmash of furniture that had clearly been purchased one piece at a time.

"Very nice," Alexsi said politely.

She undid the belt and unbuttoned the trench coat. Alexsi helped her off with it, admiring her cleavage under a tight sweater as he peeked over her shoulder.

"You can put it there," she said, gesturing toward the coat hook on the wall behind the door. Alexsi hung it up, with his own overcoat beside.

She said, "I'm going to freshen up a bit, if you don't mind."

"Of course not," said Alexsi.

"Make yourself at home. There's a few bottles of lager in the icebox, if you'd like."

She disappeared into what must have been the bedroom. Alexsi went straight for the small bookshelves, to see what she read.

His eyes dropped down below the small framed family pictures, and the hairs quite literally went up on the back of his neck. *The Communist Manifesto; Capital; The German Ideology; The Condition of the Working Class in England. Grundrisse.* Lenin. Even the speeches of Stalin, for fuck's sake.

His spy teacher Yakushev liked to say that there was no such thing as a sixth sense or a second sight for danger. Humans had been hunted by animals and other humans for millions of years, and the feeling that something was very wrong was simply your brain processing the information of all the normal senses and sending you a clear warning. And if you wished to survive you had better not ignore it.

Alexsi had no intention of ignoring it. He had been taught to seduce women as part of his training, and he was not about to die in a honey trap, as the NKVD called it.

When he first walked into the apartment he had noticed the fire escape outside the window, because that was what you did automatically: look for another way out. Now he was certainly not about to go back out into that hallway.

With one hand he slid some potted plants out of the way and had the window open with the other. He was concerned with speed, not noise. One leg out, then the other, and the window shut behind him. His overcoat was still on the hook inside. If it was a trap they would be looking for a man in an overcoat, and there was no sense in making it easy. There was nothing in the pockets of his but a pair of gloves.

Alexsi went up the metal stairs. If you were going to close off a building you certainly put someone to cover the fire escape. He was not about to drop down into a waiting lap.

The fire escape ended at the top-floor apartment. The windows were thankfully dark. Alexsi didn't need anyone shouting in alarm at his appearance. There was a rain pipe running down. He tested it. Solid enough. Grasping it, he leaned back and pulled himself up hand over hand, pushing up with his feet against the brick wall. He only had to go up a few meters before he was able to get to the top. He'd been afraid there would be a rain gutter. But thankfully there was a stone outside ridge of the roof, and he was able to reach up and grab it. Letting go of the drainpipe and swinging over to get a grip with his other hand, he pulled himself up and over.

The roof was pitched, with slippery stone shingles. Alexsi carefully scrambled up to the peak, which had a flat but narrow stone ridge running the length of it. With his arms outstretched for balance, he gingerly walked down it. It was rough stone, not slippery like the shingles, and the leather soles of his shoes did not betray him.

Each section of building was separated by a row of chimney pots in a slightly wider brick facing that ran across the entire width of the building. There was practically no room between the cylindrical ceramic chimney pots, so Alexsi had to feel his way down, as the roof gradually sloped downward and away from him, until he found two together that weren't smoking hot. Then he had to pull himself up and over, scrambling back up to the center ridge of the next room, while being choked in a cloud of coal smoke blowing up from the rest of the chimneys.

He had to do that ten more times until he finally reached the end of the building, which ran the entire length of the street. Leaning up against the final row of chimney pots, Alexsi contemplated his next move. He didn't fancy shinnying down a rain pipe—he'd had a bad experience trying that before.

Making his way down the pitch of the roof, Alexsi kept one hand on the line of chimney pots for support until he was too low. He went to sit back against the roof to slide down when his feet went out from under him. The slate shingles were like glass, and his stomach dropped as he shot down the roof feetfirst.

He grabbed at the shingles to try and arrest himself, but the first one he got ahold of came right off in his hand. It was too dark to see out in front of him, so he spread his feet out like a penguin and gritted his teeth.

Alexsi's feet slammed into the trough of a rain gutter. The impact actually bowed the gutter out away from the building, but it stopped him. Alexsi didn't move a muscle, afraid the gutter would tear away from the building. Getting his breath back, he realized that he was still holding the slate shingle in his hand. If it fell to the pavement the noise would wake the dead, so he very carefully bent his legs and inserted it into the gutter.

Should he go back up? An excellent question. If he slipped again there was no guarantee the rain gutter would hold against another impact.

Very carefully, because the gutter was wobbling, he bent his legs again, twisted, and with one hand on the gutter poked his head over the edge. No fire escape. No drainpipe. But there was a white-painted window directly below him, with a sill that looked wide enough to support his foot.

Except the window *looked* directly below him, and distances were deceiving when you were looking down from above.

Should he risk it? Alexsi didn't fancy a climb back up, and he couldn't stay there spread-eagled on the roof until dawn. These English roofs were a nightmare. How did their thieves manage it? It was enough to make you long for the roofs of Germany and the Soviet Union.

The gutter was holding his weight now; he wasn't going to wait until it decided not to. Alexsi slid down and grasped the lip of the gutter with both hands. Do or die. He swung over until he was dangling from it. It rocked but held.

The windowsill was within his body length. He got one foot on it, relieved to take some of his weight off the gutter. The window was one of those that opened outward like a door. If it was locked he was doomed because he had no knife. Like a fool he hadn't thought he needed one in London.

Of course the window had no latch on the outside. With his free hand Alexsi reached in his pocket for his hotel room key. At least English hotels didn't make you leave the key at the front desk the way German ones did. He stuck the key in the gap between the two windows, pushing it all the way in, then turned the shaft so the key bit would get a purchase on the wood inside. He pulled toward him, and both windows opened. Alexsi pushed one back shut, and opened the other all the way. He thankfully let go of the gutter and reached under the window frame to support himself. The key went back into his pocket and with that free hand he felt around the sill inside to make sure he wouldn't knock anything over as he came in.

He was inside, with the window shut, and immediately dropped down onto the wood floor so his form would not be silhouetted against the window. Sitting there, the first thing he did, faithful to his thief's experience, was take off his shoes. Alexsi tied the laces together and looped the shoes around his neck. Any movement would be done silently in stocking feet. He sat patiently until his eyes adjusted to the darkness. The apartment slowly took shape before him.

A muffled voice behind a wall, and a light came on visible under a door. Alexsi slid sideways until he was behind an armchair.

The door opened, and the light cast its shaft through the doorway into the room. Alexsi looked around for a weapon. There was a lamp on a table, but it was out of reach. He would have to be quick.

As he had mentioned to C, in his early career he never robbed from *people*, only the state. Mainly because in the Soviet Union people had nothing, and the bosses of the state had everything. But you didn't rob the bosses individually, because the greedy bastards would make it their mission to put the secret police on you. You robbed the state stores, which no one paid much attention to because crime was not supposed to exist under Communism. Also, as a practicality, Soviet housing was so scarce that apartments held more family members than there were rabbits in a hutch.

A sleepy male voice said, "All right, all right. Hold your horses."

Alexsi heard bare feet approaching the window. He did not look up. Human eyes shone in the darkness just like animal eyes.

A hand rattled the window latch. From two meters away Alexsi couldn't help but stare at the two ugliest stark white feet he had ever seen. He held his breath.

Those horned white feet spun about. A moment later Alexsi heard a doorknob rattle on the other side of the room. Then a cross male voice said, "The bloody window's shut. The bloody door's locked. Now will you go back to sleep?"

The shaft of light disappeared as the bedroom door closed. A muffled female voice was saying something plaintively.

Alexsi slid back quietly until his back was against the wall. He looked at the luminous hands of his wristwatch. An hour would give everyone time to fall back asleep. He had learned patience early, and then later that the prisons were filled with impatient thieves. An hour would also make anyone waiting outside think that he had gotten past them, and that it was time to give up and go home. This was turning out to be more complicated than he had ever imagined. His luck had been frankly terrible ever since he'd walked into the British embassy in Teheran.

The hour passed, and the apartment was dead quiet. Alexsi rose to his feet and stood there silently, letting the blood return to his muscles.

He walked to the door, one careful stockinged step at a time. No noise from the bedroom. There was an old rim lock on the door, a knurled knob to open it from the inside. No chains or bolts. The key was on a table next to the door.

Alexsi put the key between his teeth and turned the knob a millimeter at a time. Once the latch bolt was all the way back, he kept his grip on the knob with his left hand and turned the doorknob with his right. Again, agonizingly slowly so it would not squeak. His ears were cocked toward the bedroom, but nothing was stirring.

Alert for noisy hinges, Alexsi opened the door just wide enough to slip his body through. Before he did, he released the doorknob and put the key in the lock outside, retracting it all the way.

Through the door and out in the hall, he released the doorknob just as slowly as before, and then the key until the lock engaged. After removing it from the lock, Alexsi slid the key under the door back into the apartment. It would look as if it had just fallen onto the floor.

No time to waste now. He dashed down the hallway in his stocking feet, just in case a door opened. Mounting the stairway banister, he slid down the first level like a child. It wasn't an affectation. Banisters were usually solid, while stair boards creaked.

Hopping off at the first turn as the stairway followed the outside wall, he ran down. On the next floor from the bottom he stopped and put his shoes back on.

Opening the outside door a crack, he dropped to one knee and peered out. He was on the opposite street, on the other side of the building from where he had entered with the girl. And on the far end of the block. The street looked empty, covered in that wonderful London fog.

Alexsi stepped out. He crossed the street, not running since his leather heels would make too much noise, but quickly enough that any watcher would have to move fast and expose themselves to keep from losing him.

No movement on the street at all. Though between the blackout and the fog Alexsi could barely see his hand in front of his face. He stopped at the end of the next block and listened intently. Nothing.

Still not satisfied, he made a roundabout return to his hotel, going around to the rear. He watched the service entrance for some time, and didn't see any unfamiliar faces. By now he was a familiar face himself, and the night staff just nodded as he went inside. With all the "funnies" in the hotel, as the secret service people were known, no one even raised an eyebrow these days to strange comings and goings.

Back in his room, washing up, Alexsi examined his face in the mirror. He still wasn't sure whether he'd just had a narrow escape or the utter banality of life in London was causing him to crack up.

18

After going in and out of the canteen enough times to be suspicious to anyone watching closely, which they were not, Alexsi finally saw Ken sitting down to lunch.

Gathering a tray of his own, he walked over. Before he could say anything, Ken looked up and said, "Take a pew."

"If that means join you, then thank you, I will," Alexsi replied.

"The colloquial English of the English can be maddening," said Ken. "So, what may I do for you?"

Alexsi just sat there with his mouth half open.

"When a man who keeps to himself seeks me out at lunch instead of my office, it makes me think he wants to ask me something personal, and in confidence."

"Am I that standoffish?" Alexsi asked.

"Yes, but the office girls love you."

"Do they really?"

"Most definitely."

"How would I be able to tell?"

Ken laughed. "With the English, I concede it's not easy."

"Please indulge me," said Alexsi. "Why did you say what you did rather than sit quietly and hear me out? You might have learned more."

"I doubt it," Ken replied. He took a forkful of food and made a face. "Whale meat. Bloody U-boats." Turning his attention back to Alexsi, he said, "Saved us talking about the weather until you got to the point."

"I thought the English loved talking about the weather."

"No, that's only to keep from talking about anything personal. Well?"

This was certainly not proceeding the way he thought it would, but Alexsi decided he might as well get to the point. "The fellow who was at my talk the other night."

"What fellow might that be?" Ken asked with mocking coyness.

"Very well," Alexsi said, smiling back. "Philby."

"Hmmmm. What about him?"

"Yes, exactly," said Alexsi. "What about him?"

Ken grinned. "Public school boy—that's private school to you. Cambridge. You know Cambridge?"

Alexsi nodded. The prestigious university.

"Father's colonial service. India. Lawrence of Arabia to Ibn Saud. Of course keeping the service in the know all along. One of the Establishment."

"Are you?" Alexsi asked, genuinely curious.

"My dear chap," said Ken. "My name's Cohen. From the Royal Navy. I couldn't see eye-to-eye with the Establishment if I was standing atop a bloody mountain."

"You don't say."

"You don't see any of them here, do you?" said Ken, motioning with his fork. "They're all off lunching on Dover sole at their clubs, and we're eating whale meat in the canteen."

"Now I finally understand the distinction," said Alexsi. "Perhaps I should have accepted the invitation to his club. What was the name? White's?"

Ken just blinked at that.

"Thank you for your frankness," said Alexsi. "So, am I something new and exotic and interesting?"

"Speaking frankly?" said Ken.

"If we have been, why should we stop?" said Alexsi.

Ken gave up on his whale meat and went for his pudding. "If Philby's chatting you up, and you don't have a cunt? Then he wants something."

"Thank you," Alexsi said.

So that was that. Without rock-solid proof any suspicions would just be smirked at. And he barely had suspicions. As usual, he was on his own.

Alexsi had been keeping to a regular routine and walking regular routes to see if anyone else was doing the same with him. He hadn't seen anything yet, though of course anyone with a good pair of binoculars and some cover could watch from a distance.

He told himself it might just be his imagination. This Philby might just be striving for some sort of professional advancement. There might be plenty of Communist girls in England who needed men just like any other woman.

Perhaps. Perhaps he had been hunted too long to recognize safety.

But he wasn't taking any more chances. The British were not about to issue him a gun without a very good reason. And since he could not think of a very good reason they might accept, it would have to be something familiar. Familiar but not new.

He walked and found the small pawnshop in Mayfair. Alexsi peered through the crammed shelves, fascinated. There were of course no pawnshops in the Soviet Union. There was nothing private in the Soviet Union. Occasion had never brought him to a German pawnshop, since before all the Jews were deported from Berlin every one of their shops had Storm Troopers standing in front, taking down the names of those who entered.

Not seeing what he wanted, he made his way to the counter. A very thin, frail-looking middle-aged man behind it. Balding, with the lonely strands of hair plastered back on his skull.

Alexsi said, "I am looking for a knife. Solingen."

"You want German?"

The question was in German-accented English. An accent disturbingly like his own. Alexsi felt he ought to turn and walk out, though that would attract even more attention. "Yes."

"Your reason?"

"My reason is I want it," Alexsi snapped. "Do you have it or not?"

"Forgive me, sir. You see, I left Germany, and I thought I heard Berlin in your voice."

"I am not German," Alexsi said.

"My apologies, sir. If you would be kind enough to wait, I will return in a moment."

He slipped through a curtain into the back, and Alexsi thought if he had any brains or sense he would leave immediately. He waited.

The pawnbroker returned with two fabric-lined wooden trays. He set them down on the counter.

Alexsi immediately saw what he wanted. A lever-lock with a handle just slightly shorter than his hand. He pressed the catch and the spring-loaded blade flicked out. It was engraved HUBERTUS. The mechanism was tight, and the blade in good condition though it would need honing to be truly dangerous. He folded it closed again and set it down on the counter.

In the next tray was a penknife the length of his middle finger with two folding blades. He placed it beside the lever-lock. "How much for these two?"

"You want German for a reason," the pawnbroker said.

"I want these two knives," said Alexsi. "Now how much?"

"Permit me," the pawnbroker said. "I left. I was a pessimist. The optimists stayed. I fear the worst for them." He looked down at the knives. "I am not strong. I see that you are, young man. Tell me you will finish a Nazi with them, and you may have them for nothing."

Now Alexsi knew for certain the man was German. Germans were always making statements, and it seemed that German Jews did also. He reached into his jacket pocket for his billfold, and thumbed out one of the British five-pound notes that was almost large enough to be a bedsheet. "You should have something," he said. "A long time ago my auntie scolded me that it was bad luck not to pay for a knife. It cuts friendship, she always said."

19

The Abwehr liked to joke, with that German sense of humor that was as light as an anvil, that more spies had gone mad sitting in their rooms waiting for policemen to break down their doors than had been hanged after policemen actually broke down their doors.

So in a way it was a relief when Alexsi received his first hit. He was leaving MI6 headquarters at the end of the day and was on his way back to his hotel. He had been following the exact same route to give any watchers ample opportunity to set up on him and reveal themselves.

And there he was. A safe distance from MI6 on Broadway, and lounging at a bus stop. A Russian. Clearly a Russian because he was eating a bag of sunflower seeds as only a Russian would. Russians appeared to be eating sunflower seeds as if they were biting off the tip and sucking the insides out of the shell. In fact they were inserting the sharp edge of the seed between their two front teeth and cracking it by biting down. Russians were addicted to sunflower seeds.

Alexsi passed by the bus shelter without a second glance at the sunflower eater.

He walked straight now, south on Broadway, past the turn for his hotel. He would make no turns yet, because turns without a reason were a signal that you knew you were being followed. He would keep a straight route to stretch them out and lock them in behind him. Alexsi was feeling it now, that bracing tingle of adrenaline. At least he wasn't crazy. It was real. They weren't Germans, they weren't British. They were Russian. And they had definitely found him here in London. The Communist girl had been a honey trap, and he hadn't nearly killed himself scrambling across London roofs for no good reason.

It would have been comforting if they hadn't been there to murder him.

The last light was fading from the western winter sky. Alexsi thought he should get an idea of what kind of effort he was up against before it was completely dark.

An old man wearing a helmet with a luminous *W* on it and a gasmask bag slung over his shoulder went hurrying by. An air raid warden preparing to enforce the blackout.

Up ahead the first demeanor error, as the NKVD called it. Two men standing together smoking, then hurriedly splitting up as soon as they saw him come into view. So there were at least three. Sunflower seeds had probably fallen in behind. These two would flank him.

Alexsi picked up the pace just a bit now. Nothing like a run; a fast walk to panic them a bit, make them worried about losing him, make them hurry, bring them in closer.

Crossing Victoria now, the road bending into Old Pye. Alexsi made his first turn. Quickly around a corner, then stopping at a newsstand. He bought a copy of the *Daily Mirror* for a penny and watched the corner while pretending to glance at the news.

Sure enough, a Russian in a trench coat and a fedora came rushing around it. He hitched up and hesitated when he saw Alexsi at the newsstand, then recovered nicely, albeit too late, continuing down the street at a normal pace and passing the newsstand naturally. Four.

Alexsi tucked the newspaper under his arm and went back the way he had come. The brim of a hat was protruding from a doorway, and so he crossed the street. They were hugging him tighter than he would expect of professionals. But they weren't following him in Moscow, they were following him in London. Perhaps not totally familiar with the city.

A moment later Alexsi could have laughed at himself for turning into an optimist. They were obviously onto his trick of disappearing into apartment buildings and then vanishing out exits and over rooftops. And they were making very sure he did not do it again.

Now dusk was blending into night. The city blacked out, but a rising moon that was more than three-quarters. Enough to see faces by, and cast some light between the buildings. It was easier for them in the daylight, and it would be easier for him in the dark.

Old Pye until it ran out, then south to Great Peter. Alexsi had seen four, but he was sure there were at least six. During his spy training in Moscow, the NKVD had often thrown many more followers at him, but never fewer than six. He couldn't understand why they kept giving him touches; silhouettes appearing at side streets, flashes from around corners. They would appear from the side streets; a silhouette here, a pair of shoes protruding from a doorway.

Alexsi stopped suddenly, and the twisting of fear in his stomach accompanied the realization that he had been a fool. So wrapped up in the mechanics of surveillance detection that he had not bothered to consider their aim. They were not following him. They were *herding* him. Carefully bumping him southeast toward the river. If he continued on this route, they would converge from all sides to corner him at Victoria Tower Gardens and he would end the night, and his life, in the Thames.

Well, all right.

An air raid siren went off in the distance, then a succession more all across the city. Searchlights stabbed into the sky and added to the moonlight illumination as the beams reflected down off the winter clouds.

Probably alone of everyone in London, Alexsi knew exactly what this was. Operation Steinbock. They had talked about it in Berlin: inside the Abwehr they talked about everything, whereas in the NKVD anyone who asked too many questions outside his department was taken down to the basement and shot. After the British night bombing of Berlin, the leadership of the Luftwaffe met to decide what should be done. The consensus was that the production of bombers should be slowed and fighters increased, that fighter squadrons be drawn back from the Russian front no matter the cost to the armies. That an all-out defense be mounted to so increase the price of the British and American bomber offensives against the Reich that they would draw back and reassess their tactics, giving the Germans some breathing space. All of the Luftwaffe generals had agreed. But then Hitler stepped in and overruled them, stating that instead there should be a renewed bomber offensive against England. And that was that. The Luftwaffe was committed to doing what had already failed before, especially after all the bomber and crew losses of the Battle of Britain, North Africa, and Russia.

Here was the result. Alexsi immediately dismissed the idea of going down into a shelter. One might think there would be safety in a thick crowd, but he knew that would make it even easier for his followers to surround and kill him.

Not that it would be any safer above ground, with all the pedestrians drifting off the streets in search of their own safety.

Alexsi formed the diagram in his head. Two out in front, two on each flank running parallel, and two bringing up the rear. They would expect him to break from the rear.

Leather-soled footsteps came fast from his front. Alexsi's hand slipped into his pocket for the lever-lock knife.

He relaxed, slightly, when he saw another luminous helmet.

"Off to a shelter, you!" the air raid warden thundered at the sight of him.

"On my way, sir," Alexsi replied, moving quickly now, in the opposite direction, to forestall further conversation.

Antiaircraft guns began firing, off to the northeast. Many seconds later the time-fuse shells went off with a string of cracks above the clouds—so far in the distance that the sound didn't reach him until well after the flashes.

Perfect. Alexsi cut north onto Tufton, the noise of the guns covering his running feet. And soon was treated to the spectacular sight of the towers of Westminster Abbey in the searchlight-moonlight. When a suitable doorway presented itself he ducked into it. Now was the time for the hunted to become the hunter. He pressed the lever, and his knife blade flicked out from the handle. He concealed the blade against his thigh so it would not gleam.

Forefinger tapping the blade, he coldly pondered his options. There would be an overcoat, probably a suit coat, perhaps a waistcoat, then a shirt and undershirt. Near enough to a suit of medieval armor for a knife the length of his.

Footsteps. But single footsteps, which told him he had upset their orderly plan. Alexsi cursed under his breath when more antiaircraft guns went off closer, obscuring the footsteps. He crouched a bit, readying himself.

A dark figure in an overcoat appeared in the doorway. Alexsi lunged out and grabbed for the right arm with his left hand. The knife in his right, blade sideways, driven with the full force of his moving body into the center of the throat. A gasp, then a wet gurgling sound as the blade went straight in. To the untutored the neck seemed soft and vulnerable, but there was much tough cartilage there—which was why he had put all his weight behind the blow. Alexsi snapped his wrist forward, twisting the blade to the side, going for the neck artery. He did not yank the knife out, instead using it as a lever to force the head to the side. The violence of his attack had thrown the Russian up against the wall of the building.

Blood sprayed from the wound as a breath was attempted, but the windpipe was severed and there was only an airy, shuddering wheezing. Alexsi's left hand slid down the forearm to the wrist. The Russian's hand was in his trouser pocket, and it was no mystery what he was grasping. Alexsi kept his body to the side, using his shoulder to pin the arm. His right hand still grasped the knife in the Russian's throat.

A sharp explosion from the Russian's trousers as the gun there went off. Alexsi was peppered by masonry from behind, either the pavement or the doorway wall from the ricochet.

The Russian's legs went out from under him. It had seemed like minutes. It always did, in the heat of combat, but it had been only seconds. The Azeri smugglers who'd first taught him to use a knife had known what they were doing.

No time to admire his handiwork. Alexsi dragged the Russian entirely into the doorway and followed the man's dead hand into his pocket. The hole in the trousers was still smoldering, and there was a smell of burning wool. The pistol was a Russian Tokarev 33 automatic. And in the opposite pocket a spare eight-round magazine. Alexsi pulled back the slide to be sure the spent cartridge had properly ejected, and there was a fresh bullet in the chamber. It was loaded.

Alexsi had panicked at the gunshot. Not the bullet, which had come nowhere near him. The sound. But now he reconsidered his position.

The Russians would think one of theirs had done the job. When they heard the shot the procedure would be for all to freeze in place, watching for a runner in case their man had missed.

If he bolted, he would run right into one of them waiting in ambush, and the tables would be reversed.

If nothing happened, the Russians would begin moving in again to count their bag.

Alexsi made up his mind. He would be taking a huge chance, but it was still five against one and he would need a clear avenue of escape. They were hugging him too tightly to risk slipping by.

He and the dead Russian were both wearing dark overcoats. The Russian's fedora had fallen off at the knife strike. Alexsi found it on the ground and put it on his head. He grabbed the Russian by the collar and dragged the body back out onto the pavement.

Alexsi slipped the pistol into his pocket and pulled his overcoat collar up around his face. With the pistol back openly in his hand, he stood over the body and waited.

He cursed the antiaircraft guns that were still firing and drowning out the sounds of footsteps.

A moment later flares popped in the sky, blue and yellow-white. Target markers, Alexsi told himself, dropped from the German bombers. A pathfinder bomber with the best navigator would drop flares on the target for the rest of the planes to bomb on. The British did the same thing. One of theirs had practically fallen at his feet one night in Berlin, letting him know he was right in the middle of the bomb path. These were coming down over Waterloo on the other side of the river, not far away. He couldn't hear the bombers' engines over the sound of the antiaircraft guns.

The flares came down fast on their parachutes, but before they fell below the buildings they lit up both ends of the street. A figure was approaching him from the same side, cautiously. And over his shoulder another two from the opposite end.

Alexsi gave them a Russian wave. An open-fingered hand from directly beside the head. Then more typically Russian body language. A fist pounded against the chest twice, signaling triumph.

It worked. He could see them relax and pick up their pace. Especially when they were close enough to take in the body on the ground.

Alexsi turned to look across the street. That way both approaching parties were only seeing the sides of his face, obscured by the pulled-up overcoat collar. His legs were shaking, no matter how much he tensed his muscles. Now he knew what it took for a hunter to let a tiger charge close enough for the shot to count. These Russians were not amateurs. A single change in his body language and they would begin shooting.

As they drew up to him, one, obviously the leader, said in Russian, "Make sure you take his papers for proof."

Before he left Moscow, Alexsi had been shown a scrapbook of newspaper clippings. Everyone the NKVD had killed for betraying or failing them. A little something to go along with his farewell party.

The pistol was ready in his hand, and theirs were in their pockets. Alexsi swung about and shot the leader first, right in the center of the face. Then the partner right beside him.

A hand grabbed his gun arm. The singleton behind him had decided not to waste time going for his own gun, and quick as a cat had lunged at him instead. Alexsi pushed his gun elbow tight against his body to give himself more leverage. He twisted about, and struck the heel of his left hand under the Russian's nose to gain some separation. He didn't raise his gun hand, but with the pistol tight against his hip fired as quickly as he could pull the trigger.

Five rounds and the magazine ran out. Empty. And still the Russian kept coming. Bared teeth and garlic-cigarette breath in his face. Alexsi twisted out of the Russian's grip and smashed the butt of his pistol up and into his face.

At the third blow the Russian sagged back. Alexsi gave him a hard kick to the stomach, which sent him against the wall of the building.

Alexsi jumped backward, pressing the Tokarev magazine release with his thumb. The empty magazine wouldn't drop—it must have been jammed by the blows he'd delivered. Alexsi hooked a finger under the slightly protruding bottom lip of the magazine and yanked it out. Another moment to slap in the fresh magazine from his pocket, and thumb down the slide release. The slide snapped forward.

The Russian was on his side, weakly trying to get his hand into his gun pocket, so those five bullets must have done something after all. Alexsi raised the pistol, and the Russian snarled, "Traitor! Fuck your mother!"

Alexsi shot him twice in the head, then put another bullet into each Russian on the ground just to be sure. The instant he bent down to harvest more spare magazines from their pockets: the pop of a shot down the road and a supersonic whipcrack of a bullet going over his head. The other Russians were closer than he thought.

With another Tokarev and spare magazine in hand, Alexsi was off running. He knew that the direction the pair had come would be clear, and he had no intention of standing there trading shots in the darkness until his ammunition ran out and more Russians arrived. Hitting a running target with a pistol was hard enough in daylight, let alone blackout darkness.

Alexsi was running and dodging down the street, vaguely in the direction of Westminster, and at least one Russian was still behind him shooting. Knowing how the NKVD punished failure of any kind, Alexsi knew that any chance of his adversary giving up and going home was faint. But all he had to do was run, not shoot, and he was gaining distance.

Now he heard airplane motors for the first time, near enough overhead that they overshadowed the sound of the antiaircraft guns. A blinding flash lit up in front of him, and Alexsi had the sensation of a hot wave of pressure lifting him off his feet.

20

1944

LONDON, ENGLAND

Alexsi awoke with the side of his face resting against something hard and rough. He opened his eyes to find himself surrounded by ghostly white bodies. Suddenly terror-stricken, he lurched to his feet and nearly lost consciousness again as the room spun around him. He smelled fire, and his first thought was that he was dead and there really was a hell.

Reaching out, his hand made contact with a thick wooden timber that rose up into a ceiling. For some reason he doubted that there were wooden timbers in hell, and that calmed him slightly. He grabbed it and held on tightly for support.

Shaking his head to clear it wasn't an option, because his head felt as if it were about to fall off of its own accord. Alexsi blinked rapidly until his vision cleared. Though "cleared" was a relative term, since he was in nearly total darkness and the air seemed filled with either smoke or haze.

In a few moments he realized that he wasn't in some terrible afterlife. He was standing in a wrecked dress shop, and the floor was littered with knocked-over mannequins. The storefront window was gone, and Alexsi had to believe that a German bomb had blown him straight through the window and into the shop.

It didn't seem as if any bones were broken, though if he had been blown off the street through a glass window Alexsi thought he should make sure he wasn't bleeding to death. Still grasping the beam, he ran his right hand down his clothing. The hand immediately began to hurt, and holding it up to his face he saw that it was swollen, though all the fingers were working. Switching his grip, he continued to check himself.

He seemed all right, though when he touched his face it was wet, and blood covered his hand.

Lurching away from the beam, he staggered around the shop until he found a dressing mirror that had been broken. He picked the largest piece up off the floor and examined his face. A few cuts, some still oozing and some scabbed over. Trickles of blood dripping down from his scalp. Luckily, it seemed that his face pressed against the floor had stopped the largest ones from bleeding.

As his head cleared, it occurred to Alexsi that he had spent more than enough time in one place. Hopefully the NKVD assassin who had been pursuing him had suffered an even worse fate, but he could not count on that. Or the fellow not finding a public telephone and calling the Soviet embassy for more assistance.

He looked about the floor, but the Tokarev pistol he had taken from the first Russian was nowhere to be found. He told himself furiously to stop wasting time. His knife was still in his pocket, and he tossed the now-useless pistol magazines onto the floor.

Literally feeling his way through the shop in the darkness, trying not to trip over everything on the floor, he found the back room. Once safely in it, he risked igniting the cigarette lighter he always carried.

The shop did have a back door, and a heavy blow from his shoulder opened the cheap lock. Though it did his pounding head no good at all.

Alexsi made his way cautiously through the alley. He paused for a very long time before sticking his head out. The street was blanketed with fire smoke. Which was perfect for concealment, but made it difficult to orient himself. Finally he took a guess on north. His hotel was northwest but he had no intention of approaching it directly.

No one shot at him when he stepped out of the alley, so he set off slowly. It shortly became clear where the smoke was coming from. Westminster Palace had taken a bomb hit and was on fire. Trucks were spraying water into it.

At least now he knew where he was going.

This was not a good situation. He was staggering down the street like a drunkard, brain scrambled, bleeding from the face and with his right hand good for nothing. There were probably more Soviets waiting at his hotel, and he was in no condition to deal with them. Certainly no condition to be crawling up drainpipes in the back of the hotel to avoid them. Not to mention that there just might be a pair, like those two Shakespearean murderers at the British hospital in Teheran, waiting for him in his room.

Hospital. Alexsi stopped his lurching, placing one hand on the nearest building for support. His brain must truly be scrambled, that he hadn't thought of something so simple.

Now instead of skirting the firemen at Westminster, he made his way directly toward them.

"Oi, what's this?" one exclaimed in the darkness, as Alexsi stumbled into their midst. A shielded torch flashed open briefly, and hands gripped his arms.

"Easy there, mate," another said. "What happened to you?"

"I believe I was blown up," Alexsi replied.

"Boche?" a suspicious voice from behind said.

"German pilots don't fly in suits, you wanker," a dismissive voice chimed in.

Alexsi reached into his jacket and handed over his identification papers. The torch flashed again, and the bearer announced, "Czech." A moment later a hand tucked the papers back into his pocket.

"Get him to the ambulance," a new voice of authority commanded.

The hands gripping his arms led him down the street in the flickering light of the dying fire. The ambulance door opened, and they put him down onto a hard canvas stretcher. Before the door shut, a hand grasped his in the darkness and thrust a porcelain mug into it. Fortunately it was his uninjured left, so Alexsi was able to hang on to it.

He leaned onto his side and tasted, prepared to suspend his usual rule against alcohol. Tea, by God. For all they knew, he could have been bleeding to death. What could be more English? No first aid, but a nice cup of tea.

He was thirsty enough to drink it, though.

The ambulance moved excruciatingly slowly, picking its way through the streets in the blackout. On the chance that he might lose his clothes at the hospital, Alexsi passed the time by removing a few banknotes from his billfold, rolling them up tightly, and secreting them in the crack of his buttocks.

After what seemed like the rest of the night, it finally stopped. Still in total darkness, the door opened and hands grabbed the end of the stretcher and yanked him out. When it came free of the vehicle Alexsi had to shift his weight to keep from spilling out onto the ground.

A short bouncing hike in the darkness. Alexsi wondered how many of the badly wounded survived to enter the hospital.

Brushing through blackout curtains into a sudden explosion of light. Before his eyes adjusted, a terrifying female face loomed over his. "Where are you hurt?" she demanded.

"I . . . I'm not sure," Alexsi stuttered out.

The matron's face became even more terrifying. The demand became even more pronounced. "German!"

"I am Czech, miss," Alexsi said, as feebly as he could manage.

The terrifying face softened. "That's all right, dearie," she said finally, as if that was just another affliction she would have to deal with. Then, to others out of view, "Take him in."

The stretcher was set down on an examination table, and Alexsi was rolled about like a large lump of dough until his clothes were removed in record time.

"Name?" a different stern female voice demanded.

Alexsi had been thinking about it. If they found his papers he would just plead confusion, but if possible he did not want his English identity on the hospital register for any Communist to see. "Josef Zatec," he said. It was the name of the town his German infantry company had occupied during the invasion of Czechoslovakia.

They made him spell it. Then he said, "Please, what hospital is this?"

"St. Mary's dear," said one of the nurses.

"In Paddington?" said Alexsi.

"That's right."

Good. He knew where that was.

A very old doctor entered the room. The young ones were all in the army, of course.

He leaned over Alexsi and demanded gruffly, "What on earth were you doing out in the bombing, young man?"

"I don't know, sir," Alexsi replied.

"How do you mean?" the doctor said, slightly gentler now.

"I don't remember," Alexsi said.

The doctor prodded him up and down, grabbing the swollen right hand and twisting it about. Alexsi yelped.

"Right, something's amiss there," the doctor announced.

Alexsi just sighed.

The doctor shined a pen torch in his eyes, and had him look every which way. Then in his ears.

"X-rays immediately," the doctor commanded his audience. "Right hand, and . . ."

In his peripheral vision Alexsi saw the doctor tapping his head.

"After that," the doctor continued, "you can sort out those cuts. Not sure about the hand, but nothing else appears broken. We won't know about any sprains until morning, when he tries to move about." An impersonal hand patted Alexsi's shoulder awkwardly. "Good luck, young man."

"Thank you, sir," Alexsi replied without conviction. The quality of English medical care had so far failed to fill him with confidence.

After they put him in a hospital gown, they picked up his stretcher and carried him down a hallway. His head facing the wrong way, Alexsi first heard running footsteps. With no weapons available, he gripped the canvas-covered pole of the stretcher and waited for it. If a Russian had followed him to the fire, that ambulance would have been as easy to follow as a caterpillar crossing a cabbage leaf. Now there would be two shots to the head, and his assassins sprinting out the door and long gone.

Then someone shouted in one of those unintelligible British dialects, "How about some fucking attention, eh?"

At least two other complaining voices chimed in with him.

Alexsi relaxed his grip on the side of the canvas and resumed breathing. Just another drunken English idiot.

One of the orderlies carrying Alexsi's stretcher shouted back, "What are you on about, mate?"

"A doctor is what I'm fucking on about!" the shouter continued.

"Don't get in a paddy," the orderly counseled. "We'll sort this out."

"Don't you be a chopsy with me, boyo," the shouter continued. "D'ya know how long we be waiting?"

Alexsi just rolled his eyes. Whenever he thought he finally had a firm grasp of the English language, the English defeated him.

They were right on top of him now, and someone jostled the stretcher.

"Steady on," pleaded the orderly holding the back. He was the one whose face Alexsi could see, and he looked frightened.

"I'll wager this fucker has seen a medic," the shouter shouted, giving the stretcher a shake.

"Get your fucking hands off that!" the first orderly commanded.

"Don't tell me where to put my fucking hands!" the shouter shouted.

The stretcher thumped down on the floor as the shoving began.

A shoe came down right next to Alexsi's head, and enough was enough. He got up off the stretcher. The shoving match had moved slightly down, and a young nurse with a clipboard, who had been accompanying them, had pressed herself against the wall. Alexsi took her arm and they skirted the shoving match, the participants paying full attention to each other.

"You really shouldn't be up," the nurse said to Alexsi, who was padding down the floor in bare feet, his gown billowing in the back.

"There doesn't seem to be any alternative," Alexsi said. "I do not feel up to fist-fighting at the moment."

The radiographic area was just down the hall, fortunately. The nurse turned him over to the orderly there, and primly picked up the telephone. Alexsi was just about to climb onto the X-ray table when two military police and a constable came running past the door and down the hall, truncheons in hand.

They were just rolling the table from under the machine that looked like a sewer pipe bolted to the ceiling when the two stretcher orderlies spilled into the room. Uniforms disheveled, the frightened one lugging the stretcher under his arm.

The technician pulled the hard film cartridge from under Alexsi's head, and he was finally able to look up.

"Sorry, Nurse," the orderly leader said. Alexsi noticed an angry red abrasion on his forehead. "Bloody Taffs."

Alexsi couldn't stand it any longer. He had to have a translation. "I beg your pardon," he said. Everyone in the room turned to look at him. "Taffs?"

"The Welsh," the orderly explained.

Alexsi must have still looked puzzled.

"From Wales," the nurse added helpfully.

"Ah, yes. I see now," said Alexsi. "Thank you."

"Bloody people," the orderly muttered. "They'd row with Christ Almighty himself over the seating at the Last Supper."

Alexsi uneasily climbed back onto the stretcher, but there were no more confrontations. They took him to another room, where two nurses picked the glass out of his head and plastered up all the cuts.

While they were working, another old dragon came in, one of the matrons like the first he had met, that ran the place and bossed everyone. She announced that the X-ray films were negative. "You must have a very hard head," she told Alexsi with an almost frightening stained and broken-toothed British smile.

"If you only knew," he replied.

"His hand isn't broken," she announced to the world at large after a glance at her clipboard. "Just a bad sprain. So give it a wrap, and when you're done he has a bed on ward nine. Concussion observation."

"Yes, Matron," the nurses replied dutifully.

"You're a lucky young man," she said to Alexsi.

Alexsi didn't say anything. She had to be the only one in the room who thought so. For himself, his luck had been ruinous from the moment he offered himself to the British.

He ended up in a steel-framed bed in a ward with at least thirty men in it. The beds were in military rows along the walls of the room, with long narrow tables down the middle aisle to hold any equipment that was needed.

Alexsi found all the snoring, farting, coughing, and moaning strangely soothing, like background music. Especially since he had no intention of sleeping. So as he lay in his hospital bed he began putting together his plan to foil the NKVD, fittingly using the method the NKVD had taught him. First, the objective. If he valued his life, which he most certainly did, he had to get out of England. Not just London, but the entire country. Otherwise the Russians would run him down sooner or later. People who were shot for failure were not in the habit of giving up.

Next, the execution. It was war, and there was no slipping out of an island during a war. The British would have to send him.

They were not about to send him to the United States, Canada, or South America just because he asked them nicely. He could come up with no plausible scheme to convince them to. No doubt they had already shared his reports with the Americans. If they had been interested in him he would have heard of it and been asked to brief them. Perhaps he could make something up? But what? It would have to hold up under close examination. Alexsi just grunted softly. Dead end.

If he got himself assigned to a British Army unit in the field as an intelligence officer or translator, his problems would only continue. Clearly, there were Russian spies in British intelligence, and Communists everywhere. Getting close to the war zones might make it even easier for them to get him.

Alexsi shook his head at the ceiling. There was no other way. He hated the idea, but it was the only way to disappear. Disappear or die, that was the choice.

Decision made, Alexsi watched the clock until it was a half hour until first light. When the nurse finished her turn through the ward, he got up, went to the door, and peered out.

He didn't want to go wandering in his gown, and his luck turned, just a bit, when an orderly came walking down the hall.

Alexsi attracted his attention with a low whistle.

The orderly glanced over. "All right, mate?"

Alexsi motioned him closer. "I want my clothes."

"I'll wager you do," the orderly said sarcastically, and turned to continue on his way.

Another low whistle. The orderly looked over his shoulder, and Alexsi was holding a five-pound note in his hand.

The orderly turned on his heels and came back.

"Josef Zatec," Alexsi said slowly and clearly.

The orderly held out his hand. "Give it over."

The note disappeared into Alexsi's fist. "On delivery."

"Snidey bastard," the orderly exclaimed. Then, "All right." He motioned toward a door down the hall. "Wait on me in there."

Alexsi kept a grip on the banknote. He might have been a fool, but not *that* much of one.

21

Alexsi hadn't thought he'd be able to get back into C's office, and he was right. The best that Ken could do for him was a visit with the undertaker. Whom everyone called Uncle Claude, but not fondly. Alexsi had learned his last name was Dansey. The man himself preferred to be called Colonel Z, though Alexsi found it telling that no one did, except to his face.

Alexsi was ushered in by the usual pinch-faced English spinster who seemed to guard every MI6 office. Even if they really were married, they always gave you a look that was enough to send your balls fleeing back up into your body.

The undertaker was of course at his desk, head down in papers. He was wearing a slightly wider pinstripe than the last time, and of course a waistcoat. And of course he did not have the courtesy to even look up.

"Sit down," he ordered. Just as in that first meeting with C, reveling in his rudeness. "Cohen said you needed to see me urgently. Keep it brief, I'm a busy man."

Alexsi did not bother to thank him for the appointment. "I feel I have done all I can here, sir."

The undertaker glanced up at him for the first time. "You certainly look a fright. Bombing throw a scare into you? Want to run off to America?"

Alexsi kept his face neutral. "I'm sure it will please you, sir, that I was bombed in Berlin by the Royal Air Force, and it was much, much worse."

The undertaker set his fountain pen down on the desk. "Yes, happy to hear it. So what exactly is it you want?"

"To go back out in the field, sir."

That made the undertaker do his best to stare a hole right through him. "And do what?"

"Spy, sir."

He now had the undertaker's full attention. "And you think you can do that?"

"In my experience, sir, spying is like walking a tightrope. You can be taught to do it better, but you either can do it or you cannot. I can."

The undertaker decided to run the conversation in a different direction. "Well, what is it?" he demanded impatiently. "Got a bird pregnant, and the family's taken the shotgun down off the wall? Used your training to nick something and the law's closing in? You know we'll find out. We always do."

The man's rudeness really was breathtaking. Alexsi found himself almost habituated to it by now. Though he could just as easily picture the undertaker licking his superiors' boots. The bullies were all the same. "I assume you are speaking from experience, sir," he replied calmly. "But it is nothing like that. I am simply not a desk man. I prefer to be operational. I feel I can do Britain the most good that way."

The undertaker had picked up his pen again and was drumming it on the desk blotter. "I must say, I thought you were coming to tell me you'd lost your nerve. You sure you haven't?"

"The ones who have lost their nerve, sir, do not ask to go out again. They invent reasons not to."

The undertaker hummed a bit under his breath; Alexsi almost grinned, because he knew the man didn't even realize it. "While I'm thinking that over, you can tell me how you do it."

"Do what, sir?"

"When we first met you sounded like a bloody Boche speaking English he learned in a first-year course. Now you're three-quarters of the way to having a London accent. How do you do it?"

"You must speak nothing but the language you are learning, sir," Alexsi replied seriously. "A grammar and dictionary help, but you must live among native speakers every day. I am told that I have an ear for accents, as some do with music."

The undertaker grunted.

"Are you finished thinking it over, sir?" Alexsi inquired politely.

The undertaker glowered at him. "Whether I happen to believe you at the moment, you've obviously given this some thought. Let's hear it."

Alexsi had prepared his sales pitch, and it was do or die. Literally. "The problem with spying in another country, sir, as I'm sure you know, is one of impersonation. A native Englishman trying to impersonate a German, even if fluent, will be found out immediately. As would a German trying to impersonate an Englishman. You must use a native, or someone with an appropriately neutral cover. Your problem is that these people can live in a society, and tell you what is going on around them, but they have no access to real military secrets. Even someone who can pass for a native German cannot impersonate a German soldier. Armies have their own language, their own slang, their own customs. Even the slightest defect in wearing a uniform would brand them an imposter. I can impersonate a German soldier perfectly, sir, because I have been one." Here he paused, not unaware of the drama.

"Go on," the undertaker said. "Who do you impersonate?"

"A sergeant, sir."

As expected, he had thrown the undertaker off his stride. "A sergeant? Not an officer?"

Of course he would think that. There was no snob like a British snob. "I was both, sir," said Alexsi. "When counterintelligence looks for spies, they look for officers. No one looks for a sergeant. While a sergeant of signals sees every secret message, sits unnoticed in conferences, possesses the combinations to safes, and walks into offices and map rooms with complete anonymity."

"By George," the undertaker exclaimed, with real interest now. "You may be onto something here. But how do you get in?"

"Doubtless you have stock of captured German Army uniforms, sir. I know very little about the British Army, but the German wastes little time or manpower on administration. Every German soldier carries on his person a paybook that is, in effect, his entire personal record. If a sergeant of signals troops arrived at a headquarters with no baggage, saying that his transport had been attacked by Allied aircraft and scattered, no one would say a word even if he was unexpected. They would just think it was a foul-up somewhere along the line and put him to work. As long as he had the correct paybook and transfer orders. I have checked many a paybook, sir, and signed the orders for many a soldier. I know exactly what they should look like. I am certain you possess a German typewriter, sir, and some Wehrmacht paper stock. The correct stamps, well, they are an easy matter to forge."

The undertaker's eyes narrowed, as if he was pleased he had caught Alexsi in an error. "How do you get your information back to us, then? You can't very well turn up at a German headquarters shanks' mare lugging a suitcase with a wireless inside."

"You did hear me say that I would be a sergeant of signals, sir," Alexsi said with just a finely judged touch of contempt. To let this bully know who he was dealing with. "I would use the German headquarters transmitter to contact you."

"You think you could actually get away with that?" the undertaker scoffed.

"When my own radio in Berlin was captured, sir," Alexsi informed him, "I radioed Moscow using the transmitter at Abwehr headquarters."

That set the undertaker back. "You are the nervy bugger, aren't you? How the bloody hell did you manage to get away with that, with no one noticing."

"The messages were ostensibly sent from Abwehr Berlin to Abwehr Hamburg, sir. As training messages. There are training messages sent every day to maintain and test operator proficiency. Because they are marked training no one bothers to decode them, only check them for accuracy in sending. All you would have to do is listen for them."

The undertaker leaned back in his chair. "That's so simple it's positively brilliant."

"We would use a book code, sir, so I would not have to carry coding materials with me. My messages would be formatted in the four-letter groups of a standard Enigma message."

The undertaker grasped the arms of his chair tightly, as if he were trying to hold his excitement in check. "I'm still not convinced the Germans wouldn't realize something was dodgy when no word of your arrival ever turned up. Chap showed up at my door with orders and I wasn't expecting him, he'd be locked in a room until I did some telephoning."

"This is not a military headquarters, sir," Alexsi explained patiently. "In a large headquarters soldiers come and go. Signalers who can send and receive Morse and are cleared for cipher operation are very scarce and coveted. No one would refuse such a gift horse. Also, that is one of the benefits of your bombing, sir. Military mail is constantly being lost or destroyed. Mundane matters such as the transfer of sergeants are not sent by wireless."

They were all the same: Russian, German, British. Alexsi could see it. The undertaker's eyes were practically gleaming with ambition. Running his own spy in a German Army group headquarters. Of course it would be all his idea. Fine, Alexsi thought. Just like the Russians. Them having a vested interest in his success meant a vested interest in his survival. As long as it got him out of England. He could make the rest up by himself from there.

"Allow me to also point out, sir, that as a signaler I would most likely be able to send you each month's Enigma key settings."

"Yes, that would be helpful."

By now Alexsi was familiar with English understatement. But the body language, which the Russians had taught him to read, was another story. At the mention of Enigma the undertaker had unconsciously pulled his arms back into his body like a turtle withdrawing into its shell. That, and the subject matter. Normally if you offered a spymaster a way to break into his enemy's most secret codes you would expect him, in his joy, to do his best to make you pregnant.

It made Alexsi think that the British had already broken the German codes. Which the Germans considered unbreakable. The information didn't concern him at all, but he filed it away in the event he ever found himself hanging from a Gestapo meat hook. Bargaining material.

"Appears you've thought of everything," said the undertaker. "Where am I sending you to?"

"Since the invasion of Europe is doubtless planned for this summer, sir, I assume that you would want me at OB West." Paris would suit him nicely, thank you very much. No Russians; the French Communists preoccupied staying out of the grasp of the Gestapo and SD. If worse came to worse, there was always neutral Spain across the mountains.

The undertaker pondered it, no doubt imagining his future knight-hood, Alexsi thought.

Instead he rose from his chair, and with an abrupt pointed finger directed Alexsi to follow him from the room. In the outer office he pointed again to a chair and, with a brisk "Wait here," left him under the close observation of his secretary.

Alexsi just sighed inwardly. Before he sat down, he said to the secretary, "May I?," and without waiting for an answer plucked the copy of the day's *Times* from her desk.

Alexsi had made it nearly to the end of the newspaper before the undertaker returned and again bid him follow back into the office. He waited until Alexsi was in and then secured the door tightly himself. A redundant gesture, in Alexsi's opinion, considering they were inside a spy headquarters.

"Right," the undertaker announced, plopping back into his chair. "Italy."

"Sir?" Alexsi said. It was always something. For whatever reason, no one could ever manage to do as he suggested. There must be something inherently unconvincing about him.

"Italy it is," the undertaker repeated, with a tone that would brook no argument.

"Of course, sir," Alexsi replied, like a good little soldier. The undertaker had obviously just been in to see C with his brilliant new idea, and that was that.

"I tell you frankly that the Italian campaign is in the shit," the undertaker said. "It's a bloody stalemate, with the emphasis on bloody. Anzio was a debacle. Getting the Italians out of the war meant nothing—the Germans brushed the Dago bastards aside and took the country over without missing so much as a turn. If we could get a man into Kesselring's headquarters it might make all the difference in the world."

Alexsi didn't care for it one bit. To get out of Italy meant either Switzerland, over the highest mountains in Europe, or swim. But there was no way out of it. Beggars could not be choosers. "Very good, sir."

"Right," the undertaker said again, enormously pleased with himself. "We want to get this moving as quickly as possible." He began making notations on a single sheet of paper. "You'll need to be briefed on Italy. Then put together your kit and documents. Arrange with the signals people about your message coding. Then parachute training. If we put the stick to everyone we should be able to have you on your way in just over a fortnight."

He sprang up and charged around the desk. Alexsi rose from his chair automatically. The undertaker offered his hot, damp hand in an almost caressing and insinuating way that made Alexsi remember a friend from his Azerbaijani boyhood telling about the uncle his mother never let him be alone in a room with. Uncle Claude.

22

1944

SOMEWHERE IN ENGLAND

"Good morning, young man. I am the service representative for agent clothing. This gentleman here"—he indicated the man standing beside him—"is responsible for this facility, which belongs to another service. We are here to get you kitted out."

"Gentlemen," Alexsi replied. No names were given, nor did he expect any. In his mind, he named them the tailor and the storeskeeper. The tailor, who had spoken first, was a trim, dapper older man immaculately dressed in a perfectly cut suit. A regimental moustache and the upper-class way of speaking that Alexsi had noticed British tradespeople invariably mimicked. The other resembled every supply sergeant he had ever met in both Russia and Germany. Fat, red face, walrus moustache, and the fierceness that came from facing only timid clerks, not the enemy.

After approving the mission, MI6 had put him into isolation. Which was fine with Alexsi. Keep him well away from any British traitors who would betray him to Moscow.

He had been driven in a curtained auto outside of London. They were in . . . well, not quite a warehouse and not quite a clothing shop. Even though there were racks of hanging uniforms just like in a shop. More rustic were the shelves lining the walls, hammered out of rough wood, like bookcases holding items of German Army equipment.

"Your general needs have been explained to me," the tailor told him. "Please feel free to be as explicit as you are able."

Alexsi said, "We will need to begin with two . . ." In a room full of German uniforms, the German word fell from his lips. ". . . *Feldblusen.*" He caught himself and added, "Uniform tunics. One must be as new and unworn as you have, it does not need to be my exact size. The other in good condition, my size. Most important, the one in my size must match in shade and wear of shoulder straps and collar patches in the lemon-yellow piping of signals troops. Noncommissioned-officer style, not officer."

The tailor was appropriately grave as he took it all in. "I'm afraid we do not have a large selection of signals troops shoulder straps. So we should choose them first, not the blouse."

Alexsi merely nodded. The man's quiet competence was reassuring.

In a bank of cabinets with large but shallow drawers they found the shoulder straps and collar patches they needed. Plus the lightning-bolt patch of signalers, worn on the upper left arm.

"Two silver studs for each shoulder strap, please," said Alexsi.

"*Oberfeldwebel,*" said the tailor. Master sergeant.

The man knew his business.

"Then a plain private of infantry, for the newer tunic," said Alexsi.

"Much easier," said the tailor. Who then produced a tape measure and took his measurements, calling them out to the storeskeeper. The storeskeeper wandered through his racks for a while, picked out two tunics, and brought them over.

"Why must you have two?" the storeskeeper demanded, the garments clasped protectively in his arms.

Alexsi could have laughed. The sergeant of supplies was the same in every army. Their stores were like their personal property, and they absolutely bled when forced to give any of it up. "The private is for the identity documents. The branch of service color cannot be seen in a black-and-white photograph. Perhaps you are unaware of how many spies the Gestapo catch because, when they are questioned, they are wearing the exact same clothing as in their identity photograph. This is never true in real life."

That clearly gave the tailor a turn. He went from pale to slightly pink, perhaps thinking, Alexsi imagined, of how many agents he had inadvertently sent to the block.

"I shall be sure to remember that, sir."

Alexsi suppressed a smile. He had been promoted from "young man" to "sir."

He checked inside the tunic he would wear for the correct acceptance and size stamps. Just in case the British had decided to manufacture their own and missed that telling detail. No, they were correct. It was definitely captured German clothing. This was the fair-quality 1940 model tunic with more wool than rayon. The later versions had the proportions reversed.

Next the *Feldmütze,* or side cap. It had been superseded by the visored field cap, but Alexsi felt a sergeant would still be wearing one.

"We do not have a specimen with the front chevron in signals yellow, sir," the tailor announced after another consultation with the storeskeeper. "But I shall be able to sew it with the correct shade cloth strip and thread."

"That would be fine," Alexsi said.

They moved on to undershirt and underwear. All correct. Suspenders. Trousers and boots were easy. Leather belt with the GOTT MIT UNS, Nazi eagle, and swastika buckle. For some reason everyone always thought God was with them when it came to killing people.

"Decorations?" Alexsi said.

The tailor led him over to another cabinet of drawers.

Alexsi opened them all, one by one, to the storeskeeper's obvious disapproval. He was searching for things to build his legend.

He plucked out a length of thick black ribbon bordered in white and red.

"Iron Cross Second Class," the tailor murmured.

"Sewn across the second buttonhole of the tunic," Alexsi said.

"Very good, sir."

Alexsi continued poring through the drawers. He picked out a stamped black badge of a wreathed helmet sporting a swastika, over crossed swords. Wound badge. Since he already had the scar of a British bullet hole on him, why not?

There didn't seem to be anything else he could use, though he kept at it. Signalers were not heroes, after all. They received Iron Crosses in the second class only for efficiency in combat, not heroism in it. He squatted down to the bottom drawer, which held rows of ribbons. Most of them identical, since the German Army didn't give out masses of campaign medals. Iron Cross, War Merit Cross, Austria annexation. The Sudetenland Medal, which he had ironically earned himself in his previous German existence. Plenty of Africa ribbons. None of any help. He couldn't very well bump into someone who had been in Afrika Corps, wearing the ribbon and knowing nothing about it.

Ah, there it was. *Gefrierfleischorden.* The Order of the Frozen Meat. Officially the *Ostmedaille.* Given to those soldiers who had survived the winter of 1941–1942 in Russia. A broad red ribbon with a thin white-bordered black band in the center. Alexsi imagined that there were plenty of German soldiers going from Italy to Russia to replace casualties, but few the other way. Usually due to wounds. Perfect.

"I believe that will complete the uniform," he said.

"And no decorations on the private soldier tunic," the tailor said.

"None," Alexsi replied.

"Your uniforms will be altered and completed in two days, sir," the tailor said.

"Thank you," Alexsi said. "Now . . . I'm sorry, I don't know the expression in English. Wallet, wristwatch, et cetera."

"I believe 'pocket litter' is the current term of choice, sir," said the tailor.

The storeskeeper, roused to efficiency now, produced a Swiss Silvana wristwatch with the German Army DH stamp. A worn wallet and coin purse, and, to go in them, the special Reichsmark notes and coins that were only to be used by the Wehrmacht.

Alexsi's eyes fell on a fine Busch compass, and he had to have it.

Finally, he said, "Is this the correct location to inquire about arms?"

The storeskeeper stepped to the fore now. "What type?"

"Sidearms."

The storeskeeper led them across the warehouse and unlocked a metal door. He snapped on a light switch, and the smaller room was revealed to be lined with racks of weapons. Mauser rifles, MP 40 submachine guns, MG 34 machine guns. The storeskeeper opened a cabinet with pistols hung up on pegs like tools in a workshop.

Alexsi regretfully passed up his favorite Belgian Browning and chose a Walther P38.

"You're the first bloke who didn't pick a Luger," the storeskeeper said sardonically.

"Officers take the Lugers for themselves," said Alexsi. "Lowly enlisted men carry the P38. Besides, it is the better pistol. Though not as attractive, I admit."

The storeskeeper brought out a dark brown leather holster that, though well worn, would look acceptable with some polish. Two magazines, and a box of Parabellum ammunition. Alexsi opened the box and checked the stamp on every cartridge to be sure that no one had slipped in any British 9mm ammunition.

"You're a careful fellow," the tailor observed.

"The small details add up to life and death," Alexsi replied. He replaced the cover on the cardboard box. "I think we are finished, gentlemen. Thank you for your help."

"Good luck, sir," said the tailor. "The private soldier tunic will be sent along to the person preparing your documents."

The storeskeeper had no well-wishes to pass along.

"You must be special," the forger said.

"I have always thought so," Alexsi replied. "Even if others have not."

The forger grinned at that. A tiny bald man with a quiet shy voice and a Middle European accent. A Jew, which explained the tailor calling him "a person." Alexsi never understood Jew hatred. He had been in Berlin during Kristallnacht, and watched the final Jews being deported east in early 1943.

"I mean that I rarely see my clients," the forger said. "I am given the photographs and produce the documents without ever meeting them."

"Which do you prefer?" Alexsi asked.

The forger shrugged. "I was told of your special needs. I appreciate the challenge." He swept a hand over his desk. Open on it were several German Army paybooks, the *Soldbuchen*. For reference.

The room was exactly as Alexsi would have expected. The writing desk, and another drafting desk, ink stained. Cups brimming with pens and pencils and brushes. Blotters of all types. Shelves of stamps in racks, along with stacks of ink pads and bottles of ink in every conceivable shade.

"I have a few blank paybooks that were captured in Tunisia," the forger explained. "*Very* few. So we must have all the details absolutely correct before I begin work."

"I agree," said Alexsi.

The forger led him into the next room and sat him down in a chair. Examining him closely, he took a comb and some pomade and plastered Alexsi's hair down at the sides, then fluffed it up a bit on top. Looking in a mirror, Alexsi had to admit it was an adolescent German boy's hair.

"I shall make your face a bit thinner in the photographs," the forger said. "Younger."

Alexsi was glad he didn't have to tell this fellow his business.

The forger put him in the private soldier uniform tunic and stood him up against first a blown-up photograph of a stone wall, then a wooden barracks one. The German Army identity photographs were done on an assembly line basis.

The forger snapped him with a 35mm camera on a tripod, pausing only to change the hair combing slightly halfway through. "I have some real German film," he murmured, almost to himself. "It should look marvelous."

That completed, they returned to his desk, Alexsi trying to keep his hands off his hair. He hated pomade.

The forger rubbed his own hands together vigorously, and took up the pen. "Now, the particulars. I have your personal description, of course, so no worries there."

"Name: Peter Bauer," Alexsi said. It was an utterly common Bavarian name. There were probably thousands of Peter Bauers in the German Army, which was why he chose it. "Entered service Munich, January 1939. Army signal school Halle-Dölau." He borrowed the pen and wrote down the specialty codes for wireless operator, wireless repair, and Enigma cipher clerk. Passing the pen back, he said, "Army signal school instructor, December 1939." The best students were often poached as instructors for a time. "November 1940, joined Twelfth Panzer Division." He had served with the Second Infantry in Czechoslovakia, which was converted into the Second Mechanized and then the Twelfth Panzer. He knew the officers. "Radio company, divisional signals. Campaigns: Army Group North, Kursk 1943. Field hospital, Estonia. Then reserve hospital, Munich. Leave, Munich."

He fell silent, leaving only the sound of the forger's pen scratching paper. Munich because he had lived in Munich with his "Uncle Hans." Berlin was too touchy.

Alexsi knew the name of the street he grew up on, the schools he attended, and the name of his sweetheart, all ready to trip off his tongue. It was the only way to be convincing. Russia because he knew the Soviet Union and, having spied for the Soviet Union in the German Army, knew all about the war there from the reports on the German side. In London he had studied the German newspapers the British captured or obtained from neutral but pro-Fascist Spain, to be up-to-date on events from the time he had been away from Germany. Not too much, though. Soldiers at the front received their news mainly from letters from home, if at all.

"A wounded wireless man," the forger almost whispered. "Marvelous. I have already been told: Iron Cross Second Class, wound badge, Eastern Front medal."

"Can you do a *Wehrmacht-Führerschein*?" Alexsi asked, testing him.

"Army driving permit," the forger replied. "Easily. Now, if you would, please, open your mouth."

Alexsi complied, and the forger made notes on his dental condition, which was another page in the paybook.

The forger set down his pen. "That should do it. It will take me at least a week, perhaps more. Including properly aging the documents. Have you done your parachute training?"

"No." Alexsi had, but with the Germans. That was more information than he wished to spread about. The kind of information a Soviet agent looking for him would latch on to.

"Your papers will be completed by the time you finish. They send them all to Ringway Airport. You'll like Manchester."

"Will I?" said Alexsi.

"No, probably not. You'll leave soon after that, so it won't be much of a farewell."

Later, Alexsi reflected that he would have known the forger was not English even without the accent. The man never wished him good luck.

PART THREE

In the house of the hanged man, they mention not the rope.

—RUSSIAN PROVERB

23

Alexsi was so sick of the British he almost didn't mind parachuting out into the darkness. After spending what felt like a third of his life flying from England to Algeria, another third passed by flying from Algiers to Italy. The Halifax bomber shook as if it would fall apart at any moment. The navigator waved him away angrily whenever he tried to get a look at his map to see where they were. And each time he fell asleep the gunner would shake him awake and hand him a mug of tea. Quite a contrast between the German air crew who dropped him into Iran and this "special duties" flight. It made Alexsi think that the Germans would never lose a war if only they didn't persist in fighting the entire world every time. Just as this last month had made him think that the only possible explanation for the British Empire was the quality of the opposition.

The gunner weaved his way back through the narrow passage from the front of the aircraft, and Alexsi seriously considered stabbing him if there was another cup of tea involved.

Instead the gunner shouted, "Fifteen minutes!"

Fifteen minutes? Fifteen minutes' warning to jump into enemy territory? Wonderful. Alexsi picked up the X-type parachute he had carefully set out of the way and inspected it with the battery torch from his padded jumpsuit. Everything looked all right. He slipped it over his back and snapped the two leg and two shoulder harness keepers into the metal quick-release "bang box" in the center of his chest. Typical British. Brown-and-green camouflaged jumpsuit, brown parachute bag, and yet a cream-white webbing harness encircling his body. Why bother trying to conceal yourself? He might as well land waving a lit flare in his hand.

Clapping the padded cloth helmet that looked like a turban onto his head and buckling the chin strap, Alexsi waddled back to the rear of the aircraft, where the gunners had already opened the jump hole in the floor. Again, what kind of idiots would decide that it was better to parachute down through a hole in the floor of an airplane rather than out through a door in the side? The jump light was burning red for standby. The way things had gone thus far, Alexsi hoped they were at least over land.

One of the gunners plucked the static line from the pocket on the back of the parachute and hooked the V-ring to a clip overhead. Alexsi grabbed a handful of the webbing and pulled hard to make sure it was secure.

They had made him do twelve training jumps. Why, he had no earthly idea. After all, he was only going to parachute for them once—and all he needed was to know how a British parachute operated. It had been what he would call a characteristic British discussion. After the first jump he had said: All right, you can see I know what I am doing, let's move on. Their reply: You need to do twelve jumps for your certificate. Him: I don't need a certificate, why do I need to do twelve jumps? The British: You need to do twelve jumps.

After all that nonsense, Alexsi had a good idea how he would do it when there was no one to tell him what to do. Pulling the celluloid goggles down over his eyes, he sat on the floor of the bomber and braced his feet against the edge of the hole, one hand ready to guide himself out on each side.

One of the gunners shouted at him, "That's not the way you're supposed to do it!"

Alexsi responded by giving him the V-for-victory two-fingered sign, but in this case with the back of the hand facing the recipient it meant something entirely different. A convenient shorthand he had learned from the English.

The light flashed green and he went out, his hands pushing him through on both sides to keep from leaving his teeth, nose, or forehead on the metal.

The slipstream caught him, and he felt it blow him sideways. A sharp yank to the shoulders and groin told him the parachute had deployed. He grasped the risers and looked up to a full canopy. Which was reassuring, since like the Germans the British jumped with only a single parachute. If it didn't open you'd make a quick end to a long journey.

At least the British packed the parachute in a bag so the opening shock was a bit more gentle. The German parachute deploying was enough to knock your eyeballs out of their sockets.

Alexsi looked below him. Nothing but darkness. The moon was supposed to be up, to give him some light, but it was behind clouds. He looked out ahead, trying to find the horizon to judge his height. What looked like broken hills. He was supposed to be dropped in open fields. They had shown him the aerial photographs, which had been helpful, but the way things had gone he thought the only way he'd hit it was by accident.

Of course they hadn't told him the jump height, but the ground should be coming up very soon. Alexsi clamped his feet together and bent his knees slightly. The horizon disappeared, so he braced himself. No impact. This was not good—he was below the hills with no way to guess the distance to the ground.

After what seemed like forever his feet hit earth. Hard. Alexsi began to roll in the direction of the fall but it turned out he was on the side of a slope and immediately fell backward and downhill. His ankle twisted and he let out a yelp of pain. He fell onto his back and hit hard. A large rock struck him between his shoulder blades, and it was bad enough even with the thick padding supplied by the parachute backpack. His helmet hit the ground, his head bounced along with it, and immediately the parachute was pulling him headfirst down the hill.

He was being raked by bushes. Alexsi's hand went for the metal quick-release bang box at the center of his chest. He twisted the mounting hard to unlock it, then struck it with the palm of his hand. The shoulder and leg straps came undone, as advertised, and he rolled to get himself out of the rest of the harness before he was torn to ribbons on the rocks and scrub.

Then he was free. He lay there panting, looking up at the overcast night sky, blank of stars, head still pointing downhill. He twisted about so he wasn't upside down, his right ankle stabbing him at each movement.

He couldn't lie there all night, even though the air was cool but mild and there was a pleasant smell of dry grass and sage to the hillside. Alexsi reached into the pocket on the left sleeve of his jumpsuit for the gravity knife. He pressed the button and the blade slid out and locked. Ironically, it was nearly identical to the knife German paratroopers used. He cut the laces of his jump boots and pulled them off. His ankle was tender to the touch, and swelling, but he couldn't feel any broken bones. The jumpsuit had pockets throughout for all the equipment a spy would need if he or she wasn't met on the ground. His German marching boots were rolled up in one of them, and he pulled them on before the ankle swelled up too badly. He didn't bother binding the ankle first. If a German medic came to be examining it, he did not want to be wearing a British bandage. But he did take two pain pills from the medical kit, and the flat canteen of water. He would be still hurting come morning, and might need to move quickly.

He had been wrong. That white parachute harness did come in handy. Even in the darkness he could see it lying just down the hill. The parachute must have snagged on something. Alexsi just snorted through his nose. If he had kept it on it would have dragged him to the bottom of the hill. But once he got it off it just stopped.

Grimacing from the pain in his ankle, he dragged the whole parachute back up. There was a folding shovel in the left thigh pocket of the jumpsuit. A large rock jutted out from the hillside a few meters to his left, and he began digging at the base of it.

It took an hour to make a hole big enough for the parachute and jumpsuit. Stuffing the parachute in first, he grasped the double zippers of the jumpsuit, which ran from the neck all the way down both legs. To let you easily step right out of it once you hit the ground, and walk away in whatever you were dressed in underneath as if you were strolling down the road. Or in his case roll out of. Before he folded it up and threw it into the hole, Alexsi plundered one of the pockets for his silk map and wad of Italian lira. He shoveled dirt into the hole and, just before it was filled, placed the shovel and canteen onto it and used his hands to complete the job. Now everything he was wearing was German.

Strangely enough, he felt better than he had in quite some time. At least now he was the master of his own fate. And it wasn't freezing cold and raining every day.

He took stock, and rather than frightening him the first life-or-death decision energized him. Alexsi decided to stay right where he was until first light. He might be sitting on the side of a hill in the middle of nowhere, or he might be sitting in the middle of an Italian village that would come alive come morning. No matter which was the case, his ankle was in no shape for him to be wandering around fruitlessly in the darkness. His watch was still working, at least. Just after four o'clock in the morning. He wouldn't have long to wait.

Alexsi lay back and passed the time thinking of good cover stories to tell anyone who came across him at dawn. The secret to lying fluently was being prepared to lie.

24

1944

SOMEWHERE IN ITALY

There was no false dawn in terrain like this. It remained half-light for sometimes an agonizingly long time, the light increasing in intensity only gradually, until the sun finally rose high enough to make a full appearance over the tops of the hills. Even low two-hundred-meter hills like these.

Eyes fixed on the east, Alexsi could not see much for the foliage below him. Before he scrambled up the hill to get a better view, he broke a branch off a bush and swept away the signs from where he had buried his parachute. He went slowly, favoring his twisted ankle.

At the top of the hill it all became clear. It was impossible to miss the jagged pile of limestone thrusting up from the valley below. Monte Soratte. The headquarters of the German Army in Italy.

Alexsi was not terribly surprised to find that he had been dropped clear on the other side of the mountain from his planned landing site. Well, at least he was in Italy, and the right part of it.

Just to be certain of his location, he took out his silk map and German compass. There were plenty of peaks along the length of Soratte to take a bearing on. Subtracting 180 degrees from each bearing produced a line from each peak down. All three lines intersected on a spot on the map that was his current location.

There was a small vineyard on the higher slope behind him. Alexsi counted himself lucky he hadn't come down in the middle of that—it would have been like landing in a field of barbed wire. He certainly wasn't going to be walking in that direction. Down was better. The map told him there were railroad tracks and a road.

He also wasn't going to be hiking up to Monte Soratte. Not just because of the effort, and that he had no more water, but because it would be impossible to explain. You see, *mein Herr*, I couldn't get a lift so I climbed a mountain to go to work. That was just a bit too much dedication, even for a German soldier.

It was just light enough to see his footing, and the sooner he got moving the better. Before the farmers finished their milking in the barns, and they and their dogs began moving out in the fields.

Alexsi limped carefully down the hill, using his hands to steady himself. The pain pills were still working, and the ankle didn't feel too terrible. He'd been worried about his back being too stiff to move, but it just hurt enough to push him on.

He detoured around open fields, once a farmhouse, and occasionally the trees and brush were so thick he had to follow a compass bearing to keep from being turned around. It really was quite picturesque. The storm clouds of the previous night had blown away, and it was a lovely spring day.

Alexsi finally struck the railroad tracks. Carefully looking up and down, because people also used them as a walking path, he crossed them, and followed them a bit because according to the map there was supposed to be a road to his right.

There it was. Packed dirt but not a lane, bordered by brush and gnarled old trees. It was exactly what he imagined Italy to look like. All it required was a mule pulling a farm cart to come down the road.

Alexsi donned his German side cap and brushed himself off as best he could, then sat down in the shade and made himself comfortable. He'd wait an hour or two, and if nothing came along he'd walk to the next fork in the road. The only thing British left in his possession was the silk printed map. Alexsi rolled it into a tiny ball, as it was designed for, then plunged two fingers into the earth to make a hole for its burial. He felt that he had the topography pretty well memorized, and did not want to forget it in his pocket.

He must have been dozing, because the sound of a vehicle seemed to wake him up. Even though it was probably due to the pain pills, Alexsi was furious with himself for that. Falling asleep alone in a German uniform. All some disgruntled Italian would have to do was hit him over the head with a rock.

The sound and a dust cloud in the distance announced the oncoming vehicle. As it emerged from the dust, Alexsi was surprised that it was not military. He lifted the flap of the leather holster, which was worn on his left side, cross-draw, in the German fashion. Drawing the Walther, he stepped out into the road. He didn't point the pistol at the vehicle, but he made sure the driver could see it in his hand. His left was held up in the universal gesture for halt.

It was a red Fiat Balilla, open-topped. Three men. Driver and passenger in the front, another passenger in the back.

He wondered at a private automobile in the middle of a war. Did the Italians not ration gasoline? Did the Germans let the Italians have gasoline? Either the driver was a person of influence, or he had just stopped a group of honest thieves. Or Italian partisans. Now Alexsi had his pistol pointed at them, and approached for a closer look. They all had their hands up. The driver was in his late thirties, early forties, the two passengers in their late teens. Not quite army age, but close. They could have been father and sons, or just as easily could not. All were wearing suits—the teenagers' were too large for them, and in a war when nothing was made but uniforms it was hard to tell the difference between a cheap suit and a well-worn one.

Alexsi didn't see any weapons, and considering the size of the Fiat, if they weren't in sight then they weren't accessible. He relaxed. Slightly. *"Buongiorno."*

The older driver answered cautiously, *"Buongiorno, signore."*

Settling into his role as German soldier, Alexsi opened the rear door and made himself comfortable on the seat before saying, *"Portami al Monte Soratte, per favore."* He asked politely, but then again he did have a pistol in his hand.

"Monte Soratte?" the driver inquired, as if he did not understand. Both the front and rear passengers were staring straight ahead, as if they were deaf and dumb.

"Sì," Alexsi said, quite firmly, as in, Don't dream of trying to tell me you don't know the way.

"Ah, Monte Soratte!" the driver exclaimed, as if he had suddenly received a revelation from on high.

"Sì, Monte Soratte," Alexsi repeated, extending his arm over the seat and thrusting the Walther toward the windshield in an unmistakable gesture of: You may now proceed.

The driver got the Fiat moving, with a grinding of gears. The engine squealed in protest. Not seeing any weapons, and feeling enough genuine fear around him, made Alexsi confident enough to holster his pistol.

The driver, who was both driving and looking back over his shoulder, as if Alexsi were deaf and a lip-reader, favored him with a stream of Italian. The only word Alexsi could make out was *"incidente."* Perhaps the fellow was asking him if he'd had an accident. No matter. Alexsi didn't feel like fighting his way through the few words of Italian he'd memorized in England. *"Non capisco."*

"Ah, sì," the driver said mournfully, no doubt desolate over their inability to communicate. He then proceeded to have a conversation with the two teenagers in rapid-fire Italian, though perhaps "conversation" was the wrong word, because all the two boys did was nod. The driver kept looking back and smiling at him, but Alexsi was more attuned to his tone, which was not lighthearted. The only word he could pick out was *"tedesco."* German. And then *"la pistola."*

Reading the body language of the two teenagers, Alexsi was thinking that he had perhaps been hasty in holstering his handgun. The backseat was so tight the teenager was practically leaning against him, and the holster. In any case, he casually rested his left hand on top of it. His right hand went into his trouser pocket and grasped the lever-lock knife. And he had been so sure his luck was about to change. He took pains to keep his face utterly relaxed and detached while the conversation was progressing. The oblivious German among friendly Italians.

Ahead was a fork in the road. From his map Alexsi was sure that a left turn was the way up to Monte Soratte.

They stayed to the right. Alexsi was not content to wait until they reached a destination with even more friends waiting to greet him. Or for the driver to give a signal to attack. Not with three on one.

The knife was already open and hidden beside his thigh. Alexsi grabbed the hair of the teenager in front, yanked his head back, and cut his throat. The blood sprayed, and as they all did, the teenager instinctively grasped his throat with both hands, in a futile effort to try and hold everything closed.

The Fiat swerved as the driver screamed, *"Avanti!"*

The teenager in the back was already on him like a cat, correctly forgetting about the pistol and clawing for his knife hand. Alexsi fell back on the auto seat and the teenager grabbed his wrist with both hands to pry the knife out.

This was not good. Alexsi had the teenager's full weight on top of him, and could do nothing but try and keep his grip on the knife. He couldn't get his legs under him to kick the boy off.

Then the driver stood on the brakes, and both Alexsi and the teenager were lifted up and slammed into the back of the front seat. As they bounced back the teenager lost his grip, and Alexsi plunged his knife into the exposed chest.

The teenager grunted in pain. Alexsi tried to yank the knife out but it was stuck hard between the ribs. He let it go and kicked himself back across the seat, giving himself enough space to get his pistol out of the holster.

The driver had twisted around in his seat. His arm was inside his jacket and about to come out. Alexsi jammed the barrel into the back of his head and pulled the trigger. The front of the driver's face seemed to explode out onto the windscreen.

Alexsi was yanked sideways. The teenager with the knife still in his chest had grabbed his legs and was trying to either pull himself up or Alexsi down to him. He was looking up at Alexsi with a kind of animal desperation in his eyes. Alexsi pointed the pistol right between them and pulled the trigger.

The teenager went limp across his legs. Alexsi kicked him off and stood up unsteadily. The teenager in the front seat had definitely bled out. The seat was newly dyed red, and he was crumpled up on the floorboard.

The driver was slumped over the steering wheel and the horn was blaring. Alexsi grabbed him by the coat collar and yanked him back to make it stop. The third one, in the backseat, was definitely dead.

Alexsi dropped the hammer of the Walther to make it safe, and slid the pistol back into his holster. If the fools had only taken him to Monte Soratte they would have received the thanks of the German Army and a handful of MI6's lira for their trouble.

He dragged the driver's body over to the passenger side and stripped off his suit jacket to wipe the blood, brains, and a single eyeball from the windscreen since he himself would need to see to drive. When the jacket came off a small Beretta automatic tumbled down onto the seat. Alexsi drew the slide back slightly to see if it was loaded. It was. He slid the pistol into his pocket. An interesting family. How unfortunate he hadn't the opportunity to get to know them.

Curious, he removed the key from the ignition and opened the trunk. Two crates of German cigarettes, two full German Army petrol cans, and a double shotgun with exposed hammers and the barrel cut down to the handgrips. Now his questions were answered. Black marketeers driving their booty in the early hours before the army got on the roads. Pay off a friendly German supply sergeant with women or wine or whatever, then drive the goods to Rome and sell them for a fortune. Or, Alexsi thought further, trade them to the local farmers for food and sell that in Rome for even more money. It was a trade that would have interested him in his younger days in Russia. Though he was never keen on accomplices, and wouldn't have risked it over a single German soldier just to get his pistol. Now he could see why they didn't want to go up to Monte Soratte.

No matter. He was alive, and they were dead. And they had gifted him a brand-new cover story.

Alexsi got behind the wheel, and with the three bodies drove very carefully along the narrow road up the mountain. He slowed down in plenty of time ahead of the first German roadblock. The usual swinging metal bar, guard shack, and sandbagged machine guns in cross fire. At the sight of the red Fiat, military police with machine pistols came pouring out from everywhere.

Alexsi got out of the vehicle very slowly, with both arms thrust up into the air. "Good morning, *Kameraden*," he announced himself. "As you can see, I've had some trouble."

25

You could always tell a bored policeman, Alexsi thought. Bored stiff being responsible for the security of a staff headquarters far behind the lines, where everyone was on their very best behavior to keep from being sent to the Russian front. So of course here was a major of the *Feldgendarmerie* trying to fill an otherwise uneventful day by making something from nothing.

He had Alexsi's papers spread out over his desk, and Alexsi gave silent thanks to his British forger, as the man had done him proud. The paybook and driving permit had been tucked away in an agenda folder of the exact type that was sold in every German Army canteen. There were even family photographs and a school picture of a pretty girl. Just excellent work. The travel orders and transit endorsements he had typed up himself, the forger supplying the mass of official ink stamps so beloved of the Wehrmacht.

"So, once again, how did you come to be separated from your transport?"

Alexsi sighed lightly. The well-worn interrogator's trick of making you tell it over and over, hoping you'd slip up. "It is as I told you, Herr Major, the transport was attacked by *Jabos*."

"Where were you when this happened?"

"In the back of the truck asleep."

Impatiently: "No, I mean where was the truck when this happened? Its location."

"I don't know, Major, I was asleep in the back. In any case, I did not have a map."

"If you did not know where you were, then how did you get here?"

"Luck, Major. And saying 'Monte Soratte' to every Italian I came across."

There was a rustling in the outer office. Muted voices as if more people had come in. A clicking of heels, so it must have been a senior officer.

"And somehow you found your way here."

"It seems, Major, that if you are driving an automobile filled with dead men, Italians will give you the correct directions."

Deep laughter from outside the room. At least he was amusing someone, Alexsi thought.

"How many fighters strafed you?"

"I don't know, Major."

"Were they British or American?"

"I don't know, Major. I was too busy running for my life to look up at airplanes. Or count them."

"Don't be impertinent, Sergeant."

"I am not being impertinent, Major. I am trying my best to answer your questions."

"Very well. You were running for your life. And what happened?"

"As I told you, Major, I dove off the road, fell down a hill, and twisted my ankle. When the shooting stopped it took me some time to climb back up. When I did the truck was gone."

"They left you?"

"Yes."

"No one came to look for you?"

"No."

"Why not?"

What an idiot. "I don't know, Major. You would have to ask them."

"Don't be impertinent."

"I am just trying to answer your questions, Major."

"Why did you not wait by the road for another German Army transport?"

"Have you ever been to Russia, Major?"

That threw him. "What does that have to do with anything?"

"I come to you from Russia, Major. In Russia if a German soldier waits beside a road, by himself, he will never be seen again."

The major turned beet red. "Do you know what I think?"

Now, there was a loaded question. "No, Major."

"I think you were involved with those mafiosi, and that is why you shot them."

Now Alexsi sighed loudly, for the benefit of those outside the room. "Major, I come from hospital in Russia to hospital in Munich. Then convalescent leave in Munich. Then transfer here to Italy. I had not spoken to a single Italian until those three offered to drive me here. I did not know they were mafiosi until they tried to kill me for my pistol."

Red and humiliated, the major blurted out, "Only a gangster uses a knife."

The very portrait of calm, Alexsi said, "If you had been to Russia, Major, you too would carry a knife."

Furious, the major stood up from behind the desk. But before he could say anything there came a loud and angry rapping on the door.

From where he was sitting Alexsi first saw the silver trouser stripe on the uniform that was Luftwaffe blue instead of army gray. He shot to attention. Officers had no stripes on their trousers. Generals wore red. A field marshal wore silver.

Standing in the doorway was Field Marshal Kesselring, whom the troops called Uncle Albert for his ready smile and friendly manner. But he was not smiling.

Alexsi popped a sharp Hitler salute.

Kesselring strode into the room and put a fatherly hand on his shoulder, forcing him down into the chair. "Sit, Master Sergeant. Sit."

Alexsi obeyed him.

Kesselring had been rapping on the doorway with his *Interimsstab*, the silver-capped stick that was one of the emblems of his rank. Now he pointed it at the major and angrily gestured him into the other room. The major moved as if he had been shot from a cannon.

The door shut behind them. Alexsi sat comfortably and listened to the field marshal tear strips off the major.

Kesselring didn't shout. That was the way of Rommel, from what Alexsi had heard. Instead Kesselring spoke like the snapping of a whip. "A German soldier sits before you covered in the dried blood of his enemies," Kesselring began. "Have you taken him to hospital to be examined? Allowed him to clean himself? Offered him food? Given him even a glass of water after what he has been through, let alone a drink of schnapps?"

"Herr Feldmarschall . . ." the major stuttered.

"No," Kesselring went on, answering himself in the way of officers who do not want their tongue-lashings interrupted. "Do you treat him like a hero who single-handedly defended himself against three partisans and prevailed? A signaler, mind you, not a combat soldier. No, you treat him like a criminal instead. Instead of cowering in a ditch or drinking wine in a farmhouse until someone came looking for him, instead he makes his way to his duty here, covers himself with honor, and still speaks to you with dignity even as you speak to him like a dog."

"Field Marshal . . ."

"Enough," Kesselring said sharply. "Remove yourself from my sight."

That couldn't have come out any better, Alexsi thought. He was not that surprised to see Field Marshal Kesselring before him. It wasn't every day that a sergeant reported for duty driving up to your front gate in an Italian automobile filled with dead Italians. News of that would travel fast, and to the very top. It would definitely pique the curiosity.

Kesselring reentered the room, and Alexsi shot to attention again.

"Sit, sit," Kesselring ordered, taking the major's place behind the desk.

Alexsi waited until the field marshal mounted the chair before he dropped back into his.

Kesselring had picked up his paybook and was idly thumbing through it. "Ah, from Munich, Sergeant Bauer. It is always good to meet another Bavarian."

Alexsi only grinned shyly at that, as an enlisted soldier would.

"You've done a fine job," Kesselring said. "Even before you reported for duty."

Alexsi had just been given his first look at the famous Kesselring toothy grin. "Thank you, Field Marshal."

"It is I who thank you." Kesselring was still paging through the paybook. "Were you wounded at Kursk?"

"No, Field Marshal. During the Russian counteroffensive afterward."

A gentle knocking at the door. Both Kesselring and Alexsi turned to see.

A colonel poked his head through the doorway. "Please, Field Marshal."

"Very well," Kesselring said. He rose, and Alexsi along with him.

"Back to work. I look forward to seeing you about your duties, Sergeant Bauer."

"May I make a request, Field Marshal?"

"Of course," Kesselring said, picking up his *Interimsstab* from the desk.

"Field Marshal, please don't allow them to make any inquiries about the boys driving my transport. It was very chaotic. I don't think any of them had been under fire before, and it was not their fault."

"Of course it was their fault," Kesselring said sharply. "But I should have expected you would make such a request. Very well."

That would forestall any searches that might become awkward. "Thank you, Field Marshal." Alexsi gave the raised-arm Hitler salute. Kesselring might have been old school, but every field marshal was a Nazi.

Kesselring surprised him by raising the *Interimsstab* to his temple. "Good luck to you, Sergeant."

When field marshals put in a word, it became law. Because they went from not being quite sure what to do with him to not being able to do enough for him. They gave him his choice, which was to eat first. With the cooks peeking around the corners as if they were watching a wild animal, he sat alone in the mess and devoured an enormous bowl of potato soup, bubbling away in cauldrons for the upcoming lunch, and half a loaf of rye bread. Alexsi had to admit, he'd missed German Army potato soup. He had not missed chicory ersatz coffee, though.

After food, a hot shower. Because it wasn't just his uniform that was covered in the blood of those Italians.

For that reason he was glad he'd rejected all of the gadgets MI6 had offered him. Sleeve knives and lockpicks, one-time pads and miniature cameras. All a guaranteed trip to the hangman if someone took your blood-soaked uniform away while you were bathing, and happened to go through the pockets.

After the bath to medical for a look at his ankle, which was only badly sprained. Then a walk down to supply, in robe and shower shoes, feeling like a field marshal himself. To receive a complete issue with the supply sergeant swearing that everything was brand-new. Even an Italian tailor to fit and alter his uniforms.

It was an interesting place. The entire headquarters was inside the mountain, kilometers of tunnels blasted from the solid rock. The Italians had originally done it for themselves, and they had done an excellent job. The temperature, he was told, was exactly the same regardless of the seasons. Apparently the previous OB South headquarters had been bombed flat, hence the move to the tunnels. Which was fine by Alexsi. He had been bombed enough. By everyone.

None of the rooms looked as if they were hewn from the rock. They were smooth whitewashed concrete. Boxy ductwork ran along the length of the ceilings for the blown air, held up by T-shaped metal pillars whose arms the lights were hung from.

The senior sergeants' quarters were metal beds and storage cabinets along one wall, and along the opposite wall tables with long bench seats for relaxing. Alexsi had plenty of help putting his equipment away, then spent the rest of the afternoon being passed down by the officers of the headquarters signals regiment. First the chief of signals himself, a general named Jacoby who pumped his hand quickly, congratulated him on killing Italians, and insincerely extended the invitation to call upon him any time. Yes, Alexsi thought. I'll do just that.

From there it was a colonel who was the actual commander of the signals regiment. Another brief handshake and welcome, and then down to a young captain named Lang. The scholarly type, as most signalers were.

The signals regiment had almost two thousand soldiers assigned to it, but the vast majority were telephone troops manning the massive switchboards, and construction companies out stringing hundreds of kilometers of telephone and telegraph line for the partisans to keep cutting.

Hauptmann Lang commanded Abteilung 1, the radio-operating company. And looked as harassed as every signals officer Alexsi had ever seen. No one ever paid the slightest attention to the signals corps. Until communications went out, and then the entire weight of the world dropped onto the man in charge.

"I'm glad to see you, Master Sergeant," he said, not wasting any time. "I see you're fully qualified in operating, coding, and repair, which means you're exactly the man I need. What do you say to supervising the night watch?"

It wasn't really a request, but Alexsi answered as if it were. "Fine with me, Captain." It actually was. Everyone was out of your hair on the night shift.

"Excellent. All I've had is a technical sergeant, and he's over his head. The night man needs to know what's worth raising the roof over to the general staff officer on duty, and what isn't. The sergeant ran around with his hair on fire over every little thing, and I tell you confidentially it has been nothing but complaints every morning the minute I sit down at my desk. You seem like an old hand who's seen some action. It won't be as tense as the signals company in a panzer division, that's for sure. I'll trust that you made your rank so quickly because you're sharp, not a bootlicker. Show good judgment, run a tight ship, and you'll have no trouble from me. Agreed?"

"I understand, Captain," Alexsi said. "I'm your man."

"Wonderful. That's one worry off my shoulders. Take your time and get a feel for how the operation is run, then step in when you think you're ready. I'll expect a briefing from you every morning when I come on duty. Otherwise, don't surprise me with any problems. I'd rather be woken up and told right away."

"Understood," Alexsi said.

"Wonderful. If you need anything, let me know."

Alexsi walked away from that feeling good. An officer who wasn't a pig would make things so much easier.

Then he was called in to see the signals sergeant major. A quick glance at this fellow's fat cheeks and empty tunic told the tale that here was a headquarters rat who had been burrowed in with the generals since the beginning of the war. From Alexsi's point of view, that could be either good or bad.

It didn't begin well. The sergeant major left him standing. "I've decided to put you on the night watch, Bauer," he told Alexsi.

"Whatever you say, Stabs," Alexsi replied with a smile, using the army nickname for that rank.

"Sergeant Major," he was corrected.

"We're all comrades, aren't we? Stabs." Alexsi made a point of turning his smile from friendly to chilling.

The sergeant major flinched a bit at that, then said, "Don't think that being a hero is going to give you any special privileges."

"I'm just here to do a job, Stabs. I'm not about to give anyone any trouble. And I don't expect any."

"Just remember that the captain may command things around here. But I run them. Don't forget that."

Alexsi smiled again. Not friendly. "Whatever you say, Stabs."

That was going to be trouble. But Alexsi knew he couldn't handle it any other way. If you knuckled under to someone like that, you were just asking for it. Bullying always required two parties: the bully, and someone willing to be bullied.

Alexsi always had a problem with bullies.

26

MONTE SORATTE, ITALY

The next morning Alexsi was just about to have breakfast and then try to sleep in an effort to arrange his body for night work when Captain Lang at their morning meeting ordered him to quickly change into a crisper uniform and put on his more formal peaked cap. Alexsi didn't think they would have him change to be arrested, so he didn't worry himself about it. He also put on his other pair of very shiny brand-new marching boots.

A formation was held out in the fresh air, in the gravel area just outside the blast doors leading into the mountain. He was called forward, a citation was read, and Field Marshal Kesselring pinned the Iron Cross First Class on his left tunic pocket. A firm handshake and the formation was dismissed. All the staff officers lined up to shake his hand and offer congratulations. The sergeant major did also—he had to—but Alexsi couldn't help but notice him staring at the medal on his chest and not at his face. Just seething with envy.

Alexsi had never seen a medal awarded that fast, even though it was something the German Army prided itself on. But when a field marshal wanted to give you a decoration, the clerks typed quickly.

Then everyone went back to work, and Alexsi went to breakfast.

Eating his bread and jam, his fellow soldiers coming over to clap him on the back, Alexsi was alone in appreciating the irony of the moment. This was in fact the second time he had been presented the Iron Cross First Class by the German Army. In two separate identities, of course. But both legitimately awarded, and both for complete fuckups.

27

1944

MONTE SORATTE, ITALY

It was a fine life. No Russians. Safe underground from bombing. In an army headquarters that would be retreating well in advance of the front. Not to mention that the night watch was easy work.

After just watching them for a few nights, letting them wonder what he was like, Alexsi had brought all the signalers on duty together for a little chat. He told them they were doing a fine job, which they were. Efficient Germans for the most part. Then he said: Just be where you're supposed to be, when you're supposed to be, and do your jobs properly. Do that, and you'll have no trouble from me.

In his previous German life, the good sense of the Wehrmacht had made him a sergeant before they made him an officer. So Alexsi knew that the first soldier to seek him out would be the unit malingerer trying out one confidence scheme or another. He'd listened patiently to the tale of woe, the promise to inform on the other soldiers, then sent the shit off to the kitchen to scrub pots on mess duty. No one else tried him after that. The rest were good boys, mild and intelligent as signalers tended to be. Intelligent enough to know, like him, that they had a fine arrangement.

Alexsi knew they liked him when nearly every one sought him out, in private, to warn him about the sergeant major. Because he was a swine.

He didn't operate the radios, of course. Or repair them. That was why he made himself a master sergeant. If a wireless went down he ordered in the repair specialists. And supervised them, of course. Back in Russia the NKVD had sent him to a Red Army school for wireless technicians, to teach him how to build his own radio from scratch. You learned your lessons well if a failing mark meant a death sentence. He set the schedule so the operators and decoders didn't become overtired and sloppy, and if they needed relief he took care of it. Other than supervising, he collected the incoming messages and arranged them according to the recipients: operations, intelligence, supply. If a message was an alarm he alerted the staff officers on duty.

And, of course, while he was placing the messages into their proper folders in the situation room he was also getting a good look at the current situation map.

The outgoing messages that his operators were sending also included the warning orders to every German unit in Italy, telling them what they were expected to do in the next forty-eight hours.

So every few days—definitely not every day—he would write out a message of his own and encode it on his clipboard. In the lavatory. The original plain text was then burned in the toilet. Then, never at the same time, he would tell one of the wireless operators he looked tired and to take a break. Alexsi would then tap out his signal as a training message to Milan. Just to keep his hand in and his Morse sharp, he would say. Milan would send the message back and then throw it away. Of course the

British were listening in Naples. And his soldiers loved him for looking after them with the unscheduled rests.

Using junked spare parts and other odds and ends, he built a short-wave receiver for the senior sergeants' quarters. He even took the trouble to get permission from Captain Lang, to be on the safe side. Just don't put in a crystal for the BBC, the captain told him, only half jokingly, or they would all be done for. It made him the hero of the senior sergeants, and he would wire in a pair of headphones and take down a message from the British in the daytime when the quarters were nearly deserted. The British of course begged him to transmit more often. They could give a fig about him being tied to a post and shot.

He had been convinced of the futility of spying before, but that situation map every night really brought the lesson home. Because even though he was telling the British exactly where the German Army was, where they were going, and what they were doing, it barely mattered. They still had to defeat tough German divisions dug in on the high ground across the entire waist of Italy. Every time the British or Americans had a bit of success, Kesselring would move one of his chess pieces at lightning speed and plug the gap. When the pressure became too great they would fall back in good order to positions already prepared on the next row of hills, and it would all begin anew. The Allied planes ranged overhead almost unopposed, but the Germans brought up all the supplies they needed every night.

The stalemate suited Alexsi perfectly. The Germans would eventually be defeated, of course. But they would be defeated in France and Russia. He really had to thank the undertaker for sending him here. He could easily imagine himself surrendering in Italy, losing his papers, and anonymously disappearing into a prisoner of war camp under another name that neither the British nor the Russians knew.

28

1944

MONTE SORATTE, ITALY

Alexsi knocked on the office door, and was waved in.

"Sit down, Sergeant Bauer," Captain Lang grumbled.

Head down, no eye contact. The voice. Something was up. "Nothing out of the ordinary to report, Captain." Alexsi tried a smile. "Though it appears you have something."

The captain raised his head for the first time. "You've done outstanding work, Bauer."

Done. In the past tense. Alexsi felt there was nasty-tasting medicine coming his way.

"I'm not happy about this," the captain said. "I'm ordered to transfer you to Rome."

It seemed that he was never to be allowed to enjoy anything good. The problem with being a sergeant was that you were expected to salute and carry out orders, not argue about them. "I understand, Captain. Which unit am I being transferred to?"

"SD headquarters in Rome."

Now, that was a blow. SD. The SS Security Service. The ones whose harebrained scheme to kill Stalin, Churchill, and Roosevelt had sent him to Iran in the first place. "Forgive me, Captain. But that I do not understand."

Another sigh. "They require a signals supervisor who is cleared for cipher and repair."

"With respect, Captain. Why not an SS signaler?"

"The Sixteenth SS Panzergrenadier battle group has had too many casualties, and they have priority on SS signalers. With casualties in Russia, and so few SS in this theater, they have a shortage of signalers. SD Rome needs a supervisor who can do cipher, repair, and is a qualified driver. You understand they are scarce."

Yes, Alexsi understood. That was why he gave himself so many qualifications. So he would be coveted and not fucked around. Now he was kicking himself for doing it. "Will I be required to transfer to the SS, Herr Hauptmann?"

Now the captain was vehement. "Absolutely not! When I fought this I was guaranteed by General Jacoby that as soon as a qualified SS signaler becomes available you will be returned to this command."

"Thank you, Captain." Though considering what he had just heard, Alexsi would not be holding his breath waiting for that to happen.

"I understand how you might feel . . . wary, of the SS, Bauer. But you know how it is. When there's a requirement you never send your best people, only the ones you don't mind losing. Well, I sent the SS a lieutenant and a sergeant and they refused them. Refused them but never sent them back. God knows where they are right now—probably with one of the divisions at the front. General Jacoby heard from the field marshal himself on this. He's got enough problems, and he doesn't want any more with the SS." The captain made another face. "Then the sergeant major, without mentioning it to me, told the general he could spare you. So that was that."

So that swine of a *Stabs* hadn't passed up an opportunity to stab him in the back after all. Rome. Anyone else would have jumped at the chance to leave underground living behind and move to Rome. Not Alexsi. Rome was much too close to the front. Not to mention it was the one place in Italy the Allies couldn't wait to get their hands on. Not to mention that he'd be right in the lap of the SD and the Gestapo. Of all the rotten luck. For the life of him he couldn't think of a way out of it. Not if a general wanted him to go.

"I feel terrible about this, Sergeant Bauer."

He felt terrible. "When must I be there, Captain?"

"As soon as you can pack."

29

1944

ROME, ITALY

All the soldiers were poking their heads over the slats of the truck, taking in the sights of Rome. Alexsi sat sullenly on the bench beside the cab.

The truck lurched to a stop, brakes screaming.

"Via Tasso," came the call from the cab.

Alexsi threw his bags out over the tailgate.

"God in heaven," someone else said. Obviously looking up at the building. It had once been the cultural center of the German embassy. Now almost all the upper windows were closed up with brown clay bricks. Turned into prison cells, Alexsi thought.

"At least you have an invitation," chuckled some comedian in the truck, which drove off in a haze of blue petrol exhaust.

Two SD were standing guard at the front door. Gray uniforms with the SS lightning-bolt runes on their collars and the SD patch on their sleeves. Wearing helmets and carrying MP 40 submachine guns. Both first-class privates.

Alexsi pulled his orders from his tunic pocket and waved them under the nose of the nearest one. Who sneered, as if to say, So what?

This was no time to be timid. Not with these people, because they were all used to being bullies. Alexsi poked his finger in the SD guard's chest. The boy's eyes widened, and Alexsi could see his hands tighten around the MP 40. "Fetch your corporal of the guard. Now!"

The one beside him ducked in the door. Alexsi would have lit a cigarette, if he smoked. A little time in prison in Russia, watching all the smokers go mad, would cure you of any desire to take up that habit. The NKVD could get them to denounce their own mothers for the promise of a smoke.

The guard came out of the building with a corporal. The SS was so special that they even called their ranks different names from the army. For them a corporal was a *Rottenführer*, not an *Obergefreiter*. "What's this?" he demanded in a loud voice.

Just as you'd expect. Alexsi thrust his orders at him. The corporal took them and read them right in front of his face, as if he wasn't all that used to reading.

"I'm the new signals chief," Alexsi announced. He aimed a thumb back over his shoulder. "Those are my bags." Then he aimed the thumb at the two guards. "One of these can fetch them in. Or you can do it yourself. But if my bags don't find their way to my quarters, it will be *your* ass." He snatched the orders out of the corporal's hand and marched up the stairs without another word.

He heard the corporal shout to his back, with a click of heels, *"Jawohl, Herr Hauptscharführer!"*

The first thing you saw when you went in the door was a life-size portrait of Hitler on the wall. Wonderful, Alexsi thought. Hello again, Adolf.

* * *

The SS lieutenant colonel behind the desk was laughing. "Please sit down, *Oberfeldwebel* Bauer," he said to Alexsi. "When they told me a master sergeant signaler had just torn the balls off the corporal of my guard, I said: A *signaler*? But now I see." He waved a hand idly in the direction of the decorations on Alexsi's tunic. "I knew if I kept getting rid of the mice, Kesselring would eventually send me a tiger."

He was in his late thirties, with a fleshy, jowly face and a sharp nose. Not quite fat, but he had obviously been living well lately. "My name is Kappler, and I am the police chief of Rome. I'm a busy man, so let me tell you my situation. My telephones are fine." He paused at that. "Well, my telephones are Roman fine. Which means they aren't any more terrible than all the other telephone lines in this city. My wireless communications are a shambles. I have a city to control, not enough men to do it, and the wireless sets in half my radio cars are out of action. I expect you to do something about it. Quickly." He gave Alexsi a thin-lipped smile. "If you don't, I'll get rid of you too, and find someone else."

He seemed to be waiting for Alexsi to say something. Alexsi waited just long enough, then said, "I understand, Herr Oberst. Will there be anything else?"

Now Kappler was smiling with amusement, as if appreciating Alexsi's tone. "No."

Alexsi popped a rigid, straight-armed salute. *"Heil Hitler!"*

Kappler raised his right hand off the desk. *"Heil Hitler."*

The place was a nightmare. Alexsi understood exactly what the poet Dante was talking about in his circles of hell. Even though he had only read *The Inferno* in Russian. Because it wasn't really a prison, the offices were on the ground floor, and the cells were on the floors above. The screaming and crying from above went on day and night. Alexsi could only believe that the SS wanted it that way. In the Lubyanka if you so much as farted the guards came piling in and kicked the living shit out of you.

It didn't take him long to see what Colonel Kappler was talking about. Three-quarters of the SS signalers were doing radio interception, listening for spy and partisan wireless transmissions to triangulate and hunt down. Because of that, the message center was a madhouse, the wireless operators working twelve-hour shifts and falling asleep on their feet. The radios were all broken because the SD handled their radios with the same delicacy they handled their prisoners. There was nothing he could do about that, but he could do something about the repair situation. The handful of technicians were on the verge of shooting themselves because as soon as they got a set fixed another broke down, so they could never get ahead of all the other ones that were broken.

Alexsi gave serious thought to whether he really wanted to do a good job. He decided he had to. They could just as easily send him to a combat division on the front as back to Monte Soratte.

With that decision made, he also decided to follow the policy he had adopted during his previous time with the German Army. That he had not been able to follow with the British, and had unfortunately not worked on Monte Soratte. The first thing he had to do was work his ass off and make himself indispensable. Then if he ever came under suspicion, or something run-of-the-mill went wrong, then he would be given the benefit of the doubt. That seemed doubly important being stuck in the lair of the SD.

He quickly found out what the problem had been. The lieutenant they had sent from Monte Soratte was as green as spring grass, and the sergeant had been a wireless operator, not an organizer.

The SD radio cars were equipped with the standard FuG voice wireless. Instead of repairing the equipment himself Alexsi sent the cars to Monte Soratte two at a time, telling the drivers not to come back without the radios repaired, the vehicles serviced, and everything on the list of spare parts he'd given them. It was simple, but no one had thought of it.

Within a week all the radio cars were back online, and Colonel Kappler came down to the rooms used by the signals detachment and shook his hand. Alexsi had also become the hero of the repair section, who could stop pulling their hair out and go back to routine maintenance.

With that credibility in the bank, Alexsi next pulled a section of SS signalers off communications interception so he could staff the message center with three shifts, twenty-four hours a day. The pathetic part was that all he really needed on each shift was an extra pair of wireless operators so there could be another pair to run the Enigma coding machine without bouncing back and forth. With a backup to type or run messages if needed.

As soon as he did that, Alexsi kept one eye on the clock, because before the day was half over an SD major named Hass came stomping into his office.

Now, here was a real thug, with protruding ears like an elephant and white skin stretched tightly across his narrow face like a talking skull.

Alexsi, of course, stood respectfully. As a sergeant would.

Hass began, "By what authority do you take SS signalers off interception duties."

"Mine, Herr Major," Alexsi replied. He did not bother calling him *Sturmbannführer*, the SS rank.

"You will return the signalers to interception duty, immediately."

"No, Major," Alexsi said calmly.

The eyes bulged. The ghostly skin immediately took on a richer color. "That is an order."

"I understand, Major, however signals assignments are my responsibility. My reassignments will stand."

"You know I could shoot you on the spot for your disobeying an order."

Alexsi ostentatiously placed his left hand on his holster. "You could, Major, but you will not."

Hass was nearly shaking with rage, but he kept his eyes on Alexsi's pistol holster.

Alexsi enjoyed watching bullies sweat when they were checked. After letting just a bit too much time go by, he said, "May I suggest, Major, that if you disagree with my performance of duty we should both discuss it with Colonel Kappler."

"Come with me at once," Hass snapped.

On his way out Alexsi snatched up a folder that he had been saving for just such an occasion.

Of course Hass made him sit in the outer office while he went in first. He hid a smile while Hass's voice rose higher and higher in the room. At his desk Kappler's adjutant, a lieutenant, did not bother to suppress his own smile. He caught Alexsi's eye and just shook his head.

The door opened, and an angry hand waved him in.

Alexsi marched in, crashed to attention in front of the desk, and popped a perfect Hitler salute.

Kappler just raised his hand and said in exasperation, "What's all this, Bauer?"

Alexsi handed him the folder. "Colonel, I have been going through the old incoming message stack. Here are three, two from General Wolff in Brescia and one from Berlin, that I believe were not passed along to you. Fortunately they are all routine. But they were not passed along to you because the message center was not organized properly. It is now because signalers who were on interception have been moved back to their correct duties. I have only moved a few men, and if the interception teams were distributed more rationally there would still be more than enough operators on those duties."

Kappler was reading the three messages. "You are right. I did not see these. That is unacceptable." He looked up at Alexsi. "And you say the interception will not suffer?"

"There is already duplication of effort in that, too," Alexsi replied.

"Major Hass disagrees with you," Kappler said with barely concealed amusement.

Alexsi flashed a glance at Major Hass, who was quite literally quivering with rage off to the side. "I would never dream of trying to tell the Security Service their duties, Colonel. Similarly, technical questions should be properly left to technical specialists."

Kappler laughed out loud at that. "The master sergeant is telling you to stay out of his patch," he told Hass. "Which is probably not a bad idea. Thank you, Major."

At that, Hass stomped out of the office. The door cracked shut.

"Did you really threaten to shoot him?" Kappler asked mildly.

Mildly, but Alexsi could recognize a loaded question when he heard one. "I did not, Colonel. The major threatened to shoot me for not obeying his orders, and all I told him was that I knew he could but I doubted he would."

Kappler chuckled. "Probably for the best. I heard about those three Italians at Monte Soratte, you know."

Alexsi didn't say anything.

"I imagine you saw some action in Russia," said Kappler.

He had no idea, though not with the German Army. Though once again, Alexsi said nothing.

"Yes, that's what I thought," said Kappler. "Look, as long as none of my signals from Berlin are missed I'll be happy. I also expect that we also won't miss any enemy radios in Rome because of it," he added pointedly.

"We will not, Colonel."

"Good," said Kappler, returning to his paperwork. "And if you need to take a look at that area, go right ahead."

Alexsi snapped off another salute. Time to take his victory and get out. "Yes, Colonel!"

30

1944

ROME, ITALY

A head poked in the door of Alexsi's office. Actually, more of a small room that barely fit a desk, but it served. Not to mention a welcome sanctuary.

The visitor was an SS sergeant, not a signaler. "Come in," Alexsi said. "What can I do for you?" Another communications problem, no doubt.

An earnest young man. Brown hair, lean and hard, but an open and outwardly kindly face. He charged around the desk and extended his hand. "I'm Klaus Kuhn."

"Peter Bauer," Alexsi said, shaking it.

"I'm taking my section off to do some target practice, and I wondered if you would like to come along?"

"Shooting *practice*?" Alexsi inquired. He wasn't getting roped into any SS firing squads that needed another rifle to make up the regulation number.

"Yes. There's a range just over the Ponte Milvio."

As always, Alexsi was suspicious. But he might as well see what this was about. Not to mention that he had barely been outside since he arrived. "All right. Thanks. What are we shooting?"

"Automatics and pistols."

"Where can I get an automatic?"

Klaus grinned. "They didn't issue you a weapon when you checked in?"

"A signaler? Just a screwdriver."

"Come with me to the armory."

Much to Alexsi's surprise, other than Mauser rifles all they had left were Italian Beretta 38 submachine guns. He had seen nearly every single SS with an MP 40, so no wonder they were all accounted for. He signed a Beretta out, along with a German magazine pouch and four magazines.

A truck was waiting outside with Kuhn's section inside. As they drove north through the city Alexsi broke open one of the ammunition cans and began loading his magazines.

"You don't need to do that. I promise we'll let you shoot first," Klaus shouted over the road noise, laughing.

"Have you seen the looks we're getting from the street?" Alexsi shouted back.

"Italians are cowards," said one of the *Soldaten*.

"You don't have to be a hero to shoot from a window," Alexsi retorted, still loading.

When they drove onto the range, which was just an open field with targets and a few trenches and piles of sandbags, there was a company of SS troops in battle dress just forming up to leave.

"Who is this?" Alexsi asked Klaus, both the sergeants watching as their own soldiers lifted the ammunition cases from the truck.

"The Bozen."

"I'm sorry?"

"SS Police Regiment Bozen," said Klaus. "Their Third Battalion started arriving in February. This is the Eleventh Company, just coming to the city for duty."

"Bozen?" Alexsi said again. "Never heard of them."

"Ethnic Germans from the South Tyrol," said Klaus.

"The Alps?" said Alexsi, trying to remember his geography.

"Yes. When it was incorporated into the Reich, those who chose German citizenship were eligible for military service. These joined the SS as their patriotic duty."

"I see," said Alexsi. Well, patriotic duty was all well and good. But he could think of another reason. Better to volunteer for an SS police regiment and persecute your former countrymen than be conscripted into the army and be persecuted by Russian tanks.

"They're barracked over near the Interior Ministry," said Klaus. "Every morning they march up here to train in crowd control. Soon they'll be ready for us to put them on the streets."

The troops stepped off and began singing as they marched. "*Hupf, Mein Mädel.*" If you had to do it, there were much better marching songs. What a bunch of arseholes, Alexsi thought. But what he said was "They look all right."

"We need all the help we can get," said Klaus.

"They do this every day? March singing down through the streets. At the same time?"

"Yes. Rain or shine. Very dedicated."

Just asking for it, thought Alexsi.

The shooting was fun. It was good to be out in the open spring air. Good to be shooting at targets, not people. The Beretta was a fine gun. It had a wooden stock like a rifle, and was rock solid when firing automatic.

Alexsi thought it was actually much better than an MP 40, and after adjusting the sights he was hitting targets well past a hundred meters.

Driving back, Klaus had the truck make a detour and drop the two of them off. "Weapons inspection before supper," he informed his section, who of course let off some obligatory groans before he shut them off by slamming the tailgate.

The truck drove off, and Alexsi wondered what was up.

"Have you had a chance to see the Forum?" Klaus asked.

Alexsi shook his head. "Signals was such a shambles when I arrived, I haven't had a chance to even leave the building."

"I know," said Klaus, as they began walking. "You have your section running like a Swiss watch. Everyone says so. The signalers love you."

"Do they?" Alexsi said wryly.

"Don't laugh, they do. Everyone used to shit on them, and because of you none of the officers dare to."

"That is my job."

"I know," said Klaus. "All the other signals chiefs went out drinking and whoring every day and left their business to the lower ranks. You've just done your job correctly, with dedication, and it's an example to every NCO."

"If it hadn't been such a disaster," said Alexsi, "I would have had more of a chance to go whoring."

Klaus laughed. "It was important to greet you in a spirit of comradeship. All these divisions between army and SS are foolish. We are all *Kameraden,* and should meet each other as such."

Alexsi had been wondering whether Klaus was sent by Kappler or one of the other officers to keep an eye on him. Now, instead of suspecting the worst, he was instead suspecting that this was another one of those earnest Hitler Youth all indoctrinated in the concept of soldierly brotherhood.

They entered the Forum, and the Italian watchmen made themselves scarce at the sight of two German soldiers carrying submachine guns.

Alexsi found it incredibly evocative. Though he had to remind himself that little had changed in a millennium. Men in togas trying to rule the world, and men in field-gray uniforms trying to rule the world.

As they passed the ruins of the Roman senate, Klaus said, "When I walk here I try to feel as if I am standing on the spot where Julius Caesar was assassinated."

Et tu, Brute?—Then fall, Caesar, Alexsi thought, remembering the Shakespeare he had read in London. It made him want to learn more about Caesar. "I believe that took place in the Theater of Pompey, which is a bit farther to the northwest."

"Ah, a reader!" said Klaus. "I will check my Michelin map. We shall have to go see it."

"Yes," said Alexsi. "You may feel something."

"Don't laugh," said Klaus.

"I'm not laughing."

They passed the Arch of Titus.

"Do you know about this?" said Klaus.

Alexsi shook his head.

"The Romans erected it to celebrate destroying Jerusalem. One day we will raise an even greater monument."

The Jews again, Alexsi thought. Always the Jews. He had overheard the SS bragging about how Kappler had made the Rome Jews cough up fifty kilograms of pure gold to save themselves, and then deported them anyway. It was a lesson that every thief knew, about the promises of the authorities. He never understood all those Russians who meekly opened the door when the secret-police knock came in the middle of the night. Better to climb down the drainpipe in your underwear.

But then, people always expected the best. Fools.

He wondered who the Germans would blame when the Jews were

gone and the world was still shit. They would find someone else, probably. And kill them, too, to try and make a better world. It was all the same. Stalin would still be killing the politically incorrect, if the Germans hadn't interrupted him.

They emerged in full view of the Colosseum. It was a breathtaking sight. In the afternoon light it looked rose-colored. Especially since every photograph Alexsi had seen in books was black-and-white. They walked inside, and there were a few Italians there. But not sightseers. Alexsi saw thieves behind the columns meeting in private to make deals with each other. If you needed something from the black market, clearly this was one of the places. You could just tell the authorities you were sightseeing. Pickpockets were waiting for a good-looking victim to come along. They all stampeded at the sight of Germans.

"We certainly have done our bit today to fight crime," Alexsi said.

"What do you mean?" Klaus asked.

Alexsi realized that only one of them had a thief's eye. "Never mind."

They stood there, Klaus enjoying Alexsi taking it in. He looked up at the seats, imagining the crowds. Then down. The floor was gone, and he could easily see the stone partitions for the cells and cages. Men and animals waiting down below to be driven up for sport. At least the Romans were honest about it, he thought. Nothing had changed, except these days everyone liked to pretend it was something different.

"It is an example for all of us," said Klaus.

"An example of what?" Alexsi asked, genuinely curious as to what he would say.

"Of how an empire can fall. The greatest empire the world has ever seen, until now. It fell through decadence. We will not make the same mistake."

No, Alexsi thought. You'll just make all the other ones. The story of empires, as far as he was concerned, was that eventually the people they ruled decided they no longer wished to be ruled. No matter. He was not about to mention to Klaus that the one thing the Romans never succeeded in doing was civilizing the Germans. "You've been very kind," he said. "Let me buy you a glass of wine, to show my appreciation."

"That's not necessary."

"I insist."

"Very well."

"Unless you prefer Italian beer," Alexsi said. "If there is such a thing."

"There is," said Klaus. "It's thin stuff. Only better than no beer at all."

"Whatever you like."

"There's a café just down the street," said Klaus. "On our way in any case. It's less than a kilometer back to Via Tasso."

When they reached it Klaus began to take a chair at one of the outdoor tables.

"Let's go inside," Alexsi said.

"You don't like fresh air?"

"I don't like being gunned down while I'm drinking," Alexsi replied, holding the door open for him.

"You must have seen a few things in Russia. Italy isn't like that."

Whatever you say, Alexsi thought, ushering him inside. It wasn't like that until the day it was.

There were quite a few Italians there drinking. One or two began to stand up and put their jackets on as soon as they walked in. Alexsi urged them back down in their seats with a smile and a firm but friendly wave of his hand. When the word got around the street, he wanted the partisans to hold back because too many of their neighbors were in the line of fire.

He chose a table in the back, with his back against the wall. A short dash from the chair to the door to the kitchen, and he noted the number of steps in his mind's eye in case he needed to be moving toward it backward while shooting.

"Seriously," said Klaus, vastly amused by his precautions. "Rome belongs to us. The Italians are cowed. We arrest these partisans faster than

they can get organized, I assure you. We catch one and they spill everything they know about their organization. Which takes us to the rest."

Alexsi knew exactly how they obtained that information. It wasn't
by asking politely.

"I will concede that thievery is out of control," said Klaus. "But that
is war."

"If you say so."

"They are mainly Jews and Communists," said Klaus. "Which is the
same thing, if you ask me."

"A lot of Communists?" Alexsi asked warily.

"The partisans are mainly Communists," said Klaus.

A middle-aged Italian in a short apron appeared before them. He
looked to be the proprietor. Handling the Germans himself, so none of
the waiters would anger them and get him into trouble.

"Wine or beer?" Alexsi asked Klaus.

"I only like German beer. So let's try wine."

"Red or white?"

"Red."

"*Vino rosso, per favore*," Alexsi told the Italian. "*La bottiglia.*" Fresh out
of Italian words, he pantomimed that he wanted it opened at the table.

"*Sì, signore.*"

"That was good," said Klaus.

"The Italian grammar I'm studying puts great emphasis on ordering
food and wine," said Alexsi.

Klaus shrugged. "A waste of time, if you ask me. The world will be
speaking German."

Alexsi just smiled at that.

The proprietor returned with a bottle and two glasses. He showed
Alexsi the label. Alexsi nodded gravely. I did that as if I knew wine from
vinegar, he thought.

The cork came out. Two glasses were poured.

Alexsi raised his. "Prost!"

"Prost!" Klaus replied.

Alexsi took a sip, for politeness. That was rather good. He took another sip. Very good, actually. The only other time he'd had red wine was in the Lubyanka, in Moscow. When they'd let him out of the cell and began buttering him up to do their bidding. It had tasted like petrol. But that was Russian wine, he reminded himself. "I was going to warn you that I'm not much of a drinker. But this is very good."

"Are you married?" Klaus asked.

"No."

"A girl?"

"Threw me over when I went into the army." Alexsi had his answers ready, in case the officer who censored everyone's mail asked him why he wasn't writing home.

"I will have to write my wife," said Klaus. "To look for a nice girl for you."

"You're married," Alexsi said, just to get the questions off himself.

It worked. Klaus yanked his agenda book from his pocket and began spreading photographs across the table.

Alexsi nodded admiringly at the picture of Klaus's wife, the kind of astonishingly plain girl a boy marries because she was the first one to agree to fuck him at school. "Three children? What are you, twenty? Twenty-one?"

Klaus blushed deeply. "We must build the future. Nothing is sure in war."

"Nothing is sure in *life*," Alexsi said in agreement. He raised his glass again. "Is this quite excellent, or is it my inexperience?"

"I'm not much of a wine drinker, either," said Klaus. "But it is good. By the way, why did you have him open the bottle at the table?"

"So he couldn't spit in it," Alexsi replied. "Or put poison in it."

Klaus laughed uproariously. "My goodness you are a wary fellow. You must tell me sometime about your experiences in Russia."

"Trust me," said Alexsi. "You don't really want to know."

"I am from Breslau, in Silesia," said Klaus. "When the war is won my family and I will move to the new Russian territories and settle there. It will be the role of the SS to administer and police these new colonies."

"I wish you good luck with that." Alexsi took another sip of wine. Apparently he had never heard of Stalingrad and Kursk. "Perhaps we should order some food."

"With the rationing he'll tell us he doesn't have anything," said Klaus.

"There are few problems in life that a decent bribe cannot solve," said Alexsi, delving into his pocket for lira. "If he's worth his salt he'll have something hidden away in his stores for well-paying customers. So let's see what he can come up with. And perhaps another bottle."

Four hours later they staggered back to Via Tasso, Klaus supporting an uproariously drunk Alexsi, both of them singing "Lili Marlene."

The two guards at the door just raised their eyebrows as the two sergeants took an inordinately long time negotiating the steps.

31

Alexsi stared down at the cup on his desk. Ersatz coffee wasn't coffee, but chicory. It had no caffeine, which was a tragedy. At that moment he made a resolution to celebrate the first hangover of his life by becoming teetotal all over again. Even though Italian wine was very good.

He had been brooding all morning about what he might have said to Klaus when he was drunk and stupid. Because he couldn't remember a thing. The very reason, along with a drunken and violent father, why he had always abstained from alcohol. Drunk, stupid, and open-mouthed was lethal for a spy. He had always relied upon others to be foolish and talkative, and now that was him.

He hadn't needed to say anything incriminating. Just something in English or Russian would have done it.

The door opened without a knock. It was Captain Priebke. One of

Kappler's officers. A handsome fellow who was cutting his way through the upper-class female collaborators of Rome. Or so said the SS troops. Alexsi knew there was nothing the officers in a military unit could try to keep secret that the enlisted soldiers would not find out about.

He stood.

Priebke said, "Come with me."

An order, not a request. Well, it had been a good run. Alexsi fingered the hem of his sleeve, where he had sewn the British L pill. Tear the seam open with his teeth and bite down. Better than being hung from a hook and tortured for a fortnight before the execution.

He followed Priebke down the hallway, then up the stairs to the cells. He would go through a door and then they would grab him, strip him, and go to work. As he walked Alexsi was rubbing his chin with his hand, keeping the sleeve near his mouth. One bite and it would all be over.

Of course he had blathered something to Klaus, who like a good little SS had reported it as his duty. At least he was going down due to his own stupidity. As the NKVD had always said, while beating perfectionism into him: Fools die.

Priebke opened a door and went through. Alexsi put his sleeve in his mouth.

The room was empty. Alexsi whipped his arm down.

Priebke hadn't seen it. He turned and said, "You can take shorthand?"

"Yes, Captain." At the University of Berlin he had taken two private courses, in typing and shorthand. Thinking they would be helpful in school. Both turned out to be invaluable. More than the university.

Priebke handed him a pad and pencil. "There are no clerks available. Come with me."

They went through a door. Another torture room. Tiny. Clay bricks and no windows. Alexsi had been in the cellars of Gestapo headquarters in Berlin. They all smelled like piss and shit and vomit and fear. This added mold, also. There was no table with rings to strap the victim down. No field telephone to shock them. No hook from the ceiling. A terrified Italian was tied securely to a hard wooden chair. Stark naked.

Alexsi wanted no part of it. "I don't speak Italian, Captain."

"That's not what I've heard."

Good old Klaus again. "I have just enough to order wine." Not that he would ever do that again. "No more."

Priebke had never once raised his voice. He was quiet and silky, not a red-faced bullyboy like his fellow officer Hass. Alexsi found him much more frightening because of it. "I will translate what needs to be taken down into German. Sit."

No way out. There was one other chair in the room, and Alexsi took it. The air was stifling. He wanted to open his collar, but didn't.

Priebke walked up to the Italian and placed both hands on his shoulders. Which would have been a friendly gesture, except the thumbs found their way to the mastoid area right behind the ears. The Italian groaned loudly at the painful pressure.

"So, Franco," Priebke said conversationally, as if talking to a neighbor. "I'm sorry, but with me you're going to have to talk. You'll be shot anyway, but you might as well spare yourself a great deal of unnecessary suffering."

He spoke so slowly that Alexsi could understand most of it. If it were him he'd be talking a blue streak. Maybe not what Priebke wanted to know, but enough talking to keep the man from getting started on him.

Franco, however, was not going to do himself any favors. He kept his mouth shut.

Priebke just shook his head at such foolishness. He reached in his pocket and took out a set of brass knuckles. He slipped them onto his hand, and looked up at Franco as if to say, Well?

Nothing from Franco.

As if a silent starting gun had gone off, Priebke unleashed a flurry of punches around the rib cage. Alexsi could hear the dull thump of the first blow, then the screams drowned out the rest.

Priebke paused to catch his breath. Then a question to Franco, specific names spoken so softly Alexsi couldn't catch them. But he could feel the gist of it. We know all your confederates. Someone has already talked. It's over. You might just as well tell me where they are.

Franco didn't seem to feel his own self-interest the way Alexsi did. He was sobbing softly, but said nothing.

Priebke worked his way around the ribs again. Alexsi knew it was worse, because they were already broken. As if to confirm his suspicions, the screaming was even louder.

Priebke continued with his softly spoken questions. This one was terrifying, Alexsi thought. The NKVD had roughed him up during his training in Moscow, to see if he could be frightened. To see if he would break easily. Their beatings had been no worse than the ones he'd received from his father. There had been a lot of shouting, a lot of bullying. This was something else. There was no anger to it. Just a man impersonally conducting his business.

Now Priebke turned to Alexsi. He took off the brass knuckles and offered them. "Here, Bauer. Take over."

Alexsi looked up from his pad. "No, Captain."

Priebke gave him a chilling half smile. "What if I order you? I've heard you don't like to take orders. Believe me, you'll take mine."

Alexsi said, "Captain, I'm a signaler. If you order me to take down a message, I will. If you order me to take your dictation, I will. I know my duty. But I am not a policeman. I am not in the SS. There is nothing in regulations that require me to follow this order."

Priebke said, "I'm sure you can quote me all the regulations. You army types are all the same. You leave the difficult and necessary work to the SS. Very well."

In one smooth motion the brass knuckles went back on, and he delivered an uppercut directly into Franco's testicles.

Alexsi winced. The scream nearly blew his eardrums out.

Franco retched onto his chest. Priebke snatched up a bucket of water Alexsi hadn't seen and threw it onto his prisoner.

Not for relief, Alexsi realized. But so he could get close to the man without getting any vomitus on him.

He did get close. But not so close that Alexsi could not hear. And not so fast that he could not understand the Italian. "I have arrested your father. He is waiting in another cell here. If you don't talk I will be forced to shoot him. I will do it in front of you, so you can watch and he can see you're to blame."

Franco was crying now, and not just from getting his balls crushed. The words came spilling out of him, in between the sobs. Priebke got even closer so he didn't miss a word. And he quickly translated the names and addresses into German. Alexsi took them down, his pen flying.

Priebke asked a few more questions in the same quiet tone of voice. Franco answered readily. Of course Alexsi noted that the fist with the brass knuckles was still pressed up into his groin.

Priebke abruptly decided he was finished. He pocketed the brass knuckles and made for the door.

Alexsi certainly wasn't about to remain there with Franco. He followed Priebke out.

Priebke said over his shoulder, "I want that list typed out immediately."

"Yes, Captain."

Priebke whirled about. "So now you follow orders?"

"As I told you before, Captain. I know my duty."

32

1944

ROME, ITALY

Alexsi's phone rang. "This is Master Sergeant Bauer."

It was Kappler. "Report to my office at once."

"Yes, Colonel."

Odds were it was going to be a bollocking, as the British would say, for defying yet another of his officers. Alexsi told himself to take it in good spirit. It was hard enough to spend your days in this screaming house of the damned without becoming one of its inquisitors. The guards at the Lubyanka in Moscow at least received double pay and unheard-of privileges. The SS just got all the schnapps they wanted. They could have it. Alexsi's sympathies would always be toward the ones tied to the chair.

As he entered Kappler's outer office, Alexsi's attention instantly turned toward a very handsome Italian woman in her early forties. Expensively dressed. Not a new dress, but expensive. Obviously not a prisoner.

He turned and bowed. Which he would have done even if she weren't Kappler's mistress.

Clearly surprised by the action, she favored him with a haughty nod.

For whatever perverse reason it made Alexsi break into a huge smile, that he let her see. As if to tell her, Keep up the act, but you're still sitting in the outer office waiting on the son of a chauffeur. Which the troops had told him Kappler was.

It was Hitler's genius. And Stalin's, too. If you took the sons of chauffeurs and made them the king of Rome, they would cheerfully do any terrible thing you asked them to do. You kept the rich, or in Stalin's case the powerful, in check with your lack of scruples and restraint. Letting them know that in the dark of any night, if the mood struck you, you could take it all away.

The adjutant was smirking at the exchange. He motioned with a flick of his head for Alexsi to go in.

Alexsi closed the door behind him and snapped to attention.

Kappler was leaning back in his chair with his own smile on his face. As if inordinately pleased with himself. "Sit down, Bauer. I have a job for you."

"Yes, Colonel?"

"I would like you to drive Princess Santangelo home."

A princess, eh? "Yes, Colonel."

"Take one of the best staff cars." A pause. "Not mine of course."

"Yes, Colonel."

Another pause. This one more awkward.

Tired of waiting, Alexsi said, "My orders, Colonel?"

"Be polite to her. Even if perhaps she makes you feel like slapping her. Refrain from doing do. I might even say be cordial."

Didn't sound like a mistress. Or perhaps it did. "Yes, Colonel."

Kappler frowned a bit. "No, that won't do. You will require more information. You did hear me call her 'princess.'"

Alexsi refrained from sighing. "Yes, Colonel."

"The Princess Abrianna Santangelo. She is not Italian nobility, but papal nobility. Do you understand?"

"Not particularly, Colonel."

"Well, the papacy formerly ruled large swaths of Italy, how much depending on circumstances. Now reduced to that pretty little bolt-hole across the Tiber. They had their own nobility, given titles by the Pope. Some of them are Italian nobility also, but let's not make this too complicated." Kappler gestured toward the outer office. "This one's husband is a prince, also formerly a full colonel in the Italian Army. He decided to abandon Mussolini and join that group of traitors who tried to make peace with the Allies, so now he is doing useful labor in a prison camp in Germany. She comes in once a week to hound me about getting him released."

If there was hounding instead of another kind of transaction, that didn't sound like a mistress. There was another pause, as if Alexsi were expected to say something. "I understand, Colonel."

"Of course I would never release him. He's too good a bargaining chip. She, on the other hand, has connections everywhere. The elite of Rome. The partisans I'm certain, because that's how these rich bastards always come out on top—by playing both sides. Also an entrée right to the top of the Vatican. A phone call would get her an audience with the Pope himself. You can see how useful she could be."

"Yes, Colonel."

"We are dancing, the two of us, but at arm's length. She gives me as little as she can, but hopefully enough to help her husband. I make promises and press for more. Each of us is looking to spend as little of our currency as possible. Do you see?"

Definitely not a mistress, then. And Kappler was being uncommonly talkative with someone he needed to be a driver. "Yes, Colonel."

"I want you to be cordial with her, Bauer. If she wishes to go somewhere other than home, resist for a bit, then let her charm you into using my petrol. I have a feeling you've picked up more Italian than you've let on. I know you've been studying in your spare time. No, don't protest . . ."

Alexsi hadn't been about to protest. Or say anything. Other than obviously his friend Klaus was doing plenty of talking around the building.

"Pretend you don't know a word," Kappler went on. "I know you're a sharp fellow. Let her think you're a blockheaded German soldier. She'll think that anyway. Remember everything you see and hear, and report back to me."

Everyone wanted him to be a spy. "I understand, Colonel."

"Good. I knew I could rely on you." Kappler smiled. "All my officers seem to have a problem with you, Bauer. But since you reported here you've done nothing but make my life easier. Which is more than I can say for them. Please continue to do so."

"I'll do my best, Colonel." This was the essence of Alexsi's policy on spying, that he had developed during his previous stint with the German Army. Be invaluable to the man in charge. But don't worry about stepping on the toes of his subordinates, because they would be the first to become suspicious of you. Then, if they took their suspicions to the man in charge, he could dismiss them as malice because they didn't like you anyway. "If you please, I have two requests."

"Go on." Kappler seemed torn between amusement and annoyance that a sergeant would dare to negotiate with him.

"Only that you would have the adjutant pass your orders to the motor pool, so I have no argument about the staff car. And that he would have someone fetch my automatic and ammunition belt from my office and bring it to the motor pool."

"I've heard you're a wary fellow," said Kappler. "Your experiences in Russia, no doubt. But you'll have no trouble. The partisans wouldn't lift a finger against you with her in the backseat."

"I'm not worried about partisans, Colonel. But I'm sure there are several hundred Romans who would cut her head off to get their hands on the necklace she's wearing. Princess or not."

Kappler burst out laughing. "You're a man who thinks of everything, Bauer. I like that. Especially the worst in everyone. I'm like that too. Both your requests are approved. Especially so you won't have to stand around waiting for the car, and her becoming annoyed with you. Which she would, if my own wife is any example. Perfect."

Alexsi clicked his heels and saluted.

As he turned to go, Kappler said, "I think we're both going to enjoy this conspiracy, Bauer."

In the outer office Alexsi walked up to the seated lady and saluted. Not a Hitler salute. An army one. Not snapped off, but easy and appreciative. As one would salute a lady.

She looked up at him as if she was used to being saluted.

Alexsi said, "Princess, I am Sergeant Bauer. Do you perhaps speak German?"

"I do," she replied.

"I have been ordered to drive you home. Will you please come with me?"

She gathered up her purse and rose from the chair. "Thank you," she said, without a shred of warmth.

Alexsi held the door for her. As he went to close it the adjutant was still smirking at him.

He offered her his arm without thinking about it.

It stopped her in her tracks while she thought it over. After a suitably long interval, in which Alexsi couldn't imagine there were that many ramifications, she took it.

He aimed her down the hallway toward the courtyard exit and the motor pool. Of course that meant everyone gawping at them from the open office doors.

There was no argument from the motor pool. One of the best

Mercedes 540K coupes, though painted army gray, was waiting for him. The keys were already in it. His Beretta 38 and ammunition belt were lying across the front seat.

Alexsi held the back door open for her. He offered his hand for support as if it were something he did every day, and she took it. He closed the door and settled in behind the wheel. "If you please, Princess. Where am I taking you?"

She gave him the address. Alexsi pulled out the folded street map he always kept in his tunic pocket. On the Aventine Hill. One of Rome's seven.

"I would be happy to direct you," she said.

Alexsi was sure she would. "If it becomes necessary, Princess. Thank you. But I believe I have it."

They drove in silence for a bit. Then, as they swung around the Colosseum, she said, "You don't care about me being a princess, do you, Sergeant?"

Alexsi pondered his reply. "No, Princess."

"Then why do you keep calling me that? None of the other Germans do."

"For the sake of courtesy," Alexsi replied.

"Really?"

"Of course."

"Why are you being courteous?"

"That is what we owe to each other," Alexsi said. "Courtesy and kindness." He truly believed that. He only showed the lack of those qualities to those who failed to show them to him first.

"That is not German," she said.

"That is not courteous," Alexsi replied instantly.

"You are right," she said after a moment's thought. "A princess should be the example of courtesy, should she not?"

Her tone was neither resentful nor apologetic.

"So you say," Alexsi replied.

She smiled in his rearview mirror. "If you will forgive me, you are an unusual sergeant."

"I would guess you have not met many."

"A few," she said. "Enough to make the statement. If it would not seem discourteous, what is it you do for the German Army? Besides drive."

"I am a signaler."

"And what is that?"

Alexsi was fairly sure she knew exactly what that was. "I operate wireless. Though these days I supervise the operators."

"I see. And you are German Army. Not the SS like Colonel Kappler and his men."

No fool there. Alexsi reminded himself to stay on his toes. "Yes."

"How is that?"

"A shortage of signalers."

"Then you did not volunteer to come to Rome?"

Meaning: You did not volunteer for the SS torture chamber. "No, Princess."

Silence after that.

It was definitely what the Italians would call a palazzo. Limestone and marble. Screened by beautiful cypress trees. Definitely something from a picture book, Alexsi thought.

He held the door of the Mercedes, and as she stepped down she took his hand again.

Shutting the door, Alexsi said, "Good evening, Princess."

"Sergeant Bauer?"

Alexsi was frankly surprised she remembered his name. "Yes, Princess?"

"Thank you for your courtesy."

"And you yours, Princess." He gave her a smile and another slow, almost flirtatious salute.

She said abruptly, "Will you dine with us tonight?"

Alexsi was taken aback. "That is more courtesy than necessary, Princess."

"It is a sincere invitation," she said. And then she laughed. "Not an Italian invitation, given for form, that you are expected to not accept."

"Are you sure that a German soldier will not upset your table, Princess?"

Now those eyes were flashing. "It is *my* table."

She had shown him a glimpse of her steel. Alexsi could have guessed she was used to having her way. He smiled again, and bowed slightly. "Then I accept your courteous invitation."

Now she smiled, and nodded.

"Will it be all right to leave the auto here? In front?"

"Of course."

Alexsi reached into the front seat for the Beretta.

"Is that necessary?" she said.

"Regretfully, yes. I am accountable for the weapon, and cannot let it out of my sight."

"I understand. Why did you bring it?"

"For your protection. You were my responsibility."

Now she favored him with a dazzling smile. She extended her hand toward his arm, and he extended it out. She grasped the crook of his elbow, and they walked up the stairs together.

A servant in a formal black jacket opened the door. He looked at Alexsi as if the devil himself were on the verge of stepping over the threshold.

"Thank you, Paolo," the princess said in Italian. "The sergeant will be joining us for dinner."

The servant seemed on the verge of saying something, but Alexsi watched her drill him into submission with her eyes. He looked down at the submachine gun, and Alexsi just shook his head. He gave the fellow his uniform cap instead.

The princess let out a low throaty laugh. "Please excuse me. I must freshen up before dinner. Would you care for an aperitif?"

"Thank you, no," Alexsi said. "May I use your telephone? I must tell my command what I am doing, or they may turn everyone out to search for me." Or not, he thought.

"Of course." She then explained in Italian to Paolo.

The princess went up the central staircase. Which had been lined with paintings but now showed several empty spaces. If Alexsi had not put aside the little Russian thief he had been, he would have snickered at the sight. Having to sell off the art to make ends meet. No doubt the fellow making money off the war was laughing behind his sleeve at the royalty coming to him with their treasures. And your magnificent house would be gone tomorrow if Kappler showed up with a section of SS and decided he wanted it. The only tenet of Communism Alexsi had ever abided by was to own nothing. And he had been proven right time and again. From the Whites of the Russian Revolution to the Jews of Berlin during Kristallnacht. Sooner or later someone with a gun would show up at your door, and you would have to go out the window anyway. Or your attachment to all your things, which would be taken from you anyway, would put you in a truck on the way to a camp.

The entry was unbelievable, designed to be that way, with a laced marble floor and a massive chandelier. Alexsi was led to a sitting room with rich silk and velvet furniture that made him anxious about even sitting down, and in an instant a telephone was produced and plugged into the wall.

Aware that everyone in the house was listening in, Alexsi had the switchboard at Via Tasso put him through to the adjutant. Kappler of course had left for the day. Alexsi was a bit surprised to be given permission, but no doubt the adjutant had already been briefed by Kappler.

When he was finished with the phone another servant made it disappear. He made himself comfortable . . . or as comfortable as you could be in a chair you were afraid of even farting on. Alexsi had the distinct feeling that there was a servant just out of eyeshot to make sure the German didn't pocket anything. He had to admit that a house like this made him want to be a burglar again. In Russia he could live for a year on what he could carry away from this place in his arms.

Forty-five minutes later the princess swept into the room. In another dress, this one for evening. Just as expensive as before, but also not new. The Germans had the Italian clothiers hard at work, but not making evening dresses.

"I asked them to show you about," she said, mildly annoyed.

"I will go out on a limb and say they were afraid to," Alexsi replied.

"I hope you didn't think me discourteous," she said playfully.

"No," said Alexsi. "You've gotten much better about that."

She gave him a sharp little look. Alexsi just smiled back at her. He'd already guessed that she was used to getting her ass kissed. Double, because she was a good-looking woman and a princess. There was no harm in being a different commodity.

Recovering, she took his arm and led him to the dining room. Her son and daughter were already seated, and Alexsi imagined already warned to be on their best behavior. Emilia was fourteen and uncharacteristically fair. She colored a deep umber whenever spoken to about anything. Francesco was seventeen, and a dark-haired, dark-eyed male analogue of his mother. He refused to speak a word, just smoldering in adolescent fury at the German at the table.

Alexsi thought it hilarious.

They began with grace said by the princess. In German. Speaking as if everyone knew the language. Which they probably did. Since he was playing a Bavarian Catholic, which he had learned to be with his uncle Hans in his other life, he crossed himself along with everyone else. He noticed the princess noticing it.

They began with bread toasted and topped with olives and something else chopped in oil. Alexsi was given a glass of wine that he took a single sip from out of politeness, even though it was excellent. And shook his head each time a servant appeared to refill it.

The soup was egg cooked in broth, with cheese.

Alexsi hardly said a word, except to answer. He was the topic of conversation, the princess interrogating him much more skillfully than Captain Priebke and his brass knuckles. Alexsi told himself absolutely no more wine, since if he slipped on a single detail in his legend she was sure not to miss it.

The main course was spaghetti dressed with cheese and black pepper. Incredibly simple, and also incredibly delicious.

"Tell me," the princess said, "what you think of Rome."

"Beautiful," said Alexsi.

"But too tied to the past," she said.

"Worse if the past were covered over," said Alexsi.

"I wish these Roman ruins were all covered over," she said vehemently. "They were fine when they were just here for tourists to photograph and spend money on. Their tragedy is that they give people like Mussolini . . ."

And Hitler, Alexsi heard her imply, though not out loud . . .

". . . the idea to try and re-create it. Even though there was a reason it died, and has been dead for a millennium."

Alexsi just twirled spaghetti onto his fork, as he had seen the Italians do.

The boy Francesco spoke for the first time. In German. "You say nothing."

"Since I wear the uniform of Rome's latest conqueror," said Alexsi, "what is there to say?"

Francesco only snorted. His mother glared at him.

"Do you know what is the nice thing about being a sergeant, young man?" Alexsi asked him.

Francesco opened his mouth to speak.

"You do not have to reply," said Alexsi. "The question was rhetorical. Sergeants do not start wars. They do not send men out to die—they are sent out to die."

"And yet you are here," said Francesco. "With your gun."

"We are all at the mercy of forces more powerful than us," said Alexsi.

"Yet you Germans are all so good at following orders," said Francesco.

"Francesco!" his mother snapped.

"This I concede," Alexsi said.

"Since we are all at the mercy of power and orders, what about choice?" Francesco demanded.

"Francesco," his mother warned.

"Sometimes survival is the only choice," said Alexsi.

Francesco snorted again.

"You may leave the table," the princess said to him.

Francesco slapped his napkin down on the table and stalked off.

"I apologize," the princess said. "You are our guest."

"I remember being seventeen all too well," Alexsi replied. Though he had always been a survivalist, not an idealist.

There was no dessert, and Alexsi knew why. Sugar in wartime was worth its weight in gold. Instead the servants brought little cups of coffee. It looked like real coffee, which Alexsi imagined was why the cups were so small. He waited until the others did so, then took a sip.

He thought his eyeballs might explode from his skull. It was coffee in a concentration until now unknown to him. He could feel it rushing through his brain, especially after so many mornings of German ersatz.

The servants cleared away the dishes. Alexsi knew little of Italian food, though he knew poor people's food. And this had been poor people's food, no matter how perfectly prepared or served upon fine porcelain and eaten with silver utensils. It was like back on the kolkhoz in Azerbaijan, where the paint came out from under lock and key only when a boss from the district soviet was due to inspect.

Except this hadn't been for him. It was their way of persuading themselves they were still as rich as their house.

He turned to the princess. "Thank you for a wonderful meal, and your hospitality. Perhaps I have imposed upon it too much."

"Absolutely not," she said. "Let us take our coffee, and I will show you about as I promised."

Alexsi stood. The silent daughter was about to bolt anyway. He bowed to her. She blushed deeply again and dashed off.

The princess walked him through the house. Each room was more magnificent than the last. Alexsi allowed his imagination to run free, envisioning merchants and cardinals from the Renaissance wandering about.

The lights suddenly went out. Not an unusual occurrence in wartime Rome.

The princess took his arm. "Let us go out to the garden while candles are lit. We will not have to worry about the blackout."

She led him through paneled double glass doors. There was a light breeze, and Alexsi could smell the fresh green of the early spring plants. Kesselring had declared Rome an open city. Though there were still Germans using it, so the Allies were still bombing it. They were quite careful, however, by the standards of bombing. Alexsi had to give them that.

"I'm sure there would be quite a view," he said. "If we could see anything."

She laughed beside him.

As his eyes adjusted to the darkness, Alexsi saw shadows moving very slowly. "Are any of your people out here?" he asked.

"No," she said, her voice showing her puzzlement at the question. "The gardener is of course at home, and the rest of mine are clearing from dinner and lighting candles."

"No watchman?"

"No," she said, concern in her voice.

"Plug your ears," he said.

"What?"

In one smooth motion Alexsi unslung the Beretta and brought it up to his shoulder. He thumbed off the safety catch and placed his finger on the rearmost of the double triggers.

He fired the first short burst just over the top of the shadows in the garden. As he paused, there was loud shouting and the shadows began running. Alexsi fired another burst to speed them along.

An instant later three dark shapes went over the light-colored garden wall. Alexsi fired a last short burst into the wall beside them, to speed them on their way.

His ears rang, and his nostrils were filled with the smell of gunpowder.

Alexsi swapped out the magazine for a fresh one, even though he had used less than half. The Beretta was slung back over his shoulder before the princess took her fingers out of her ears.

Servants came running out of the house, and the princess spoke quickly and reassuringly to them in Italian. Two of them began crossing through the garden and beating the shrubbery with sticks.

"Thieves," Alexsi said. "Your people won't find any bodies there. I was just shooting to give them a good fright and send them on their way. They won't bother you again. They'll look for something easier."

"Thank you," the princess said simply.

The head servant spoke to her behind them.

"The candles are lit," she said. "Shall we go back inside? I think I have lost my taste for the night air."

"As you wish."

"Let me show you upstairs."

With one hand on the banister and the other on his arm, she gave him the names and brief histories of the descendants whose portraits marked the route up. Alexsi held the candlestick they used to see by.

Down a long hall lined with enough paintings to make a museum. At the end the princess opened a door and led him through.

Alexsi swept the candle in a circle to take it all in.

"This is my bedroom," she said. Standing in front of his candle very small and slightly afraid, as someone who had made a decision and wondered if what happened next would be good or bad, comfortable or humiliating.

Alexsi found himself standing on the tightrope again. He said, "My name is Peter."

Her face softened into a smile. "Please call me Abrianna."

She took a step forward. He leaned down and she kissed him. That was the way to describe it, Alexsi thought. She kissed him, not the other way around.

"Excuse me for a moment," she said.

When she disappeared into the bath, Alexsi leaned the submachine gun against a side table and tucked the ammunition belt away underneath it. His Walther, however, went underneath the mattress. No sense in being completely stupid.

She emerged wearing a sheer nightgown, again expensive. Alexsi just stood there smiling warmly at her in the candlelight. As part of his spy training, the NKVD, with their Russian practicality and Communist lack of scruples, had put him through a course of instruction in making love to women. First classroom training and then practical application with the instructor sitting there watching him with the poor girls they had recruited for that task. Like all their courses, it was one that you did not dare fail. Though if you lacked sexual endurance, which he certainly did at seventeen, a dour secret policeman critiquing your staying power was exactly what the doctor ordered. It had taken Alexsi two weeks to orgasm at all, let alone normally, after that class was over.

The princess walked up to him and kissed him again. Alexsi pressed his hand gently but firmly between her legs, and kept it still. She moaned during the kiss and pressed harder against him. As they kissed she unbuttoned his tunic. If she wanted to undress him, he would stand back and let her. He kept his hand where it was.

With his suspenders off and trousers unbuttoned, he stepped out of his boots. Underwear off. She had him in her hand, appraisingly. Women liked to see if they had that immediate power over you. Even if it hadn't been a long time, she was a beauty.

Alexsi kissed her again, and with one hand opened the buttons of her nightgown.

"Let me blow out the candle," she whispered.

Alexsi smiled at her and shook his head. "Not a chance, Princess."

She looked up at him openly. He swept the nightgown off her shoulders. Taking both her hands, he took a step back to view her in full, smiling appreciatively. She dropped her eyes, but he cupped his hand under her chin and kissed her again.

She led him over to the bed and turned it down, his arm around her waist.

She lay down on her back, and from the way she positioned herself he could see that her husband had been a man of limited imagination.

Alexsi lay down beside her, took her in his arms, and whispered in her ear, "Tell me what excites you."

It wasn't something the Russians had taught him. He had once asked a woman that in bed, really just out of politeness, and she had opened up like a beautiful flower.

She pulled her head back to look him in the eyes, and took his face in both her hands. Looking at him like no man had ever asked that question, which they probably hadn't. Then she kissed him and leaned forward to whisper in his ear.

She got him a silk scarf and he blindfolded her. Stretching her hands over her head, he held them down gently with one of his as he went exploring down her body.

Alexsi was always curious about why people were the way they were. He imagined this might be a Catholic thing. Since she was being made to do it, she was without sin. It could also have been being made to do it by a German soldier. Though he had also seen the same thing in aristocratic Iranian ladies in Teheran. They spent all day bossing the servants and their children, and in bed they wanted the opposite. Usually their husbands were ineffectual.

He was fine with a light spanking, but had been beaten enough by his father to balk at hurting anyone even for their own pleasure. But that wasn't what she wanted.

He decided to take advantage of the blindfold to surprise her. Which he did. He worked his way down her body with his mouth and free hand, taking unexpected turns. Soon she was squirming and moaning. He whispered to her not to move.

When he needed both his hands he told her to grasp the headboard and not let go. With his head between her legs and both hands free, she went wild. Though she did not let go of the arms of the headboard. Clearly, despite the reputation of the Italian male, this was not something her husband was interested in.

She came twice, and then he urged her on top of him.

"I can't," she said.

"I know you're sensitive now," Alexsi told her. "But if you just push past it, it will be all right."

He had her mount him from above. Still wearing the blindfold. Which let him keep surprising her with his hands.

She moved very slowly, taking her pleasure. "You were right," she murmured.

The things the husbands of the world did not concern themselves with, Alexsi thought. Their own loss. He had to thank the Russians for this, at least.

He could feel her getting close, but her pace did not alter. As if she did not quite know how to get there. Alexsi took her hands in his, and she gasped at that. Then he kept her still, poised above him, and began moving faster and faster himself.

Her moaning became louder and louder, and he could feel her tension building. He went as fast as he could, and then she exploded. That was the only word for it. A noise came from her that was close to a scream. Her entire body spasmed; her back arched, and then she collapsed upon him, shaking.

She sobbed on top of him. Alexsi wrapped his arms around her and whispered in her ear that it was all right.

It was something men were supposed to be notorious for, but she fell asleep right on top of him. He gently slid her off him, and rolled onto his side. Might as well take a little sleep for himself. It had been a long day.

Alexsi awoke with the movement of the bed. Someone getting off it. His hand automatically went for the Walther under the mattress.

"You are a very light sleeper," the princess said, standing beside the bed in the darkness.

"An occupational hazard for a soldier," Alexsi replied. Not to mention a spy.

"Tell me," she said. "Do you love me?"

"Of course not," Alexsi replied, half into the pillow. "I've only known you for a few hours."

She laughed uproariously, and Alexsi was afraid she would wake the house.

"An Italian man would be professing his undying love. How marvelous the truth is. I never thought I would find so much to like about the Germans."

"I warn you, I'm not your typical German." That at least was the truth.

"I had already come to that conclusion," she said. "Don't fall back asleep. When I return from the bathroom, we should continue our discussions."

That was a nice way to put it, Alexsi thought, watching her sway off naked in the moonlight through the open window. The candle had burned down. He probably ought not hold out any hope for more sleep.

Before dawn he was dressing in the darkness. She stirred, and he whispered in her ear. "I must return to report for duty this morning."

She lifted herself up on one elbow, hair falling down across her eyes. "I understand."

"I hope we will see each other again," Alexsi said. "I will understand if we do not."

"From now on," she said, "if Colonel Kappler wants something from me, you will bring me the message."

"I would like that," Alexsi said. "Thank you for your courtesy, Princess. And your hospitality."

She fell back upon the pillow, laughing. "Peter, when you write to your family, please thank them for the good manners they gave to you."

Despite his best efforts, Alexsi felt his face become serious. "What good manners I have, came from my aunt."

"Then please thank her, from me."

"She is gone now."

"That is sad," the princess said.

"Yes," said Alexsi. "Yes it is."

33

"Did you fuck her?" Kappler demanded.

"Yes, Colonel," Alexsi replied.

Kappler hammered the desktop with his fist, in pure delight. He bounded up and practically skipped around the desk. "Fantastic! Both for you and for me."

Alexsi held back a yawn.

Kappler placed both hands on his shoulders in an almost fatherly gesture. "Now, you're a good-looking fellow, Bauer. And I'm sure quite a charmer. But I don't want you to think she fell in love with you at first sight."

"No, Colonel," Alexsi said.

"After all, you're the signals chief of my headquarters. I'm sure she wormed that out of you, didn't she?"

"Yes, Colonel."

"You're the man who sees every message, sent and received. If I was going to recruit a spy, it would be you."

Alexsi kept his face very still.

"So now she's going to use you to find out what's going on here," said Kappler. "And she'll use what women always use to get their way."

"I understand, Colonel," Alexsi said. "You do not want me to see her again."

"No, no, no," Kappler moaned, squeezing Alexsi's shoulders as if to squeeze some sense into him. "You *must* see her again. It is imperative. She will think she is getting information out of you. But you will actually be working for me. A double agent."

"I'm sorry, Colonel," Alexsi said, maintaining his straight face. "A double agent? I don't know what that is."

"Look, sit down," said Kappler, leading him over to a chair and then standing over him. "I know you're a signaler and don't understand these matters like an SD man. Which is why I chose you for this job. Try to follow me, now. *She* will think that you are spying on me, for *her*. Because you are sympathetic to her, and she is fucking your brains out. But actually, you are working for *me*. Spying on her. Whatever *she* asks you, you will tell to me. And that will tell *me* everything I need to know about *her*. A double agent. Are you following?"

"I think so, Colonel." And then, plaintively, "But Colonel, as you said. I am a signaler, not an SD man. I am over my head in these matters. What if I should do something wrong? Say something wrong?"

"You will be fine," Kappler said authoritatively, though still in his fatherly voice. "All you have to do is act besotted by her. I doubt this will be difficult. Whatever she asks you, just play dumb. Tell her you don't know, but you will try and find out for her. Let her keep fucking you. Then come back and tell me everything. I will then tell you what to tell her. It will be easy, you see?"

"I don't know, Colonel . . ." Alexsi said, playing hard to get.

"I'm counting on you, Bauer," Kappler said. "You told me you were my man. Isn't that right?"

"Yes, Colonel," Alexsi said grudgingly.

"Good. Believe me, you will come to enjoy this intrigue. Plus, I'm sure you will be getting more sex than anyone in this building besides Priebke. And you will not have to pay for it."

Alexsi was certain he was going to have to pay for it, one way or another. "I'm sure with your help I will be able to grasp it, Colonel."

"That's the spirit," said Kappler.

The phone on his desk rang. He picked it up. "Yes?" He listened for a moment. "What? Are you sure? All right, turn out everyone available. Yes, including Koch's Italians. Everyone. Have my staff car out front. Yes, now!"

He hung up the phone. "Bauer, have the wireless truck manned and waiting out front at once."

"Yes, Colonel."

"Something has happened on the Via Rasella."

34

The acrid smell of TNT hung in the air of the narrow street. It would be hard to convince anyone but a soldier that blood had a smell, Alexsi thought. But if there was enough on the ground you could definitely smell it. There was enough on the pavement here that the soldiers were splashing through it like rain puddles. Clinging to that was another odor, of spilled bowel. Again understandable, considering the circumstances.

Gunfire kept ringing out, Alexsi trying not to flinch at each shot. The German troops who responded had lost their heads. Even as their comrades were turning the residents of the street out of their apartments, they were shooting up at the windows even though no one was shooting back. A woman was hanging half out of a third-floor window, dead, her blood staining the wall below her. Shot while sticking her head out to see what was happening, Alexsi thought. Killed by curiosity.

The shell-shocked survivors of the Bozen police regiment were lurching about the Via Rasella picking up the bodies and pieces of their comrades from the cobblestones and laying them out with Germanic order in a neat row along the sidewalk. A sergeant was walking up and down, tears streaming down his face, carrying a human arm and looking for the correct body to reunite it with.

They were the same dumb singing bastards he had seen that day on the range with Klaus and his men. Alexsi had thought at the time that they were just asking for it, and now he had been proven right. Especially today. It was the twenty-fifth anniversary of Mussolini founding the Fascist movement. A perfect day to be marching the same route through Rome, bellowing their stupid marching songs. The partisans had very carefully planned a party for them down this tight little street. And, by all appearances, pulled it off beautifully.

The SS and Italian Fascist police and soldiers were herding all the civilians they had been able to lay their hands on down the other side of the street, lining them up in front of the gates of the Barberini Palace.

Alexsi made his way down that slaughterhouse of a street until he saw Kappler. Who was standing listening to the military commandant of Rome, Luftwaffe General Mälzer.

As he drew closer, Alexsi could hear Mälzer raving like a madman. "You see, Kappler?" he bellowed. "You see what they have done to my boys? Now I'm going to blow all these houses sky-high!"

My God, Alexsi thought to himself. The general hadn't gone mad. He was drunk. Crazy drunk. He could barely stand up straight. But nonetheless deadly serious. Farther down, German Army pioneers were unloading crates of explosives from their trucks. He was actually going to do it. And of course the engineers, as good German soldiers, would follow their orders to the letter.

Alexsi only thought about how he would compose his wireless message to the British about this. Just the facts. Because if he told them that the military governor of Rome, deep in his cups, was tearing about like the Red Queen in *Alice in Wonderland,* screaming "Off with their heads," no one would ever believe him.

The general might have been deadly serious, but Kappler was deadly calm. He waited until Mälzer paused for breath, then said, "General, my men and I will proceed with the investigation into this outrage. I believe it would be best if you returned to your headquarters. You will need to keep the field marshal informed, and I'm sure they will need your guidance in the hours to come."

"No, damn it!" the general shouted drunkenly. "My place is here! I want to watch this street go up in smoke, with all the rats who live here inside!"

Kappler was still calm, but now there was ice in his voice. "General, you must go. You will be needed at your headquarters. The entire situation in Rome must be monitored. There may be further attacks."

Alexsi watched Kappler, without much effort, making Mälzer frightened. The general was sweating alcohol right out his pores. "All right, all right," Mälzer said.

Without another word Kappler took the general's arms and guided him toward his staff car. Halfway through the door, Mälzer stood up and waved his hand up and down the street. He shouted, "They are all to be shot!" Then he fell back into the vehicle.

Kappler made a quick motion to the driver, who was no doubt just as anxious to be gone, and the staff car roared off.

Kappler sighed and turned about. "Yes, Bauer, what is it?"

Alexsi said, reading from his message pad, "Colonel, Field Marshal Kesselring is visiting the front lines at Anzio today. He will be out of touch until later this evening."

"Probably just as well for now," Kappler said. "General Mälzer will be able to . . . calm himself, as he waits."

Sober up, you mean, Alexsi thought. The general had dredged up memories of his father, who when drunk would certainly have blown something up if he'd been able. Instead, he usually beat someone up. Usually him.

Captain Priebke walked up, staring coldly at Alexsi.

Kappler said to him, "Fetch that engineer officer over here."

Priebke returned in a moment with the lieutenant of pioneers, who saluted sharply.

Kappler said, "Pack up your men and equipment, and return to your base."

"Colonel?" the lieutenant said, puzzled.

"You're not blowing up Rome today," said Kappler. "Go home."

The lieutenant saluted and dashed off to his men.

Alexsi breathed a silent sigh of relief.

Priebke motioned for Kappler to follow him.

Kappler said, "Bauer, get me a count of the dead and wounded. Exactly, if you please."

"Yes, Colonel."

Alexsi walked down the line of dead on the sidewalk, ticking off the numbers on his pad. The surviving Bozen were staring angrily at him. "I'm very sorry, Comrades," he said. "I have orders to list your losses."

"We knew something was going to happen," said one. "It was the first time the streets were ever empty."

"Italian bastards knew it was coming," another spat.

Alexsi returned to Kappler. "Twenty-six dead, Colonel. Somewhere between a hundred and one hundred and ten wounded. The count is inexact because some of the unwounded may have taken the rest to hospital already."

"Out of how many?" Kappler asked.

"One hundred and fifty-six," Alexsi said.

"Then they are wiped out," Kappler said flatly.

He and Priebke were standing over what seemed to be the only evidence. A red flag and a mortar bomb with what looked like a home-made impact fuse in the nose.

"The bomb is Italian," said Kappler. "So no English commandos like everyone is bleating about. Definitely partisans. Bauer, what do you think?"

Alexsi knew Kappler was doing that just to get Priebke's goat. "I am only a signaler, Colonel."

"Yes, so you always begin," said Kappler. "But based on your experiences with partisans in Russia. Bombs thrown from the roofs, and then gunfire shooting down, eh?"

Alexsi decided to tell the truth, if only to keep those two hundred Italian civilians lined up at the Barberini Palace from receiving the death penalty for not being shrewd enough to take to their heels after the first shot was fired. "I think if you look down that way, Colonel," he said, pointing, "you will see there is a crater nine meters across in the street. And another blown out of the wall opposite it. I would say a very large bomb in a cart or something similar, then the mortar bombs from the roofs. After that firing from both ends of the street, to cover the retreat."

Kappler thought it over. "Reasonable. Though the Bozen say they were fired upon from the rooftops. Why could the bomb not have been launched from up there?"

"As I said, Colonel, I am just a signaler." A signaler who would not have been stupid enough to haul a bomb all the way up to a roof if he could set it off down on the street. But let the idiots think what they wanted.

"Yes, I know," Kappler said dryly. "And the partisans? In your signals opinion?"

"Long gone, Colonel."

"On that we agree." Kappler turned to Priebke. "There will be a reprisal ordered, of course. But we will use the ones we already have locked up, under sentence of death. Not have all of Rome up in arms after wiping out an entire neighborhood."

Priebke nodded. He aimed his head questioningly in the direction of the Italians at Barberini Palace, who had been goaded by the trigger-happy sentries into keeping their hands over their heads for hours.

"Turn them over to the Italian police for interrogation," said Kappler.

"They'll be released," Priebke said.

"I'm counting on that," said Kappler.

Priebke nodded and walked off in that direction.

Kappler said, "Bauer, I am going to the Corso d'Italia. I will use the communications there. Bring the wireless truck back to Via Tasso and stand by. I want copies of all incoming communications on my desk for when I return."

Alexsi saluted. "Yes, Colonel."

Corso d'Italia was General Mälzer's headquarters. Kappler was going to keep a very close eye on that clown of a general, Alexsi thought. To keep him from doing anything stupid.

He looked down the street again. The partisans had done this to provoke an outrage from the Germans. To turn the city out against them and cause chaos that would require more troops to restore order. Troops that would have to be taken from the front, and therefore weaken it.

If Alexsi knew his Germans, they were going to do exactly what the partisans wanted.

35

ROME, ITALY

The Via Tasso was a madhouse, and gave every sign of being one for the rest of the night. Kappler was back from General Mälzer's headquarters, sequestered upstairs with his officers. Signals and telephone calls were flooding into the communications center like a tropical storm. Alexsi had to keep the previous shift of signalers on duty just to keep up with it. No sleep for anyone tonight.

It meant that there was no way he could sneak in a message letting the British know what happened. A training message at a time like this would have everyone doing more than wondering.

He was having a hard enough time keeping ahead of the incoming messages himself. After the news of the attack reached Kesselring's headquarters, his chief of operations immediately passed it along to Hitler's

Wolf's Lair headquarters in East Prussia. Hitler was told, and went absolutely mad with rage.

Alexsi flipped through the message carbons. Staff officer at Wolf's Lair told Kesselring's 1A that the Führer demanded a reprisal "to make the world tremble." The next message was the Führer's order to blow up an entire quarter of Rome, and shoot thirty to fifty Italians for every German police officer killed.

More messages. Kappler and General Mälzer, now sober, speaking to General Mackensen, Fourteenth Army commander. They all decide on a more reasonable number of ten Italians to be shot in retaliation for every German killed. Kesselring confirms: ten for each one. Those to be executed were persons already in custody and sentenced to death or life imprisonment.

Alexsi guessed that was what they were doing upstairs. Putting together the death lists and planning the logistics. Hitler had ordered that the reprisal take place within twenty-four hours of the attack, and that much murder was going to take time. The clock was ticking.

Wireless messages in hand, Alexsi wandered into the switchboard room and thumbed through the telephone log. Kappler to his SD superior, SS General Harster in Verona. Kappler to the justice of the German military tribunal in Rome. Kappler covering his ass, Alexsi thought. Making sure everyone was in on it, and on the record.

A clerk had been sent up with all the prisoner record cards.

By now thirty-two of the Bozen SS policemen had died, so that was three hundred and twenty Italians. Alexsi knew there were fewer than three hundred prisoners total, men and women, both here in the Via Tasso and in the wing at Regina Coeli prison the Germans had taken over for their use. And only a handful of those under death sentence.

Alexsi took his stack of messages down the hall, and ran into Kappler also going into his office.

Kappler said, "Anything new, Bauer?"

"No, Colonel. Nothing new to report. These are just all the messages to date. I will leave them with the adjutant."

"Good, good." Kappler was preoccupied, and said nothing more.

Alexsi followed him into the outer office, remaining there while Kappler went through his own door. It was a fog of cigarette smoke, and Alexsi saw all the officers crammed in there.

Kappler announced to them, "I have just been to the *questore*. I have a promise of fifty from the Italians. Along with the Jews scheduled for deportation, we have it."

So they weren't going to shoot the women, Alexsi thought. How chivalrous.

The door shut, and Alexsi dropped the stack of messages on the adjutant's desk. Hanging around there any longer would be too suspicious.

It was late morning and Alexsi sat staring at the bare top of his desk. He had no desire to see three hundred and twenty people put up against a wall and shot. But he had no good practical ideas on how to prevent it. Especially since the only thing he wanted even less was to see himself put up against a wall and shot. What could he do? Setting fire to the building to delay things would only mean the SS running out to save themselves and standing there laughing while all the prisoners burned alive. Good job saving them, Alexsi Ivanovich. Such men were also not likely to be moved by him delivering a passionate speech on the morality of the summary execution of civilians.

Still no way to get a message to the British. Not that it would do any good, other than make them pleased to know what was going on. But it was a worry. They were just moral enough to think he ought to have done something, a view easy to take from the comfort of an office in London.

This would not be a problem if he were still working for the NKVD. They would insist that three hundred and twenty souls was a small price to pay to maintain a spy's cover. The Abwehr would not care either way.

The other worry, more immediate, was being dragooned into being one of Kappler's executioners. There weren't that many Germans at the Via Tasso, and they had already tried to make him a torturer. Alexsi had no idea how they were going to kill three hundred and twenty people, but he wanted no part of it. Not only because he might end up back with the British, and it would be very difficult to explain away becoming an SS war criminal.

Rather than say no again, and being firmly ordered to this time, he ought to get out of the building before it happened.

That ignited an idea. Perhaps a way to kill two birds with one stone, without killing anyone.

Alexsi grabbed his Beretta and ammunition belt and stopped first at the armory for two egg grenades to go in his pockets. Just in case he had to break up a roadblock.

Then it was off to the mess. As he could have predicted, when he told the cook sergeant he wanted a twenty-kilo bag of flour there was a fight.

"Going into the black market along with everyone else?" the mess sergeant scoffed. "At least you're not sneaking in here to steal it like the rest. Absolutely not."

"Look, I'm taking the flour," Alexsi said. "It's for a mission authorized by Colonel Kappler personally. And when he's less busy you can tell him all about it. Or, you can go upstairs and tell him now, and see what happens to you."

That hit the mess sergeant like a shot between the eyes. Alexsi watched him think about going off to be a cook on the front lines, as a private. "You'll sign for it," he said finally.

"I'll sign for it," Alexsi said.

Heads turned as he made his way to the motor pool with the sack of flour over his shoulder. "I need a vehicle," he said to the transport sergeant.

Who shook his head definitively. "Colonel Kappler's orders. All trucks and staff cars on hold. Nothing leaves."

"For fuck's sake," Alexsi blurted out. "It's urgent. What can you give me? Besides a bicycle."

"You can have a motorcycle."

Alexsi just looked at the sack on his shoulder as if to say, Can you believe this? "Tell me you have one with a sidecar."

"I have one with a sidecar," the motors sergeant said. "You'll have to sign for it."

"I'll sign for it," Alexsi said.

Exactly what he wanted to be doing. Driving through a city full of emboldened partisans and surly Italians on a motorcycle. With a sidecar holding a large sack of flour.

Alexsi kept waiting for a wire to come up across one of those narrow Roman streets and take his head off. Otherwise, he pushed that motorcycle as fast as it could go. And like both a typical Roman and a typical German soldier, he ignored every traffic sign and regulation.

He breathed a sigh of relief as he went up that familiar drive on Monte Aventino. They had probably heard the motorcycle a block away, because the head servant was at the door before he pulled his helmet and goggles off.

As he came up the steps, the servant said, "The princess cannot see you."

Alexsi took the final step up, reached out, and grabbed him at the junction of the neck and shoulder with his left hand. His right had the Beretta in it. The servant's eyes went wide. Clearly the Italian upper crust did not manhandle their servants, and he was not accustomed to it.

Alexsi said, in Italian, "My friend, I have no wish to be angry with you. I must see the princess. Now. I do not care who she is with, and I do not care to see them. I will wait in the garden. Are we in accord?"

The servant nodded.

"Fetch her immediately."

Alexsi went around the side of the palazzo to the back. In the daylight he could both see and hear the chicken coops. Obviously a recent addition, and incongruous with the elegant gardens. But with the Germans shipping Italy's food back to Germany, and Rome starving, they were a more inviting target to thieves than the art treasures inside the house.

The sight of the chickens pecking through the garden for insects brought back a memory of the kolkhoz in Azerbaijan. Except farming under Communism meant that you raised the chickens, the government took the eggs, and then they gave you no eggs. So if you wanted any eggs for yourself you had to steal them. And if the government caught you, you went off to a prison camp to do free labor for the state. It was a fine system if you were a party boss, who ate the eggs. Not for anyone else, though.

The head servant ushered the princess onto the portico. She looked upset, and Alexsi knew this would require careful handling. He said over her head to the servant, "There is something in my motorcycle for the household. Please remove it."

The servant nodded and tactfully disappeared, probably because he was feeling the princess's anger also.

She walked up to him, her eyes flashing but otherwise under control, and said, "Peter, you cannot—"

Alexsi cut her off. "You have heard about Via Rasella?"

Absorbing his tone, she only nodded.

"Colonel Kappler is going to execute three hundred and twenty Italians in reprisal," Alexsi said. "It will be done before the day is out."

She gasped. "Three hundred and twenty?"

"Already in custody."

"Will they do it at Fort Bravetta?" she asked.

That question told Alexsi he had come to the right place. He decided to play dumb. "I'm sorry?"

"That is where they do their executions," she said. "By firing squad in the prison yard."

"I do not know," Alexsi said. Then, pointedly, "The trucks will come out of both Via Tasso and Regina Coeli prison." So if the partisans wanted to put a stop to it, that was where they had to ambush. It wouldn't be hard. A couple of grenades and a spray of gunfire. The guards scatter—those prisoners with any brains at all run away. Even the ones they recaught wouldn't die that day, at least. But Alexsi wasn't going to offer to do their planning for them. What he had just said was the best he could do.

The princess suddenly clasped his face in both her hands and kissed him hard. "Wait here. I will return in a moment."

"Do not speak of this over the telephone," Alexsi warned. "The Italian police have five hundred listeners at the Rome telephone exchanges." Kappler would surely have them listening to her line.

She nodded and turned toward the house.

"Do not say where this information came from," Alexsi said.

"I will not," she replied.

Alexsi doubted that. But at least he could make the case that she fucked it out of him. He sat down on an ornately carved marble bench that looked as if it had taken a couple of talented fellows with hammers and chisels a month to complete. He gave the cool marble a pat. The men who made it were dust, and the pretty bench was still there to be sat upon. He looked out over Rome. The view was even better than he thought it would be last night. Strangely enough, it made Alexsi recall a line from *Father Goriot* by Balzac. The French writer's novels were not banned in the Soviet Union because the Communists always looked to the French as fellow revolutionists. Alexsi had no head for mathematics, so for a reader there was only literature because in Communism history was nothing but lies. *The secret of great fortunes without apparent cause is a crime forgotten, for it was well done.* The princess's ancestor must have been a brilliant thief, Alexsi thought.

A chicken came over and stood on his boot. Alexsi picked her up and stroked her feathers. Just like back on the farm. You had to get them used to being held when they were chicks, so it was less trouble getting the eggs later.

The portico door opened, and despite herself the princess had to laugh at the sight of Alexsi with a chicken on his lap. She sat down on the bench beside him, and he gently shooed the bird on its way.

The princess took his hand in hers. "I knew you were a human being even before I invited you into my home."

Alexsi said nothing. Merely squeezed her hand back.

She let out a disgusted breath. "Men. They always have a perfect reason for doing nothing."

Alexsi had expected that. The ones who had done the Via Rasella attack had wisely gone into hiding. No one else had the balls to do anything about the reprisal. It had already occurred to him that the bastards might even *want* a reprisal, to bring in new recruits, or even get the Romans out in the streets in an uprising.

"The Pope is silent," she said, still holding his hand. "The Holy Father is always silent."

Alexsi always sympathized with women. Always had. From sitting at the kitchen table with his mother, before she died, waiting in mutual terror for a father to return home explosively drunk and expecting food to instantly appear before him because he was hungry. To his aunt Emma, so smart and capable, who still had to defer to her husband Otto, nice but definitely not so capable, and all the male idiots who ran their kolkhozes. That didn't mean they weren't dangerous, though. In fact, they were far more dangerous than men. A girl named Aida had taught him that, all too well. But he still liked them more than men.

"Is there anything you can do?" she said.

"Unfortunately, I am only a sergeant," Alexsi replied. "That is my perfect reason for doing nothing."

She let out a bitter chuckle. "There is nothing I can do, either. The Italians may hate the Germans, but they will never hate the Germans more than they hate the Italian from the next village."

Alexsi imagined that had more than a little to do with who she was inside talking to. They were both playing their parts very well, he thought. He was not about to ask any questions that might make her think he was anything other than the besotted lover who was upset about a Nazi reprisal and had come to drop off a bag of flour and get another look at her. "Actually, I am here so I will not have to be part of it," he added, for emphasis.

"You may stay as long as you like."

"I will have to return eventually," he said. "I would like to time it so they will have already left."

"Of course."

They sat there quietly for a while, holding hands. The chickens were talking excitedly to each other in the background, pecking away in the garden.

"I have a statement to make," said Alexsi.

"That is a funny way of saying something," she said. "Not really in German, but it would be very difficult in Italian. More like a speech."

"It is about what I can do," said Alexsi. "You are not foolish. It will not be a surprise when I tell you that Kappler has more than suspicions about you."

"You are right," she said. "It is not a surprise."

Very cautious, Alexsi thought. That was good. "Do not keep anyone or anything here that you would not want Kappler to find. He has informers everywhere. Even if there are not betrayers, he arrests people every day and makes them talk. He will arrive one day and search your home."

She just squeezed his hand again.

"If I telephone and ask to speak to you on the phone, and ask you if it is all right to come over, then everything is normal. If I tell you I am on my way here, and hang up like a rude German, that will mean Kappler is coming. I will say nothing else on the telephone, because others will be listening. Your servants answer the phone for you. If they tell you the German sergeant is on his way, not that I am making a request to speak to you, you will know. That will be the best that I can do."

By way of an answer, the princess leaned over, wrapped her arms tightly around his neck, and kissed him deeply.

36

1944

ROME, ITALY

"Shit!" Alexsi said out loud. Shit, shit, shit.

He had thought to take a cautious turn by the entrance to the Via Tasso motor pool, to see if the trucks had left. But Kappler had the whole building guarded like Hitler's headquarters, and as soon as his motorcycle came down the street everyone saw him.

And the killers were late. As Alexsi parked the motorcycle they were still loading prisoners into the trucks. The Italians all had their hands tied behind their backs, and two burly SS guards were literally picking them up and throwing them in.

Captain Priebke was standing in the courtyards before the trucks, a clipboard in his hands, checking off names.

Alexsi saluted.

Priebke just stared at him, and said, "You should be shot for abandoning your post, Bauer."

Alexsi replied, "Since I was not under orders to maintain a post, I doubt it, Captain."

Furious, Priebke spat, "You signalers are such smart-asses. The spoiled brats of this place. I'd like to do something about it."

"I'm sure you would, Captain." Alexsi saluted again.

"Report to Colonel Kappler," Priebke shouted behind him.

Inside the doorway, two SS sergeants had overheard and were still laughing about it. "That was good, Bauer," said one.

"He'll fix you if he has the chance," said the other.

"He'd do that anyway," said Alexsi.

Kappler was standing before the mirror in his office, buckling on his pistol belt.

Alexsi forced his face into total neutrality.

"Where the devil have you been, Bauer?" Kappler demanded.

"I went to see the Princess Santangelo, Colonel," Alexsi said. "I thought that if there was a partisan attack planned for our headquarters, she might warn me."

"What did she say?" Kappler demanded.

"Nothing outright, Colonel. I received the impression that you were correct, the partisans are on the run and in hiding after Via Rasella and that no attack is planned on us. I brought her some flour from the mess to smooth my way, and she was very friendly. I'm sorry I didn't ask you, but you were incredibly busy. I made sure the message center was fully staffed before I left."

The trick to being an excellent liar was to tell yourself the story first, so it slid out smoothly. If necessary as many versions as you could think up.

Kappler put his cap on, and tilted it slightly for effect. Alexsi thought that made the silver SS death's-head emblem on the front look like it was smirking at him. "You know, Bauer, as always I go from very angry with you to very pleased with your good judgment and initiative. You did well, and this is at least one weight off my mind."

"Thank you, Colonel. I was worried that I had done wrong in not checking with you first."

"Ordinarily yes, but not today. Don't make a habit of it, though."

"No, Colonel."

"Right. Follow my staff car with the wireless truck."

Thinking quickly, Alexsi said, "Are you certain you wouldn't prefer me in charge of the message center here, Colonel? I could notify you by voice radio if anything important comes in."

Kappler thought about that for only a moment. "No. When this job is done coded messages to that effect will have to be sent out immediately. I will need you to do that. The Führer himself must know that his orders have been carried out."

Defeated, Alexsi said, "As you order, Colonel."

37

1944

ROME, ITALY

They drove south, slightly more than ten kilometers. At the edge of the central city the density of the buildings lessened, and there was more green. From the map in his head Alexsi realized they were not going toward Fort Bravetta, which the princess had mentioned as the preferred site of executions. Instead they were driving down the old Appian Way. Again from his Michelin map Alexsi remembered that they were approaching the area of the old catacombs where the early Christians had interred their dead.

With Kappler's staff car in the lead, the trucks came to a fork in the road. With a chill Alexsi realized that this was exactly the spot where they said the Apostle Peter had stood and asked his vision of Christ which way he should go.

They took the right fork, and in less than two kilometers turned in to a narrow road between trees. The sign said VIA ARDEATINA. It ended in a large clearing facing the side of a hill exposed in stone with green on top. There were three entrances in the side of the hill that looked like the mouths of caves.

Dear Lord, Alexsi thought automatically. He had once before been confronted with that canto from Dante's *Inferno*. As a prisoner in the Lubyanka in Moscow, during his first meeting with his spy mentor Yakushev. Given the choice between service or death. Yakushev, the devil, had expected him to recognize the quote, since the NKVD had trapped him at the library at Baku and of course knew which books he checked out. He'd been so frightened that when Yakushev demanded that he think up his own code name, he had picked Dante. Alexsi would not forget the quotation.

"Through me is the way into the woeful city of woe,
Through me is the way into eternal woe,
Through me is the way among the lost people.
Justice moved my lofty maker:
The Divine Power, the Supreme Wisdom and the Primal Love made me.
Before me were no things created,
Unless eternal, and I eternal last.
Leave every hope, ye who enter!"

The sign at the gates of hell.

Alexsi looked at his watch. It was just before two thirty.

"Schnell!" came the shout.

Alexsi climbed out of the small wireless truck with his two junior signalers. Dieter and Horst, the Enigma coders. The rest he had left behind at the message center.

At the top of the hill he could see some regular army soldiers, who he guessed had been brought in to secure the perimeter of the site.

Kappler and the more senior officers were huddled together on the other side of the clearing. The shouting was coming from SD Captain Shütz, who apparently had been put in charge for the moment. Kappler had picked well, Alexsi thought. When a prisoner he had been torturing defiantly told him he had the eyes of a hyena, Shütz was so flattered he bragged about it in the mess for the rest of the day.

Shütz was haranguing the SS enlisted. As Alexsi and the signalers joined the formation, Shütz was shouting, "Everyone is ordered to take part! Any soldier who refuses will be shot along with the Italians! Is that understood?"

At that Alexsi took his two signalers by the arms and led them back to the wireless truck.

"Do you think he was telling the truth?" Horst asked.

Alexsi refrained from rolling his eyes. "No. He's just trying to frighten you so no one will give him any trouble."

"He did a good job of it," said Dieter.

The trucks that had transported the SS drove off. The troops milled about.

A few minutes later the prisoner trucks began to arrive. Metal-sided trucks that the Italians used to deliver meat. They rolled the doors open and the prisoners were ordered out, blinking at the sun after the darkness of the trucks. They were tied together in pairs.

Alexsi had slightly rolled up the canvas covering of the wireless truck, and was watching through the wooden slats. Some of the prisoners were heavily bruised from recent beatings. He could see their body language deflate as they took in the black entrances to the caves and the SS brandishing their rifles. Only a fool wouldn't be able to guess his fate.

One of the prisoners cried out in a loud voice, in Italian, "Father, bless us!"

As Alexsi watched, another prisoner began thrashing in his bonds. And, unbelievably, managed to break free from the ropes. Alexsi expected him to run, or attack the guards, but instead the man dropped to his knees and began to pray. He raised his hand like a priest to bless the prisoners, who all began to rush in close to him. Some also dropped to their knees.

The SS rushed in, shouting and clubbing with rifles and pistols.

"Should we help?" Horst asked anxiously.

"If you like," Alexsi replied. "You won't get a medal for it, though."

Both signalers stayed put.

In the confusion Alexsi watched the prisoner who had been tied to the priest break out of the melee and rush off up the side of the hill, trailing his ropes. Good luck to you, my friend, Alexsi thought. They may shoot you, but not as a sheep.

Alexsi rubbed his eyes. It had brought back the memory of a night when, much too young, he had first seen all the horrors of the world. The reason why, though he might be a killer when he had to be, he would never be an executioner. Never. No matter what it cost him.

"Are you all right?" said Dieter.

"I'm fine," Alexsi replied. "I'm just tired."

38

Alexsi had never even sat in an automobile before. He subtly bounced around a bit on the padded seat, which seemed incredibly luxurious even though he was occasionally jabbed by a protruding spring.

He leaned over the front seat and carefully watched how the secret policeman changed gears and used the foot pedals. In the newspapers they posted on the wall of the school, because of course there was only one copy, they were always talking about tractors. But neither their kolkhoz nor any of the other farms he knew about had one. He'd only seen pictures.

The driver watched him watching him in the mirror and smiled. "What is your name again?"

"Alexsi, Comrade." He had always been taught to use his patronymic when making introductions, but Alexsi Ivanovich no longer had any desire to use his father's name.

"Alexsi. You may call me Viktor."

Alexsi had known he was a Russian, not an Azeri. And he spoke as if it wasn't his real name. "Thank you, Comrade Viktor."

Again silence passed between them. Comrade Viktor said, "Usually boys your age never stop asking questions. You don't. That is good."

Alexsi had learned that listening was always better, because at best whenever he asked a question he was ignored. Most of the time he was hit. Except for the Shulzes, and at school.

"The drive will be long," Comrade Viktor told him. "Use the blanket under the seat and try and get some sleep."

The blanket was good quality wool, and clean. Alexsi had been afraid it would smell like the seats, but it didn't. He guessed that the Chekists kept it for themselves. They probably didn't care if the enemies of the people were cold or not. Which at least meant that he wasn't an enemy of the people. It wasn't easy to get to sleep, because this automobile bounced worse than a pony. Especially as the dirt roads became even poorer and they left the solid green farming belt of the Kura River basin behind, moving through foothills that varied between green pasture and rocky desert.

Alexsi stared out the back window. Pyotr on the kolkhoz had taught him to find Polaris to navigate by at night, and the stars were brilliant tonight. They were heading roughly east. The moon was the color of bone, and made the brown hills shine blue. He had a general idea where the roads were, and it was said there were nearly none in the desert country. Perhaps they were going to Baku. He had always dreamed of seeing the city. Without an internal passport you were not allowed to go away from the kolkhoz, and you would never get a passport because the authorities knew that otherwise everyone would move away from the kolkhoz. When they got drunk people called it the Russians' second serfdom. Most of the older boys planned to get away by joining the army.

They passed through villages that looked even poorer than his, with not a single lantern showing in the darkness. Even the most violent bouncing over rutted roads was not enough to keep a thirteen-year-old boy awake for long, but the car coming to an abrupt stop did.

"Are we there?" Alexsi asked sleepily. Though he had no idea where "there" might be.

"No," Comrade Viktor replied. "The auto needs petrol."

Alexsi sat up. They were inside a small walled compound. A uniformed secret policeman was closing a metal gate behind them.

"Do you need to piss?" Comrade Viktor asked.

"Yes, Comrade."

That seemed to pose a dilemma that required Comrade Viktor to think it over. "You cannot come inside the building. Go against that wall over here," he decided, pointing. "Come *right* back to the car. Do not wander around, do you understand?"

"Yes, Comrade."

"You may walk around the car to stretch your legs, but it is forbidden for you to leave the area of the car."

"I understand, Comrade."

"Be sure you do." He slammed the door behind him and went into the building with the policeman who had closed the gate, the two of them talking.

Alexsi bounced out of the car. Another gate guard was standing there, looking him over. He seemed to be as large as a wall himself. "He told me I could go piss by the wall, Comrade."

"You'll have to" was the answer. "You cannot go inside. Were you told not to wander about?"

"Yes, Comrade. Piss and then back to the car."

"See that you do." Then, as an afterthought, "Shit in my compound and I'll break your head, see?"

"I understand, Comrade."

"Wait until you're back on the road to do that."

"Yes, Comrade."

Alexsi walked over to the wall, looking around all the time, and pissed in the corner. The building seemed small, not more than fifty meters long. And there was obviously not much storage room inside, because the compound wall was lined with drums and stacks of wooden crates. He picked at the wall with a finger as he leaned against it, and a chunk fell away. Too much sand, not enough cement. Same as the farm. There was never enough concrete allocated to do the job, so everyone always put in more sand to make it go further.

The top was covered in barbed wire. He listened carefully. All the sounds of people living. From the sounds it seemed they were in the middle of at least a village, if not a town.

Alexsi looked back at the car. The secret policeman who'd been watching him had disappeared. The only light at the front of the building was on the entrance, where the car was parked. There seemed to be another faint light at the back, and flickering shadows as if something was going on. He looked down the wall, and back at the car again. Buttoning his trousers, he began moving down the wall, as quietly as if he were hunting rabbits.

He slipped in between two rows of steel drums, close enough to see the far corner of the building. A truck with a canvas top was parked near a back door, and a light higher up on the side of the building shone down on it.

A man wearing dark coveralls came around the side of the truck and knocked softly on the door. A moment later it opened and a man stumbled out, as if he'd been pushed. He straightened up and held a hand to his eyes, as if the light was blinding him. An instant later another man stepped out of the shadows behind him and raised a revolver.

There was nothing but a loud metal snap, and Alexsi thought the pistol had misfired. The old hunting shotguns on the farm sometimes did that; the hammer would fall with that same snap but something was wrong with the shells and they wouldn't go off. But here the man the pistol was aimed at crumpled to the ground as if his spine had been broken.

Alexsi watched open-mouthed as the man in coveralls was joined by another, identically dressed. They picked up the body by the shoulders and feet and, swinging it to and fro to build up momentum, heaved it like a sack of seed into the back of the truck.

One of the coveralls rubbed the small of his back and spoke for the first time, to the man with the revolver. "Why in hell don't you have them climb into the truck, and then do it for them then?"

The executioner wore a uniform, but no cap. "And if the bullet goes through his neck into the truck, what then?"

"Who gives a shit? At least we won't have to lift his carcass in," said the second coveralls. He turned toward the light and Alexsi could see from the bloodstains why they wore what they wore.

"Fuck your mother," the executioner informed him. He stepped back into the darkness.

The two coveralls looked at each other and shook their heads. One disappeared from sight, and the other knocked on the door again.

Another victim was pushed out the door and shot in the back of the head. They threw him into the truck.

"You fat son of a bitch," one of the coveralls groaned.

The other turned toward the truck and sniffed loudly. "Ah, one of these shit himself."

"Before or after?" the first coverall said, snickering.

"Fuck your mother, and yourself for free," the other said louder. "You can wash the truck out afterward."

"You'll both wash the truck," the executioner said flatly. He was dropping fresh cartridges into the cylinder of his revolver. "There had better not be many more. I feel the silencer clogging up."

A silencer. Alexsi had wondered about the thick pipe on the end of the revolver, that made it look so different from the ones of all the Che-kists he'd seen lately. That was why there was no sound, and no flame from the barrel like a shotgun.

"So what?" one of the coveralls said.

"You won't say that if it blows up," said the executioner, gesturing with the revolver. "You don't know what it was like before they *finally* filled the requisition for this. Having to take them out to the desert *alive*, and after you did the first one all the screaming and praying?"

"If we had a nice soundproof cellar like every other station we wouldn't need to worry about anything," said a coverall. "Have a couple of prisoners load and unload the truck, then get rid of them out in the desert."

"Then dig a cellar, you bastard," said the executioner.

"He doesn't even want to load the truck," the other coverall said, laughing. "How is he going to dig a cellar?"

"Fuck your mothers," the injured party told them.

Alexsi was transfixed. It was just like listening to a group of demons discussing their work. And except for doing murder they sounded just like the men on the farm.

Finished with the reloading, the executioner closed the cylinder of his revolver with a loud snap. It had been so quiet before; Alexsi jumped at the unexpected sound and his shoulder hit an empty steel drum behind him.

"Did you hear that?" one of the coveralls said.

"Hear what?" the other replied.

But the executioner was already running toward the sound, his pistol leveled. He reached the barrels and clicked on his torch. The dying bat-teries cast a faint yellow light between the barrels. Nothing there.

The executioner whirled and swept his light across the compound. At the edge of the beam there was just the briefest darting shadow at the far corner.

Alexsi was sitting in the car when the executioner tore open the door and dragged him out by the hair.

"I'll teach you to spy, you little shit."

The executioner had blond hair and a pale face that looked like a skull in the half-light. Alexsi was forced down onto his knees. He felt the silencer pipe jabbing into the back of his neck and began shivering uncontrollably. He heard the click of the pistol hammer cocking back.

"Stop!" came a shout from off to the side. It was Comrade Viktor. "What the devil do you think you're doing?"

Alexsi was looking down at the dirt. His eyesight seemed to have gone fuzzy, but for some reason his hearing was crystal clear.

"This little rat was spying on us," the executioner shouted.

"Spying on *what*?" Comrade Viktor shouted back.

The executioner dropped his voice to a hiss, as if to keep a secret. "We were doing wet work back there. And he saw it." Shaking Alexsi's head for emphasis.

Alexsi was used to being shaken, but it seemed like all his muscles were gone and he was being held upright only by his hair.

"You were doing the work *where*?" Comrade Viktor demanded.

The executioner was pointing with his pistol. "The back of the building."

Comrade Viktor looked at the open car door, and then down at Alexsi. "And he saw all this from . . . the back of the *car*?"

The questions were making the executioner even angrier. "We heard him, and then we found him here. Where the hell were *you*, anyway? Letting him roam around loose."

"Oh, you *heard* him," Comrade Viktor said calmly, as if now more sure of his ground. "You heard *something*. You didn't *see* anything. So it had to be him." He lightly prodded Alexsi in the stomach with his boot. "Eh, so what were you doing?"

"I went to piss against the wall, like you told me to," Alexsi muttered at the dirt, his teeth chattering. "Then I came back to the car, like you told me to."

The executioner bent down and shouted into his ear. "Liar!" Then he straightened up and took a different tack. "What are we arguing about? Just get rid of him. Why take a chance? We'll take care of everything."

"The boy is not a prisoner," said Comrade Viktor. "I have orders to deliver him. And I *will* deliver him."

"You just want to get out of here so your mistake doesn't come to light!" The executioner had gone back to shouting.

The front door of the building slammed. Everyone looked over. Alexsi's head was jerked in that direction when the executioner shifted his body.

An officer was walking across the courtyard with a sergeant, who had obviously fetched him. The officer was still buttoning his tunic, and his pistol belt hung open at his front. His face said that he'd been woken up, and he was angry the way people are who are woken up before their time.

Everyone saluted.

The officer ignored them, still buttoning up his uniform. "What the hell is going on here?"

The executioner, taking advantage of home field, began to shout his accusations.

The officer silenced him with one finger held up. "My hearing is perfectly fine, Voikov."

For the first time the executioner was subdued. "Sorry, Comrade Lieutenant." He then repeated his accusations in a calmer tone, occasionally rising as his agitation heated up.

Then Comrade Viktor presented his case, much more calmly.

The lieutenant looked down at Alexsi. "You, boy. What have you been up to tonight?"

The executioner jerked Alexsi's head up so he was looking eye-to-eye at the lieutenant. Alexsi had stopped shaking, but his shirt was wet with perspiration. "Your Honor, I was told to go piss against the wall and go back to the car. I pissed against wall and went back to the car. Nothing else."

The lieutenant kept looking at him, and Alexsi held his gaze.

"Give me that torch," the lieutenant snapped at the executioner, who had to let go of Alexsi's hair in order to hand it over. Suddenly without support, Alexsi weaved about and might have fallen over except that a moment later the hand violently grabbed his hair again.

The lieutenant clicked on the torch as he walked over to the wall. Then the beam went out. He banged the light on the heel of his hand, swearing loudly, and it came back on even dimmer. He examined the wet piss-stain circle on the wall.

The enlisted men cautiously eyed each other.

The lieutenant aimed the beam toward the back of the building, then returned, his boots crunching on the packed gravel.

They all waited while he thought it over.

Finally the lieutenant pointed to the executioner. "Voikov, get back to your work and make sure you finish before the sun comes up." Then the finger spun around to Comrade Viktor. "You, get your petrol and be on your way." And then he turned on the sergeant. "The next time I have to get up and do your job, I'll find someone else to do your job."

They all saluted, but he was halfway back to the building.

The sergeant turned on the executioner. "The next time you make trouble for me I'll have your balls." Then he stalked off.

Comrade Viktor allowed himself a smug smile in the executioner's direction.

Furious, the executioner released his grip on Alexsi's hair with a shove that sent him hurtling face-first into the ground. Alexsi both heard and felt his boots crunching off.

"Get in the car," Comrade Viktor said coldly.

Alexsi practically leaped into the backseat and curled up into a ball with the blanket wrapped over his head for protection.

Comrade Viktor went back for the two petrol cans he had set down, and poured the petrol into the car. Then he got into the car, beeped the horn for the gate to open, and drove off without another word to anyone.

Huddled under the blanket, Alexsi knew that the only reason he was still alive was because Comrade Viktor had no choice but to defend him or get into trouble for leaving him alone.

They drove in silence until the sun came up and Comrade Viktor stopped the car by the side of the road. "Don't bother pretending you're asleep," he said.

Alexsi came out from under the security of the blanket. In the distance were wooden oil derricks, the first ones he had ever seen outside a book. He prepared himself to be dragged out of the car and beaten.

Instead Comrade Viktor handed him a military mess tin and a spoon. The tin was warm and heavy. Alexsi undid the folding latch and carefully pried off the metal top part, that was like a big cup. The prospect of eating from a mess tin was so wonderfully exotic that he'd almost forgotten his brush with death.

The bigger bottom container was full of soup. He gave an exploratory stir with his spoon. Meat soup! He'd never seen that much meat in a soup before. It wasn't too hot, so he blocked off the contents with the spoon and drank off the liquid so he could see how much was in it. The entire bottom of the tin was filled with chunks of lamb and onions and carrots. He wanted to eat them slowly, but he couldn't. The lamb was so tender and delicious, not like the hearts and lungs, left over from the slaughtering, that he was used to. No wonder the Chekists were all so big.

"Don't eat so fast, I don't want you throwing up," Comrade Viktor grumbled, handing him a third of the large loaf of black bread he'd just cut, and a mug of black tea from a thermos. "And don't spill anything back there."

It all must have come from the death compound. Then it had definitely been worth almost dying. Alexsi broke the bread up evenly and distributed it in his pockets, just in case there was no food later.

He only handed the mess tin back after he'd scraped it empty with his spoon and wiped it clean with a small piece of the bread. He'd finished long before Comrade Viktor, and waited until the after-meal cigarette was lit. They both pissed along the road and then continued driving.

Now they were in pure desert, with no plant life at all except brown scrub bushes.

Suddenly out of the sandy hills more oil derricks came into view, and Alexsi nearly fell out of the car window looking at them. He could actually smell the oil in the air. He was feeling more confident now that he wouldn't be punished for what had happened in the night.

The oil workers' clothes and faces were all black from the oil. At least, Alexsi thought it was that. He didn't think that only black men were made to be oil workers.

Alexsi wondered how Comrade Viktor could keep driving for so long; it was hard for him to even sit still for that long. But Comrade Viktor was smoking many cigarettes and drinking nearly all of the tea.

Near noon he thought he could see the outlines of Baku in the distance, but he'd thought that before and been wrong. Tantalizingly short of the city they turned off the main road onto a narrower one. The new road was lined with trees so thick that he could barely see through them. After many twists and turns they came upon an amazing house. It was made of white stone and it was huge, bigger than anything Alexsi had ever seen before. There were actually three floors and a massive peaked roof. It looked like the pictures of the homes of the aristocratic exploiters from books. He'd never understood why the government put them in books, because such houses made you want to be an aristocratic exploiter.

"We are here," Comrade Viktor announced.

Alexsi didn't yet feel confident enough of his position to ask where "here" was. He got out of the car only after Comrade Viktor did. The pale stone shone in the early-morning light. There was a darker stone fountain in front. Birds were chirping. Maybe it was going to be a reward, like in a fairy tale. Then he thought of the bodies being heaved into the truck, so maybe not. In the Brothers Grimm stories, something that looked good at first had a way of turning out to be something bad. But at least it would be something different. It seemed he had always fended for himself, in one way or another, so he wasn't terrified of that the way another boy his age would have been.

He stood there looking up at that huge, grand house, and Comrade Viktor came around the car and up behind him.

Then Alexsi was grabbed by his jacket collar and twisted around. Comrade Viktor took hold of the jacket lapels and hoisted him nearly off his feet, though he had bent down so they were nearly face-to-face.

"You have oil on the back of your jacket," Comrade Viktor said.

Alexsi's stomach began to hurt.

Comrade Viktor laughed softly. "Little liar. You saw it all, didn't you?"

The cigarette breath washed over him. Alexsi was too frightened to speak.

Comrade Viktor laughed again. "That's all right. Maybe you learned something about what happens to people who can't keep their mouths shut and do what they're told. So tell me, little liar, did you lie about *everything*?"

Alexsi felt like he was going to throw up the soup.

Comrade Viktor gave a little jerk on his jacket, as if for emphasis. "Don't worry, little liar. I don't care. We have a quota to fulfill, just like you do on the farm. And stool pigeons like you only make it easier to meet the norms." He released his grip on Alexsi's jacket and straightened up. "Remember this. The only people who won't be arrested are the bosses and the ones they need to arrest the enemies of the state. So you'd better stay in line."

He gave Alexsi a shove to get him moving toward the front door of the mansion, and raised an expansive arm in its direction. "This is an orphanage. It is your new home. And Comrade Stalin is your father now."

Alexsi wasn't sure how much of an improvement that would be. But at least his debt to the Shulzes was paid. He didn't like being called a stool pigeon. He'd never tattled on anyone before, and wouldn't have needed to if there had been another way to justice, or he'd been big enough to kill them all himself. As they approached the house he saw that the fountain was cracked, and had no water in it.

Comrade Viktor stopped just shy of the front door. Alexsi obediently did the same. "A word of advice before we part, little liar," said Comrade Viktor.

Alexsi turned and looked up at him.

"You had better be ready to fight."

39

1944

ROME, ITALY

More trucks arrived in the clearing. Alexsi heard one of the SS milling about say that these were the ones from Regina Coeli prison. He glanced at his watch. It was just before three thirty.

Kappler was gathered with his officers again. When he was finished speaking, five of them broke off and grabbed five prisoners. With Priebke leading them with his clipboard, they entered the middle of the three caves. Minutes later a volley of muffled gunfire could be heard. Only the five Germans walked out.

Kappler led the second group of five in. Again a ragged volley of gunfire. Then another.

Kappler had brought a case of cognac, and the SS broke it open and began passing the bottles around.

One of the prisoners balked at entering the cave, kicking and screaming when the SS tried to drag him. After a short struggle the guards gave up and beat him to death with their rifle butts in full view of all the others. They dragged the body into the cave. After that the Italians waiting their turn seemed to decide that a bullet was preferable. The crying and praying had mostly stopped. Instead there was a stunned silence from the prisoners, as if they were in shock. It might have been because the SS grew louder and more vicious the drunker they became.

Alexsi sat in front of the wireless with his headphones on so no one would bother him, idly twisting the frequency dial and half listening to the streams of Morse passing through the ether. Even though most of it was in code and therefore gibberish, the staccato beeping was strangely comforting.

Suddenly Captain Shütz appeared at the back of the wireless truck, shouting, "Get out and do your duty!"

Dieter and Horst immediately leaped out past him. German-soldier reflex.

Alexsi didn't move a muscle.

Shütz waved his Mauser pistol threateningly and screamed, "You too, Bauer! Don't think you're special!"

Alexsi reached across his body and jerked the Walther from his holster, slapping the pistol down hard on the table next to the Morse key. With his hand resting on it, he just stared at Shütz. And in one of the rare times in his life, he allowed his face to reveal exactly what he was thinking.

Alexsi could see Shütz thinking it over, and watched the fear and uncertainty pass across his face. Finally Shütz yanked the canvas covering back across the rear of the truck and disappeared from sight.

Alexsi took his hand off the pistol, though he left the pistol there out on the table. The bullies were all the same. He took the headphones off so he could hear anyone coming now.

The gunfire continued. Alexsi heard trudging feet approaching, and put his hand back on the Walther. But then there was a sound of retching near the ground. He glanced over the tailboard, and Horst the signaler was on his knees vomiting onto the sand. Dieter climbed into the back of the truck, looking weak and pale. Alexsi noticed the bloody handprints on the bottom of his blouse where he had wiped his hands off. His hands were still faintly stained red. It made Alexsi think of Macbeth. *Blood will have blood.* He missed Shakespeare. He wouldn't dare read him now, not even in German. He passed Dieter a canteen, though not his.

He cocked his head in the direction of Horst down in the dirt, and asked Dieter, "Not as easy as you thought?"

"We should have listened to you," Dieter said, putting down the canteen, his breath ragged.

That was how every expression of regret ever began, Alexsi thought. Should have listened.

"When we went in the bodies were in a heap, blocking the way," Dieter said. "They made us try to drag them out of the way. But they were too heavy to move."

Alexsi immediately regretted asking the question. "I really don't need to hear about it."

"We couldn't move them," Dieter went on, as if *he* hadn't heard. "Some of them had their heads blown all the way off."

Alexsi just sighed. One of those who was going to have to confess his sins out loud.

"So they made the next group of Italians climb all the way up on top of the pile," Dieter said. "We had to climb up behind them to shoot them. There were noises coming from the pile, as if some of them weren't dead yet. There were brains on the roof of the cave."

Done puking, Horst climbed into the truck and collapsed weakly onto the bench.

Dieter put the canteen into his hand. "Horst was shaking so badly he missed his man completely. The fellow fell onto the pile of bodies and began screaming. Everyone else had to shoot him. It took him forever to die."

At that Horst dropped the canteen and vomited over the tailboard. The water went spraying out, and then he was dry-heaving.

"Look," Alexsi said. "Why don't you shut up and go find yourselves a drink? It will calm your nerves."

If not your consciences, he thought to himself, after they both jumped down from the truck again.

Another trudging of feet. What now, Alexsi thought. He was expecting Kappler or Priebke. Shütz was just the kind of weasel who would run off to them.

The canvas pulled back, and a head appeared.

"Ah, Klaus," Alexsi exclaimed. "Somehow I was expecting you."

Klaus climbed into the truck.

Alexsi was immediately engulfed in a fog of cognac. Oh, wonderful. A drunken heart-to-heart talk about murder.

Solemnly. "Peter, you must do your duty."

"Klaus, my duty is to send and receive messages. That is what I am doing."

"I am talking about your duty as a German soldier."

"Yes, I know."

"We all have to do these hard things. For a better world."

"Do we, Klaus?"

"Then you will join me at the next turn?"

"No."

"But you killed three partisans with a knife."

"Actually, I shot two of them," said Alexsi. "But fundamentally correct."

"Yet you won't do this."

"Correct."

"But these are partisans."

"Are they?" Alexsi didn't add that it didn't seem to make any difference either way.

"German soldiers were killed. You will not avenge them? You will not prevent another massacre?"

"Which massacre?" Alexsi asked. "That one? Or this one?"

"I don't understand you."

"I know you don't, Klaus."

"Why don't you explain yourself, at least?"

"It's not my habit." Plus, he thought, you'd just blab it to everyone.

"Yes, I know," Klaus said angrily. "That is the way you always talk, isn't it? Plenty of conversation. Plenty of questions. Get everyone talking about themselves, but not you."

I honestly didn't think you were smart enough to notice, Alexsi thought.

Klaus shook his head. "I cannot believe a soldier with an Iron Cross will not do his duty like the rest of us."

Alexsi said, "I did not need to be drunk for that. Why don't you go have another cognac and leave me alone?"

"You want me to leave?"

"I have been hoping for that since you began talking."

Klaus poised himself dramatically over the tailboard. "We are no longer friends."

Alexsi turned to the wireless, therefore turning his back on him. "Your choice, Klaus."

After that they left him alone. It seemed that Kappler did not have time to deal with him. Listening to the shouted conversation going on out in the clearing, he gathered that Kappler was in a dither because the fifty men the Italian Fascist police had promised him to make up his count had not arrived yet. He sent two of his lieutenants in a truck to Regina Coeli prison with orders to bring back the remaining number immediately.

The sun was dropping in the sky. The shooting went on, and the number of Italians in the clearing steadily diminished. Kappler was pacing back and forth, looking at his watch.

Horst and Dieter climbed back in the truck, carrying a bottle of cognac. They sat on the bench, sullen as schoolchildren, passing it back and forth. Alexsi didn't say anything. At least it kept them quiet.

After nearly two hours the two SS lieutenants returned from Regina Coeli with thirty more Italians locked in their truck. Alexsi watched Kappler counting them out and then speaking animatedly with the two lieutenants. Only thirty, Alexsi thought, after making his own count. Twenty short. After what Alexsi presumed to be a tongue-lashing from Kappler, combined with some vigorous body language, the two lieutenants drove off again.

As the sun set, Kappler ordered a few of the vehicles to turn their shielded blackout lights on, so they could see what they were doing. For the first time in his life Alexsi hoped for bombers to be flying overhead. Torches bobbed back and forth as the Italians were led into the cave five at a time.

They were down to only five more waiting to be killed when the truck returned from Regina Coeli with the last twenty.

The final five died at eight o'clock by Alexsi's watch. Kappler had made it under Hitler's twenty-four-hour deadline, so his job was saved. A platoon of German Army engineers moved in to blow the tunnel entrance shut and seal all the evidence from view.

Kappler gathered them all in for a final address. Alexsi jotted it down on a message pad. "The reprisal has been carried out. I know that this has been very hard for some of you, but in cases like this the laws of war must be applied. The best thing for all of you to do is get drunk."

Quite a joke, since most of the killers were already so far gone they could barely stand. But for Alexsi the final bitter joke was that Kappler forgot all about the wireless truck. He had been forced to watch this

nightmare take place all afternoon for nothing. It was yet another example of life's insanity, as if he had needed any more. Instead of just stepping
up and shooting some poor bastard in the head, who was going to die
anyway, he had taken a moral stand. For what good it had done. Now he
was a marked man, with everyone's eyes on him. Exactly where a spy did
not want to be.

Kappler didn't send out his message to the Führer until later that
night from the military headquarters at the Excelsior Hotel. The head of
the SS police in Italy, General Wolff, had flown in that afternoon to hear
the news, as Himmler's personal representative, and of course Kappler
had to tell him first.

40

1944

ROME, ITALY

Alexsi's office door flew open. He was about to exclaim "What the devil!" as a prelude to tongue-lashing the un-knocking lout when he looked up and saw Captain Priebke in the doorway. Instead, he respectfully stood to attention.

Priebke left him in that position, leaning over the desk and carefully leafing through all the papers.

"May I help you with something, Captain?" Alexsi asked respectfully.

Priebke didn't say a word until he picked up the novel lying on the desk. "So you like Karl May, eh?"

"Yes, Captain." Nineteenth-century cowboys and Indians by a German who had never set foot in the American West.

Priebke carefully fanned through the pages as if looking for something. "A very old edition of *Winnetou IV.* I read that as a boy."

"May I help you with something, Captain?" Alexsi repeated.

Priebke tossed the book back onto the desk, scattering the formerly neat stack of message forms. "Report to Colonel Kappler immediately."

"As you order, Captain."

Without a single change of expression, Priebke faced about and walked out.

Alexsi took a moment to breathe. Everything that he used to send messages to the British was sitting on the desk. A chosen page and line number from the May novel, with an identical edition in London's hands, was the basis for his double-transposition message code. Fortunately, he was once again saved by the disciplines of his mentor Comrade Yakushev, forever warning against complacency. The book was never marked, not even a dogeared page. The messages were never composed and coded in his office.

That was a bit warm, though. As he'd feared, he had gone from being an object of dislike among the officers to an object of suspicion. He would have to become familiar with having Priebke looking up his ass.

Alexsi opened his desk drawer and removed the little Beretta pistol he had liberated from the black marketeers. He made sure it was loaded, and the hammer safely down, then slipped it into his right trouser pocket. If he was arrested going through the door, and they took his Walther, then at least he could do something about it once they dropped their guard.

The adjutant's face was usually a clue as to what was happening in the office, but his desk was empty. Alexsi thought it over for a bit, then knocked on Kappler's door.

"Enter."

Kappler was alone, sitting behind his desk. Alexsi clicked his heels and saluted.

Kappler said, "Sit down, Bauer."

Alexsi casually moved a chair off to the side so he could see both Kappler and the door. Also within range of the window. Then he sat and waited.

"SS Polizeiführer Wolff is in Rome," Kappler announced.

Since it was a statement and not a question, Alexsi just sat there attentively.

"He desires a private interview with the Pope," Kappler said.

Again, another statement. Alexsi remained silent, though he sensed it was annoying the colonel.

"I am expected to arrange this," Kappler said. "And I am sick of trying to go through these black-robed bureaucrats of the Holy See, who think it perfectly reasonable that they should take a hundred and twenty-five years to decide that the earth spins on its axis."

Ah, the career was on the line again. But at least no executions for now. Not wanting to provoke him any further, Alexsi said encouragingly, "Yes, Colonel?"

Kappler looked as though he wanted to beat someone, to calm his nerves. "The Princess Santangelo will not accept my telephone calls. She is always conveniently and courteously indisposed." He stood up and began pacing. "I would like to send a couple of men to that haughty bitch's home and drag her here by the hair." He stopped pacing and fixed Alexsi in his gaze. "But unfortunately I cannot. If she wants to, she can facilitate this audience with a single telephone call. If she doesn't then there will be a hundred perfectly good Italian excuses why it cannot be done." Kappler gave him an icy smile. "So I am sending you to arrange this."

"Yes, Colonel," Alexsi said.

That brought Kappler up short. "That's it?"

"Yes, Colonel. A private audience between General Wolff and the Pope. Unless you would like me to do something else."

Probably against his will, Kappler's smile went crooked with amusement. "No. That will be sufficient."

"She will give me her price, Colonel. Shall I telephone you to see if it is acceptable, or would you rather I stay off the phone lines and tell you in person?"

"There is no time to waste," Kappler said. "Telephone me. Otherwise she will think it is a trick if you agree to anything without my authority."

"Yes, Colonel. May I bring them some food from the mess to smooth my way?"

"You mean your cock will not be enough?" Kappler demanded. Then he burst out laughing at his own wit.

Silence from Alexsi.

"Yes, yes, of course," Kappler said. "Whatever it takes. You know, I almost feel bad about this, Bauer. I hope she's all right in bed, because that snotty bitch annoys me so much I would need Spanish fly."

"With your permission, Colonel, I will leave immediately. I will telephone as soon as possible."

"And I will call for a staff car so you do not have to take a motorcycle this time."

Letting me know how much he knows, Alexsi thought.

"Efficient as always, Bauer," Kappler said, though the smile had turned chilly again. "Keep it up. Your efficiency covers a multitude of sins."

41

"Rome is starving," the Princess Santangelo said sadly, as her servants unloaded the flour and canned meat from Alexsi's staff car.

That was why Alexsi had brought the food. Some women had rioted at a bakery that had no bread. It had spread across the city, and then some women and children attacked a bakery in Ostiense that served the German Army. Thinking that being women and children would let them get away with it. His former friend Klaus's SS section dragged ten of them onto the Ponte di Ferro and machine-gunned them into the Tiber. In the cause of a better world, of course.

"The Allies bombed the rail yards to stop the munitions trains," Alexsi said. "Supplies can only come up in trucks, and most of them are being sent to the front."

"I know," the princess said. "The planes strafed some trucks belonging to the church, that were painted with the red cross."

She was quite well informed. "The army was painting red crosses on ammunition trucks," said Alexsi. "The Allies got wise to the trick." He didn't mention that it might have been his reporting.

"So Rome will starve until the Allies come," the princess said. "And the Allies do not come." She looked out over the city. "How could they have been stopped at Anzio, where it is as flat as a slice of bread? They must have wanted it that way. Let the Germans clean out the resistance, terrorize the old authority, weaken the church. That way when they arrive there will be no one to challenge them, and they can put in power whoever they wish."

As a Russian, Alexsi had lived among the world's most dedicated conspiracists. In Communism every misfortune was the result of spies, saboteurs, wreckers, counterrevolutionaries. For himself, experience had taught him to believe in incompetence, not conspiracy. But if you mentioned that to anyone who believed in conspiracy, they then regarded you as part of the conspiracy. Always better to keep your mouth shut. In everything.

The princess turned back to him and broke into a laugh, clasping his face between her hands and kissing him deeply. "I am a princess without courtesy, as you correctly pointed out," she said. "I have not thanked you for your gifts. I have not welcomed you to my home. I have not even said how glad I am to see you." She kissed him again, and her tongue found its way into his mouth.

"I think you just took care of all that," said Alexsi.

"Let us go inside," she said. "Italians with their sharp eyes and wagging tongues."

With the Italians you always had to eat first. Alexsi didn't know if that was just their way, or they wanted you full of wine before the bargaining began. In any case, he thought there ought to be a statue erected to the princess's chef. No one else could make German Army canned ham taste like that, with angel hair spaghetti and oil and garlic.

It was just the two of them lunching in the garden. When they were finished, the servants cleared the table and left them with their wine. Alexsi definitely felt softened up. It was a good thing he didn't care about making a good deal for Kappler.

The princess was all business, though. "What does General Wolff want with the Holy Father?"

"I don't know," Alexsi said. "And I don't think Kappler does either. Wolff has Himmler's ear, so it must be important."

"The church must know, then." She began to rise.

Alexsi's outstretched hand urged her back into her chair. "Before you do this, Kappler is waiting for you to present your bill for service." He could see her thinking it over. "May I advise you?"

She smiled warmly. "Of course. Every other man would tell me what to do. You advise me."

"Do not ask for your husband," Alexsi said. He did not fail to see her eyes flash. "Not because I am jealous. Kappler will agree, of course, but then throw up so much red tape and excuses that he cannot get higher authority to give him up. Ask for something he will really give you."

"Like what?" she asked.

Now it was Alexsi's turn to shake his head. "I have no idea."

She smiled at him again, as if he had passed a test. "The son of one of my dear friends was being held in Regina Coeli. Now no one can find him. She fears he was one of those killed at the Ardeatine Caves. The Germans have released no names of those they killed. They do it to torment everyone who has someone imprisoned."

"Was he arrested by the Italians, or the Germans?" Alexsi asked. He wanted to make it easy for her.

"I do not know."

"If it was Germans, and he was arrested before the reprisal, I must tell you he is probably dead."

She put her hand over her mouth. "Were you there?" And then, almost immediately, "Never mind. I did not ask that."

"No," Alexsi said.

She nodded, and the warm look that returned to her eyes justified his lie. Not much of a lie, Alexsi thought. Since she really wanted to know if he killed anyone.

"Are you sure that is what you want to spend your capital on?" he asked. "If this son is misplaced, Kappler can find him and release him. But if he is dead or deported to Germany, he is gone with no recourse. You could instead have Kappler owe you a favor for yourself."

"No. If it was my son, I would want to know."

Alexsi took a message pad and pencil from his pocket and passed it to her. "Give me his name."

She scribbled it out, and one of the servants took him to a room he had never been in before, and plugged in the telephone. Alexsi wondered if there were rooms in that house, fully furnished, that no one had ever spent a moment in. He also envied the electrician who had put in all the phone plugs. A single telephone line, but a plug in every room. The fellow must have made some money.

The switchboard at Via Tasso had to have had orders, because they kept him on hold for a long time while they tracked Kappler down. Alexsi gave him the name, and Kappler replied curtly, "I'll ring you back." At that Alexsi knew he was out of his office, because he would have had the death list Priebke was so diligent in checking off right there.

Alexsi waited by the phone, passing the time trying to put a black-market price on everything in the room.

The phone rang. Kappler said, "He's dead."

Alexsi said, "They will ask me if the family can have the body."

"If they want to get some picks and shovels and go mining in the cave," Kappler said lightly. "Looks like I got the better of the bargain, eh?"

"Yes, Colonel" was all Alexsi said, fighting to keep his voice even. "I will call you back with word from the Vatican."

"I'll be waiting." Kappler made it sound like a threat.

When Alexsi returned from the garden she knew from his face. "*Morto.*"

"I'm sorry," Alexsi said.

"The caves?"

He nodded.

He expected her to cry. She didn't. And from her face, he wondered why he had expected her to cry.

"I cannot tell her this on the telephone," she said. "I will tell her tomorrow."

She looked out at the view of the city, and when she turned back to him her face was rearranged. "I will call the Vatican now."

Alexsi sipped his wine and listened to the birds singing. At least they were enjoying the war. The famous cats of Rome had all disappeared in the last month. Eaten. At least that was one thing he never had to eat. Then he told himself not to speak too soon.

The princess returned, and gave him a classic Italian shrug. "We shall see. The cardinals, well . . . they are cardinals. They will need to have a conclave over it." A pause, then a sly look. "Are you expected back?"

Alexsi grinned. "No. Kappler made you my work today."

"Hmmm. So you are working for me?"

"You could certainly say that."

"So how should I put you to work?"

"My auntie used to say that idle hands are the devil's workshop."

"I am sorry I will never meet this woman," the princess said.

In her bedroom she sat him down on one of the elegant chairs. But she did not undress. She put a record on her player, and an opera began.

"What is that?" Alexsi asked.

"Puccini. *Fanciulla*."

Alexsi didn't have a great history with operas. But when in Rome.

Standing before him, she said, "If you laugh I will kill myself."

"You are not the suicidal type," Alexsi said. "And I will not laugh."

She placed her hands on his shoulders and closed her eyes. "I am at the opera. In a box by myself. You enter and lock the door behind you. You do not say a word. You look at me hungrily for a long time, and it makes me afraid. I ask you what you are doing, but you say nothing. You sit down beside me, moving the chair very close. I get up to leave, but you push me back down. You lift up the bottom of my dress and put your hands on me."

She licked her lips and rubbed herself.

"Do you need me for this?" Alexsi asked politely. "Because you seem to be doing fine on your own."

"*Basta*," she whispered. "You unzip the back of my dress, make me stand up before the audience, and it falls away. I am naked. You make me kneel before you, open your trousers, and satisfy you. When you are ready you have me sit in your lap and move to the music. You still say nothing."

She opened her eyes and looked at him with equal parts trepidation and arousal.

Alexsi said, "Will I need to change into evening clothes for this? Or will imagination suffice?"

She chuckled. "Trust me, there is nothing here that would fit you."

42

1944

ROME, ITALY

The late-afternoon sun was spilling through the window. The princess was dozing in bed beside him.

Alexsi was wondering if it was normal to not have any sexual fantasies. Because other than thinking about having sex itself, he didn't. Everyone else certainly seemed to, though. People were incredibly complicated about that. The Russians had taught him about sexual fantasies, as part of their course of instruction. He had originally thought they were joking, though the NKVD was not generally noted for its sense of humor.

There was a soft knock on the door, and an equally soft male voice said, "*Signora? Telefono.*"

Alexsi shook her lightly on the arm until she came awake. She looked at him wildly for a moment.

Alexsi pointed to the door and said, "Telephone."

She came alive at that, calling out, *"Un momento."*

The princess dressed and checked her hair and makeup in the mirror before going out the door. Alexsi just chuckled into the pillow. Whoever it was would just have to wait.

She returned with a surprised look on her face. "His Holiness will meet with General Wolff on the tenth of May. At noon. The only condition is that the general will wear civilian clothing, not SS uniform."

"They moved pretty quickly, wouldn't you say?"

"For the Vatican? Like lightning," she replied.

So the Pope wanted to meet with General Wolff just as much, if not more. Alexsi knew that when he radioed them the British would become all excited and demand to know details of the meeting. As if he would be invited to sit there with the two of them. A meeting like that would not usually be reported in a wireless message. But if it was, he would read it.

"Will you call Kappler?" she asked.

Alexsi shook his head. "If I do now, I'll have no reason to stay. Sweating over his career tonight will do him good. I'll call tomorrow." He grinned at her. "But if you want to throw me out, I'll call now."

"Not a chance," she said.

43

Alexsi was sitting on the toilet in the latrine, composing a message to London. That Wolff had met with the Pope, and no one but the two of them knew what had been said. Also the location of the vulnerable-looking unit boundary between the German 362nd Infantry Division and Hermann Göring Panzer on Monte Artemisio. It might do someone some good.

From the Karl May novel he selected a random word, noting the page, line, and number in the line for the message prefix the decoder would use. "*Schlucht.*" "Valley" in English. He wrote it across the top of a single sheet of tissue paper on his clipboard, dropping the second *c* and *h*. The message underneath it in rows under each letter. Above "*schlut*" the alphabetical order of each letter, 412365. Then turning each column down into a line across, in the order of one through six. With that complete, a second transposition of that coded text, using the randomly selected keyword "*hohepunkt*," or "summit." He was halfway through when the door banged. Alexsi immediately balled up the paper and fired it through his legs into the toilet.

Captain Priebke appeared around the corner. Alexsi had his message clipboard across his knees, the Karl May novel open upon it.

Standing over him, Priebke snatched the clipboard and the book. "What are you doing?"

Alexsi reached back over his shoulder and yanked the chain, flushing the toilet. "Are you serious, Captain?"

Priebke was thumbing through the clipboard.

"Captain," Alexsi said in a patient voice. "If you are searching for a particular message, would it be possible to wait until I am finished here, and then we may look for it in my office?"

Priebke thrust the clipboard back into his hand. "Never mind."

He vanished around the corner, and the latrine door banged shut again.

Alexsi waited a few minutes, then pulled up his trousers. He had to splash some cold water on his face. Things were getting a bit too hot, he thought as he examined his face in the mirror. Next Priebke would be observing closely, either personally or with an informer, while he sent his test messages at midnight. The walls were closing in once again, and the British would have to live without their spy for a while. All praise, though, to the disciplines of Comrade Yakushev, who insisted that every secret message be composed and coded where the evidence could be disposed of immediately.

Back in the message center, Horst, who had spilled his guts at the Ardeatine Caves, said, "I'm glad you're here."

"What is it?" Alexsi asked.

Horst handed him a message.

Alexsi glanced at it. Just a standard wireless message, still in code.

He was about to ask why it hadn't been decoded yet when his eyes fell on the unencrypted message heading. Which listed the sender's and receiver's call signs, the time the message was created, the fact that there were four parts to it, that this was the first part, that it had two hundred and five characters, and then . . . there was an extra three-letter code.

"I've never seen this urgency code before," Alexsi said. "What is it?"

Horst handed him the bound Enigma codebook, and pointed to the correct three-letter group.

"'Commanding officer only decode,'" Alexsi read. "What sender call sign is this?"

"Berlin," said Horst. "*Reichsführer* SS."

Alexsi gave a low whistle. Probably from Himmler himself.

"Something big," said Horst.

"That we are not meant to see," said Alexsi. "All right. Good job. I'll take it in to the colonel. Have the other three parts come in yet?"

"Not yet."

"When they do, have them ready."

When he went through the office door, the adjutant only looked up and raised one eyebrow. Alexsi held up the message.

"Go ahead," the adjutant said.

Alexsi knocked on the door.

"Enter."

Kappler was at his desk signing papers. "What is it, Bauer?"

"Colonel, this message has just come in from the headquarters of the *Reichsführer*. It is required that you decode it yourself."

Kappler looked up, and Alexsi saw that he had his full attention.

"Since I have never done this before," said Kappler, "I assume that we have never received such a message."

"No, Colonel. Shall I have my men bring the Enigma here?"

"No," Kappler said after a moment's consideration. "I will come to you, to see how this works."

They went down the hall to the message center, then into the wireless room.

Horst leaped to attention.

Kappler returned his salute casually.

Alexsi said, "Take a break, Horst. I will listen for incoming messages."

The Enigma looked like a large typewriter in a wooden box. It had keys just like a typewriter, but above them was a lamp board in the same letter configuration as the keyboard. Above the lamp board were the three rotor dials positioned vertically in a row.

Kappler peered at the machine as if he expected it to blow up at any moment.

"Shall I instruct you in the operation, Colonel?" Alexsi asked.

Kappler shook his head. "I certainly don't have time for that. You will do it, and explain to me as you go along."

Too lazy to do the work, but he wanted to know how in case anyone asked him later if he had done it. Kappler would make a decent spy, Alexsi thought. "Very good, Colonel."

Alexsi handed him a pencil and a clipboard with a blank *Funkspruch* form in it. The standard blank message form, graphed in groups of five to code and decode messages. "When I key in a letter, the decoded letter will flash in the lamp board. You will have to write it down."

Alexsi clipped the message to the tilted board beside the machine. "The heading of the message shows the rotor start position is JDU. I turn the rotor wheels to J, D, and U. The second three letters in the heading are KEB. I type in those letters." When he did, the lamp board flashed RXK. "RXK is my rotor setting to decrypt this message." Alexsi spun the rotor wheels accordingly. "Now, when I type in each letter of the coded message, the lamp board will flash with each decoded letter."

"What an incredible pain in the ass," Kappler exclaimed. "You have to do this with every message that comes in?"

"Yes, Colonel. Each day at midnight I take the monthly key sheet from the safe. I install the correct wheels, the correct ring settings, and the plug connections on the keyboard for that day. I then lock the machine. The operator is only authorized to select the rotor start position." Alexsi didn't mention that was when he sent his test message to make sure the day's key setting was correct. And then when he had something to report, after that a practice training message that the German operator on the other end would not bother to decode. But the British would.

"The things we have to do to keep the Allies from reading our mail. You must remind me to send some schnapps to your signalers."

"Yes, Colonel."

Alexsi began typing in the coded message.

"Slow down, slow down," Kappler muttered, the pencil scratching paper as he strained to keep up.

"Yes, Colonel."

When the message was finished, Kappler was frowning at the paper. "All right, what is FRAGE?"

"The machine only processes letters, Colonel. FRAGE is a question mark. ZZ a comma. X is a full stop. Numbers are NULL, EINZ, ZWO . . ."

"All right, now I have it," said Kappler, making corrections with his pencil.

When all four messages were decoded, Kappler gathered up all the papers and the original messages. "Let's go back to my office."

Alexsi opened the door and said, "You may return, Horst."

Kappler sent the adjutant away and locked his office door, quite melodramatically, Alexsi thought. Though he was used to it by now.

"You signalers are sharp fellows," Kappler said, settling into his chair. "Now I see why. I know you were watching those lights flash. You probably have the entire message in your head, don't you?"

"Colonel . . ."

"Don't worry, don't worry," Kappler said soothingly. "I was the one who ordered you to decode it, wasn't I? I'm going to need some help in this anyway, and you're just what the doctor ordered. Now, to summarize. Reichsführer Himmler has learned about General Wolff's meeting with the Pope."

Kappler's wolfish grin left no doubt as to who had passed that information to Himmler. "The Reichsführer is not satisfied with General Wolff's explanation for this incredible meeting, which he did not authorize. He feels that General Wolff may be trying to ingratiate himself with the Pope to gain some absolution for his sins in the event Germany loses the war. Perhaps even trying to enlist the Pope to negotiate a separate peace with the Americans and British. This of course is treason."

Alexsi saw Kappler trying to arrange a vacancy for an SS general, which he would be the perfect man to fill.

"The Americans and British are making their final push on Rome," Kappler said. "They are less than seventy miles away. If the front crumbles the Führer will decide the final fate of Rome. If he orders the city destroyed, it will be destroyed. If it is left up to Kesselring, I suspect that he will not wish to go down in history as the man who destroyed Rome. He will do what he always does: fight like the devil, then make a quick withdrawal to another fortified line behind him, leaving the Allies punching air. When Mussolini went down last year, the Führer was on the verge of having the Pope seized and taken out of Italy under our control. Our craven diplomats convinced him it would cause a general uprising among the Italians."

Kappler snorted in derision at that.

"If we are leaving Rome, it makes no difference," he said. "I will propose to the Reichsführer that before the Allies arrive I go into Vatican City and take control of the Pope and as much of the church archive as I can get my hands on. We will say that the Pope has asked to be put under our protection for his own safety. There will be no one to say otherwise—the Pope will not be giving any more press conferences. It will be the work of one night. We can clean all the spies out of the Vatican with a single blow! I have some scores to settle with them."

Kappler clapped his hands together with finality. "Now, do you know why I am telling you all this, Bauer?"

"I have no idea, Colonel," Alexsi said.

"Don't disappoint me," Kappler warned.

"You will need me to code the messages to the Reichsführer?" Alexsi said.

"Yes, partly," Kappler said, only slightly appeased. "I will make the plan, but no one will be told of it until the order is given. It must be kept absolutely secret. Whatever legwork needs to be done, you will do it for me." He favored Alexsi with one more wolfish smile. "Only you and I will know about it. So if word leaks out, I will know exactly who did it."

44

Alexsi was back in his office, all of Kappler's messages to Himmler spread out across his desk.

As far as he was concerned, Hitler holding the Pope in comfortable captivity in some castle in Liechtenstein was not going to make the slightest difference to the course of the war. And so was definitely not worth risking his neck over.

Unfortunately, the Germans persuading the Pope to talk on the radio about the German Army's fight against Communism was exactly the sort of thing that would make every politician in London, Washington, and Moscow go completely mad.

It was a consideration. Not one worth risking his life over, but a consideration nonetheless.

So the question was: How to sabotage this scheme?

The easiest thing would be to mention to Princess Santangelo that the Pope ought to take off his vestments, dress as a regular priest, and take a powder until this all blew over. Would the Pope do it? Well, that wasn't his problem. His problem was that even though the church was good at keeping secrets, this was still Italy. Eventually the word would get out that the Pope had skipped town. And Kappler would know exactly who the stool pigeon was.

Another option would be to mention to the princess that perhaps a thousand Italians needed to start camping out in St. Peter's Square to keep the Pope from any harm. The church would certainly feed them.

Alexsi immediately dismissed that. Kappler would just shoot ten of them, in front of the rest, who would then go home and leave him with a free hand.

There didn't seem to be any other solution. The Pope's Swiss Guards probably had some guns rusting away somewhere in the basement, but those nice Catholic boys in their cute Renaissance costumes certainly weren't going to stop the SS, even if they knew the SS was coming.

Alexsi leaned back in his chair and put his feet up on the desk, thinking that it was easy to be a saint only in paradise. One of the message forms stuck to the heel of his boot, and he had to rock forward to pull it off.

Holding it in his hand, he laughed out loud. He had been playing a German so long that he was beginning to think like one. Always choosing the most complicated solution to every problem.

All he had to do was not transmit Kappler's messages to Himmler. Kappler would never move a muscle without permission. And Himmler couldn't approve a scheme he knew nothing about.

It was perfect.

Alexsi briefly considered substituting his own message from Kappler to Himmler, just something like Kappler saying he understood and was working on the problem. He just as quickly dismissed that as too much

German complication. Kappler might telephone or send another message, and Berlin might refer back to that one. And the jig would be up for Alexsi Ivanovich. Too risky. No, not sending anything at all would buy plenty of time, especially considering how many messages went to Himmler on a given day. And if Berlin got impatient and wanted to know what was up in Rome, it would be their fault they misplaced Kappler's communications in the first place. Because Rome had certainly sent them.

Hopefully by the time it was retransmitted it would be too late.

In retrospect, it was fortunate that Kappler had kept it between the two of them, even though it had scared him to death at the time.

Alexsi was definitely not about to tell the British anything about this. They might decide to do something stupid like publicly warn the Germans to leave the Pope alone, which they had done before when Mussolini was overthrown, and that would be his head.

He carefully considered all the possible permutations. No, it seemed perfect. He scooped the messages up and walked over to the wireless room.

Horst was still on duty.

"I have to code and transmit these myself for the colonel," Alexsi said. "Go grab a smoke and make sure everyone knows not to come in until I'm finished."

The more corroborating witnesses, that weren't really witnesses, the better.

Alexsi locked both doors to the wireless room. Sitting down at the Enigma, he coded the messages as if he were really going to send them. Then typed all the code onto outgoing-message forms, as if he were really going to send them.

But instead of that he just stamped the messages sent. Adding a notation in his own hand that the originals were in the hands of Colonel Kappler. He dropped them into the sent-message basket, for the clerk to file at the end of the day.

Then he stamped Kappler's originals, adding the date and time they were transmitted, and his signature.

Alexsi sat there twiddling his thumbs, glancing at his watch for the time it would have taken to transmit, had he actually done so.

He unlocked the door and stuck his head through. "I'm finished, Horst. You can come back in."

Up the hall to Kappler's office, feeling much better about things.

The adjutant held up one finger to stop him, then buzzed Kappler on the phone. Hanging it up, he nodded for Alexsi to go in.

Priebke was in there with Kappler. All the better, Alexsi thought. He handed the original message forms across the desk. "These have all been sent, Colonel," he announced. "I did not want to trust them to the signals safe. So I return them to you for safekeeping."

Kappler thumbed through them and noted all the sent-message stamps. "Good thinking, Bauer. Thank you."

"Is there anything else, Colonel?"

"I wish to be informed immediately if any reply comes in about these. Day or night."

"I will make sure all the signals shifts are made aware, Colonel."

"Thank you, Bauer. Carry on."

Alexsi saluted and left the office. When he turned to close the door, there were Priebke's eyes staring right at him.

45

1944

ROME, ITALY

Alexsi could always tell when they were getting ready to make a raid. The alarm section went pounding down the hallways to the armory, then pounding out the door to the motor pool. When that happened, the prisoners in their cells all went suddenly quiet, knowing something was about to happen but not knowing exactly what. And fervently hoping it was not going to happen to them.

His phone rang.

Kappler said, "Gather your arms and meet me at the motor pool."

Nothing to do about it but reply, "Yes, Colonel."

If it was another reprisal, Alexsi wasn't sure he wanted to be the odd man out again. He felt as though he had pushed his luck to the limit at the Ardeatine Caves.

He buckled on his ammunition belt and checked his submachine gun. He thought about a helmet, then decided not. He donned his soft field cap instead. Better to look like a noncombatant than like someone who wanted to be a combatant. He did slip the little Beretta pistol into his trouser pocket, though. Just in case.

Kappler was standing in the Via Tasso courtyard with Priebke. Alexsi walked up to them and saluted.

Kappler said, "We've received a hot tip. Some people we want are gathered at the Princess Santangelo's house. I'm going to send you in while we surround the place. It's up on the top of that stupid hill. If they see us coming you can tell them we're hitting another house on the road. This will give us surprise."

Alexsi didn't see how sending him in first was going to surprise anyone, but he could feel Priebke staring at his face like he was an Italian cinema actress. Without any change of expression, he said, "As you order, Colonel."

Kappler slapped his thigh and said to Priebke, "You see? I told you."

Alexsi hoped Priebke had to pay some money after losing the bet over his disobedience. "Just so you know, Colonel, the princess has said that I must always telephone before I come over."

Kappler had been pleased. Now he frowned at that. "I don't know. Should we make it a complete surprise, and see what happens?"

Priebke said, "I have an idea. Let's get there and surround the place on all sides. From a distance. We find a phone nearby and Bauer calls, as if he was here. All these old palaces have secret hiding places. They'll think they have time enough to run. Bauer's call flushes all the rats right out of the house and into our hands. That way we won't have to worry about missing someone in there."

Kappler's mood brightened, and he slapped his thigh again, with delight. "Wonderful, Erich! Wonderful! We will do just that. Bauer, hop in my staff car."

Alexsi got into the front seat with the driver. Resigned. He had told her that he would do the best he could. This would probably be it. Regardless of Kappler's hot tip, he hoped she had taken the advice he had given before and didn't have any contraband, human or otherwise, in the house.

Priebke pulled a map from his pocket and went to each truck to give the SS their orders. When he was through, he got in the backseat with Kappler, and they drove out through the gates, the trucks following.

They raced through the streets, not that any Italian still driving an automobile would be foolish enough to get in their way.

Alexsi hoped the Italians had someone at the bottom of the road as a lookout, though he doubted it.

Heading up the road to the palazzo, Priebke had the driver stop at one of the houses farther down. "This one looks rich enough to have a phone," he said to Kappler.

Kappler just nodded. He was looking at his watch, to give the other trucks time to get around the hill.

Priebke rapped on the door with the butt of his little Mauser HSc pistol. Alexsi stood slightly behind him, fervently hoping someone would shoot through it.

No such luck, which was no surprise the way his luck had been running.

Also no answer. Priebke rapped on it again, more vigorously this time.

The door was inlaid wood and wrought iron. A beautiful door, Alexsi thought, though now much less beautiful after Priebke hammering gouges into it.

An old lady opened it. Alexsi thought that a smart move. If there was an SS officer pounding on his door, and he had an old lady available, he would have her answer it.

She was frightened out of her wits. "Yes?"

Priebke snapped, in Italian, "You have a telephone?"

"*Si*," she said, stammering it out despite the lack of vowels.

"Take me to it," Priebke ordered, pushing his way through the half-opened door. He had the old lady by the arm, dragging her along as if he were the one who knew where the telephone was.

Fortunately for the old lady's legs, it was sitting on a table in the entrance hallway.

Priebke waved a hand, as if to say, Get on with it.

Alexsi dialed the number. The connection clicked, and the ringing began. Three times, then it was picked up.

"The residence of Colonel the Prince Santangelo."

Alexsi recognized the voice of Paolo, the chief servant. "This is Sergeant Bauer. Would you please inform the princess immediately that I am on my way."

"Yes, sir."

Alexsi hung up.

"That was it?" Priebke demanded.

"You didn't tell me to say anything else," Alexsi replied. "The servants answer the telephone, not her."

"You're too polite," Priebke told him, already halfway to the door. "You need to give these Italians orders. That's all they understand."

As they passed her, Alexsi bowed and said to the old lady, "*Grazie per la sua cortesia, signora.*"

She nodded to him.

Priebke just snorted through his nose.

The staff car raced up the road.

Kappler said, "I have another idea. You will get out before the gate. When they let you in the door, keep it open so they cannot bar it to us. If we don't have to break it open, it will get us in there without delay."

"As you order, Colonel." Though Alexsi suspected that he was going in first to absorb any potential gunfire that might otherwise have come Kappler's way. Then, after he was dead, they could stand off and shoot the house to pieces without any danger to themselves. Since he didn't think there was much chance of that, he wasn't about to argue.

The staff car stopped, and Alexsi unbuckled his ammunition belt. He left it on the seat, along with his Beretta.

"You're not taking your automatic?" Priebke said, amused by it.

"If I'm going in alone, I might as well look like I'm going in alone," Alexsi said. "My pistol will be enough."

Kappler just laughed.

But Alexsi opened one of the Mauser pouches on the belt, and removed an egg grenade. He put it in his pocket.

"What the hell?" said Kappler. "What do you have that for?"

"Roadblocks when I'm driving alone," said Alexsi, wasting as much time as he could.

"No, I mean why are you taking it now?" said Kappler.

"Just in case someone starts shooting, and it takes you too long to reach the door," Alexsi replied.

Kappler laughed again. "You've got balls, Bauer, I'll give you that."

"Get moving!" Priebke ordered.

As soon as he reached the door, Paolo opened it, obviously terrified. Either the princess had told him, or someone had seen the SS getting into position. Or both.

"Remain calm," Alexsi told him. "Just be meek and do whatever they say."

Paolo nodded.

"Oh, leave the door open," Alexsi said. "And for heaven's sake stay away from it, or you'll get a rifle butt in the teeth."

Paolo vanished as fast as he could without running.

The princess came out of a side room. Looking only slightly less upset than Paolo.

"Is everyone out?" Alexsi whispered.

She shook her head furiously. "Hugh is down in the cellar."

"Hugh who?"

"Monsignor O'Flaherty."

Oh, wonderful, Alexsi thought in despair. O'Flaherty was an Irish priest who hid Jews and escaped Allied prisoners of war all over Rome. One of Kappler's personal nemeses. He had Vatican diplomatic immunity, so Kappler couldn't go into Vatican City after him. Not that he wouldn't be one of the first to get the chop if Kappler got permission from Himmler to grab the Pope. O'Flaherty wouldn't stay in the Vatican, though. He ran all over Rome, sometimes in disguise like the Scarlet Pimpernel of the English popular novels. Kappler had never been able to get his hands on him. If Kappler caught him here, both the priest and the princess would have a long talk with Priebke and his brass knuckles and then be shot while trying to escape, before the Vatican could pull strings to get them back.

"Which way to the cellar?" Alexsi hissed. "Quickly!" Kappler and Priebke had just about reached the steps, right behind two SS with submachine guns.

The princess tossed a glance toward one of her servants standing in the far doorway, awaiting her. A man with more loyalty than sense, unlike Paolo.

To keep up the act Alexsi drew his pistol. "Take me to the cellars! At once!" He grabbed the man by the collar and quite literally ran him to the back of the house. Through the kitchen that was bigger than the house he grew up in, then a drab door and stairway down. "Get out of here," Alexsi ordered the loyal fool, and headed down himself.

On the stairs he kept his Walther ready. If anyone was going to be shot by a priest under vows, it was him after this year he had had.

No lights. Just some vague illumination from a few narrow windows above the foundation. With a start Alexsi was reminded of the British embassy in Teheran. It was enough—he wasn't about to turn any electric switch on. He crept along, listening for noises. There was no time for this. "Father!" he said in English, in the loudest possible whisper he could manage. "Father O'Flaherty! Are you here?"

A rustle from a corner, then a faint gleam on light in eyeglasses as the priest stepped out. "Who is it?" he whispered.

Alexsi realized that his German uniform couldn't be seen in the darkness. That would be all he needed, for the priest to start shooting as soon as he came into view.

"I am a German soldier," Alexsi said in English. "But I will not arrest you."

"God bless you, my son."

At least that was what Alexsi thought he said. The Irish accent was nearly as bad as the Scots one. Alexsi holstered his pistol. The priest was very tall, nearly two meters, with a nose like a potato and wire-framed eyeglasses. Alexsi couldn't imagine anyone less distinctive in Rome. How Kappler hadn't caught this fellow was beyond him. "Are you armed?"

"Of course not."

Of course not. "The SS will be in the house at any moment. We have to find you a hiding place." There was no way he was going to get out of the house, not with it surrounded by an SS cordon.

"I've been looking for that myself," the priest said.

There was an incredibly loud bang, and an only slightly less loud rumbling.

Alexsi and the priest both nearly jumped out of their skins. "Shit!" Alexsi yelped.

"Jesus, Mary, and Joseph." The priest crossed himself, though Alexsi didn't think it was on account of his profanity. The bang was metal, not like a gunshot. The rumbling was something not metal hitting metal, but like an earthquake.

There was a short stone hall between two sections of cellar. Alexsi drew his pistol again and dashed down it to see what the noise was.

They were delivering coal, for the kitchen stoves. Shoveling it down the chute to the bin in the cellar.

The priest had followed him.

Alexsi said, "God is definitely with you, Father."

"Of course he is, my son."

Alexsi wished he had that amount of confidence. "Look, take off your . . ." At the moment he couldn't think of the word in English. "Uniform. Take off your eyeglasses. Rub coal all over yourself. Crawl up the chute and leave with the coal men. I'm sure you can persuade them if you tell them you're a priest."

"We are thinking exactly alike, my son."

"Good. Good luck. And good-bye."

The priest insisted on shaking his hand. "God bless you for your humanity, my son." Then he made the sign of the cross over him. "May God, the Father, Son, and Holy Spirit bless you and keep you. May his blessings remain forever with you."

"Thank you." It was all Alexsi could think to say.

He ran back up the stairs and into the kitchen. Two of the SS were just coming through. "Anything?" one of them asked.

Alexsi shook his head.

Kappler was in the sitting room, or one of them at least, with the princess. "Where the devil have you been, Bauer?"

"I thought I saw someone running through the house, Colonel. But I searched and could find no one."

"The princess is adamant that no one was here except she and her servants," Kappler said. "We shall see."

Alexsi holstered his pistol and made to leave.

"Wait here, Bauer," Kappler ordered.

Alexsi stood at rest.

"Colonel, why will you not believe me?" the princess said.

"I don't know," Kappler replied. "There is just something about you I don't find trustworthy."

Alexsi wished she would keep her mouth shut. But he had never known a woman to give up the last word.

Priebke strutted into the room. The body language was unmistakable. "How many fish did we net?" Kappler inquired.

"Five," Priebke said with a satisfied smile. "All on our list."

"Wonderful," Kappler exlaimed. "The Irish priest?"

Priebke shook his head.

"Shit!" Kappler said. "Well, you can't have everything. We'll still turn the house upside down and give it a good shake."

"You'll enjoy this," said Priebke. He snapped his fingers and in came Francesco, the princess's son. With a burly SS man gripping each arm.

Alexsi had to give her credit—she kept her composure.

One of the SS handed Priebke a cloth sack. He emptied it onto the table with a clatter of metal.

Alexsi winced. It was an exquisite table.

Half a dozen handguns. A smaller sack of bullets for them. And banded stacks of lira notes. Quite a sum, from the looks.

The young fool, Alexsi thought. Should have hidden it in the house.

"What do you know," Kappler said, clearly delighted. He nodded to the two SS. "Put him in the truck."

"Nazi bastard!" Francesco shouted. Then turned his head to Alexsi. "All of you!"

All it took was a look from Kappler and one of the guards silenced him with a hard punch to the solar plexus. Francesco bent over, still in their grasp, and vomited onto the floor.

The princess, looking stricken as a mother would, was biting her knuckle to stay silent. But she did stay silent.

"Oh, dear, my feelings are hurt," Kappler said facetiously. "What about you, Bauer?"

Alexsi did not say anything.

"Get him out," Kappler ordered.

Going out the door, Francesco got his wind back and shouted, "*Salve Italia!*"

There was a scream, and Alexsi would have bet that they had thrown him down the stairs. He hoped the brief satisfaction had been worth it.

"Ah, the spirit of youth," Kappler said.

He turned to her. "Princess, you are also under arrest. We shall take you to Regina Coeli." Kappler turned to Alexsi and smiled. "We would not want anyone at Via Tasso to feel softhearted about you and do something foolish. Your son will assist Captain Priebke in his investigations. If he is not helpful, then we shall call you in to fill any gaps in his information."

He nodded to Priebke, who crossed the room and yanked her up roughly by the arm.

Kappler pointed to Alexsi. "Princess, before you leave I want you to know that this man was working for me all along. My agent. I sent him to you, and I sent him to your bed."

Stone-faced, Alexsi sagged inwardly as he watched her eyes flash at him for just an instant before Priebke dragged her out. An Italian conspiracist offered a conspiracy. That was unfortunate. But he had done the very best he could for her.

"I think I shall take a stroll around this lovely house," Kappler said. "And see if anything strikes my fancy."

46

1944

ROME, ITALY

Alexsi didn't need to read the message traffic to know what was happening. All he had to do was look out the window. The German Army was streaming through Rome. But not in the direction of the front. Retreating away from it.

They were retreating in Mark IV tanks and armored half-tracks, army and civilian trucks, stolen automobiles and farm carts pulled by tired horses. They were not stopping, and Alexsi knew the reason they were not stopping was that someone was right behind them. The message traffic said that the Americans had cracked the Caesar Line and taken Velletri on the first of June. Now it was Saturday the third and their way to the city was open except for a few desperate rear guards who could only hope to delay, not stop.

Of course the Via Tasso had made no preparations for an orderly evacuation. That would be defeatism, and defeatism was punished by sentencing to a penal battalion.

Alexsi had no intention of being the last German to leave Rome, and in his nightshirt at that. Kappler was locked to his telephone seeking orders that would no doubt come too late. So Alexsi had issued his own to pack up all the signals equipment and load it onto trucks. The wireless was still operating because he was running it from a truck in the courtyard, and except for one ten-line telephone switchboard and an operator on duty everyone and everything was ready to move on a moment's notice.

Now there was nothing to do but drop by the switchboard to get the latest gossip. Which telephone operators were always good for. General Mälzer, the military commandant of Rome, was drunk as usual and raging like King Lear. The diplomats had run either north or into the Vatican for sanctuary. Captain Priebke had packed off his German wife and children to Verona, then jumped into a confiscated Fiat two-door to say good-bye to his Italian Fascist mistresses.

Alexsi had thought long and hard about what to do next. And decided to remain with the German Army. Once he was free of Rome and these SS animals he would find his way back to Kesselring's headquarters. Once there he would hold Captain Lang to his promise to return him to that nice safe headquarters signals company. That way he could retreat north through Italy until the war was over. If he went over to the British now he would only be making himself a sitting duck for every Russian spy in their ranks. The Soviets were unforgiving and relentless. Sooner or later one of them would put an end to him. Whereas if he stayed with the Germans he could radio the British regular reports to keep them happy. Then, when the war was over, collect his British passport for services rendered and vanish. It was the only solution.

After lunch he and his submachine gun took a cautious stroll around the neighborhood to see what was happening. The military traffic through the city was tapering off, though there were still traffic jams, and it was making him nervous. The streets were otherwise empty. The Romans, including it seemed the partisans, were remaining indoors until the situation became clear. Alexsi approved of their sense. That was what he would have been doing.

Returning to Via Tasso, he waited patiently all afternoon. Then into evening. By then it wasn't a matter of reading messages for situation reports. He now could hear the rumble of artillery to the south. And then the more isolated crack of heavy-caliber tank guns. That was enough. Kesselring had two of his best divisions as rear guard to delay the Allied advance into Rome. The Fourth Parachute and Hermann Göring Panzer. They weren't going to break and run, but if you could hear the fighting then the hour was already late. Time to take matters into his own hands. If these SS were going to fiddle while Rome burned, he needed to give them a nudge.

In the now-empty signals room he wrote out his own message, as if it had come from Kesselring's headquarters. Ordering all units in Rome to evacuate the city and ensure that none of their signals equipment fell into the hands of the enemy.

The adjutant looked like a man about to shit a cobblestone. Kappler's door was open, and he was sitting at his desk with his head in his hands. Alexsi handed him the message.

"So that's it," Kappler said. "Bauer, how soon can you have all your equipment packed?"

"It is already on the trucks, Colonel."

Kappler's eyes narrowed. "Then where did this message come from?"

"We are using the wireless truck in the courtyard, Colonel. Tied into the antenna on the roof."

Kappler's face relaxed, along with his paranoia. "I should have guessed. Efficient as always. All right, if that's the case then you and your people may leave."

"Yes, Colonel." Alexsi turned to go.

"Wait!" Kappler blurted out, immediately transitioning into a panic. "My papers! I cannot leave them here. We have to burn them."

Alexsi did not say: *Now* you're thinking of that, you fucking idiot? What he said was: "I will send some men up to you, Colonel. They can burn them in drums in the courtyard."

"Yes, yes, good," Kappler said, calming himself slightly.

Alexsi relayed that order to the first SS lieutenant he ran into, who just shook his head and stomped off to find some soldiers.

Time to go. Alexsi turned the corner and nearly bumped into a line of prisoners filing out of the building. Their hands were tied behind their backs and their heads were hanging down.

"Where are you taking them?" Alexsi asked the SS corporal bringing up the rear of the formation.

"North," the corporal said.

"Why are we evacuating prisoners instead of Germans?" Alexsi demanded.

"Don't worry," the corporal said. "We're getting rid of them along the way."

That stopped Alexsi in his tracks. "What about the rest?"

"Thirty more for the big truck," the corporal said. "That will get all of these rats out of our hair. We won't have to listen to their sniveling day and night. They're getting rid of the ones in Regina Coeli, too. No sense letting the Americans have them back to do more mischief."

"I see," said Alexsi. He followed them to the door. Yes, they were loading these fourteen onto one of the smaller trucks, while a large meat wagon they had used at the caves was standing by.

Shaken, Alexsi went to the toilet and splashed some water onto his face. Son of a bitch! He kicked the wall so hard his boot went right through. He furiously shook himself free, and cleaned off his boot with a towel. Then he grasped both sides of a sink, leaned forward, and looked at himself in the mirror.

After Priebke made him talk, which hadn't taken much, Abrianna's son Francesco had been sent off. Alexsi presumed to Regina Coeli. So both of them were there.

Snarling his frustration, he shook the sink so hard the plumbing nearly came loose. He looked up again into the mirror. Well, what are you going to do, Alexsi Ivanovich? The man who had his future so carefully planned out?

You know, he told himself, they would never have been caught if their tradecraft had been even halfway competent. The only people who had ever done anything for *him* out of kindness were dead, and he owed nothing to anyone.

It was no good. His own gaze would not even release him. That foolish Irish priest and his blessing for humanity. Where was God when all the others went to the wall?

Alexsi drew in a lungful of air and blew it out hard. Shit. Shit, shit, shit. It was probably too late anyway.

He kicked the door to the toilet open and charged down the hallway. Sticking his head into the switchboard room, he told the operator, "Leave all the lines open and get out to the courtyard."

His tone set the private to flight, as if the enemy was right at the door. Dashing down the hallway in front of him.

Alexsi stepped out into the courtyard. Pitch black, with the occasional flash of a hooded torch as someone went by. A mild roar, though, as all the SS troops gathered together were gossiping hard. Knowing soldiers, Alexsi could only imagine what outlandish rumors were flying about.

His troops were huddled around the signals trucks. "Corporals to me!" Alexsi shouted, shutting off all the conversation.

They all came running up. A lot of the other SS, too, hovering within earshot in the background. Trying to hear what was going on.

"Get everyone loaded and get out of here," Alexsi ordered. "Head north and attach yourselves to the strongest column you see. When the sun comes up keep a sharp eye for air attack."

"Aren't you coming, Sergeant Bauer?" one of them asked a bit plaintively.

The others laughed at him.

"I'll catch up to you later," Alexsi said. "Get moving at once."

As they turned, he said, "Wait. Who has pliers?"

Of course one of the repair technicians did.

"Thanks," Alexsi said. "Now get going, and good luck."

He stood and watched them leave, the signalers in the back waving to him.

He could hear the other SS muttering, wondering why the devil *they* hadn't gotten orders yet.

When the last truck turned onto the street, Alexsi walked up to the meat truck and quickly rolled underneath. He flicked on the cigarette lighter he always carried but never used, and clipped the ignition wires near the dashboard. Leaving a gap that was too great to be twisted back together. He rolled back out, and if anyone had seen him in the darkness it hadn't caused any alarm.

That was the best he could do for the remaining prisoners.

Back in the building, the offices were largely deserted. Alexsi poked through them until he found what he was looking for. One of the SD lieutenants had an extra uniform hanging up, that was close enough to his size. Alexsi took the tunic, trousers, and cap. He would use his own boots and pistol belt, thank you very much. Tucking the clothing under his arm, he brought it back to his office and hid it in his desk.

Next stop was his quarters, where he had a cheap set of Italian civilian clothing tucked away in a paper sack. Suit, shirt, tie, trousers, stockings, and shoes. All of his available Italian lira and German Army marks went into the bag as well.

He checked his watch. Two o'clock in the morning now. That was both good and bad.

Down the hall, troops were moving in and out of Kappler's office, straining under armloads of paper. The adjutant was gone, and no one took any notice of Alexsi sweeping up a handful of SD Headquarters Rome orders papers, the rack full of official stamps, and the ink pad. Back to his office with the loot, and then off again for a typewriter. He had sent his off with the signals trucks, which was a firm rebuke to his German efficiency.

At his desk, Alexsi typed out an official order for the release of prisoners Abrianna and Francesco Santangelo. A careful proofreading to check for any format errors that would catch someone's attention. It looked good. Uncapping a fountain pen, he finished it with the cramped gothic signature of Herbert Kappler, Lieutenant Colonel, SS. The typewriter of course had an SS lightning-bolt key. Alexsi had seen a few of these real orders, and for something like this the signature was just "Kappler." He imagined that "Herbert" wasn't martial enough.

He carefully folded the orders and buttoned them into the SS uniform tunic. As the Russians had taught him, he then sat quietly for a moment to collect his thoughts, review his plans, and inventory all his goods. Sometimes you had to go out the window, but if you didn't then it was all too easy to make mistakes while dashing about in a frenzy. He was sure he had everything he needed. The SS uniform went into the paper sack on top of his Italian clothes. He buckled on his ammunition belt, slung the Beretta submachine gun over his shoulder, and tucked the sack under his arm.

It wasn't quite every man for himself yet, but the activity in the courtyard was frantic enough that no one in the motor pool bothered him when he grabbed the keys to a staff car.

Alexsi was out of the courtyard before anyone could ask what he was doing.

He parked near the Circus Maximus and changed into the SD uniform right in the street. There was no one around to ask him what he was doing. The uniform was a little tight, but acceptable.

Fully costumed, he looked at his watch. Just after three o'clock. Good. Anyone with any authority left work before the sun went down. More so in Italy. The less rank that was there in the prison in the early-morning hours, the fewer questions.

Alexsi was standing there beside the staff car, smoothing out his SD uniform, when the distinctive put-putting of an Italian engine sounded down the otherwise empty road. Open-mouthed, Alexsi watched as Erich Priebke, in uniform, sped by him with a friendly wave to another SS uniform. Then the Fiat braked hard and Priebke was standing up in the seat of the open-top, shouting, "I knew it! Traitor!"

Alexsi already had the Beretta nestled in the pocket of his shoulder, and he gave the Fiat and Priebke the entire thirty-round magazine without pause. Priebke disappeared below the seat. While Alexsi was reloading there was a grinding of gear and squealing of rubber tire, and the Fiat sped down the street.

Son of a bitch! Alexsi tossed the submachine gun onto the front seat and slid in behind the wheel. There was no time to waste. Priebke might decide to save himself. Or he might decide to find help and return to look for him.

Back on the road, Alexsi crossed the Tiber on the Ponte Palatino. Regina Coeli was on the western side of the river, just south of Vatican City. There was still military traffic moving on the roads, but fortunately he had gotten around it.

The prison vehicle gate was unmanned when he drove up. It was a huge wooden gate in the wall, which had to have been first planned to accommodate a team of horses. Alexsi honked the horn. A guard came scurrying up out of the darkness. Probably sleeping, Alexsi thought. That was good if there weren't a lot of visitors tonight.

The Italian looked surprised as he opened the gate. Alexsi fervently hoped there weren't any real SS or Gestapo already there in the prison. And that after all this, he wasn't too late.

47

"Have any other Germans been here today?" Alexsi asked the Italian jailer escorting him into the building. Just making conversation.

"Earlier, Excellency. To take five prisoners to Fort Bravetta." The Italian gave him an ingratiating grin, then pointed his finger and made machine-gunning sounds. Loud laughter followed.

Alexsi's stomach compressed itself down into a tight little knot.

They reached the prison offices, and the grinning escort took his leave.

Alexsi had no idea why, in every prison he had ever been in, the walls were cream-colored. Probably to make it easy to see the blood.

Another jailer unlocked and opened the door. He nodded his head slightly, which passed for a bow, and motioned Alexsi toward a long desk. Alexsi handed the forged order to the sergeant behind it.

The sergeant looked the paper over, then called out, "Captain?"

The captain emerged from his office, uniform coat unbuttoned and open, eating a sandwich. Still eating, he looked insolently at Alexsi, then took the paper from the sergeant. He read it deliberately slowly, word by word, handed it back, and nodded.

The sergeant thumbed through a roster on his desk. "The woman is here," he announced in German. "The man is not."

"I want to know where he was sent," Alexsi said. "I also want a list of everyone who was sent to Fort Bravetta."

The captain bent over the sergeant's desk. "The German is yesterday's news," Alexsi heard him mutter in Italian. "Yet he still expects us to dance to his tune."

Without a word Alexsi slid over the desk and rammed the barrel of his submachine gun into the captain's ample stomach. The man folded in half, and a piece of the sandwich came flying out of his mouth. Alexsi grabbed him by the coat and threw him back into a chair. Now the muzzle of the Beretta was inside the captain's open mouth.

This was how the SS acted every day. Alexsi would have preferred not to, but he also would have preferred not to be fucked around all night long. He said to the sergeant, "Call for the woman prisoner. If I see anyone but her and her escort come through the door I'll paint the wall with his brains. Then I'll deal with you." And then to the door locker, "You just sit there and don't make a nuisance of yourself."

With his free left hand he removed an egg grenade from his belt pouch and set it on the desk. "If I have to wait too long I'll pull the cord on this and leave it here for you to deal with. *Capisce?*"

The sergeant snatched up the telephone and called for the prisoner to be brought up immediately. "It is done, Excellency," he said in German.

"Thank you," Alexsi replied. "Now I want the lists of everyone who was sent to Fort Bravetta in the past two weeks."

The sergeant tore through the papers on his desk and handed them over.

Alexsi read them while still holding the submachine gun in the captain's mouth. "Try to stop shaking," he advised. "It is bouncing my finger on the trigger."

A wet stain began spreading across the crotch of the captain's trousers.

"All I required was a little cooperation," Alexsi said to the captain. "And it had to come to this."

"Please, please . . ." the captain was begging, though the words had to be indistinctly formed around the barrel of the gun.

"Look, as long as I get what I want, you'll be telling this story to your wife tonight," Alexsi said. Then, glancing down, "While she washes out your underwear." Over his shoulder, he added, "Sergeant, would you please sit still? You're making me nervous and putting your captain in jeopardy."

"Yes. Yes, Excellency."

"Forget that," Alexsi said. "Everyone tonight is moving like a caterpillar across a cabbage leaf. Instead make another call and hurry them along."

The sergeant shouted into the telephone this time.

"I almost forgot," Alexsi said. "Make another call and have her clothing brought here, also."

That storeroom must have been closer, because the bag with the princess's clothing arrived only a few minutes later. The jailer who brought it stared with his mouth open at the captain with the gun in his.

"Get back to work and forget all about this," the sergeant told him.

"No," Alexsi said. "Join us. Sit down and relax."

The store man did so dutifully.

Forty-five minutes later another jailer appeared with the princess. Coming through the door, she froze in place at the sight of Alexsi in his SD uniform.

"Take the handcuffs off her," Alexsi said.

He stood up and removed the gun barrel from the captain's mouth. The captain immediately fainted dead away.

"When he awakens tell him I pardon him for drooling on my gun," Alexsi said to the sergeant. He pocketed the egg grenade and handed the sack of clothes to the Princess Santangelo, who had yet to say a word. After he motioned with the Beretta, the sergeant rushed to unlock the door for him.

Alexsi said, "Thank you, Sergeant. Now, if any one of you do anything foolish—if I hear any alarms, see anyone running about, have any doors locked to me, or am hindered in any way—I'll come back here, blow this door open, and make all your wives widows. *Capisce?*"

"Yes, Excellency."

"Good. I'm sure you'll enjoy working for the Allies tomorrow even more than you did us today."

He took Abrianna by the arm and pushed her through the door. As he shut it he whispered, "Say nothing until we're out of here."

The staff car was parked in an inner courtyard that separated the administrative building from the prison itself.

His original escort was there at the door. Alexsi looked out over the automobiles there. "Say, who does that Alfa Romeo belong to?"

"Captain Benedetto."

"The one inside?"

The escort nodded.

"Do you like him?" Alexsi asked.

An Italian shrug that was better than a no.

Alexsi looked the Alfa over. It was a 6C 1750, red. The keys were in the ignition. Alexsi opened the passenger door for the princess. "Have a seat."

She primly sat down without a word, the paper sack of clothes in her lap.

Alexsi took his own sack of clothes and handed them to her also.

Then he took the petrol can from the staff car and filled up the Alfa, just in case.

The guard was watching like it was the best show in town.

Alexsi flipped him the keys to the staff car. "You can tell Captain Benedetto that I traded automobiles with him. And of course I had a gun, so there was nothing you could do about it."

Now the grin was so wide that all the missing teeth were apparent.

Alexsi also handed him some lira. "For your trouble."

"Thank you, Excellency. Excellency?"

"Yes?" Alexsi said.

"Forgive me, but you are the finest German I ever met."

"Well, there's a reason for that," Alexsi said.

48

1944

ROME, ITALY

The princess said, "Where is Francesco?"

Alexsi had certainly been expecting the question, just not for it to be asked that calmly. "I don't know. He wasn't at Regina Coeli. He's not at Via Tasso. He wasn't taken to Fort Bravetta. He's not on any execution lists. I couldn't find him anywhere. I'm afraid he was sent north to a labor camp."

Her composure finally cracked, and she burst into sobbing tears.

"There is hope," Alexsi said. Though not much. They would be building fortifications for a new defense line to the north. The brat would have to learn to keep his mouth shut and survive, which would be particularly hard for him.

Far enough away from the prison, Alexsi pulled the car over at the Piazza di San Giovanni della Malva. He got out and checked up and down the streets. The Romans were still staying indoors. "Change into your clothes."

The tears were still streaming down her face. "What? Here?"

"Sorry, no dressing room. In case you hadn't noticed, the sun is coming up and you're wearing a prison gown."

He stood guard while she changed. Thinking about what would be the best option for him. A German uniform was going to be a target for everyone soon. Less risky in civilian clothes. He would keep his army paybook, though. If they were stopped by the Germans, it had his assignment to the Via Tasso in it. He would say he was on a secret mission for Kappler, who had probably skipped town already.

The princess had changed, and now she held the prison gown in her hands in a questioning pose. Alexsi motioned for her to get rid of it. She threw the gown into the gutter and spat on it.

While he was changing, she said, "Are you really SS?"

The conspiracist again. "Of course not," Alexsi replied. "I stole that to get you out."

"Kappler did not order my release?"

Alexsi laughed out loud at that. "He would have been overjoyed to shoot you himself. But he's very busy right now, so I typed your release and signed it for him."

That took a moment to register, and then she said, "Thank you."

Alexsi was knotting his tie in the auto mirror. "I was wondering how far into the morning we would get before I heard that."

She burst into tears again. Covering her face with her hands, she spoke through them. "I am ashamed. As you always say, I have no courtesy."

Alexsi slid behind the wheel and patted her knee. "By now I've gotten used to it."

Now she laughed through her tears, leaning over and kissing him on the cheek.

"Much better," he said.

"Where are we going?" she asked, as he pulled back onto the road.

"I'm taking you home. I don't know if the German rear guard has orders to fight all the way through the city or not. Better to lie low until it's over."

"But my house," she said. "What about Kappler?"

"Believe me, he has bigger things on his mind right now. Besides, for all he knows you're in a prison cell."

She squeezed his thigh.

"Shit," Alexsi blurted out loud, swerving the wheel. He had been about to turn onto the Ponte Sublicio to get back across the river. But there was a 37mm flak gun sitting on it.

He sped down the Via Portuense, looking back over his shoulder to see if the cannon barrel was swinging around. It wasn't.

"So much for an open city," the princess said.

"Don't believe everything you hear," Alexsi replied.

The sun was full over the horizon now, and the thunder rumble of artillery to the south was even louder. Time for another decision. Alexsi said, "I'm worried there might be another gun on the Ponte Testaccio. Or that we won't be able to get past the slaughterhouse. I don't want to go too far south and bump into the fighting, but I think we should see if we can cross at the Ponte Industria and perhaps detour through Ostiense."

"Are you asking me?" she said.

"Why not?"

"It sounds all right. I don't know what's going on, though. I've been in prison."

"No one knows what's going on," Alexsi said. "That's what happens when cities change ownership. And don't worry. We'll have time for you to tell me all about prison later."

He slowed down and approached the bridge cautiously. There was nothing on it that he could see. But that didn't mean anything. Infantry didn't defend a bridge by standing atop it in plain sight.

"No choice," he said out loud, and gunned the Alfa over. Though ready as always to stand on the brake and start talking fast, just in case.

They crossed without problems. This was an industrial area. Alexsi drove slowly, nearly standing up behind the wheel to see as far out ahead as possible.

He suddenly dropped down and swerved to the side of the road. "Get your head down," he said, pushing her below the dashboard.

A few hundred meters up ahead a Tiger tank was clanking up the Via Ostiense, with German paratroopers riding atop it like a cluster of ants. "Keep your head down," Alexsi hissed again, as she tried to rise and see what was going on. Combat soldiers would begin firing as a reflex if they saw any movement at all.

The Tiger disappeared through the intersection, heading north. Seconds later it was followed by another, also covered with *Fallschirmjäger* in their distinctive helmets and camouflaged smocks.

If they were pulling the Tigers out with infantry, then the Allies weren't far behind. The trick would be to safely reach the princess's house without bumping into either.

"Take the Via della Conce," the princess suggested.

Good idea. It was the next left, a smaller road just before the Via Ostiense. He pulled back out and made the turn. They immediately went under the huge railroad bridge.

The road was narrow. The next intersection was dangerously close to the Via Ostiense. Alexsi felt it would be better to go slow and get a good look rather than race through at high speed and trust to luck. The Germans might have dropped off flank guards to secure their route out, and there might be an armored car or assault gun sitting right there.

Alexsi edged up to the intersection. There was a circular piazza out in front that would definitely slow him down once he crossed. He decided to stop the Alfa and get out on foot to take a look around the corner.

He said to Abrianna, "I'm going to . . ."

Just then doors opened on both sides of the street and more than half a dozen armed Italians dashed out.

Shit. They were too close for him to toss a grenade and race off without getting himself shot, and too spread out to risk taking on with his automatic without also getting himself shot.

"Red armbands," he said out loud.

"Partisans," the princess said in a low voice. "*Comunisti.*"

Wonderful. It would have to be Communists. If he spoke to them in his German-accented Italian they were just going to start shooting.

Idiot, Alexsi chided himself. Talk to them in English and tell them you're a British intelligence officer. Which had the happy advantage of actually being true.

Not enough time to explain things to her, and he didn't want them to hear him speaking German.

"Don't worry," he whispered in Italian. "I'll handle this."

They had their guns on him, so Alexsi wasn't even going to make a demonstration with the Beretta propped up on the seat beside him.

He was just about to open his mouth when one of the Italians pointed to Abrianna and shouted, "I know you! You're the black princess Santangelo!"

"Fascist whore!" another chimed in.

"Capitalist bitch!"

All Alexsi got out of his mouth was "I . . ."

Abrianna shouted, "He's a German soldier! He's taking me prisoner!"

When he heard that, Alexsi was now the one who could only look at her with his mouth hanging open, like an imbecile. He grabbed for the submachine gun, but something hit him on the back of the head.

49

Alexsi woke up fighting. For all the good it did him. A rope circling his waist pinned his arms to his body. Wrists tied together in front. A gag in his mouth. A splitting head.

His instinct was to get up and run. A good one, except his ankles were tied together.

The smell of shit was so strong in his nose that it felt like he was lying in a latrine. As his head cleared he saw that he was atop one of the carts they used to clean the streets.

He looked up, which was all he really could do, and saw that he was underneath the arch of what looked like a very old brown brick bridge.

Alexsi threw himself up into a sitting position, and it felt like his head would explode. He was sitting on the cart with three Italians and a German soldier in uniform, all tied up like himself. A bounce as the cart was pushed forward a few meters, and then ropes began dropping from the sky. Ropes with nooses tied in them. Alexsi saw now that it wasn't a bridge. He and his unfortunate new friends were about to be hanged from the old Aurelian city wall of Rome. Definitely not the first to have that happen, he thought.

There was a big crowd all around them. All Italians, so they were all talking, and the noise was like a roar. There was one standing on the street just below the cart. He had a red armband like the others and a rifle slung over his shoulder. The fellow had his German Army paybook in his hands. He held it up and wagged his finger at him.

Yes, I am definitely a bad boy, Alexsi thought. And a stupid one, to have not at least hidden that away in the automobile so no one could find it. He tried to say something in English, but it was a very good gag and all these Italians were gabbing too loudly.

Partisans jumped up onto the cart and began pulling them to their feet. Alexsi tried to shout in English through his gag, but they were paying no attention.

He didn't see Abrianna anywhere. Probably made good her escape. Saved herself by looking out for herself, Alexsi thought. There was a lesson there for everyone. Just as well he never got a chance to see what she would do to her enemies, since she had done him in pretty well.

There was no sense giving in to panic—thrashing about and kicking up a fuss. That was just a good way to be the first to be hanged.

Even though his heart was thumping through his chest, it was time to start thinking. Especially since he didn't think prayer would do any good. His mind was racing through his options. Without being able to speak, or anyone willing to listen, there didn't seem to be any. He was willing to try crying or screaming if it would do any good, but it wouldn't. They would just laugh and mock him.

Might as well try something. He began speaking from behind the gag. In a normal voice. He kept on as if he were making a speech. With any luck the Italians would get curious about what he was trying to say, and take the gag off.

Instead they just started screaming at him. "Why don't you shut up?"

So much for that.

Suddenly there was a stir, and a section of the crowd in front of him began to move. Someone was pushing their way through to the cart, and the Italians, uncharacteristically, were actually giving way. A man dressed in black finally emerged from the throng, and Alexsi could scarcely believe his eyes. It was the Irish priest O'Flaherty. The man absolutely turned up everywhere. Hope flowed through him like a surge of electricity.

O'Flaherty pointed to the cart and began speaking to the partisans in Italian. Due to the crowd noise and his position atop the cart, Alexsi couldn't make out what they were saying. But the frantic body language from them all was telling the tale. O'Flaherty was arguing with the partisans, and they in turn were shouting back at him.

The crowd began shouting along with them, because there was really no such thing as a private argument in Italy. Some were crossing themselves.

Alexsi was not feeling good about this. Now O'Flaherty had one of the partisans by the arm, and the Italian shook him off angrily.

One of the partisans fired his pistol into the air, joined by two more with their rifles. The crowd ducked almost as one, and fell back a bit. O'Flaherty was standing in the space they had left, immovable, with an implacable expression on his face that reminded Alexsi of a fighting dog.

The partisans were now pointing their guns at the priest. The classically Italian hand gestures were not working, so two of them leveled their rifles and jabbed them at him, forcing him back into the crowd. The crowd closed in around them, and the Irish priest vanished from sight.

Alexsi told himself he should have known. Communists were not about to be moved by either Christian argument or the threat of eternal damnation. Of course it was his luck to be captured by the only Italians who would not be either impressed or persuaded by a priest.

There was only one other thing he could think of. Something he hadn't had to use in a while, because he'd become a lot better at not getting caught. Until now.

The old trick he'd learned as a boy from tribal smugglers in Azerbaijan. It was the way he'd gotten a knife into the Lubyanka, which had deeply impressed the NKVD.

It was a trick he could try because he'd purchased two knives back in that pawnshop in London. He was certain that the lever-lock in his pocket was long gone by now. But the little penknife was still sewn into a pocket in the front of his underwear. Alexsi wasn't sure if he could get to it. And if he could, what good it would do. But it wasn't as if he had anything to lose. During British parachute training some idiot had asked what he should do if his parachute didn't open. The instructor thought long about it, then said, "You might as well try to fix it on the way down."

The noose went around his neck, and some helpful soul cinched it tight.

One of the Italians next to him began thrashing about as they tried to put the noose on him. The partisans on the cart were all shouting insults as it bounced back and forth. Alexsi bent his knees and shifted his weight drastically, as if he were on the pitching deck of a ship. Trying desperately not to fall off the cart and hang himself.

Finally the partisans got the rope on the thrasher, yelling, "Hold still, you dirty bastard!" They threw him off the cart. Now he was thrashing in midair.

I could have told you, Alexsi thought.

"Don't worry," a wine-soaked voice said in his ear. "You won't need a priest to tell you a bedtime story before you go to sleep. There's nothing out there anyway. It's all dark."

It was what he'd expect to hear from a Communist. Now, there was some irony for you. They had finally gotten him, and they didn't even know it. At least the NKVD would still be wasting their time searching for him.

The partisans all jumped off the cart. It was funny. Alexsi couldn't even hear the crowd now. Just his heart pounding in his ears.

Some comedian began rocking the cart up and down. One of the Italians slipped off and began kicking.

The cart was less crowded now. No one's neck would get broken today. Just strangling slowly for the amusement of the public. Without making a show that would provoke them into throwing him off the cart, Alexsi began twisting his arms back and forth to see if he could get a little slack in his bonds. If he could only manage to bend his wrists up a bit, he could get them next to his waistband.

He had no idea how long you could remain conscious while hanging by the neck, though he didn't think it was very long. So he absolutely needed a bit of warning.

He felt the cart moving a bit, as if people behind were grabbing it and getting ready to pull.

Someone yelled, "Time to meet the devil, you Fascist bastards!"

Definitely time. Alexsi worked his thumb under his waistband. The cart moved more drastically, and he plunged his hands into his trousers. The crowd was roaring at that, and pointing.

But he couldn't get enough slack in his bonds. The rope tying him was taut, and the knife was just tantalizingly out of reach. With the rope around his neck he couldn't bend at the waist. Why oh why couldn't he have faked having a fit and pitched himself down onto the cart before the rope went on?

The cart began to tip.

Alexsi's feet slid out from under him, his shoes skittering down the shit-slick tilted wood of the cart. All he could do was tense his neck muscles. Then his feet were in the air and all his weight was hanging from his neck. It hurt like the devil. Air was cut off, and the world went gray as he felt himself blacking out.

He hit the ground like a sack of coal. Alexsi had no idea what had happened, but as the dirt in front of his face came back into focus he re-alized he was alive and bent over and could reach the knife. At least with his wrists tied together he could get the blade unfolded. It was honed like a razor, and with an upward sweep of the wrist his hands were free.

Alexsi yanked his hands out of his trousers. He got the blade under the rope girdling his waist and swept it outward. Even though it felt as if he'd sprained his ankle again, he was up on his feet with the knife outstretched. He could see the partisans frantically unslinging their guns.

A submachine gun went off right behind him. Alexsi spun around, and there was an American soldier, a lieutenant, aiming a Thompson straight at his heart.

Alexsi tore off the gag with his left hand. He tried to speak but he couldn't. That goddamned rope. He took a ragged breath and croaked out, in English, "I . . . am . . . a . . . British . . . intelligence . . . officer."

The lieutenant was standing sideways, his submachine gun leveled. Alexsi could see the red arrowhead patch on his shoulder. "What did you say?"

Alexsi rasped, "I said: I am a British intelligence officer."

A rifle shot cracked to one side of them. The Italians were shouting and pushing in. Not out of the woods yet was Alexsi's first thought.

Then more deeper-sounding rifle shots and the lieutenant was sur-rounded by more American soldiers, leveling their rifles at the Italian partisans. The lieutenant raised his Thompson into the air and ripped off another burst, sending the crowd scattering. "Back the fuck up!" he bellowed at them.

The American soldiers began pushing the crowd back. More were coming up now, and Alexsi saw the partisans slinking away. Good at hanging, but more timid when confronted by anyone else with a gun. They'd proved that by staying well-hidden while the German Army was retreating only a block away.

A soldier with two stripes on his arm had a wicked-looking double-edged dagger in his hand. The man who cut him down, Alexsi thought. He gave the knife an admiring glance.

The soldier slipped the dagger into a brown leather sheath on his cartridge belt and thrust a wine bottle into Alexsi's hand. "You look like you could use this."

Alexsi took a large gulp of wine. Which was welcome, even though his throat hurt like the devil. Better to never use the devil's name again, he thought.

There, standing before him with an enormous grin on his face, was Monsignor O'Flaherty. "I thought I recognized you, my son."

Alexsi managed to croak out, "Saying it is good to see you again would be an understatement, Father."

"Yes, well . . ." O'Flaherty's smile faded, and he said, "Excuse me for a moment." He pushed past them.

Alexsi looked back over his shoulder. His four new friends were crumpled up on the ground with their hanging ropes splayed about. O'Flaherty was making the sign of the cross over them.

Once again the sole survivor, Alexsi thought. He had been hiding the wine bottle behind his back. He passed it over to the lieutenant. "The priest found you, didn't he?"

The lieutenant drank the remainder, tossed the bottle, and wiped his mouth with his sleeve. "Yeah. And he wasn't about to take no for an answer, either."

Alexsi managed his first weak smile of the afternoon.

The lieutenant said, "So you're a spy, huh?"

"Yes," Alexsi replied. "I am a spy."

"You better be one of ours, or they'll hang you all over again."

"Fair enough," Alexsi replied.

The lieutenant's gaze abruptly dropped down, and he began laughing uproariously.

Alexsi was afraid the fellow had gone mad from too much combat.

Then he looked down at himself. In his haste to cut the rope off his wrist he had also slashed his trousers wide open. The waist was draped down over his shoes. There was also a prominent slash in his underwear, hanging wide open. The only good news was that his genitalia seemed to be intact, and he wasn't bleeding down there.

"I'll say this for you, my friend," the lieutenant offered. "You got balls."

"As you can see," Alexsi replied. He folded his knife back up, and dropped it into his shirt pocket. Now that everything was over, the cold sweat had soaked it through and it was stuck to his skin. His hands were shaking, so he bent down to pull up his trousers, examining them to see what could be done.

"Thank you," Alexsi said.

"Don't mention it, buddy."

There was an entire crowd of Italians around them, dead silent. Listening intently to the conversation, without understanding it.

O'Flaherty was suddenly beside them again. "I must take my leave of you, my sons. More of this madness will be happening today, and there must be a stop to it." To the lieutenant, he said, "Thank you, my son, for your help."

He raised his hand in the sign of the cross, and to Alexsi's surprise the lieutenant dropped to his knees as if he'd been shot.

O'Flaherty said, "May Saint Michael the Archangel defend you in battle, and be your protection against the wickedness and snares of the devil. May God Almighty bless you and keep you, and return you safely to your home and family."

The lieutenant crossed himself, and then used the butt of his submachine gun to push himself to his feet.

O'Flaherty turned to Alexsi, and another bright smile lit up his face as he made the blessing. "May God, the Lord of heaven and earth, who so graciously has accompanied you on this pilgrimage, continue to keep you under His protection."

It was as if he knew, Alexsi marveled. He shook the Monsignor's hand, and O'Flaherty's eyes twinkled at him holding up his trousers with the other. "Thank you again, Father."

"God was with *you* today, my son."

"So you recognized me from the cellar."

"That I did," O'Flaherty said.

"But you would have helped me even if you hadn't."

The smile never left the priest's face. "Of course, my son. There is good in every man. Never forget that. Now good-bye and God bless you."

And then he was gone in the crowd.

"Quite a guy," the lieutenant said.

"Quite," said Alexsi.

"Mind if I ask you a question?"

"Of course not. You saved my life."

"Okay. If I wasn't here, and you did get that knife out, what did you think was going to happen after you cut yourself down?"

"Die quicker than hanging, certainly," Alexsi replied. "Otherwise, who knows? Perhaps I could have persuaded them. Perhaps I could have put my hands on a gun, and they would decide to run away." He shrugged. "One thing at a time."

The lieutenant's opinion on that was expressed with a simple shake of the head. "Glad the Monsignor found me, then."

"So am I. I hope you're not punished."

The lieutenant frowned. "What do you mean?"

"Have you ever heard the expression 'No good deed goes unpunished'?"

"Yeah. Why?"

"It's true," Alexsi said.

AUTHOR'S NOTE

As I did in *A Single Spy*, I feel that I should close by emphasizing that this is a work of fiction. But since I have freely used actual historical figures and events, I'd like to provide some context.

Unlike in the James Bond movies, the head of the British secret service was always known as "C," not "M." During World War II the service was also generally known as MI6, while today it prefers the Secret Intelligence Service (SIS). Sir Stewart Menzies was C from 1939 until 1952, when he retired at age sixty-two. Modern historians regard both him and wartime MI6 much as Alexsi did: amateurish and mostly ineffective. However, Menzies was highly regarded by the British government at the time, mainly because he was a skilled bureaucratic operator who managed to keep the incredibly successful Bletchley Park code-breaking operation, and its product, under MI6's control. His insistence upon recruiting from the upper class and the well-connected opened his service to Soviet penetration from a number of British traitors. He died in 1968.

His deputy, Sir Claude Dansey, was regarded by everyone who worked for him as "a total shit." He retired in 1945 and died in 1947.

Field Marshal Albert Kesselring's conduct of the Italian campaign is considered a masterpiece of defensive warfare. His cold-blooded and brutal reprisals against Italian civilians and the atrocities committed by the troops under his command led to his being put on trial by a British military court in Italy in 1947. He was convicted and sentenced to death. By that time Italy had abolished the death penalty, so the sentence was commuted to life in prison. A campaign by the West German government and some British military figures who regarded him as a chivalrous opponent, to uniformed soldiers at least, led to his release in 1952. He wrote his memoirs, which are self-serving even by the standards of the German generals of World War II, and died in 1960.

SS General Karl Wolff was a nimble figure cut from the same cloth as his fellow SS general Walter Schellenberg in *A Single Spy*. A member of SS leader Heinrich Himmler's personal staff, deeply involved in the Holocaust, he was transferred to Italy as supreme police and SS leader after angering Himmler for divorcing without his consent. By his own account his private meeting with Pope Pius XII on 10 May 1944 was an attempt to enlist the Pope's help in arranging a separate peace with the Western powers, but not the Soviet Union. He described the Pope as characteristically equivocal. A year later he would make contact with Allen Dulles, the head of the Office of Strategic Services, in Switzerland, and negotiate the unconditional surrender of the German armies in Italy one week before the actual end of the war in Europe. This, and his role as a witness for the prosecution in the Nuremberg trials, allowed him to escape indictment as a war criminal. Eventually he was tried by the new West German government and sentenced to four years in prison. In the 1970s Wolff appeared on the British television series *The World at War*, and later publicized an alleged German plot to kidnap the Pope before the Allies captured Rome. From the surviving historical record it is clear that Hitler would vent on numerous occasions about wanting to get his hands on the Pope, Vatican City, and the Vatican archives and treasures. It is also clear that the German officials on the ground in Rome habitually deflected these initiatives out of a genuine fear of an uprising in Rome and uproar in the entire Catholic world if the Pope were taken prisoner. I have given Alexsi a very small and fictional role in this. Wolff died in 1984.

Herbert Kappler was arrested by the British in 1945 and turned over to the Italian government in 1947. He was tried by an Italian military court and sentenced to life imprisonment. His wife divorced him while he was in prison. In 1972 he married, in a prison ceremony, a German nurse with whom he had carried on a lengthy correspondence. In 1975, at the age of sixty-eight, he was diagnosed with terminal cancer. He was transferred to an Italian military hospital and his wife, as a nurse, was allowed almost unlimited access to him. In August 1977, she carried him out of the hospital in a large suitcase and both escaped to West Germany. The West German government refused to either extradite or prosecute him, on the grounds of ill health. Kappler died of cancer at home in Soltau, West Germany, on the ninth of February, 1978. Aged seventy.

Erich Priebke escaped to Argentina at the end of the war with the help of a network established by the pro-Nazi Austrian Catholic bishop Alois Hudal and the Argentine bishop and later cardinal Antonio Caggiano, who arranged for Vatican, Red Cross, and Argentine travel documents that enabled a large number of wanted Nazi war criminals to establish new comfortable lives in South America and the Middle East. Priebke lived freely and openly in Argentina for fifty years until confronted by an ABC News television crew in 1994. After a tortuous extradition to Italy, an equally tortuous trial and acquittal, appeals, and a new trial, he was finally convicted and sentenced to life imprisonment at the age of eighty-five. He remained totally unrepentant about his actions during the war, and was put under house arrest due to his age. He died in Rome of natural causes in 2013, at the age of one hundred. His remains were refused by both Argentina and Germany, and finally his coffin was taken to a military base in Rome and buried in a secret location so as not become a shrine for neo-Nazis.

SS Major Karl Hass was taken prisoner after the war, but rather than being prosecuted for war crimes was employed by the U.S. Army Counterintelligence Corps to spy on the Soviet Union. In 1953 he was fired after CIC concluded that he was also working for Soviet intelligence. After Priebke's extradition Hass traveled to Italy to testify against him, presumably as a safeguard against his own indictment. On the night before his testimony he had a change of heart and tried to escape his hotel by climbing down an outside balcony. He fell and injured himself, giving testimony to court officials in the hospital. Based on his testimony he was tried and convicted for his role in the Ardeatine Caves massacre and sentenced to life in prison in 1998. Due to his age and health he was held in limited house arrest in a retirement villa in Switzerland, where he had lived previously, until he died in 2004 at the age of ninety-two.

The SD and Gestapo headquarters on the Via Tasso has been preserved as the Museum of the Liberation of Rome, with cells and prisoner graffiti intact. It is open for public viewing, and has on at least one occasion been subject to an anti-Semitic bomb attack.

The Ardeatine Caves are an Italian Memorial Cemetery and National Monument. Each year on the anniversary of the massacre a commemoration takes place in which each of the 335 victims' names is called out. There were actually five victims over and above the 330 ten-for-one ratio demanded in the reprisal order, due to a clerical error by Kappler and Priebke. Each of whom blamed the other for it.

The account of the massacre in this novel is based on the historical record, except that every one of Kappler's men participated. The only survivor was an Austrian deserter from the German Army named Joseph Raider, who had been arrested days before carrying fake Italian identity papers and was thought to be an Allied spy. He maintained his imposture as an Italian and found himself at the Ardeatine Caves. Raider was tied to Dom Pietro Pappagallo, a Catholic priest betrayed by a woman who came to him begging for false identity papers. She collected a reward, and he went to the Via Tasso. When Father Pappagallo broke free of his ropes in order to bless the other prisoners about to die, Raider made a break for it up the hill in the confusion. He ran into the German Army troops guarding the perimeter, but they recognized him as a deserter from their own unit at Anzio. He was put back on a truck and returned to Via Tasso alive, since he was a German. His place was taken by one of the Italians dragged out of Regina Coeli in the later afternoon to make up the final number, some of whom were signing the paperwork to be released when they were arbitrarily thrown into a truck by the SS. I was unable to determine Raider's eventual fate, though the German Army was not charitable to deserters.

There is a literal mountain of literature debating whether Pope Pius XII's relative silence in the face of the crimes of Nazi Germany was due to the impossibility of his position or his blinding anti-Communism, anti-Semitism, and personal lack of courage. Readers who are interested in this subject can make up their own minds. The wartime actions of his church ranged from willing collaboration with evil to almost unimaginable heroism, personal self-sacrifice, and Christian charity.

Any account of Rome in 1944 would be unthinkable without at least a mention of Monsignor Hugh O'Flaherty, and I am sorry that I could not give this gallant priest more of his due. He deserves to be much better known. He was a citizen of neutral Ireland and a Vatican diplomat, and a perfect thumbnail of the man is that he was Italy's amateur golfing champion even though there were diocesan strictures at the time against priests playing golf. O'Flaherty apparently knew everyone in Rome. As an Irishman he originally considered the British no better than the Germans, but was radicalized by the Nazi treatment of the Jews of Rome before their eventual deportation to Auschwitz. O'Flaherty hid escaped prisoners of war, Jews, partisans, and Italians wanted by the Fascist authorities all over Rome in monasteries, convents, hostels, private homes, and the Vatican itself without the permission of church authorities. He would stand on the steps of St. Peter's and wait for refugees to come to him. One evening he was approached by a Jewish couple who expected to be deported any day. They gave him a very large solid gold chain in exchange for hiding their seven-year-old son. O'Flaherty obtained forged identity papers for them, hid the son, and tossed the chain into a drawer in his quarters. At the end of the war he reunited the parents with their child, and gave them back their chain.

He was the personal nemesis of Herbert Kappler, who attempted to assassinate him on several occasions, once inside the Vatican. When he left the confines of Vatican City he was subject to arrest, and would disguise himself as a postman or laborer. Before the war he had regularly said very early mass for the trolley car drivers of Rome, and they faithfully moved him all around the city. His escape with Alexsi is based upon an actual one he made solo from Palazzo Doria Pamphilj, while Kappler was searching the building for him.

This remarkable man survived the war, even testifying on behalf of traitors in his own network who were on trial as collaborators. Because, as he said, they had done wrong but there was good in every man. He was made a Commander of the British Empire, and awarded the U.S. Medal of Freedom with Silver Palm, though he sent all the decorations to his sister in Ireland with instructions to just put them in a box. The Italian government offered him a lifetime pension, which he declined. His church career was hindered by envy at his wartime accomplishments, which he rarely spoke of, and he retired as a domestic prelate.

While an inmate of Gaeta prison, Herbert Kappler had only a single visitor. Hugh O'Flaherty would visit him every month. In March of 1959 he baptized Kappler into the Roman Catholic Church.

After a long period of heart disease O'Flaherty died in Ireland on the thirtieth of October, 1963. Age sixty-five. A grove of Italian trees stand in Killarney National Park as a monument to him. Another tree stands in his honor at the Yad Vashem World Holocaust Remembrance Center in Jerusalem, along with the title "Righteous Among the Nations."

I have taken the liberty of placing American soldiers in Rome on the fourth of June, 1944, even though the recognized liberation of the city is the fifth. Although there is much disagreement among the units involved, I believe the first troops to enter Rome were from the First Special Service Force: a U.S.-Canadian elite unit known to the Germans as the black devils of Anzio due to their preference for fighting exclusively at night with blackened faces for camouflage. Arguably the toughest soldiers of any army in World War II. An advanced patrol of the Devil's Brigade had made it as far as the Cinecittà movie studios on the third before being pushed back by a German counterattack. Given their predilection for fighting in dispersed small groups, I don't think it beyond the realm of possibility that there were Forcemen in Rome on the morning of the fourth of June. They were as wild in moments of calm as they were fearsome in action.

Alexsi was incorrect, but understandably so considering the circumstances. The Force shoulder patch was not an arrowhead but a red spearhead with the words USA and CANADA embroidered upon it. The current shoulder patch of U.S. Army Special Operations Command is a red spearhead with an inner representation of the distinctive Force double-edged fighting knife.

Rome officially fell to the Allies on the fifth of June, 1944. The sixth of June was D-Day, the invasion of Europe. And after that the Italian campaign was as good as forgotten.

ACKNOWLEDGMENTS

This book was written during a difficult time in the world, and I apologize to the readers of *A Single Spy* for its delay.

It's hard to properly express my appreciation for my editor, Keith Kahla of Minotaur Books. Not only for his professional skills, which are extraordinary. His patience, empathy, and kindness are definitely not job requirements, but a testament to his personal character. I'll never forget how you handled what we went through, Keith.

As always, my agent, Richard Curtis, is the rock I rely upon. Not only a great agent, but another great human being.

My family and friends know, I hope, how much they mean to me.

Readers can reach me at christieauthor@yahoo.com, williamchristieauthor.com, or Author William Christie on Facebook.